GW01003531

WILL THERE BE WINE?

Happy reading! ♡

Will There Be Wine?

WHITNEY CUBBISON

Will There Be Wine?
Copyright © 2022 by Whitney Cubbison
All rights reserved

This is a work of fiction. Names, characters, businesses, places, events, locales, and incidents are either the products of the author's imagination or used in a fictitious manner. Any resemblance to actual persons, living or dead, or actual events is purely coincidental.

Designations used by companies to distinguish their products are often claimed as trademarks. All brand names and product names used in this book are trade names, service marks, trademarks and registered trademarks of their respective owners. The publishers and the book are not associated with any product or vendor mentioned in this book. None of the companies referenced within the book have endorsed the book.

No portion of this book may be reproduced, stored in a retrieval system, or transmitted in any form by any means—electronic, mechanical, photocopy, recording, or other—except for brief quotations in printed reviews, without prior permission of the author.

First Edition

Paperback ISBN: 979-8-9868960-1-4
eBook ISBN: 979-8-9868960-0-7

To my dad,
who read it anyway.

"Where there is no wine there is no love."
Euripides

CHAPTER ONE

The City of Love

Paris was supposed to be the epicenter of romance where all great love stories began, but for Austen Keller, it was where her marriage died. It was a slow death dragged out over two long years, made longer by Parisians' penchant for PDA—public displays of affection. Nothing truly puts heartbreak into focus like seeing countless couples making out in every absurdly charming café and on every cinematic street corner. In Paris, love was oxygen, and Austen was gasping for breath.

The final death knell rang as Austen and Brad emerged from the Palais de Justice courthouse on an unseasonably warm Indian summer day in September. They had just signed their divorce papers; she was officially a divorcée. They walked together silently toward a nearby bar. After ten years together and an amicable divorce, the moment needed to be marked somehow. But she didn't plan to stay at the bar for long. There was no need to dwell. Brad was leaving Paris for good the next day, to move back to the States to rebuild his life. They ordered double shots of whiskey—the hard stuff—nothing else seemed appropriate.

"Here's to the memories," he offered, raising his glass.

"May we remember the good ones and learn from the rest." Austen threw back the shot.

She returned to the apartment alone—the one she had up until four months ago shared with Brad. It was a beautiful Haussmanian apartment, the quintessential Parisian style of 19th century architecture, with herringbone wood floors and crown molding fit for royalty.

They moved to Paris when she'd landed a job as a speechwriter for François Vinet, a high-powered sales executive at a large technology company. Living in Paris had been her lifelong dream, so Brad had begrudgingly agreed to leave San Francisco, the only place he'd ever wanted to live. The day they'd moved in, she'd wondered how anyone could be unhappy in such a beautiful apartment. She'd thought it was going to be their fresh start.

And yet, here she was two years later, a divorcée.

She kicked off her heels and walked toward the large bouquet of red and purple flowers and another small package that had somehow appeared on her dining table. *The concierge must have signed for them,* she thought as she opened the card with the flowers.

"It's a new dawn. It's a new day. It's a new life. And I'm feeling good."

She smiled warmly, immediately recognizing Nina Simone's lyrics.

"Here's to new beginnings for you. Can't wait to see you for NYE. Love, Sam."

Damn. That man sure has timing—and style.

Sam and Austen first met five years earlier in California while working at a boutique public relations agency. She was on the client-facing side of the business, and he was the finance director. They'd immediately become good friends and had maintained a close relationship. She (and most of their mutual friends) believed he'd always secretly pined for her. The flowers more or less confirmed it for her.

The last thing she wanted right now was a boyfriend who lived on the other side of the world. Her new Parisian life as a single woman was just beginning. She smelled the flowers somewhat guiltily. She quietly loved thinking of him wanting her from afar and was grateful the distance between them would keep things at bay, at least for a while. He and a few other friends from the States were coming to Paris for New Year's Eve.

The package was from her college friend, Liz. *Who knew divorce came with so many gifts?* Flimsy lacy thongs in an array of bright colors tumbled out of the box, and she dug through them, searching for the card.

"You may now go get laid… finally!"

Austen laughed loudly at Liz's crass message. Liz was the crazy one back in their university days. She had no filter. She always said the things others only dared to think about. It was what Austen loved the most about her.

Between their gifts, Sam and Liz had nailed it. Austen was sure there was no better way to start her new life than with a bouquet of beautiful flowers from an admirer and a set of lacy thongs from a wonderful friend.

Her phone rang while she poured herself another whiskey. It was François, her boss. *Can't a girl get a day off to get divorced?*

"Bonjour, François. What can I do for you?" She dropped ice cubes gently into her drink, hoping he wouldn't hear them clinking in her glass.

"Where are you? I haven't seen you all day. I wanted to start brainstorming with you on the speech for the conference in Vienna next month." He was talking fast—a tell-tale sign of when he was feeling impatient.

François was the head of international sales for the company, so he was constantly on the road, working hard to close multi-million-dollar software deals. Her job as speechwriter was to make sure his message was the right one for the audience du jour, which ranged from C-suite executives one day to government ministers, developers, or the press the next. On most days, Austen loved her job, but today, being professional was not high on her priority list.

"I got divorced today, remember?" She tried not to sound pathetic.

"Oh, shoot. Sorry. You have today off. I forgot. Go. Drink. Do whatever you need. You'll be back tomorrow?"

"Thanks. I'm already drinking, and yes, I'll see you tomorrow." She forced a smile into her voice.

"OK, Austen, don't drink too much. Hang in there."

She'd been "hanging in there" in her marriage for years. Today was the day she could finally let go. She pushed François and Brad from her mind and walked out onto her balcony, whiskey in hand and Eiffel Tower in center view, and texted her Paris tribe—Daphne, Chiara, and Isobel—in their group chat.

Girls, it's done. So it's all just beginning.

And tonight is a whiskey night. Come over?

Austen knew that they would be central to her new single life and wanted to spend the first night of her next chapter with them. Also, she was certain the whiskey in her glass wouldn't be her last of the evening, and it was bad to drink alone.

The next morning, she rolled into the office, determined to power through the hangover that was dulling all her senses. A breakfast burrito with eggs, bacon, hot salsa, and lots of sharp cheddar cheese would have fixed it, but there was zero chance she'd find that in Paris. Mexican food never caught on in France, for reasons she still didn't understand. So, she settled for a café au lait and a croissant instead. She bit into the delicate, buttery croissant, which she loved as much as the next girl, but it didn't do the trick on a hangover day.

"Good morning."

The voice startled her so much that she nearly spilled coffee all over her desk. It was Bastien, François's chief of staff, and he was hovering.

"Two things. First, Aurore Blanchard from Société Générale just put in a late RSVP for tomorrow's lunch. I was thinking I'd squeeze her in next to Jérôme Lafont from INSEAD at the front table. François told me to ask you for some reason." He looked at her intently, waiting for an explanation.

"That'd be a great idea if they hadn't gone through a contentious divorce last year."

Divorce is the theme of the week, apparently, she thought.

"Really? How do you know these things?" Bastien studied her like she was a circus oddity.

"I'm paid to know things, Bastien. And we have a very helpful CRM database. You should consider using it from time to time."

"People's divorces are in our CRM database?"

"No, I read about their divorce in *Paris Match*," she said deadpan.

"Right, OK. Well, I can never tell if you're serious, but I'll come up with a plan B. Thank you." He ran his fingers through his jet-black hair and looked at his tablet. "Next, there's a new event on the docket three weeks from now in Stockholm. François will need a new speech on data sovereignty for it."

Austen nodded for effect as she zoned out. *Why are his fingers always in his hair? Is it a nervous tick that helps him think better? A sign of stress? I bet his wife hates it. Or maybe she loves it. He does have a nice head of hair.* She shook her head and tried to refocus on Bastien's words.

"You can call Malin in the Stockholm office for more details so you can get moving on it ASAP. Also, François wants the final draft of the Dubai speech before the end of the day."

"No problem. I'm on it."

In truth, she was relieved at the amount of work Bastien had just dumped on her. She wanted to disappear into her job—the only place she still felt in control of her life. François was the only person who knew why she'd taken the previous day off. The last thing Austen wanted was words (or even looks) of sympathy from her coworkers over her failed marriage. Thankfully, Bastien's "all business" attitude reassured her

François had been discreet. If anyone had heard, it would have been Bastien.

The word "failure" had prominent placement on the flashing neon marquee that described her love life, but it wasn't part of her professional vocabulary. At work, she was a fixer and regularly made the impossible possible. That was the only way she wanted anyone in the office to see her.

Since arriving there two years earlier, she'd maintained a clear divide between her personal and professional life. When her marriage started falling apart, she hid her sadness behind her highly polished exterior wall. Her colleagues couldn't know about the one thing she couldn't fix—her marriage.

CHAPTER TWO

Sexpectations

Three weeks later

Austen made plans to meet Daphne and Chiara for dinner as soon as she returned from François's speech in Stockholm. She always looked forward to catching up with them after her business trips, hearing about their lives, and discovering new restaurants. Tonight's rendezvous was at a quietly trendy bistro behind the Musée d'Orsay called Cinq Mars that Chiara had chosen.

A handsomely rugged waiter with two days' worth of stubble ushered her to the table. She was the first to arrive and took advantage of her time alone to surreptitiously watch him. He moved around the restaurant, chatting easily and confidently with the customers.

He looks like he genuinely enjoys his job, she thought. *Also, he could probably charm the pants off just about anyone—including me.* The mere idea sent a spark through her body. She hadn't allowed a stranger to ignite anything inside her for a long time.

She snapped out of her reverie when Daphne arrived. She stood up to greet her friend, with kisses on both cheeks. They'd met 20 years earlier in Toulouse, a beautifully quaint city in southwest France, during their junior year study abroad program from Stanford. They'd lost touch after school but reconnected as soon as Austen moved to Paris. Daphne had been living there for five years, was married to a lovely French man named Jean-Marc, and worked as a pastry chef at the ridiculously glamorous Ritz Hotel.

Austen settled into her chair. "So, what have I missed?"

"Last weekend, I made 100 hand-painted sugar flowers for a wedding cake and 250 more for individual chocolate cakes the bride and groom gave their guests as party favors," Daphne grinned. "That cake was a work of art. The bride nearly passed out when she saw it."

Austen clapped proudly. "Let's see pictures."

Daphne was fishing her phone out of her purse when Chiara arrived.

"Sorry I'm late. Work is a terror." She dramatically collapsed onto her chair.

They greeted her with air kisses across the table, and Daphne handed the phone to Austen.

"Wow, it's stunning," Austen declared, scrolling through the photos. She passed the phone to Chiara. "Look at Daphne's latest epic confection. I still don't understand how it's possible to create something that beautiful with sugar and flour."

"Daphne, this is divine," Chiara said. "And now I'm starving. These pictures are making my mouth water. What are we eating?"

As if on cue, the handsome waiter breezed by their table to drop off menus, flashing a sly smile at Austen. She couldn't help but smile back, her curiosity rising. *I want to know his name. Why don't French waiters introduce themselves like they do in the States?* Back there, it would have all started with, "My name is Jim, and I'll be taking care of you tonight." In Paris, it just wasn't done. She smiled at the idea that his name was Jim. *So American. He is definitely not a Jim.*

Austen and Daphne met Chiara three months earlier at a networking event. She was a petite Italian brunette who designed handbags for Chanel and spoke 10,000 miles an hour, always with dramatic hand gestures, as all good Italians do. About 20 minutes into their meeting, Austen and Chiara discovered they both loved wine and were both getting divorced. They bonded instantly and committed to drinking as much French wine as they reasonably could to drown their divorce sorrows and make the most of their adopted city. Chiara was the perfect sidekick for the adventure Austen currently found herself in.

"So, Chiara, any good dates lately?" Daphne asked once they'd made their choices for dinner.

A devilish grin spread across her face. "Well, as a matter of fact, yes, although it wasn't a date. I met someone salsa dancing last week. Nico. He's way too young for me, but my God, he can move. The body. He was simply not to be resisted."

Austen raised an eyebrow. "Just how young are we talking about?"

"He's 28. It's scandalous," Chiara whispered. "I'm a soon-to-be-divorcée in my forties with a boy toy. How did I get here?"

She feigned shock, but Austen could tell Chiara was delighted by the latest development in her love life. *As she should be,* Austen thought. *The newly divorced deserve some fun, don't we? Lord knows I do.*

In his second display of impeccable timing, the attractive waiter returned to the table, ready to take their order. Daphne went first and then Chiara, leaving Austen to complete the round.

"And you, madam? What would give you pleasure?"

She blushed at his innocently feigned question and ordered the scallops. *There are a few other things that would give me pleasure, and they all involve you.* He smiled in acknowledgment and headed toward the kitchen.

"Well, that's interesting," Daphne said, looking pointedly at Austen.

"Right? I felt some electricity between you two." Chiara nodded conclusively.

Throughout the evening, he was exceptionally attentive— recommending wines, making small talk, and checking in often to make sure they were having a great night. The corners of his mouth turned into a smile each time he caught Austen's eye, and her body temperature rose with each stolen glance between them. By the end of the night, she was drunk on the idea of him and admittedly on the full-bodied Bordeaux he'd been pouring all night. But she knew it wasn't just the wine making her giddy. She felt desired for the first time in a long time.

"So how was everything, Charlie's Angels?" he asked, handing them the check.

The three women looked at him and each other quizzically.

"The brunette, the blond, and the beautiful redhead," he said, looking at Chiara, Daphne, and Austen in order as he spoke. They laughed warmly at his American cultural reference as his gaze seared into Austen's smiling face.

"Everything was delicious. Thank you," she said calmly while her pulse raced wildly.

By the time they'd settled the bill, Austen was a ball of nerves. "OK girls, what's my move here? I can walk out and never see him again, or," she grabbed her wine glass and tossed back its remnants, "be bold and take a chance?"

"You know this is how Jean-Marc and I met. It can work. Just give him your number on the way out the door," Daphne suggested.

She makes it sound so simple, Austen thought, drinking in her friend's encouraging words. She'd been out of the game for a very long time. The last time she'd considered how to approach a man "out in the wild," she'd been in her twenties and living in the U.S. Back then, courtship rituals still involved speaking to one another on the telephone. But times and technology platforms had changed, and she felt like a fish out of water.

"Go for it. You have nothing to lose. If he calls, great; if not, we'll never eat here again." Chiara zipped her purse. "I mean, it was a great meal, but I'm willing to sacrifice this restaurant if needed, for the possibility of you finally getting laid because that's the kind of friend I am."

Austen's nerves edged her forward. As Chiara and Daphne gathered their things and made their way out into the street, Austen took a paper napkin from the table and walked to the bar where he was standing alone.

"Can I have a pen?" she casually asked. He handed her one and watched with curiosity as she wrote "I'm Austen" along with a smiley face and her phone number on the napkin. "Thank you." She handed him back the pen and paper. She walked away quickly, trying to look cool while her insides were on fire.

"Nice to meet you, Austen," he called after her.

She looked over her shoulder as she walked out the door and saw him grinning from ear to ear. Daphne and Chiara watched the whole thing from the street through the restaurant window, and the three collapsed into laughter as soon as they were out of his view.

"Well done you," Daphne said. "You're officially back in the game."

Austen was buzzing. She'd connected with someone and proactively made a move to explore it. Maybe nothing would come of it, but tonight she felt two things she hadn't felt in a long time—wanted and empowered. She was taking her life back.

Chiara draped her arm around Austen's shoulders as they walked away. "That was a big step. The first time I got back into the dating game after splitting from Giovanni, I was a nervous wreck. Starting over is hard, but we're doing it together. It's going to be so much fun."

Austen gave her friend a grateful squeeze.

A blue light lit up Austen's dark bedroom, awakening her from her wine-induced slumber. She looked over to her nightstand, where the phone continued to buzz lightly, demanding her attention. It was him.

Hi Austen. It's Alain from the
restaurant. Did you want to
get together?

His name is Alain. She smiled sleepily and checked the time. *Three a.m. Is he serious?* She sat up in her bed, trying to decide whether her excitement was enough to overpower her sleepiness. She didn't want to seem too eager but was nervous she might never get a chance to see him if she didn't see him tonight. *I can't have a three a.m. booty call as my re-entry into single life. If it's meant to happen, it will. Another day and at a more civilized hour.*

> It's late. Another night
> perhaps.

She settled back into her pillows fitfully, staring at the dark ceiling and hoping she made the right call.

A few days later, her phone buzzed, and his name appeared on the screen.

So, how about tonight?

It was 11 p.m., and she was in Amsterdam for a speech François was delivering the next day.

> I'm in Amsterdam. Damn. 😊
> Wish I could.

Great city. Are you there for
work or pleasure?

> It is. I love it here. It's work
> this time.

What do you do for work, by
the way?

> I'm a speechwriter. The guy
> I write for has a big speech
> tomorrow, so I'm just putting
> the finishing touches on it now.

Impressive! Sorry to miss you
tonight.

Me too. I'll ping you when I'm
back in town?

That would be great. Hope
the speech goes well.

Thanks. Goodnight Alain.

Bonne nuit, ma belle.

"Ma belle." My beauty. She thought "my" was a bit posses-
sive since they'd never had a real conversation, but part of her
liked it. *Time will tell if I'm going to be yours, Alain.*

She texted him again a few days later, opting for late afternoon when she thought he might have a break between the
lunch and dinner shifts. She wanted to change the late-night
booty call text dynamic.

Bonjour Alain. I'm back in
town. Any chance you're free
tonight?

I can't tonight. I have my son.

You have a son? How old is
he?

He's eight.

Meeting guys with kids was inevitable when dating at her
age, but this was something Austen hadn't yet considered. And
here it was, straight out of the gate. *A kid. How would that
work? Obviously, I don't have to meet the kid tomorrow. I've barely met the man. One thing at a time.*

Good age. OK, have a nice
night with him. Another time
perhaps.

I really would like that. How
about you come back to the
restaurant for dinner next
week. Maybe Friday?

I'll be on a plane back from
Brazil on Friday night. Sorry.

*My habit of planning far ahead might make dating diffi-
cult,* she thought. Her calendar was usually packed weeks in
advance between her work trips and the busy social schedule
she liked to maintain whenever she was in town. *Must plan for
more spontaneity.* She rolled her eyes at herself for the utterly
ridiculous thought.

Now it's Brazil?! I used to live
there for two years when I
was in my twenties, working
as a club promoter. And
then lived in Canada for six
months after that, doing the
same thing.

A man of the world, I see. 😊
That's cool!

Is this business again, or
pleasure this time?

Work again.

You don't stay in one place
for very long, do you?

I spend a lot of time on
planes. It's true.

OK, enjoy the trip to Brazil.

She was suddenly nervous about losing him. Her mind flashed back to the night they met in the restaurant and the spark she'd felt between them. It felt worth chasing.

Thanks. What do you think
about me coming in on
Saturday night instead?

Sounds perfect. Looking
forward to seeing you again.

She called Chiara. "Saturday night. Please say you're free. I need you."

"I love to be needed. What are we doing?"

"We're going to Cinq Mars for dinner. Alain and I have been texting." Austen couldn't keep the nervous excitement from her voice. "He invited me, and I can't go alone. He's going to be working, of course, so please come keep me company and counsel me through it?"

"Wouldn't miss it for the world. And it is a fabulous restaurant. Is Daphne coming too?"

"I thought about it, but wouldn't it be better to keep it to just the two of us, to keep things small and intimate?"

"Intimate?" Chiara asked, adding a sultry tone to her voice.

"Shut up, that's not what I meant," Austen threw back at her, laughing. "Scratch that. It's absolutely what I meant. I can't wait to see him again. Oh, but I learned one important new detail—he has a kid. An eight-year-old son. How do we feel about dating men with kids?"

"I'm dating inappropriately young men, so it hasn't come up. I have no idea," Chiara replied. "How do *you* feel about it?"

"I suppose that when dating in your late thirties, everyone has baggage. The important question is—what size? I think mine is carry-on sized: one divorce, no kids, no drama. Kids definitely equals checked baggage. So, Alain has checked baggage. I can work with that."

"I always check a bag. It's going to be fine." Chiara sounded confident.

On Saturday night, the two women arrived at the restaurant, and Alain greeted them warmly, with kisses on the cheeks and a soft hand on Austen's back as he guided them in.

He showed them to the table they'd sat at on their first night there. She was glad he hadn't put them at a table for two. She hoped the extra space meant he would sit next to her by the night's end.

As he told them about the specials, she noticed his hazel eyes had tiny gold specks. He exuded warmth, and she wanted to be wrapped in it. She felt nervous, but it was the good kind of nerves. Butterflies. It was a sensation she hadn't felt in a decade, and she happily welcomed the little flutterers back into her life and belly.

While Alain was pouring their wine, a man walked into the restaurant and came directly to their table. Alain set down the bottle and greeted him warmly.

"Ladies, allow me to introduce you to my friend Patrick," Alain said. "This is Austen and Chiara." Hellos and air kisses on both cheeks were exchanged around the table. Austen found it strange that in France, people meeting for the first time kissed each other on both cheeks. It felt familiar for a first encounter—much more so than an American handshake—but it was the French way.

"Austen is a unique name and very not French. Is there a story behind it?" Patrick asked.

"My parents obviously didn't consider that I might live here one day," she said, playing back her standard answer. "My mom wanted to name me after Jane Austen, the author who she loves. But my dad hated it. He thought it was plain and didn't want me to be a 'plain Jane.' Austin is the capital of Texas where we're from, so they settled on Austen—spelled with an 'e' instead of an 'i'—as a nod to Texas and the venerated Ms. Jane."

"It's unique, just like you," Alain said.

"I like it," Patrick declared, as he turned toward Alain. "I was just in the neighborhood, so I thought I'd drop in and have a drink and maybe a bite."

Alain looked cautiously at Austen and Chiara. "Would you mind if Patrick joined you since he's here alone?"

Patrick seemed so non-plussed by the suggestion that Austen suspected this was a pre-orchestrated plan. They invited him to sit, and Alain returned to his duties looking satisfied.

"How do you know Alain?" Chiara asked.

"We grew up in the same town. We've been friends since we were kids," Patrick replied. He turned to Austen and continued, "So I can assure you he's a stand-up guy."

Yep. Alain invited this guy to tell good stories about him. A for effort, she thought.

The wine, the conversation, and the laughs flowed freely throughout the evening. Alain joined them as much as he could, while keeping an eye on the other guests. It was getting late, and only a few clients remained in the restaurant when Austen mentioned she was in the market for a new watch.

"What kind?" Alain asked.

"Gold and silver, but otherwise, not sure. I'll know it when I see it." She shrugged.

He pressed further. "Round face? Square face? I'm kind of a watch guy. Maybe I can help."

She told him she wasn't sure, and Chiara moved the conversation to a more sensitive subject.

"Alain, I hear you have a son. What's his name?"

"Timothée. We call him Tim. He's eight," Alain replied.

"And this 'we' you mention is your ex-wife?"

Chiara was a good friend—prying so Austen didn't have to.

"We were never married, so she's just the ex." He looked toward Austen and said reassuringly, "I'm not married."

"Divorced," she said, pointing to herself. "Just last month. When did you separate from Tim's mom?"

"Well, technically, we haven't separated yet. We all still live together, but I'm on the couch. It's not ideal, but we're in a custody fight. I'm trying to keep his life normal while I work to get him full time. His mom is a bit unstable." Alain paused, looking intently at Austen.

He's searching my face for a clue on how I feel about this news. How do I feel?

"He's going to win. Tim will be so much better off with his dad," Patrick said, doing his best to make his friend look good.

"Wow, that's a lot to have on your plate. I hope it all goes your way." Austen made her best attempt at a kind smile.

"Thanks, me too," he replied, scanning the room. Another table flagged him down for the check. "Sorry, be back when I can." He walked away reluctantly.

"Patrick, can you excuse us for a moment, please? Austen and I need to go to the ladies' room." Chiara stood up and pushed in her chair.

Austen took the cue and followed her friend upstairs to the restroom. She needed a minute to process this information—and to pee.

"Remember the baggage theory? He doesn't have checked baggage," Austen whispered loudly over the bathroom stall door. "There's a third kind of baggage in my analogy—the odd-sized other window baggage. That's the window where you pick up golf clubs, skis, or lunatic ex-wives who you share kids with. He's an odd-sized other window guy. Should I be terrified?"

When she came out of the stall, Chiara was washing her hands, looking at Austen through the mirror. "It's a tiny red flag. Not going to lie. But he's been perfectly charming tonight, and I think he really likes you. I say put it out of your mind for now and enjoy the evening."

When they returned to the table, the restaurant was empty of other guests. Alain was wiping down glasses at the bar, and Patrick stood near the door. "I'm going to head out," he said. "It was lovely to meet you both. Thanks for letting me join you."

Austen looked over to Chiara, telling her without words that she could go too. She wanted to be alone with Alain.

"I think I'll walk out with you, Patrick. Bye Austen. Call me tomorrow. And good night, Alain. Thank you for another delicious evening."

"My pleasure," Alain replied across the bar, before turning to face Austen. "Keep me company while I shut this place down? I need 15 minutes."

She nodded and watched Chiara and Patrick walk their separate ways, then took a deep breath to calm her nerves before turning to face Alain.

An open bottle of *Chinon* in hand, he asked, "A last glass for you while I finish?"

He didn't wait for her answer, but it was a yes. She watched carefully as he poured. *Strong hands. God, I hope they're on me soon.* She sipped her wine while he stacked chairs on top of tables, put away cutlery, and settled accounts at the cash register with the two other waiters. She saw from the way they interacted that he was the boss and that they respected him.

A few minutes later, the rest of the staff was gone, and they were finally alone.

"Thanks for waiting. I need to put this money into the safe upstairs, and then we can go." He became very still, his gaze intensifying. "You're beautiful. Don't move a muscle." He bolted upstairs.

Austen felt the energy in the room start to buzz like a thousand neon signs lighting up what had been, for the last many years, a dark and fairly dreary corner of her life. She was swimming in the sensation, eagerly anticipating his return and trying desperately to play it cool.

"Let's get out of here," he said when he reentered the dining room. "Want to walk for a while? It's a nice night."

She happily agreed, and he locked the restaurant door behind them. Fall had arrived—her favorite season. The night air was crisp, and the blast of cool air helped level her head.

"It was fun tonight. I'm glad we could make it work. Patrick is certainly a fan of yours," she said as they made their way toward the Seine.

"And I'm a fan of yours," he replied.

She was grateful for the cover of night, hoping he couldn't see her blush. She looked at her feet as they navigated the cobblestones. She couldn't stop smiling.

They turned a corner, and the Seine came into view, moonlight reflecting off the water. She snapped a photo with her phone to cement the memory.

He took her hand as they crossed the street onto the quai and then onto Pont Neuf. He stopped halfway across it, took her other hand in his, and pulled her softly toward him. "Can I kiss you?"

Her head spun slightly from the red wine and the nerves of the impending first kiss on the oldest bridge in Paris. *Is it weird that he asked to kiss me, or is it polite?* She wasn't sure but chose to consider it polite. And romantic. And sweet. And several weeks and many texts in the making.

"I've been hoping all night that you would."

He pulled her toward him and kissed her softly at first and then with more urgency. It was a scrumptious kiss that left her wanting more. As he leaned back, she could tell by his breathing that he wasn't done either. They walked hand-in-hand to the end of the bridge, and she steered them left toward her apartment.

"Where are we headed?" He squeezed her hand lightly.

"My place?"

As soon as the words were out of her mouth, he hailed a taxi with his free hand.

At her door, he stood behind her and kissed down the side of her neck with his hands on her hips as she fumbled for her keys. He would be her first since the divorce. It had been a long time, but she wasn't nervous. She opened the door and led him straight into her bedroom.

He unbuttoned her navy-blue silk blouse, peeled it slowly off her shoulders, and looked at her red bra with its subtle snakeskin pattern. It was her "sexy bra." She watched his eyes move downward, anticipating his reaction.

A look of disappointment crept onto his face. "Hmm, I was expecting something sexier. Much sexier."

A sound went off in Austen's head, like the needle on a record player violently scratching off its vinyl track. She looked down to verify that she was indeed wearing her sexy bra. *Confirmed.* She looked back up to meet his gaze, which still showed disappointment. The imaginary record player in her head crashed to the floor with a violent thud.

She'd gone into the evening prepared for this exact outcome. She hadn't expected it, but she was prepared, just in case. She had sexpectations. There had been a lot of beige items in her lingerie drawer in her married days, and the red snakeskin bra was a new purchase she'd made specifically for this type of occasion. It perfectly matched one of the new lacy thongs from Liz.

Did the temperature in this room just drop ten degrees? The hurt crept onto her face as she tried to process his comment and decide what to do with it.

Alain noticed the change in her mood and quickly tried to recover. "But it doesn't matter. You're still sexy," he purred into her ear as he slipped the offending bra off and onto the floor and kissed her again.

She kissed him back. The only thing she wanted more than to erase the previous ten seconds was to finally get laid. She swept the comment away onto the floor with her discarded bra and wrapped her arms around Alain.

First lesson learned in the "dating French men" game: It's all about the lingerie. Get thee to Aubade *toute de suite, madame.* She'd learned the lesson the hard way and gotten her pride hurt, but Alain was hell-bent on making her forget, and she let him.

CHAPTER THREE

The First French Boyfriend

It was a bright and chilly morning when they woke up the next day, and they stayed cozy and warm in bed talking, bragate forgotten after a very satisfying night.

"What are you doing for the holidays?" he asked.

Like, in December? I don't even know his last name, and he's asking about my holiday plans? It is barely October, for the love of God.

She had her second minor freak-out in fewer than eight hours because American men—the only ones she'd dated until now—would never ask such a thing after one night together.

"I'm going back to Texas to see my family for Christmas and will be back here for New Year's Eve. What are you planning?" she asked tentatively.

He propped himself up on his elbow. "Every year around Christmas, we rent a beach house in Brittany for a few days. It's always been me, Tim, his mom, and my mom. We spend our days walking on the beach or curled up by the fireplace drinking wine."

"The beach house and fireplace sound dreamy," she replied.

"It's always good to escape the city for a few days. Shame you can't join. Although I'm not sure what will happen with Tim's mom. The next few months will probably be messy," he admitted.

Austen's mind was in overdrive, unsure how to process the easy way he spoke about their future.

All the family drama, less dreamy. So not ready for that. Can't believe we're even talking about me joining his family at Christmas. But it is sweet he wants me there. Assuming I get some new lingerie by then, of course. Wait. Did I just wake up in a relationship with this hunky Frenchman? "Life is messy," she conceded.

"It can be. I will look forward to New Year's Eve with you as my light at the end of the tunnel." He buried his face in her tousled hair.

Sam will be here for NYE. I'll think about that later, she told herself as Alain pulled her body on top of his.

They met up again a few days later for their first "real" date. It was *Toussaint,* a French public holiday, so she wasn't working, but he was. The restaurant business never sleeps. He suggested she come by the restaurant between the lunch and dinner shifts, so they could hang out for a few hours. She turned onto his street and saw him standing outside the restaurant, talking on his cell phone. He grinned when he saw her.

"My God, you're sexy," he said when she was in earshot, covering his phone with his hand.

Bra-gate forgotten, she smiled flirtatiously and gave him a twirl before leaning into his arms and quietly pressing her lips to his neck. He quickly wrapped up his call, slipped his phone into the pocket of his dark, perfectly fitted jeans, and kissed her deeply.

He pulled back but kept her face cradled in his hands. "Do you want to go look at watches? I found you the perfect watch."

"Really? I can't believe you remember I was looking for one."

"I'm paying attention." He pulled two helmets from a bag leaning against the restaurant's steps. "How do you feel about scooters?"

"If you're driving, I feel great about scooters," she confirmed.

He put a helmet on her head and fastened the strap below her chin, kissing her quickly before putting on his helmet and climbing onto the blue Piaggio scooter parked on the street. She climbed on the back and wrapped her arms tightly around his waist as he pulled away from the curb and headed toward the Seine. After a short ride onto the Right Bank, he parked, and they walked toward his chosen destination—Cartier on the Rue du Faubourg Saint-Honoré.

Austen never would have waltzed into Cartier to look at watches—not in a million years. She didn't spend money like that on jewelry.

Alain reacted to a mix of fear and shock in her eyes. "I know this may be a bit out of your price range, but if you see something you like, I know a guy who could get you the same thing, slightly used, for a good deal. So, we'll just look."

"OK, we'll just look," she repeated, taking a breath. *I slept with the guy once. He's not going to buy me a Cartier watch. I mean, I'm good, but I'm not that good,* she laughed to herself. *And even if he tried, I'd never let him.*

They walked in, and Alain told the elegantly dressed salesman they wanted to see the ladies' Tank model.

He escorted them to a small table and two plush red velvet armchairs and, to Austen's delight, offered them champagne.

Of course. Let's swill champagne while fake shopping for stupidly expensive jewelry. As one does. She was using all her self-control to keep the silly grin off her face. *I could get used to this.*

The salesman returned to their table and presented them with the watch on a square red velvet tray. Austen picked it up nervously and slid it onto her wrist. Alain leaned in to examine it closely and then rested back into his chair with a proud smile, clearly pleased that he'd selected the obvious winner.

"You should try the next size up, just to be sure." He winked.

Austen nodded, playing the character of a serious shopper. "We should be sure. Of course, you're right."

The salesman left to retrieve it, and they took advantage of the moment to steal a kiss and a giggle. She was in awe. *Is this what dating is like in Paris?*

When it arrived, she tried on the larger model, but they both agreed the original choice was the best. Despite the headiness of the entire experience, Austen was nowhere near prepared to throw down that kind of cash, so they finished their champagne, graciously thanked the salesman, and left the store.

Alain wrapped her in his arms as soon as they were on the street and kissed her sweetly. "You should buy the watch. It was made for you."

She kissed him back, melting into him. "I'll think about it. I promise."

They spent the next month in a haze of new-couple bliss. Alain took her to fabulous restaurants all over Paris where he always knew the chef. They did their best to balance his work and family commitments with her travel schedule. When she returned from day trips to Brussels or London, he greeted her on the train platform whenever he could, whisking her into the Parisian evening. She stopped by the restaurant for a nightcap on nights when he worked. They fell into a comfortable and happy pattern.

One night over dinner and a bottle of Chianti Classico at Oxymore, a perfectly charming pizza place near Bastille, he told her about his three best friends in Paris. Patrick was the only one she had met.

"Have you told the other two about me?" she asked.

"Of course. They were shocked by how we met. They think you're amazing, which you are." He kissed her hand across the table and took a long sip of Chianti.

She rested her chin in her hand. "Why shocked?"

He leaned toward her and mirrored her movement, placing his chin in his hand. "No French woman would've approached a man like that. It's just not done."

It was her turn to be shocked. "What do you mean?"

Picking people up in bars and restaurants isn't a universal thing? Who knew?

He laughed at her question, but not unkindly. "To be clear, I love the story. I admire your courage. Honestly, I can't tell you how much I needed that experience at that moment. But no French woman would've ever dared. You are most definitely unique."

She didn't understand but chose not to care. She took her last sip of wine and leaned across the small table to kiss him. The wine and his tongue circled her mouth. When they pulled apart, she whispered to him, "Take me home. Take me to bed. And tell me what else I can do that no French woman would ever do to you."

He accepted the offer with a low growl emanating from his throat.

Without understanding it, Austen had found Alain in the eye of the storm of his life. The court date was imminent for his custody case, and the gale force winds were building. She should have sensed it, but she was too enamored to notice the clouds rolling in until the skies opened. It hit her in the form of a text.

I won full custody. I'm moving him out of her apartment tomorrow and into a new school. It's going to be a rough couple of days or more likely weeks for him, so between him and the restaurant it's going to be tough to break away to get to you.

Of course, I totally understand. Go take care of your son. I don't think there's much I can do to help, but if there is, just ask.

Merci chérie. Life just changed a lot.

I know. Congratulations. He's lucky to have you, as am I.

🖤 I'll talk to you soon.

Austen met up with her British friend Isobel that night for dinner. The two women settled into the terrace of Le Compas, Isobel's favorite café on the Rue Montorgueil, and ordered wine. She definitely needed wine.

The waiter brought olives and a bottle of *Pic Saint-Loup* and gave them a French pour—less than half a glass each. Isobel rolled her eyes as he walked away and grabbed the bottle, unabashedly filling the glasses to the top.

"God, it annoys me when French men fill your glass halfway and then swat your hand away if you try to refill it yourself. If he's going to make me wait for him to refill it, he should fill it up," Isobel moaned.

This "rule" was especially troublesome at dinner parties. French men did *not* like women to fill up their own wine glasses. When Austen first arrived in France, she'd been baffled when men had repeatedly pried a bottle from her hands, insisting she let them refill her glass. At first she'd wondered if they were trying to flirt, but then she understood it to simply be the norm.

"It's a very strange form of gallantry," Austen agreed. "And a bit inconvenient for you and me, given how often our wine glasses turn up empty. They always seem to have a hole."

Isobel laughed. "Why do we always get the glasses with holes? Anyway, I haven't seen you since you started dating the new man. Tell me everything."

"It happened fast," Austen replied. "The morning after our first night together in early October, he was already talking about holiday plans. I nearly fell out of bed. Who does that?"

"French men. You sleep with them, and the next morning you find out if you're a one-night stand or a girlfriend." Isobel said it as if it was common knowledge.

"Really? That's normal?"

"Yes. Most Frenchies meet through friends or work and then casually hang out in groups until they fall into bed together. If they wake up the next morning and the other one is still there, they're a couple. That's how it started with Luc and me."

"Gotta love the clarity. It's so much less complicated than in the States," Austen said. "Over there, you can sleep with someone for months, but you're not a couple until you have 'the conversation' to make it official. It is a time-honored dating tradition."

Isobel laughed and patted Austen's arm. "You Americans are savages. It doesn't work like that here. The French don't even have a word for 'dating.' That should've been a clue."

That's a great point, Austen thought, nodding to Isobel in acknowledgment. *I'm out of my depth.*

"It's been a little over a month, and we're having fun. He's adorable. But he's been in a custody battle with his ex over their eight-year-old kid, and today he won—full custody. Gulp."

"Well, that's fucking crazy," Isobel said. "It's rare for a man to win full custody of a kid. What a mess the mother must be."

"That's the impression I get, but I don't pry. It's still too early in the relationship for me to be mixed into the weird family dynamic, right? Or am I being an ostrich with my head in the sand, avoiding reality?"

Isobel's boyfriend, Luc, had a daughter, Amélie, from a previous relationship, so Austen was eager to hear her perspective.

"Listen, you both have to do what feels right. This is tricky territory. Clearly, he needs to prioritize his son right now, so it's just a matter of how patient you want to be while this shit gets sorted out."

Austen took a deep breath. "I've only been divorced for a few months, and that relationship tapped me out of patience.

Is it horrible that all I want right now is sex, spontaneity, and champagne?"

"You want what you want. Don't apologize for it. But do be clear." Isobel took a sip of wine and swallowed slowly. "If you're not sure you're in, don't meet the kid. I didn't meet Amélie for the first six months, and by then Luc and I were madly in love. Are you guys in love?"

"No. And I think being in love is an excellent prerequisite for meeting the kid. Definitely going to hold off on that," Austen declared.

Thank God I'm going to Prague soon. It'll take some pressure off and give them time to adapt to their new rhythm.

"Yes. Wait until you're sure. I love Luc, and I love his daughter, but being a stepmom is no fucking joke," Isobel said. "That man better marry me soon."

The next two weeks passed quickly as Austen prepared for Prague. François had an important speech and a press interview to give, in addition to five customer meetings that Bastien would manage. The speech would showcase how technology can be applied to digitalize patient records and improve patient care while meeting the strict data privacy regulations of the European Union. He would also announce a new deal between their company and a local hospital to bring virtual reality into its operating rooms to assist surgeons. They worked around the clock to prepare.

The jet took off from Paris at the crack of dawn with the three of them on board. François peppered Austen with questions about the speech as soon as they reached cruising altitude. She felt undercaffeinated but confident.

"How many people are in the audience?" he asked.

"Around 150. It should be about 30 percent hospital administrators, and the rest are doctors, nurses, and other healthcare providers," she said.

"How many press?"

"Just the one outlet—a reporter and a cameraman. We've given CT24 an exclusive on the news, so as soon as the speech ends, we'll take you to meet the reporter privately so she can ask a few questions. This is her," she said, handing him the reporter's bio and photo. "They'll also shoot footage during the speech, and it's expected to be on the nightly news tonight."

François continued. "What percentage of the Czech population is over retirement age?"

Austen's strength was words. Bastien's was numbers. *Please know the answer,* she silently begged him with her eyes as she started to sweat.

"Twenty percent," Bastien replied without missing a beat.

You're a magical creature, she thought. She exhaled and shot him a grateful smile. François got twitchy when his questions went unanswered.

"Austen, add that stat into the talk track, just after I mention the importance of improving care for aging populations on page three."

It wasn't a request.

"No problem. Will do." *Why do I wear heels when I know I have to run ahead of him from the car to get the final changes loaded on the teleprompter in the two minutes between our arrival and when he gets on stage? Must buy some flats.*

He kept reading. "This is a cool virtual reality deal we're announcing for remote assistance in surgery, but how on

WILL THERE BE WINE?

Earth do I pronounce the name of this hospital? Czech is an impossible language."

"See that embedded file by the hospital name in your script?" she asked. "Click on it. That's an audio recording I made of the account manager pronouncing it for you."

"Clever. Thank you." He listened to the recording three times and repeated it out loud to help it sink into his brain. "And this doctor I'm mentioning, Dr. Cabelova, she'll be in the room?"

"In the front row, the first seat on the right center aisle. And she will join you after to meet the reporter to take any questions about their plans."

François nodded his thanks and turned his attention to the customer meetings and Bastien. Austen turned to the coffee machine. *I'm going to need a continuous caffeine drip to survive today.*

Austen and Bastien sat in the front row while he delivered the speech. She tracked François's comments against the script on her laptop, making notes when he deviated from it, even if the change was minor.

"You really do catch every word, don't you?" Bastien whispered to her mid-speech. He was watching her work. His question interrupted her focus, so she simply nodded and returned her attention to François.

When the speech was over, they waited for him as the stagehand untucked his lapel microphone wire from his jacket and then walked him down the hall to meet the reporter.

"I noticed you changed a few things. We can talk about those on the flight home if you want to, for next time. Every word matters," she said, handing him a water bottle. "On that note, before you sit down with this reporter, remember to avoid the word focus. Use emphasis instead, OK?"

"Did I say focus on stage?" he asked.

"You did. No biggie. Just don't say it in the press interview. And good luck." She ushered him into the room where Dr. Cabelova and the journalist were waiting.

Austen and Bastien sat on a bench in the hallway to wait. She reached for her phone. *Still no message from Alain,* she noticed, disappointed. They hadn't seen each other since he'd won in court two weeks prior, and she hadn't heard from him in two days. She was giving him space, despite wanting him nearby. *I hope he's OK. I hope we're OK. Two weeks is a third of our relationship. Are we still in one?*

Bastien interrupted her thoughts with a question. "What's wrong with the word focus?"

"Have you ever heard François say focus with his French accent?"

"I don't know. What am I missing?" Bastien replied with a blank stare.

"The accent makes it sounds like he's saying 'fuck us.' I told him he wasn't allowed to use the word. Imagine the press coverage," Austen explained with a smile.

Bastien dropped his forehead into his hands, laughing. "That would be bad indeed."

As they sat on the jet at the end of a long day waiting to leave Prague, Austen was anxious to get home. She wanted to see Alain. He had just moved into an apartment close to his retired mother, who'd agreed to watch Tim when he was at work. That was important, practical relief. Austen wanted to offer a different kind of relief—in the form of sex and champagne. She texted him from the tarmac as the plane pulled back from the terminal.

About to hit the skies. Back in
Paris in 2.5 hours. I miss you.
Hope to see you soon.

Alain's reply came in the morning, her buzzing phone jolting her awake.

"Bonjour, ma belle. Welcome home. How was Prague?"

"Went well, thanks. I'm glad to be back and to hear your voice." She leaned back into her pillows and pulled her comforter to her chin. "How are you?"

"It's been tough, but I'm OK. I miss you. How would you feel about coming to my place for lunch with me, my mom, and Tim on Saturday?"

Austen pushed her hair from her face and rubbed her eyes, unsure how to respond. Panic crept in. It was too soon.

"I want to see you, but do you think it's a good idea to introduce a new woman into the mix so soon after all that's happened?"

"Let me worry about that," he replied.

What would we even talk about? God, how awkward. She decided honesty was best. "A lot has happened since we saw each other last. I'd love to find some time for us to be alone. I'm just not sure it's the right moment to meet everyone."

"I know you're nervous about meeting them, but it's the only way I'm going to be able to see you for a while longer. Just come," he pleaded.

"I understand that. I do." She carefully considered her next words. "But it doesn't feel right to me. I think you're looking for a new mom for your son, and I'm not ready to take the job. I'm sorry."

He exhaled. "I don't want to lose you."

"Timing is everything, and I think ours is off, at least for now. I respect and agree that you need to prioritize Tim right now. But I've just come off a marriage where I was neglected for a long time, and I need to be with someone who can prioritize me," she explained, with more honesty than she'd planned.

"I wish I could, chérie, but I just can't right now," he conceded.

She heard the sorrow in his voice and knew it was over.

She was surprised to feel relief when she hung up. As much as she liked Alain, she didn't want an instant family and the responsibilities that it implied. She knew it was selfish, but it was time she put herself first.

Her first dating experience post-divorce had been relatively easy. She saw someone she liked, went for it, and it had worked, at least for a while. She resolved to no longer date single dads with full custody of young kids and keep things light and fun with the next guy. She decided that Alain was just the first of the many great and sinfully romantic Parisian love stories that lay ahead.

CHAPTER FOUR

The Holidays

December 30th

Austen sat on her couch, waiting for Liz (of the lacy thongs) to arrive. She and Andrew had flown in from San Francisco that morning. While Andrew took a power nap at the hotel, Liz was on her way to Austen's apartment so they could catch up before the group dinner that evening. While she waited, an email from Brad appeared on her phone. The subject line read "Money."

She looked at it with dread, hesitating to open it. When she got the job in Paris, Brad quit his job to move with her. He didn't work while he was there, so she paid him in the divorce. They settled on an amount each thought was fair, but Austen was a good negotiator. He could've gotten more if he'd pressed.

She double clicked on the message and read.

Austen,

The money discussions leading up to the divorce weren't pleasant for either of us, so I hesitate to reopen them. But something has been bothering me, so I need to get this off my chest. I feel that we didn't land in the right place in our settlement.

One of the reasons I decided it was OK for me to leave my job was that your company was going to pay our rent in Paris, so our expenses would be lower. I've now been out of the job market for two years, and it's proving tough to find something new. I'm looking but haven't found anything yet, so I'd like to ask you to send me half of your rent allowance (1500€ per month), until I find a new job. Think about it as alimony. I would ask that it be backdated to October when I left Paris.

As soon as I find a job that's comparable to the one I left, you can stop the payments, of course. I hope you'll do what I think is fair. My bank details are below for the transfer.

Brad

She read it twice, anger bubbling up from deep inside her gut. *Is he fucking kidding me?* Austen screamed into a couch pillow, repeatedly. Their split was clean. She was proud that they had handled a tough situation with grace. *And now we're just another divorced couple who fight over money and hate each other.* She was fuming when the doorbell rang.

She buzzed Liz into the building and waited in the hall-way as her ancient elevator creaked its way up through the building's spiral staircase. Her anger at Brad was momentarily displaced by her excitement to hug her friend. The elevator door opened with a ding, and Liz jumped out and threw her arms around Austen's neck.

"Bonjour. We made it. Happy almost New Year," she cheered.

"I'm so glad you're here. Get inside." Austen directed her friend into the apartment and helped her out of her coat. "How was the flight? Did you sleep?"

"I drank a tiny airplane bottle of wine, popped an Ambien and slept the whole way. I'm officially ready to party," Liz declared. "Tell me you have champagne."

Austen stepped into the kitchen and pulled the champagne flutes out of the cabinet.

"Have we met? Of course I do. House rule: always have champagne on ice in case something needs celebrating. Your arrival most definitely counts."

Liz leaned onto the counter, looking satisfied. "Fab. Now give me the scoop on everyone in the party crew for this weekend."

"I will, but first, you'll never believe the email I just got from Brad." Austen finished pouring the Ruinart and then handed Liz her phone. Austen watched her friend's face as she read.

"How thoughtful of him to include his bank details," she scowled.

"I think my head spun around *Exorcist*-style when I read it. Thank God he's on the other side of the planet. If he were here, I'd punch his lights out," Austen exclaimed, as they settled into the couch with their champagne. "He did nothing for two years, and now I have to pay more?"

"He did move here for you, without speaking French. It wasn't obvious for him," Liz said with some pity.

Austen's blood had returned to a slow boil.

Liz raised her hands as if in surrender. "OK, I see that look on your face. Hang on. I'm on your side of course."

"He had the golden ticket. I earned enough for us both, so the only thing he had to do was be happy. And yet, he was miserable," Austen vented. "He wasted the opportunity of a lifetime, and now wants me to compensate him even more for it. He sucks."

A thoughtful look passed across Liz's face. "Didn't you tell me he got less than he could've in your settlement?"

"Yes, but he agreed to it. This is just so typical. The man lives in a constant state of uncertainty and regret. If he'd asked for more money before the divorce was final, he would have gotten it, but it's too late now, Brad," she screamed.

"It is too late. You have no obligation to pay. So why are you so mad? Want to know why I think you're mad?"

"Yes please, oh wise Liz. Why am I so mad?" *Let's see what she's got.*

"Because you finally *can* be. You spent two years being angry at him because he was miserable in your dream city. You tried to help him thrive here, which he was determined not to do." She put a hand on Austen's knee and continued. "You pushed all that emotion down because you were in 'fix it mode' trying to save your marriage."

Austen crossed and uncrossed her arms, watching the bubbles rise to the top of her glass, as she listened to her friend's theory. *She's not wrong.*

Liz continued. "It's like you've been holding a beach ball underwater. The farther down you pushed it, the more force it created to be ready to pop back up. This stupid money thing gave you permission to finally let go."

"That damn beach ball just went soaring into the sky. I never want to see him again."

"That's entirely your call. For now, let the ball hang up there in its anger-orbit for as long as it needs to." She pointed upward with both index fingers. "And one day, when you least expect it, it will fall and land in front of your face. Because—" She paused for dramatic effect and flipped her fingers downward. "Gravity. And then you'll know you're not angry anymore."

"I'm so happy you're here." Austen hugged her friend. "It's almost New Year's Eve. It's entirely too cold outside to even think about beach balls, so screw Brad. We're going to throw on some faux fur and ring in this New Year in style."

"And with a shit ton of champagne," Liz shouted, raising her glass.

It snowed in the early evening, dusting Paris in a thin layer of white as Austen got ready for dinner. She was still somewhat shocked the group had grown to its current size so quickly. It all started when Sam offered to come ring in the New Year with her when she told him she was getting divorced. He called a few days later to inform her their mutual friend Peter, who had recently moved to London, had invited himself to join. Liz and her husband, Andrew, signed up soon after, and since then, the crew had grown to nine people, including Daphne, Chiara and their respective beaux, Jean-Marc and Nico.

Christmas lights still twinkled all over the city, and La Gentiane was decorated for the season. The restaurant had a low-key vibe, delicious food, and friendly staff. It also had a disco ball hanging above the bar which often came on after hours. The owner was known to crank things up a few decibels when his guests were in a festive mood, so it was a perfect dinner spot for any eventuality of the evening.

Tonight will probably be mellow, but it's good to have a plan in case they're already in party mode, Austen thought.

She walked through the doors and spotted Liz, Andrew, Sam and Peter, already seated. She shimmied out of her coat as she crossed the room and embraced each of her friends tightly, her cold cheek getting warmer as she pressed it into each of theirs. Sam's hug was tighter than the others. *He smells good,* Austen thought as she claimed the seat next to him.

"*Bienvenue à Paris, mes amis*[1]." She looked around the table and took in the scene. "I can't believe you're all here."

"Thanks for hosting us and for arranging that nice snowfall." Sam gestured to the window.

She flashed him a smile. "Thank you for noticing. I spared no expense."

Daphne, Jean-Marc, Chiara, and Nico arrived, and introductions were made between her old friends from the States and her new Parisian posse. The waitress handed them menus, and Andrew used one to cover a yawn.

Peter looked toward him, Liz, and Sam, who'd all arrived that morning from San Francisco, and declared, "You guys need to rally. There's only one way to manage jet lag, and that's to power through it."

"Careful who you challenge, Peter." Austen pointed at Liz. "That girl coined the phrase 'water is for quitters' when someone asked for a glass at a party once. She was born to rally."

"Damn straight, Austen. Thank you for your faith in me." Liz raised her wine glass toward her friend, then kissed her yawning husband on the temple.

---

1   "Welcome to Paris, my friends."

"We're going to get you guys some amazing food and wine and keep you up until at least 11 p.m. It's the only way you're going to make it past midnight tomorrow," Austen said while flagging over the waitress. "The after dinner rager is optional tonight."

Andrew nodded and then dramatically groaned into his palms.

"Do you want coffee? We can get you coffee," Peter offered, trying to help.

"Coffee is for after the meal, you crazy American. You can't have coffee before we eat," Nico declared.

"They can do whatever they want to. Stop being so French." Chiara playfully smacked his hand. "You try to power through a nine-hour time difference after a transatlantic flight in coach."

Sam cocked his head at Chiara. "Coach? What's that? Business class all the way, baby."

Austen expected nothing less from him. "Then I guess you have no excuse and will lead the charge for the rager tonight?"

"You know it. I'm recruiting Liz as party co-chair, and we're going to get that disco ball going." He reached across the table to shake Liz's hand and seal the deal.

Chiara's laughter and *oh là làs* reverberated off the restaurant's stucco walls as Liz and Sam shook on it. The weekend's shenanigans had officially started.

Austen and Sam always sat next to each other, in any room. At work or social events during her San Francisco years, they were like magnets, always drawn together. She was married to Brad then so treated it as friendship, actively ignoring the thought that he might want something more. She felt the magnetism again at the small Parisian table, and this time, things were different.

"Divorce looks pretty good on you," he said, putting his arm around the back of her chair.

"Why thank you, kind sir." She nervously picked at the breadcrumbs on the table.

"How is single life as an American in Paris?" He leaned back into his seat. "Seeing anyone?"

That question didn't take long.

"I'm adjusting rather well, thank you. I've already started and ended a first new relationship with a Frenchie, which fell into the short but sweet category. His name was Alain." She flattened the tablecloth in front of her with her palms. "He was lovely but in the middle of a heated custody battle with his ex, and it was a bit more than I felt like taking on. But it was good for getting me back into the dating game. So that's something."

She turned to him and asked without needing to, "What about you? Anyone special?"

"You know me. Workaholic. No time for that. Of course, you're a workaholic too, yet somehow you manage to do both. I should learn from you." He adjusted his collar. "So, your first Frenchman, huh? Is dating in Paris as romantic as the movies would have you believe?"

From across the table, Chiara chimed in. "He was lovely, I can confirm. I was there the night they met, and this man could not take his eyes off our dear Austen. And he took her to Cartier on their second date."

Sam's mouth dropped open. "What did he buy you?"

"Oh no, nothing. We were just looking," she offered dismissively, intentionally leaving out the details.

I love Chiara for introducing that little anecdote.

"At what? Engagement rings?"

She rolled her eyes at him. "You're hilarious. No, watches."

I love that's where your head went though.

"Nothing would surprise me with you." Sam shook his head.

"I mentioned I was looking for a watch, and he had a suggestion for me to consider. I'm still considering," she told the table.

Everyone's attention had turned to her story.

"Well, sounds like a classy move. Score one for the Frenchie," Sam said.

She couldn't help herself and tilted her head to the side. "Well, yes. He definitely scored."

Sam threw his head back, laughing. "Look out, Paris. Austen's single and ready to mingle." He took a big gulp of his wine.

"I'm loving this new single Austen and all the crazy sex you're going to be having with French men." Liz smiled broadly and raised a finger toward Austen. "Don't you dare settle down again any time soon. It's time for you to have fun and clear those cobwebs out of your vagina."

"Sounds like Alain took care of that," Andrew deadpanned.

Daphne and Chiara both became wide-eyed at the exchange. Liz noticed their reactions.

"I'm a doctor. I can talk about body parts. And he's used to me by now," she said, gesturing toward Andrew. She looked at Austen for backup.

Austen obliged. "She's a sports medicine doctor for the San Francisco 49ers so not sure it's relevant, but she did indeed go to medical school. And I told you she has no filter."

Everyone around the table laughed nervously and took sips of wine.

Peter broke the silence. "Maybe don't have tons of crazy sex with French men *this* weekend. We did all travel here to hang out with you."

Austen quipped, "I'll try my very best not to fall into bed with any French men this weekend. No guarantees. But I'll try."

She let her smile fade and glanced toward Sam, who was investigating the contents of his wine glass, looking unamused.

The group ended the night at 11 p.m. on the dot. The disco ball never came on. Liz, Andrew, and Sam took Peter's jetlag-beating counsel to heart. They said their goodbyes and agreed to meet at Austen's apartment in the early evening the next day for champagne and pre-funk. For dinner, they were booked into a classy restaurant called Vesper which had advertised a fixed New Year's Eve menu, a DJ, and free-flowing champagne.

Austen awoke on December 31 feeling excited about the night she had planned and thrilled to be spending it with good friends, both old and new. She spent the day primping—face mask, manicure, waxing—the works. Daphne texted her around lunch time.

What are you wearing?

> New dress—slinky, backless, and black. With my red Louboutins. What about you?

Va va voom! Sounds perfect! I'm wearing black leather pants and a white silk halter, with gold jewelry and gold heels.

> Love it. Can't wait to see you.

Will there be wine?

Daphne's closing text didn't need a reply. It was their inside joke—used every time they talked about going anywhere. There was always wine.

The out-of-town contingent arrived at her place right on time, which was early in Paris terms. She was barefoot and without lipstick or jewelry, but otherwise, everything was ready. She poured Veuve Clicquot for everyone, then walked to the balcony doors, opening them dramatically.

"There she is," she said as the Eiffel Tower revealed itself, in all its glory. Her friends gasped like the tourists they were and hurried out into the wintery air, glasses in hand. Austen took hers and hurried back to her room to complete her finishing touches.

Her pulse was racing as she sat on her bed and doubled over to strap on the painfully tall Louboutin heels. She fastened the last buckle and flipped her long red hair back to find Sam leaning against the doorframe, champagne in hand, watching her. He looked dashing in a dark suit, white shirt, and deep blue tie which matched his eyes.

"Nice shoes," he said, blatantly admiring her.

She raised one foot and turned her ankle in both directions, giving him a good look. "Wildly uncomfortable, but worth it. You may have to carry me home." *Only half joking. He may.*

She moved to her dresser and put on her earrings and red lipstick while he watched. Her lipstick matched her shoes. "Now I'm officially ready to ring in the New Year." She placed a hand on her hip and let him take her in.

"You're stunning. Need a date?" He offered her his arm.

She linked her arm through his to walk back down the hallway to join their friends on the balcony. "Why yes, I do."

WHITNEY CUBBISON

The *maître d'* showed them to their table, and Sam pulled out Austen's chair. The table was scattered with silver and gold star confetti and tea light candles, with fairy lights twinkling across the ceiling. She snapped photos of every detail. When everyone was seated, a waiter poured the champagne Austen had pre-ordered.

"In France, you must look everyone directly in the eye when you clink their glass," Daphne explained. "Otherwise, it's seven years of bad sex."

"I think we can all agree no one wants that." Jean-Marc raised his glass and toasted his wife, exaggerating his eye contact.

The rest of the group followed their lead, intentionally and methodically locking gazes and toasting across the table. As the champagne hit their tongues, the effervescence of the bubbles leaked into the atmosphere, bringing smiles to all their faces. It was magical, and Austen was quietly thrilled to have put together this evening for her friends.

"So, how did everyone here meet?" Chiara asked, as the first course of foie gras on toast was served.

Peter started. "Sam and I worked together at Pixar 20 years ago and have been buddies ever since. I guess we both met Austen around the same time, back in San Francisco. But she was married and boring then, so we didn't really run in the same social circles." He gave her a playful look.

"I was never boring." Austen kicked him lightly under the table.

"Pixar, the animation studio?" Nico asked.

"I worked on the dull side of the house in finance, and Peter worked on the creative side in production," Sam explained.

Nico nodded his approval, looking impressed.

"I moved to London about a year ago for a production job with Disney, and since Austen comes there pretty regularly for work, we've had the chance to bond over the crazy ex-pat experience." Peter shifted in his seat, looking reflective. "London and Paris are really different, but it's been good to have an American friend in the time zone to commiserate or celebrate, depending on the day."

Sam spoke next. "I met Austen through work too but at a different job in a PR agency. We've known each other for maybe five years? I can confirm she was never boring. But it's sure fun to see this new side of her coming out as a Parisian princess."

She leaned in and kissed him on the cheek, leaving a faint red lipstick mark, which she quickly wiped away with her thumb.

"What about you two?" Sam asked Daphne and Chiara.

Daphne placed a hand on Jean-Marc's shoulder. "We met here in Paris in a restaurant by sheer luck and happenstance, and Austen and I studied abroad together in the South of France during university." She sat up straighter in her chair and continued. "But we were not friends back then. Austen actively avoided all the other Americans for the whole year, and we all thought she was a total snob."

Austen nodded, acknowledging the truth of Daphne's story. "I was focused on learning French, and you had nothing to offer on that front."

Thank goodness the universe allowed me to correct that error.

"We reconnected a few years ago when Austen and Brad moved here," Daphne explained.

Austen bristled at his name. *The money. The damn beach ball. No, stop,* she told herself. *Don't let him ruin tonight. He's ruined enough.*

"We all lived in San Francisco after Stanford, and Brad and I had a few friends in common, so we saw each other socially from time to time. He knew I lived here, so reached out when they arrived. But truth be told, I always liked Austen more than I liked him." Daphne raised her glass to her friend.

"As it turns out, I like you a lot more than I like him, too." Austen threw Daphne a sincere smile and raised her glass in return.

Chiara jumped on the momentary silence to share her story. "I picked up Austen and Daphne, and Nico for that matter, in a bar, albeit under different circumstances."

Liz leaned in and gestured to Chiara. "I knew I liked her."

"We met salsa dancing." Chiara put her hand on the back of Nico's neck. "As for the girls, I went to a networking event in a different bar and noticed them talking, clearly having more fun than anyone else in the room. So, I inserted myself into their conversation, which was the best decision I've made since I arrived in Paris."

Both Austen and Daphne let out simultaneous "awws" as the three women grasped hands across the confetti-strewn table.

"Andrew and I win for knowing Austen the longest," Liz interjected. "We all met freshman year at Stanford when we were 18 years old. Mere babes. Been friends ever since. We were at Austen and Brad's wedding, so we decided we had to be here for the divorce coming out party."

"Oh, is that what this weekend is?" Austen asked, laughing.

"Hell yeah, it is," Sam and Peter both said almost in unison, raising their glasses to her.

The night passed in a blur of incredible food, wine, and more champagne. Once the dinner plates were cleared, the group made their way into the bar area, where the DJ was already playing music. Liz grabbed Austen's hand and spun her around on her heels. She twirled right into Andrew, who was never more than a step away from Liz. He grabbed her shoulders and turned her toward Daphne and Chiara, who were bouncing to the beat. The guys followed their lead, and soon, the whole group was dancing.

The DJ stopped the music to start the countdown to midnight. *"Dix. Neuf. Huit. Sept. Six. Cing, Quatre, Trois. Deux. Bonne Année,"* he shouted.

"Happy New Year," Austen shouted toward the ceiling. She looked around the room at her friends, as all the couples leaned in for their New Year's kisses. She lunged at Peter with a hug. He hugged her back and kissed her on the cheek before quickly heading to the bar.

She turned to find Sam, but he had already found her. He leaned in and kissed her squarely on the lips, holding the back of her neck gently. To Austen, the whole thing happened in slow motion while the music blared, and everyone celebrated around them. He released her slowly, watching her for a reaction. She could only smile and then slowly squeeze her lips together to suppress it, even while her eyes smiled into his. Words escaped her.

He ran his hand lightly down her bare back, then grew conscious of the room and drew his hand away. He planted a quick peck on her cheek and peeled away, breaking the spell. As he walked toward Peter at the bar, Austen stood immobilized, slightly stunned by the kiss, and very buzzed by the champagne. *Did anyone see that?* She scanned the room nervously, but everyone appeared to be caught up in their own celebrations.

Then she saw Chiara, standing in the corner of the room, staring at her wide-eyed. She flagged her over.

Austen covered her mouth with her hand, in a reflex defense, as she walked across the room to her friend. Chiara knew all the stories about Sam, so the significance of the moment wasn't lost on her.

"I saw that," Chiara shouted over the music, shaking Austen's shoulders lightly. "That was your first kiss, no?"

"It was. There was no tongue, but it wasn't a quick peck either." Austen grabbed her friend's arm, realizing her hand was shaking like a leaf.

Chiara reached for a champagne bottle and filled Austen's glass. "Drink. Breathe. It's a new year, and the night is young. There are no rules on New Year's Eve."

The dancing resumed. Austen and Sam never let the other get too far away. She didn't want things to be too obvious, but resisting the pull felt like hard work. *We've got our very own magnetic field going here,* she thought. *And magnets are impossible to keep apart.* She wrapped her arms around Daphne and Liz as they danced, to counter the force.

Austen's aching feet eventually led her to a barstool, where she sat with her back against the bar, talking to Peter, Liz, and Andrew. Sam was nearby talking to Daphne and Jean-Marc but caught Austen's eye as she gave him the tiniest of head nods, asking without words for him to join her. He meandered over, grabbing a champagne bottle on the way and filling her glass when he reached her. He put the bottle down and rested his arm on the bar behind her.

Daphne grabbed her phone. "You guys all get together. We need a picture."

As they squeezed together and smiled for the camera, she felt Sam slide his fingertips inside the deep V of her backless dress, his thumb rubbing just below her shoulder blade. She was instantly alert. His fingertips were only on her for a few seconds, but her skin was burning from it for the rest of the night.

When the restaurant staff eventually kicked them out, Daphne, Chiara, and their guys hopped into cabs, and Austen walked the out-of-towners back to their hotel. She and Liz walked at the front of the pack.

"It's been too long since I've seen you smile and laugh like you did tonight," Liz said, wrapping her arm around Austen. "I knew you'd come out of this whole divorce mess stronger, so I was never worried about you. But I'm so happy to see you in a better place. You deserve it, you know."

Austen stopped and wrapped her arms tightly around her friend. "I love you dearly," she declared into her chestnut hair.

Liz whispered into Austen's ear. "Is this Sam thing finally happening? You two seem cozy."

"Shh. Not now," Austen chided, her arms still wrapped around her friend. She saw over Liz's shoulder that the guys were right behind them.

"Break it up, you two," Andrew shouted. "This happens every time they're together and have some alcohol in them, which is basically every time," he explained to Sam and Peter. "We may be getting to the stage where they need to be fireman carried home."

"We're fine," Liz and Austen squealed in unison, champagne still effervescing through their blood.

Just in case, Andrew took Liz by the waist, and Peter and Sam locked elbows with Austen for the rest of the walk back.

When they were in front of the hotel, Andrew hoisted Liz over his shoulder, delivering on the fireman's carry he had threatened. "Good night, revelers, and Happy New Year," he shouted over his shoulder as they entered.

Liz waved goodbye from her precarious, upside-down position and shouted, "I love you guys."

"Great night, Austen, thanks," Peter said, hugging her and shaking Sam's hand. "Goodnight, buddy."

"I'm walking you home." Sam was insistent. "I will do the fireman's carry if needed."

"Not when I'm wearing this dress," she laughed, pulling down her hemline. "But I will gladly take your arm."

He put his arm around her waist and held on to the crook of her elbow with his other hand, as she teetered down the sidewalk in her high heels.

As they walked, her mind started to race. *Is he coming in? Do I want him to come in? What would that mean?* By the time they reached her grandiose Parisian doorstep, she had no answers to her questions. She stood at the doorway, not opening it and faced him wordlessly, until they fell into one another and started kissing. *Magnets.*

The kiss continued for what felt like an eternity, this time with a whole lot of tongue. It was intense but not urgent. But even in her champagne-fueled state, something in her mind clicked mid-embrace.

I can't invite him in. I'm not ready for this.

She pulled back slowly and took both of his hands in hers, squeezing them lightly. "Tonight was incredible. But I don't think you should come up."

He searched her face and then, with one finger, slowly returned a fallen spaghetti strap of her dress to her left shoulder. "OK. Happy New Year, love. I'll see you tomorrow?"

She nodded. She had made lunch plans with the out-of-towners for the next day.

"Sleep well." He kissed her lightly on the lips and then walked in the direction of the hotel.

She woke up the next morning with her head reeling from a combo of hangover and wow-that-really-happened-so-now-what stupor. She replayed the kiss over and over. She'd wondered what kissing Sam would feel like so many times. *It finally happened, and I sent him home. Why? He's such a good kisser.* But the longer she thought about it, the more certain she was. *It was the right call.*

Austen's heart was in her throat as she entered Au Pied de Cochon for lunch. Peter, Sam, Liz, and Andrew were already seated when she arrived, and the open chair for her was on the same side of the table as Sam, with Peter between them. She blew kisses around the table at everyone as she took her seat. Sam smiled quietly when their eyes briefly met.

"Brilliant night, Austen," Peter said. "Thanks so much for organizing everything. It couldn't have been better."

"Best New Year's Eve I've had in ages," Liz declared. "We should all come back and do it again next year."

"Sure, why not. I might even be over this hangover by then," Andrew laughed, holding his head.

"Let's get you something greasy," Austen said.

They talked and laughed over warm, cheese-covered French onion soup with crusty bread, soaking up the previous night's alcohol and memories. Everything about the room was warm and calming, so Austen settled into the vibe. A conversation with Sam was inevitable. *For now, don't worry about it. Just enjoy the soup and your friends*, she told herself.

After lunch, as the group lazily wandered back to their hotel, Sam again offered to walk her home.

Once they had peeled away from the group, he said, "You do remember us kissing at your door last night, right?"

She looked at him surprised. "Of course, I do." *Did I seem that drunk?* "And on the dance floor too," she added, to reassure him her memory of last night's events was intact.

"There was an off chance you didn't, so I just wanted to check," he smirked back at her.

She had been searching for the right words ever since she woke up.

"I do remember, of course, and it'd been coming for a long time, I guess. But—" She looked down at her boots, momentarily hypnotized by the monotonous sound they made clicking down the cobblestone streets.

"But?" Sam inquired.

She took a deep breath and turned to look at him. "I've only been divorced for a few months, and you live in San Francisco. I didn't invite you in because there's too much love between us for this to be casual and too much distance for it to be serious."

He ran his fingers through his dark brown wavy hair and nodded again. "I get that, and you're right. I don't want to risk our friendship. You're too important to me."

"Thank you for understanding," she said, hugging him.

"It was a Happy New Year kiss. Doesn't need to mean anything. It was just another epic evening with you, of which I'm sure there will be many more."

As she walked away, she replayed the conversation. *That went well. Too well? If he was upset that I shut things down, he sure didn't show it.*

She decided to simply be grateful for his maturity and look forward to a new year and a clean slate.

CHAPTER FIVE

The Internet, Round One

One week later

When all the out-of-town guests were gone, Austen met Daphne and Chiara to debrief over mulled wine under the heat lamps on the terrace at La Palette. There was a lot to discuss.

"It was a perfect New Year's Eve. What a great group. Nico and I both had a blast," Chiara offered. "Sam is really great. And oh my God, that kiss."

Daphne had missed it. "Wait. What kiss? You two kissed?"

"*Siii cara,*" Chiara squealed. "I saw it happen. No tongue, but they didn't even need sparklers to ring in their New Year. There was electricity enough in that kiss."

Daphne clapped excitedly. "You two seemed super comfortable together, and yeah, nice guy. Jean-Marc and I talked to him a lot. So, what happens now?"

"She only saw the warm-up act," Austen admitted, gesturing to Chiara.

Chiara's hands flew into the air. "What? Did you sleep with him?"

"No, we didn't. But he walked me home at the end of the night, and we kissed again. With tongue. A lot of tongue. It was kind of amazing, but then I didn't invite him in," Austen said, dropping her forehead into her hand.

She recounted her conversation with Sam and their decision to bury the kiss.

"Wow, that's very adult and rational of you both," Daphne offered. "How're you feeling about it all now?"

Austen interlaced her fingers and put her hands under her chin. "It was the only sensible choice. A long-distance Paris to San Francisco romance would be about as spontaneous as the one I would've had with Alain. I can't have a boyfriend nine time zones away. It's crazy."

"You made the right call," Chiara said. "But you two do have good chemistry. That much was obvious. I'm not sure this story is over."

Austen nodded. "We've been good friends for so long that if something started, it'd go from zero to 100 in no time at all, and I just can't do serious again so soon after Brad. But he's wonderful." She closed her eyes and shook her head. "If he ends up with someone else any time soon, I'll kick myself. But I just can't do it now."

"If it's meant to be, it will, when the time is right," Daphne declared. "You've been off the market for a decade, and you're in a new country. You should be enjoying the local flavors. Trust me. I'm a chef."

"New Year's Resolution: I will only date French men." Smiling, Austen banged her fists on the table for emphasis.

"It's time for me to get properly integrated into the Parisian single-girl lifestyle. Bring on the frogs."

Chiara waved her phone in the air. "I think it's time for you to get online," she said with her signature devilish smile.

The world of online dating was known to be a wild roller-coaster ride the whole world over, and Austen was sure France would be no exception. Alain showed her the tip of the Parisian dating iceberg, and even that small glimpse taught her several important things. First, French men and American men are not the same when it comes to dating culture. Second, when texting is the primary form of communication, and one is communicating in a second language, it's easy to misunderstand things. Third, one doesn't learn the vocabulary for sex and flirting in school.

"Once, I tried to tell Alain via text that he made my toes curl." She shook her head, remembering the embarrassment. "My literal translation did not work. He could tell I was trying to be sexy, but he had absolutely no idea what I meant."

"You'll learn as you go," Daphne reassured her. "I had a lot of fun getting Jean-Marc to teach me all of that vocab. Embrace the challenge."

She was willing to give it a try. *On the plus side, it will be great practice for my French writing skills.* Her job was international, so she worked only in English and hadn't written in French since her university days.

After a careful exercise in joint editing with her friends, her online dating profile was live on Bumble. She focused on the things that she thought wouldn't intimidate potential suitors. *I'm not lying about who I am. It's selective disclosure. No one is totally honest online, right?* She chose to play down the powerhouse elements of her job, and herself. She simply said she worked "in communications." She left out that she'd traveled to more than 70 countries. She didn't even *think* about including her alma mater, Stanford.

Later that night, she sat on her couch and scrolled through the online dating minefield. If anyone had been watching her through the living room window, her facial expressions would have been cause for alarm. They alternated between wide-eyed-WTF, twisted in horror, jaw dropped open, and the rarer look that casually combined inherent doubt with cautious optimism.

These guys need serious help in self-marketing. What are they thinking with some of these photos? I need some rules. She started a list for herself.

> THE RULES: Do not swipe right on anyone whose photos include:
> 1. Multiple car selfies. So vain.
> 2. The "in bed" shot.
> 3. Shirtless bathroom mirror selfie(s).
> 4. Nothing but selfies.
> 5. A hat and/or sunglasses in every picture. Definitely hiding something.
> 6. Smoking in any picture. Filthy habit.
> 7. A kid in picture number one. Allowances can be made for a kid in later photos.

Her experience with Alain led her to believe that any guy who put a kid in his first picture in his dating profile was looking for a new mom for said kid. *A girl should get the chance to fall for the guy first before taking on the family.*

But even with this initial screening process in place, Austen went on many dates over the next two months that ended up in some form of tragicomedy. Her friends were equally amused and horrified by her stories.

Isobel came to her apartment one night in early February, to hear about the latest nightmare date.

"You should start a blog," she declared, sitting on the couch sipping Pinot Noir from a recent wine tasting trip to Burgundy. "Honestly, you just can't make this shit up. It's too good not to be shared with the world."

Austen loved the idea, but her practical side dampened her enthusiasm. "It'd be a lot of fun. But I'd never get another date."

"Make it anonymous. Oh my God you're going to be the next Banksy, cranking out one genius thing after the next, with everyone absolutely gagging to know who you are."

"I'd be horrified if anyone from work discovered it," Austen admitted. "I've seen guys' profiles online with no photos, where they explicitly say they've not included any to avoid discovery at work. I get it."

"Ooh, speaking of pictures, I have another idea. You should take one for each blog post, from wherever the dates happen," Isobel said, her energy rising. "Your Instagram is divine. You've got a brilliant eye for photography."

The creative side of Austen's brain started to fire. "Paris does offer an impeccable canvas. I probably already have pictures I could use from most of these wretched evenings."

She forced herself to take photos of beautiful things whenever she had a bad day, as a reminder to appreciate the small stuff. Most of her dates tipped the scale to "bad day," and in Paris, beauty was everywhere.

"It could be a small detail of the venue—a pattern in the floor tiles, a candle on the table, the jars of drink garnishes at the bar. But no faces. Anonymity or bust."

Isobel put an index finger to her lips, as if to shush someone, and then pointed strongly at Austen. "You'll have to be discreet taking the pictures. Otherwise, the guy will notice and might expose you if he ever came across the blog."

"With the stories I have, no man will want to admit he's the subject. I think I'll be safe on that front." Austen leaned back into the couch with confidence.

"You make an excellent point," Isobel said. "You simply must do it."

She thought about it for another week and then decided Isobel was right. *I'm going to take these horrid misadventures and create something entertaining. If nothing else, it will distract me from how wildly unfulfilling my dating adventures actually are.*

On a rainy Saturday morning, she plopped onto her plush forest-green couch with her laptop to research domain names and read "how to start a blog" advice. It didn't take long for her to find an appealing blog template and purchase her URL. By Sunday evening, the blog was live.

Welcome to Dating Disasters.Paris!   February 16

Lots of people don't know this, but Paris has two names—
the better known "City of Love" which I have found to be
the result of some truly nefarious marketing, but also the
"City of Light." This second moniker was earned during
the Enlightenment, when Paris was a central locale for big
ideas and progressive thinking. The city was home to some
of that era's greatest poets, philosophers, and scientists.
These were the kind of men (let's face it, they were all men)
who held rooms—and women—utterly rapt for hours, pon-
tificating on all manner of things with elegance, depth, and
sophisticated charm.

Let's just say that something catastrophic happened since
the late 18th century to the men of Paris. I'm convinced "that
something" is Internet dating, as it has given everyone the
attention span of goldfish. I would like nothing more than to
be held rapt, totally absorbed, spellbound by the intelligence
and wit of a handsome man across the quaint Parisian café
table from me—and to feel that I too hold that same power
over him. Because it is the 21st century after all, and because,
well, equality! Sadly, Paris is not cooperating. On most of my
dates, I struggle to get past one glass of wine without wanting to bolt, and I *really* like wine. Even worse, if I stopped
to look over my shoulder, I'm pretty sure no one would be
chasing after me.

So, what's a girl to do? Start a blog, apparently. No, I won't tell
you much about me, other than I'm an Anglophone in my late

thirties. But I will tell you about what it's like to be a single girl on a quest to find my own version of both love and light in modern-day Paris. Frankly, I hope this blog doesn't last too terribly long and Monsieur Right is just around the corner, but in the meantime, buckle up, Internet friends. This is going to be a bumpy ride. Oh, and all names in the blog are changed to protect the guilty! Let's do this!

#parisdatingdisasters

Charles, the Cheapskate   February 16

Charles and I said our bonjours and ordered a glass of Bordeaux each at Les Éditeurs in the 6th near Odéon with cute red chairs and white tablecloths. The chairs turned out to be cuter, and even more interesting, than the man. The hour of conversation that followed consisted entirely of small talk and never took the slightest hint of a turn toward anything amusing, flirtatious or even remotely interesting. The vibe at our little café table was lackluster, at best. Honestly, it was so dull it's not even worth recounting. It felt like watching paint dry.

After one drink, I fabricated some dinner plans and said I had to go. The check arrived and was placed on his side of the table. He looked at it, then looked at me and asked if I wanted to see him again. He looked sad, like he already knew the answer was no.

Shocked at the timing of this question, my only thought was to be honest. It's my default mode. "Sorry. I don't think so," I replied, with an attempt at kind eyes.

He pushed the check into the middle of the table and said, "OK then, let's split the bill."

Charles is an accountant, and I must say, the accounting side of him was definitely not his most attractive. It was two glasses of wine. Ten euros, total.

"No, let me get it," I insisted.

He let me.

For the record, readers, I'm not one of those girls who expects the man to pay. I'm all for equality and perfectly happy to go Dutch, but who *openly* bases their decision on how to pay a bill on whether there will be a second date? No class whatsoever, Charles.

Thank the Lord for girlfriends. Mine were only a short "SOS" text away. Bless their hearts; they promised me the next one would be better. It wasn't.

#parisdatingdisasters

Philippe, the Ultra French   February 23

Philippe looked like he should be in a classic Parisian art house film and acted like it too. All he needed was a beret to complete the image you probably have in your head right now, dear readers. I admit, I was into it. We are in Paris, after all. It felt like the "real deal" experience.

We met at Le Café des Officiers near École Militaire and were chatting along pleasantly about work and life, in "getting to know one another" mode, or so I thought, when he said, "I can't believe you talk like this."

I took a beat to try and make sense of his comment. But despite the best efforts of the wheels spinning in my head, I really didn't get it. So, I just asked him. "Like what?"

"You just say what you mean," he told me, staring at me across our tiny French café table, as if I was some sort of alien. He lit a cigarette as he stared, completing the perfect French stereotype.

"And?" I stammered. I genuinely had no idea what was happening.

"I don't know anyone who talks like this," he told me, with a look of genuine confusion and a hint of bemusement on his face.

I couldn't help myself. I just had to ask what the hell this Frenchie was talking about. Eventually I pulled out of him that, apparently, French women simply never say what they actually mean. They speak in some sort of undecipherable code that French men are meant to figure out through some lengthy and painstaking process of discovery that—allegedly—adds to the intrigue.

He spoke of it as a very charming and enjoyable game that everyone universally understands to be the de facto way to get to know someone. All of this "just saying what you mean" was clearly not to his taste. Too easy, apparently. How boring. How pedestrian.

I was raised on "be yourself." It seems this is NOT the way to go in French dating. Philippe has led me to spend more than a few hours since, desperately seeking the answer to one critical question: How can one possibly succeed in a game where they simply don't understand the rules?

Recounting this story to French friends at a few dinner parties in recent weeks, I have gotten many knowing nods in recognition of this mysterious little game that's apparently played between all eligible Parisian bachelors and bachelorettes. But tragically, not one of them has offered to explain the rules. I'm probably screwed. But I will play on.

#parisdatingdisasters

Pierre, the Mansplainer   March 5

Part one

Let me start by owning the fact that this story truly should not have two parts. It should have been a "one and done." But I was having an off day and got blindsided. It happens, right?

I met Pierre at 7 p.m. at Le Bombardier near the Sorbonne. I was already seated when he arrived, looking flustered. He said bonjour and then quickly told me that the zipper on his jacket was stuck. He couldn't get out of it and asked if I could help—because I have tiny fingers, he said.

The guy seriously asked, as his opening line, for me to help with his zipper. It wasn't his pants, but still. I took one look at the jacket zipper and knew it wasn't coming unstuck, so suggested he just slip it off over his head. I watched as he awkwardly wiggled himself out of the jacket, tossing it on the chair and settling into our table. What a weird start.

I ordered a glass of Bordeaux. He ordered tea. Who drinks tea at 7 p.m. on a date? In retrospect, I should have left immediately based on that choice alone.

He then proceeded to rapid-fire questions at me for 54 minutes. I clocked it. The questions were about my work, my studies, my family, and my ex-pat life in France. I never had the chance to ask him anything because I was apparently being interviewed for a job—the job of being his girlfriend. But it turns out it wasn't so much an interview as it was a pre-screening. After these strange 54 minutes, he put some money on the table, quickly stood up and said, "Well this has been fun. You're really interesting. I have a dinner to get to, but I'd like to see you again. How's Saturday?"

Had my brain been firing at full speed, I could-have-would-have-should-have simply said "no merci" and put myself out of the impending misery, but as mentioned, I was having an off night. I uneasily agreed while he clumsily struggled to get his zipped-up jacket back over his head. None of it was graceful.

"Great, I'll text you," he said, as he bolted out the door. I sat there stunned for a solid minute wondering what the hell had just happened, and then resigned myself to part *deux*.

Part two

Saturday arrived, and Pierre suggested that we meet at the Grands Boulevards Metro. In my experience, meeting at a Metro stop means the guy has no plan so we inevitably spend the first 20 minutes of the date wandering around (usually on cobblestones with me in heels) to find an acceptable spot. Between this and the less-than-auspicious part one of this encounter, I was not jazzed about the evening. But at this point, I was committed.

I got on the Metro, and while en route, he texted saying he was going to be 15 minutes late. It was raining, so I asked (always hopeful) if he had a place in mind. I suggested I could head directly there, rather than waiting at the Metro stop in the rain. I ended the text with a smiley face emoji because that softens it, right?

He replied saying he didn't have a place in mind but maybe he would only be five minutes late after all. Subtext: you'll wait in the rain. Deal with it.

Charmed, I'm sure.

I huddled under the awning of the Metro station until he arrived, and we emerged into the rain together. We wandered into two places that were fully booked before eventually landing in a small Italian restaurant that was completely devoid of charm. The fact is that on Saturday night in Paris, reservations are required for any place that's even remotely nice. I wasn't expecting a Michelin star, but I do appreciate it when someone takes the time to actually *plan* a date. Is that so much to ask?

We were looking over the menu when he proclaimed, "They have ravioli. You know, the pasta with stuff inside." There was an accompanying hand gesture to demonstrate the putting of stuff into the pasta pocket. Or was he pantomiming sex? I instinctively cocked my head to the side like a dog trying to understand its human. Did he really just mansplain ravioli to me?

All this happened in French of course, so I took an extra second or two to be sure I understood what was happening. When my brain confirmed that it was the disaster it seemed to be, it was too late for a snarky reply, so I simply went with,

"Yeah sure, ravioli." I somehow managed to keep my exaggerated eye roll on the inside.

Suffice it to say the conversation didn't improve, so by the time dinner was over, I was desperate to escape. I told him I'd take the Metro home, and because he lived in the same direction, he said he'd join me. It was my lucky night.

In the Metro, he asked if I was a natural redhead. I told him I was not.

He then mansplained, "Because you know, there *are* natural redheads in the world."

Yes, dear readers, he mansplained ravioli and redheads in the course of 90 minutes, and then asked if I wanted to go home with him. I did not.

#parisdatingdisasters

Austen posted the first four entries and shared it with a dozen trusted friends in Paris and the States. She picked people who agreed to protect her anonymity but also knew how to build an audience. She didn't care deeply about her blog going viral. She only wanted to entertain some people with her miserable dating experiences. Misery loves company, after all.

Her audience numbers grew slowly but surely. Comments and likes started to roll in. Unsurprisingly, Anglophone women were shocked to learn that not all Parisian men were the romantic legends of their cinematic or literary dreams. The momentum of the blog encouraged her to keep swiping on Bumble, even though the resulting dates continued to disappoint. And so, she continued to blog.

Paul and the Pheromones   March 14

Paul was an architect, and we had some interesting conversation online leading up to the date, so I went into this
evening pretty optimistic. I was so optimistic, in fact, that I
suggested we meet on the opening night of an art exhibit at
a small gallery near the Opéra. It was curated by a friend of
mine and its subject was the art of the Kama Sutra. Kinky,
I know.

But in record time—literally seconds—it was painfully clear
that we would never be entwined in any kind of kinky pose
whatsoever. He smelled. Terribly. It wasn't B.O. It was pheromones. From the second we did the traditional French bises
(the double cheek kiss hello) at the museum entrance, I wanted to bolt. Everything was just *off*.

Pheromones. Of all the freaking reasons a date could go
wrong, this was one I'd never even considered, and yet, there
it was, violently accosting my olfactory system. He was cute
too, damn it, but *just no*. It was impossible from go.

I did my best to keep a reasonable distance between us as
we walked through the exhibit, and after about 20 minutes
of artful avoidance, I started to question myself. Was it really that bad? I decided to take a second sniff as he was
admiring an etching of two people tangled in a position I'd
never even thought to consider. I walked up to the point
that our shoulders were touching and very nearly gagged

before slinking far away. I had no choice but to speed up my pace to reach the end of the exhibit, graciously thank my friend the curator, feign an upset stomach, and flee into the night.

#parisdatingdisasters

Simon, the Snoozer   March 18

Yep. I'm still going, and it's still ridiculous.

Simon was a divorced software sales guy with two kids, who seemed very sweet. He even offered multiple options for bars we could meet in, all in my arrondissement, which he had kindly researched for my convenience. So thoughtful. So promising.

Or was he just trying to get close to my apartment in case things went well? I chose to believe it was the former and picked Les Timbrés from his lovely little list. It was a tiki bar I have walked by a million times and never noticed. There's a tiki bar with fruity drinks in tiki hut-type glasses in Paris. Who knew? It was cute and quirky and unusual, and I was optimistic. I like unusual.

Our first 20 minutes of small talk turned to a discussion of our hobbies, and he shared that he was a big movie buff. He told me he went to the movies almost every day.

I expressed some surprise that he was able to find a movie he wanted to see in the theater almost every day and guessed he must have a really broad set of interests. It was a leading statement to try to investigate his passion.

"Well, not really," he admitted. "Sometimes, I just go there to take a nap."

Umm. Say what? Is he homeless? Why can't he nap at home? And why on Earth did he just confess this? I was thrown. "Unusual" had just gone south.

As my eyes dropped down to my tiki drink and I considered all the oddities of this twist in my night, I thought of that weird early 90s Tom Hanks and Meg Ryan movie *Joe Versus the Volcano* where he accepts an offer to throw himself into the volcano on a tropical island. Maybe poor Joe had just been on too many bad dates. I get it, Joe. It's a jungle out there.

#parisdatingdisasters

Robert, the Ghost   March 25

I suggested to Robert that we meet at a cute bar called Rosie
in the 18th arrondissement. This place is on the other side of
town from where I live, but I really like the vibe so decided to
venture across the Seine. I left work a bit late and headed in
that direction, and shortly after, Robert texted saying he was
running 30 minutes late. I replied saying no problem. I was
going to be 10-15 minutes late myself, so all good.

I arrived, and at the "30 minutes late" mark, he texted again
saying he was *really* late and maybe we should just reschedule.
I asked where he was. He was near Alésia, closer to my
place. Frustrated but not ready to let the night fall apart before
it even began, I proposed that I head back in his direction, and we could meet somewhere in the middle. I asked
him to pick the place, thinking it was the least he could do
to make up for his incredible lateness. He replied saying he
really didn't know the neighborhood, so asked me if I could
pick. So, everything was going *super well.*

Unimpressed, I texted him the address for Le Dôme near
Montparnasse. He replied to say he'd be there in 15 minutes.
I got back on the Metro and headed that way. I was about
ten minutes out when he texted saying he was there—at our
second meeting point. By this time, it was nearly 9 p.m., so I
suggested that he order food for both of us—anything would
do—and that I'd be right there. He agreed.

I arrived shortly thereafter and looked high and low for him,
inside and out on the terrace. No sign of Robert. On the off

chance he looked nothing like his pictures online, I texted him saying I was there, asking where he was. No reply.

I waited ten minutes, standing on the sidewalk in front of the restaurant and then left in a huff, descending into the Vavin Metro, baffled, and hurt, imagining the worst-case scenario: that he'd seen me and left. I wore a dress and everything. Or maybe he was never there. Maybe he was sitting at home petting his six cats the whole night while I traversed Paris, twice. I'll never know.

In the Metro, I decided to check Bumble, just in case he had sent me a message there. Opening the app, I discovered he had unmatched me at some point in this wild goose chase across Paris. I sat there, fuming, and texted my best girl-friend, to rage about the whole ordeal. I was texting so furi-ously that I missed my Metro stop to get home. When I finally looked up and realized where I was, I'll admit I let out a long string of colorful expletives under my breath, jumped off at the next stop and took an Uber home to get the night over with as quickly as possible.

I was still texting with my friend when I got home. Her texts flew back with the righteous indignation only a bestie could have. She asked if I'd sent him a nasty message for sending me on a wild goose chase across Paris. I told her that I didn't want to give him the satisfaction of my fury. The only thing I really wanted to say at that point was, "Your mother must be very proud."

And, I wasn't sure that would translate.

After Robert, dear readers, I think I'm going to give this app a breather. I've had enough of the Internet. It hardly seems worth it. I'm now officially holding out for a meeting in the real world. These seem rare, by all accounts, but I'm an eternal optimist, and the app must go.

But I promise to keep writing, with any juicy stories of real-life encounters, so stay tuned, and here's hoping! And in the meantime, good riddance, you bastard, The Internet.

#parisdatingdisasters

A few days after the "good riddance" post went live, Austen opened the dashboard on her blog and discovered it had amassed more than 300 followers. *Three hundred fellow members of the lonely-hearts club*, she thought. She flipped into the comments section and started to read.

"Oh, girl I've been there," one reader wrote.

"You can't be serious. My Paris dating dream bubble is bursting," another commented.

"What the actual fuck?" a third asked.

Austen laughed out loud. At least her dating mishaps were giving other people some giggles. Sharing the stories, even anonymously with strangers, made her feel less alone. She was an extrovert to the extreme; she got energy from being around other people. Yet, at the end of every failed date as she made her way home alone, she felt the energy draining out of every finger and toe. Thinking about the blog, what she could share from the night's experience and how her readers might connect to it, brought some of that energy back to her.

Maybe I'll keep swiping. The next one could be the one, she thought.

The next swipe revealed none other than Alain. Proving her rule about kids in profile photos, there he was, posing in photo number one with his son. *Ugh. OK, the next one could be the one?* The next swipe revealed Charles the Cheapskate, the dull-as-dishwater guy from her first blog entry.

"It's official. I've reached the end of the Internet. There are no more men," she said out loud to no one, before tossing her phone violently into the armchair in the far corner of her living room. She felt numb. She stared at the wall for a solid 20 minutes, before getting up to retrieve her phone and deleting the app in frustration.

CHAPTER SIX

The Bodyguard

Early April

Off on another jet set work adventure, Austen was headed to Senegal for two days. It was the usual group—François, Bastien and herself, plus a new communications colleague, Georges. When they landed in Dakar, she watched from the window as two black armored SUVs pulled up next to the jet on the tarmac. Austen emerged from the plane and saw two security guards, both clad in *Men In Black* suits and Ray-Bans, each standing by a chauffeured car. One was shorter and built like a tank. The other was tall—a gorgeous God of a man with dark hair, olive skin and broad shoulders, and he was coming straight at her.

"Hello, Ms. Keller." He extended a very capable-looking hand. "I'm Matt. I've got you and Mr. Martin with me in car two. My colleague, Carl, has your other colleagues with him."

She met his grip with one hand and tried with the other to tame her hair, which flew wildly in the tropical tarmac wind. Her insides pulsed to the same wild beat.

I'm going to like Senegal. I can feel it already. "Nice to meet you, Matt. Please don't call me Ms. Keller. Just Austen."

"Very good, Austen." He nodded his head with military precision.

Georges had heard his name and moved toward them. "I'm Mr. Martin. Call me Georges. Thank goodness we're in the fun car."

"The fun car?" Matt raised an eyebrow, calling attention to his piercing blue eyes, as he opened the back door.

"François and Bastien will be talking about business non-stop for the next two days," Georges said, climbing into the back seat. "When we're with them, we have to be in that mode too, but without them, this is automatically the fun car."

A crooked smile spread across Matt's face as Austen slid into the back seat next to Georges. Moments later, she watched him settle into the front passenger seat and adjust four rearview mirrors, from which he could monitor all angles. The mirrors also helpfully provided her with multiple views of Matt's face.

"This is our driver, André," Matt said, gesturing to the man next to him. André turned and gave them a silent nod.

"So Matt, tell us absolutely everything about you," Georges said, as both cars rolled toward the exit.

The tone of his voice was just a bit too interested. *Georges isn't blind. Of course, he's drooling too. Who wouldn't be?*

"Not much to tell. I'm based out of Johannesburg but grew up in French Polynesia," Matt replied.

"How exotic," Georges declared. "I've lived my whole life in Paris and will surely die there too."

"Paris is a great city. There are plenty of worse places to spend your days. In my line of work, I've been to most of them," he said, as his eyes scanned the road ahead.

"I thought I detected a slight French accent." Austen tried hard not to sound as interested as Georges.

"*Je m'appelle Mathieu, au fait*[2]. Matt just works better in South Africa," he explained, before quickly switching gears into work mode. "I have your itinerary for both days, and we're on our way now to your first meeting at Banque Atlantique Sénégal. We should be there in 18 minutes."

André shuttled them around Dakar all day, from one meeting to the next. Matt opened and closed every door they passed through, whether car, building or elevator. His eyes were always scanning, alert to their surroundings. When she didn't have to be "on" with François, she tried to be subtle about watching him work, stealing glances whenever she thought he wouldn't notice. He caught her almost every time. He was watching her too, but she couldn't be sure if his interest was personal or entirely professional.

He's obviously very good at what he does. I bet he could kill someone with his bare hands. Well, that's terrifying. Think about something else. I bet he can do other things with those hands too.

Her eyes were fixed on the clear, curly cord that stretched from his earpiece down his tan neck into his jacket collar. It'd been five months since things had ended with Alain, and she'd had only horrible first dates since. She missed being touched. Between her inner monologue and the outside temperature in Dakar, Austen felt pleasantly over-heated for most of the day.

When they arrived at the hotel that evening, Austen and Georges settled into couches in the hotel lobby to finish the prep for the next day's press conference. François and the Senegalese Minister of Education were set to introduce new collaboration technology for the country's teachers and

---

2   My name is Mathieu, actually.

students, and during the flight, François had requested changes to his talk track and the press release. Both had to be sent to the Minister's office for final approvals before nine p.m.

As the sun was setting, sending warm light pouring through the lobby windows, Matt approached.

"Sorry to interrupt. Just wanted to let you know I've taken your luggage up to your rooms. You're both on the fourth floor. I'm headed up, turning in for the night." He held his hand out to Austen, palm open. "Let me plug my number into your phone in case you need anything."

The request wasn't unusual for corporate security protocol, so she handed her phone to him without a thought. He quickly programmed in the number and wished them both a nice evening. She watched him walk away and then turned to Georges who was looking at her wide-eyed and open-mouthed.

"What?" she asked, unsure why he was gaping at her.

"He gave *you* his number but didn't even pretend to want to give it to me."

It was true. He hadn't. The realization turned her face a particularly elaborate shade of crimson. Georges, on the other hand, turned green with envy.

About 30 minutes later, Bastien came out of the elevator, looking frazzled and running his fingers through his hair more frantically than usual. He saw Austen and Georges and walked quickly toward them.

"I left my laptop in my room when I was grabbing a bite to eat, and I just went back up there, and it's gone. I think it was stolen."

Austen picked up her phone. "Let me call Matt. He'll know what to do."

He answered after one ring. "Matt speaking."

Very professional, very sexy voice. "Hi, it's Austen."

There was a pause just a beat too long, and then, "Hi. Is everything OK?"

His words were all business, but Austen detected pleasant surprise in his tone.

"I'm afraid not. Bastien's laptop has gone missing from his room. We're down in the lobby."

"I'm on my way," he said quickly, now in full business mode.

Moments later, Matt emerged from the elevator looking serious but dressed down in jeans and a t-shirt. The tattoos snaking up his exceedingly well-defined arms immediately caught her attention. Bastien crossed the lobby to meet him, and she watched as they spoke briefly with the hotel manager before they disappeared into the elevator, presumably headed to Bastien's room.

Austen and Georges returned to their work, but their concentration was once again disturbed ten minutes later by the ding of the elevator. Matt followed the hotel manager toward the back office. Their eyes caught briefly as he crossed the lobby.

He's always scanning. Professional interest only, Austen told herself. She turned her shoulders away from the office door and concentrated on work.

She was lost in her PC screen 20 minutes later when Georges blurted out, "Austen, girlfriend, that man is done dealing with Bastien's shit, and he is lurking around this lobby waiting for you."

She looked up to see Matt standing by the elevator, typing into his phone. "He's probably filing a report about Bastien's laptop. He's not waiting for me."

"You're blind. He's been tracking you all day. And he keeps looking over here. As much as I hate to admit it, he's not looking at me," Georges said, with an exaggerated pout.

"Well, we're not done, so shut up and let's finish," she said, trying hard to keep the smile off her face.

"If you don't go for it, I will," he smirked.

She couldn't help but giggle.

They were in town for only one night, and while it would break all professional protocol if something happened between them, Georges's words had her wheels turning. When the final edits were sent to François and the Minister's office, she went up to her room, tossed her laptop bag onto the chair and made the quick decision to shave her legs. *Nothing ventured, nothing gained*, she thought. She put on a cute pair of shorts and a tank top, sat cross-legged on the bed, and sent Matt a text.

> Hi, it's Austen. Just thought I'd let you know I'm back in my room, and everything is exactly where it should be.

She saw the three dots dancing across her screen and waited impatiently for his reply.

> So glad to hear it. I still can't believe what happened with Bastien.

> That definitely wasn't how I wanted the night to end.

She took a sharp breath and held it in. *Is he saying what I think he's saying?* She exhaled and typed her response quickly before she lost her nerve.

> I, for one, am still trying to
> decide how my night will end.

She stared at her phone waiting for a reply. A minute ticked by, then two. Then, she heard the faint ding of the elevator, which was directly across the hall from her room. *He knows what room I'm in. Could it be?* She flew to the door and looked out the peephole. There he was, standing very still inside the elevator and staring straight at her door. She gasped silently, waiting for him to make a move.

The elevator door started to close, but he stuck out his arm to stop it, and took two steps into the hallway. Another three steps would close the distance to her door. He stood frozen, until the elevator door once again started to close behind him. He quickly turned on his heels and stopped the door once again with an urgently outstretched arm, his back to her door. Austen held her breath, watching his mental gymnastics play out through the peephole.

I could open my door and say his name, and this would be game on, she thought. *But he's clearly hesitating. Decision has to be his. This could probably get him fired.* She saw his head subtly shake no, as he stepped back into the elevator and let the doors close behind him.

She spun around, leaned into her door and slid down it until she was sitting on the floor, phone still in hand. Her pulse and her mind were racing. *Damn. Georges was right. That almost happened. Holy hell.*

Her phone buzzed.

I hope it ends well! Don't
work too hard. Have a great
night and call me if you need
anything.

Didn't I just do that? She stared at his text for several minutes, looking for an opening that simply didn't exist. Disappointed, she peeled herself off the floor just long enough to flop back onto the bed and let out a sigh. *Why does he have to be so freaking professional?*

The next day, Matt accompanied her and the team to and from all their meetings, and he was all business. The press conference went off without a hitch, and the rest of the day progressed like any other. But now she knew he wanted her. And he didn't know that she knew—that she'd seen his "should I or shouldn't I" turn outside her door.

Knowledge is power, and damn if I'm not feeling powerful today, she thought. *If only we had another night.*

During the last meeting of the day, she struggled to focus. She imagined him sitting outside in the car waiting to escort them back to the airport. She wondered if his body had other tattoos. *I'll probably never see him again, so I've got nothing to lose.* With that thought, she sent another text.

You should keep my number
in case you decide you want
to visit Paris. I'd be happy to
take good care of YOU next
time around.

He replied quickly.

What a nice offer. Thank you.
I miss Paris. Haven't been
back in years. So I just may
take you up on that.

I hope you will.

To have that man in my world. Oh, the glorious possibilities, she thought.

When she and Georges exited the meeting room, Matt was waiting. He escorted them to the car, and when he opened the door for her, his cool professionalism warmed a few degrees. His smile was bigger than before and the sparkle in his eyes was dazzling.

And now I'm leaving. Double damn.

When they arrived at the airport, they made their way into the lounge while Carl and Matt brought in their bags and spoke with the airport staff. A few minutes later, Carl approached and said to François, "I'm sorry sir, but we've just been told there's a mechanical problem with the plane, and it may be a few hours before you're able to take off. The mechanics are on their way."

"A couple of hours? Really? We were already getting in so late." François sounded exasperated as he pulled out his laptop. "Keep us posted please."

Carl walked out of the room, leaving Austen and the team with Matt.

"I don't even have a laptop to work on," Bastien said to no one in particular.

It had never been found in the hotel. He sat down in a huff in an armchair near the window and stared at his phone. Georges let out a frustrated sigh and dove into his laptop. Austen sat down next to him on one side of the taupe L-shaped couch that dominated the center of the room. Matt settled in on the far side of the L, with Georges in between them.

"I'll be here until you guys take off," he said when she looked his way. His words were all business, but his voice conveyed something softer.

Fate is intervening. I've got a few extra hours with this man. What do I do with it?

The wheels in her head were in overdrive. Her options felt limited in the confines of the small room and the suit she was wearing. She unzipped her suitcase and pulled out a pair of perfectly fitting jeans and a casual but fashionable black top. She went to the bathroom to change, and as she returned to the couch, she watched as his gaze traveled all the way up and down her body.

She sat down and pretended to work on her laptop, but her mind was elsewhere. After 45 minutes of feigned, quiet professionalism, she gave in, feeling emboldened by the twistiness of fate and the idea of flirting openly—albeit quietly—while surrounded by colleagues. *I feel naughty. I'm going for it.* She picked up her phone to send another text.

> Everyone in this room is
> so annoyed but I'm going
> to choose to have a sense
> of humor about it all and
> decide that this "mechanical

> problem" is just some
> elaborate scheme by you to
> keep me here for another
> night.

She watched him carefully out of the corner of her eye as he picked up his phone and read her message. He raised a hand to cover his mouth, trying to hide his smile. Then he typed.

> You're fearless. I'm
> impressed.

With you, I think I could be fearless, she thought to herself.

He oozed confidence, and she liked the idea of being with someone who had an above average chance of survival if shit ever really hit the fan. Austen wanted to see the world—even the dodgy parts. She fantasized about the two of them travel-ing to magical places far off the beaten path, swimming naked in pristine lakes in the middle of nowhere and mingling with the locals in a way she would never do on her own, for the sake of security. The appeal was extreme.

She was jolted out of her fantasy when Carl returned to say, "Great news, guys. The problem wasn't as serious as they thought. You're ready for takeoff."

François, Bastien and Georges let out audible sighs of re-lief while gathering their bags and making their way to the doors. Austen lingered back and moved toward Matt. She reached out to shake his hand and shut off all her professional tendencies, looking at him with her best bedroom eyes. "Well, Matt, it's been an adventure. Thanks for everything."

WILL THERE BE WINE?

He shook it slowly and with a tender grip. "I'm walking you to the plane. Door-to-door service. Give me your bag please."

Their hands brushed as she handed it over, and she could swear the touch generated an actual spark.

Door-to-door. If only you'd taken those few extra steps to my door last night, she thought.

They walked the short distance to the plane without speaking. He walked as close to her as was possible, without touching. She felt heat coming off both him and the tarmac, in waves.

Once there, he took her bag to the back to load it, along with the others. She hesitated at the bottom of the plane's stairs but couldn't think of a reason to linger. *Is this how it's going to end? A wave through the plane window? Ugh.*

François was heads down in a newspaper and Georges was on a call when she boarded the plane and flopped into her seat across the aisle from Bastien. Two minutes later, Matt's head and shoulders leaned in through the plane's door. He looked down the aisle and waved goodbye directly to her with a strained look on his face.

Is that regret I see? She mouthed "bye" at him, her heart contracting, as he disappeared down the stairs.

"What was that?" Bastien asked quietly, as his fingers pushed their way through his hair.

Austen reached for her phone in her purse, trying to be casual. "What was what?"

"That little wave goodbye just for you. And it wasn't lost on me that his number was in your phone when my laptop went missing. Good for you."

He almost sounds jealous.

"You're crazy. I'm sure you have Carl's number in yours. Standard protocol," she replied flatly. She looked down at her phone to try and end the conversation. *Busted.*

She texted Matt one last time as the plane started to pick up speed down the runway.

> I've never wanted a flight to be canceled so badly in my life. Oh well. It was super lovely to meet you. Hope our paths will cross again someday.

He didn't reply, and she couldn't help but feel disappointed. Game over.

A few weeks later, Austen was asked to attend some meetings in Johannesburg. *Matt is there.* She sent him an email the same day.

Subject: Hey there

Hi, Matt. Hope all's well and that you don't mind me reaching out.

Maybe you're married. Maybe you've got a girlfriend. Maybe you're wildly uninterested.

But in case none of these things are true, I thought I'd let you know that I'm going to be in Johannesburg in two weeks' time.

Hope to hear from you.

Austen

She never did. She played her cards, and he packed his away. Game over indeed.

But she felt as fearless as Matt believed she was. She took a risk. It didn't pay off, but now she didn't have to wonder, "what if I'd just asked?" It also proved to her once again that real-life encounters were possible. The vile apps weren't the only way to meet people.

It wasn't love or even a kiss. Damn. But the game sure was fun.

CHAPTER SEVEN

The Internet, Round Two

Two months later

Back in Paris, meaningful "in real-life" encounters continued to evade her, so to the Internet she reluctantly returned for a second round. The blog audience was waiting, after all.

She revisited her online dating profile and decided to get a bit more real about who she really was. She added Stanford as her alma mater, which was a cautious step toward reality. *Most French guys have probably never heard of it,* she told herself. *If they haven't, it won't matter, and if they have, maybe it could even be a plus? Surely some French guys are attracted by intelligence.* That hope was confirmed when she noticed the word "sapio-sexual" appearing in some men's profiles. It meant they were turned on by intelligence. *That is a concept I can get behind,* she thought.

She had also spent time reflecting on her learnings from her last stint online, so to her initial list of rules, she decided to add four more. She restarted the blog by sharing the full set, along with some color commentary.

The Rules   June 1

I'm back, dear readers. The real-life Parisian meet-cutes just aren't happening, so I've reinstalled the evil dating app. As I head into round two, I thought I would share my rules for how I try to weed out the un-dateable, based on their profile pictures. I'm trying to make a science of this. Ignore at your own peril.

Do NOT go out with guys who have any of the following:

1.   Multiple car selfies. This is clearly vanity run amok.
2.   The "in bed" shot. One guess what he's after.
3.   Shirtless bathroom mirror selfie, especially when the bathroom is gross.
4.   Nothing but selfies. Does he have any friends? Also, see comment to rule #1.
5.   A hat and/or sunglasses in every picture. Is he in witness protection? He's definitely hiding something.
6.   Smoking in any picture. Kissing a smoker is like licking an ashtray. Amirite?
7.   Posing with his kid(s) in his first picture. Can't we decide if we like the guy before we have to like his progeny? (Later photo with kid(s) is OK. That's good disclosure.)
8.   Posing with a tiger or large cat of any kind. It's shocking how many of these exist.
9.   Posing with a woman who isn't clearly marked as his relative or best friend. Quite a few couples seem to be using dating apps to find threesomes. Is this a French thing or universal? Insights from my readers are welcome here.

10. The "thoughtful" pose with chin on fist. You know the one. Cheeseball.

11. Proposes meeting at the Metro stop. No plan = no date.

For the sharp-eyed amongst you, you'll notice that rule #11 has nothing to do with profile photos and more to do with dating etiquette. This rule was put in place after "Pierre the Mansplainer." (Please refer back to the entry from March 5, and you'll understand why.) I reserve the right to add additional rules to the list as my dating disasters continue. Your suggestions are welcome!

Into the abyss I return, with these rules as my guide. Pray for me.

#parisdatingdisasters

Michel, the Zealot   June 3

I met Michel for a Sunday afternoon coffee near Palais Royal at the perfectly charming café, Le Nemours. The guy wasn't bad looking and worked as a government statistician—an interesting job. He's probably great to have on your team for a pub quiz. I do love a pub quiz. But I digress.

About 30 minutes into the date, he shared that he was thinking of buying a house in Greece. I told him I loved Greece and asked why he had picked it.

His response was a real doozy. But before I tell you what he said, allow me a sidebar. I'm going to misquote him here simply because I was too dumbfounded to retain the actual year he mentioned, so please note that what I cite as "20-whatever" was actually a specific year in the not-too-distant future. With that as context, here is his reply.

"Statistically speaking, by 20-whatever, France will be majority Muslim so will inevitably fall to Sharia Law. So, I think it's better that we leave now and move closer to the cradle of Christianity."

After a casual effort of picking my jaw up off the table, I said to him, "Wow. Sharia Law. In France. You think?" Surely, he was joking, right?

Wrong. He looked me straight in the eyes and said, "I don't think. I know. It's happening." He then proceeded to explain the stats on Muslim versus non-Muslim birthrates and other factors that go into radicalizing a Muslim community. This explanation lasted for a solid five minutes.

Who knows. Maybe he was right, and France is going to be the next Afghanistan, but is that really good conversation for a first date? Or, maybe he was very wrong. I couldn't say. Regardless, he was a bit too religiously motivated for this single girl.

I finished my coffee and made my excuses to go. A few hours later, he sent me a text saying he'd enjoyed meeting me and hoped to see me again soon. I know it's super rude so please don't shout at me in the comments, but I decided not to reply.

To his credit, he sent me a text a few days later saying, "They say that no news is good news, but I think in your case, that's probably not true."

Touché Michel! I responded to that one, wishing him well in love and in Greece. The statistics were definitely not in his favor with me, but at least he had a sense of humor, which isn't obvious in France, I'm discovering.

#parisdatingdisasters

Albert, the Anxious   June 18

Albert had promise. He was a good-looking French guy with an MBA from Harvard and CEO of his own homewares company. On paper, he had it all.

Over dinner at Buvette in the 9th arrondissement, we spoke about how we both worked quite a bit. I said I thought it was OK to work a lot if you love what you do.

"That's not why I work all the time," he quickly replied.

So, I asked him. "Then why do you?"

"To avoid my life."

In my mind, I suddenly saw red flashing lights and heard ambulance sirens wailing. I couldn't tell if the lights in the restaurant had just dimmed, or if it was perhaps my spirit dying a little. I sensed an impending disaster.

He continued, "I'm going to share something really intimate with you."

My first thought upon hearing that was, *Oh God, please don't.*

He continued, despite my silent request: "I can't sleep without an earpiece in my ear with talk radio going, because if I wake up and don't have someone saying boring shit in my ear, I get lost in my own anxiety and can't get back to sleep."

I'm all for honesty, but really.

Too.Much.Information.For.A.First.Date.Dude.

#parisdatingdisasters

Gildas, the Anti-Gun   July 8

Gildas was a filmmaker, so I should have expected an over-active imagination from the beginning, I suppose. We met at Paris's Museum of Music that's tied to the Philharmonic Orchestra concert hall, which I found to be a delightfully creative choice for a date.

He was cute and smart and seemed to have a great sense of humor, so I was having a really nice time walking and talking, while looking at some truly remarkable old instruments. I was relaxing into it and being myself—that person I never know if I should or shouldn't be when dating in France.

"So, you're from Texas," he stated, confirming a fact I'd already shared. I nodded yes, and he continued. "Is it true that if someone breaks into your house there, you can legally shoot them in self-defense?"

I confirmed this strange Texan trivia and then told him that there were ten guns in my parents' house—a range of rifles and handguns all dutifully cared for and used by my dad, mostly for hunting. It should be noted that guns are very uncommon in France, so in retrospect I realize that this is where things went sideways.

He looked at me with genuine concern and asked, "Has your dad ever shot anyone?"

"Well, not since the last guy I brought home," I replied.

Poor Gildas. He blanched and then decided (hoped?) I must be joking and tried with a very fake laugh to move on. He looked so uncomfortable.

For the record, I *was* joking, although when I was in high school, my dad did once answer the door shotgun-in-hand when a boy picked me up for a date. I left that last anecdote out of the conversation because I wasn't actually trying to scare the bejeezus out of him.

Sadly, Gildas' sense of humor wasn't as strong as I'd thought. He picked up the pace of our museum visit, suddenly rather desperate to escape my presence. I guess he really didn't want to meet my dad.

#parisdatingdisasters

Victor, the Desperate   July 30

Things with Victor started out well enough. We chatted on-line, building up to the first date. When the day finally came, however, he made a fatal mistake. He broke rule #11 about meeting at the Metro stop, which I set after the debacle two-part date with Pierre the Mansplainer. The text exchange that ensued just has to be reprinted wholesale. There's really no other way to tell this story.

Hello Austen. How is it going?
Still up for a drink tonight?

> Yes indeed, monsieur. Where shall we meet?

Wherever is convenient for you.

> I work in the 9th and live in the 15th but am up for meeting wherever. Your pick.

How about something near Motte Picquet?

> That works. Do you have a place in mind?

Then there was radio silence for three hours. The day was winding down, Happy Hour was approaching, and I was all dressed up with nowhere to go. So, I tried again.

> Hi. Me again. Any thoughts?

7:30 at the Motte Picquet Metro and then we're going to wing it. OK?

I hesitated. There are plenty of decent options near Motte Picquet, but it was pouring down rain. Also, why create rules just to break them? I knew it wasn't going to go over well, but I decided to hold my ground.

> Actually no, sorry. I promised myself I'd never go on another date where the guy proposed meeting at a Metro in bad weather. It shows a lack of thoughtfulness or effort, so I think it's best we cancel.

Given the totally snarky tone of my message, I was surprised by his quick and rather practical reply.

What? Why? Let's go to Primerose. It's nice. I'll see you there at 7:30.

I hesitated again because Primerose is one of my favorite places. I considered whether I should just unclench and go. But while I considered it, the texts started to roll in, one every 30 seconds, for the next ten minutes. I watched, my mouth agape, as his messages appeared, one after another.

Austen please!

That's not fair.

I want to see you.

Please Austen!

Austen please I want to meet you.

It's a bit harsh to judge me on the fact I did not know immediately where we should meet.

I'm really busy today. So, I admit I didn't take time to think about it.

But is that a reason to decline my invitation?

I think that's unfair.

I'm very sad that you don't want to meet me anymore.

Really

I might have not showed up with a perfect place for a drink, but I had an idea for a restaurant.

I love creperies and the Creperie Framboise is very good. I promise.

But judging me on the fact
that I didn't suggest an
accurate bar, isn't it a bit too
harsh?

You might've had bad
experiences in the past, but
should I pay for those fellas?

I don't think so.

I was so happy to see a pretty
American girl with a good
education.

I had to give him points for using the word "fellas," as a
Frenchman but the madness had to stop, so I replied.

Sorry, but no. You're
misunderstanding my
reasons, and I know it
seems harsh, but it's just a
no. I wish you lots of luck in
your search. Hope you find
someone great.

I was expecting that would be the end of it, but no such luck.
He continued at the same rapid pace.

No, I did understand what you
said, and I'd like to apologize.

However, Austen please give
me a bloody chance.

At least one.

Oh, I was so happy to see
you tonight.

Honestly, Primerose is a very
good place for a first date.

And I wanted to come to the
15th as it was convenient for
you but obviously you didn't
notice that.

> At that point, I just couldn't take it anymore. I tried once
> again, very directly, to shut it down.

Pls stop. Respectfully, no.

OK Austen.

Apparently, I'm just not good
enough for you.

I'm really disappointed and sad.

Really

You cannot imagine how bitter
and frustrated I am.

Have a good evening, Austen.

> Twenty-nine messages, basically begging. Where's your pride, man? Again, I recognize the rule might be harsh. I recognize that he apologized. I was reconsidering my whole strategy before the onslaught of his 29 desperate messages.
>
> I double down on rule #11. No Metro stop dates.

#parisdatingdisasters

Austen met up with Chiara and Daphne for dinner at Le Vauban, one of their favorite terraces in the shadow of the gold dome of Invalides, a few days after posting the blog about Victor the Desperate. Neither had read it, so Austen recounted the story to them, in full detail.

"Twenty-nine text messages. Can you believe it?" Austen still couldn't.

"I do think the 'no Metro stop' rule is tough, but it clearly saved you from Mr. Wrong in this case," Chiara said. "Desperation is a bad look on everyone."

Daphne was about to chime in when an American woman sitting at the table next to theirs leaned over toward Austen.

"I'm so sorry for eavesdropping, but I couldn't help overhearing your story. You're the author of that blog *Dating Disasters,* aren't you? I just read that one last night."

Austen was floored. It was her first time meeting a subscriber. "I am. Wow, I've been outed. So much for anonymity."

The woman continued in a conspiratorial whisper, "Oh don't worry. Don't you dare tell me your name. You'd be so vulnerable if people knew who you were. You'd never get another date." She leaned over the space between their tables to shake Austen's hand. "I'm Hilary. It's so nice to meet you. I just love that you tell it like it is. Online dating is the worst."

"The absolute worst," Austen concurred.

"I'm all paid up, so I'm headed out." Hilary stood and pushed in her chair. "For the record, I fully support the no-Metro-stop rule. Have a great evening and keep blogging! We single girls need the comic relief."

As she walked away, Daphne asked Austen, "How many readers do you have on this blog? How wild that you just met a fan."

"About 1,000 last time I checked. And yes, it's totally wild. Improbable, really." Austen leaned back into her chair and took a sip of her *Côte de Brouilly*. Hilary's comment on being vulnerable stuck in her mind—but more on the professional front than the personal.

"Have either of you ever been told that you should show more vulnerability at work?" Austen asked her friends. "At some point last year, two different people told me I needed to, and I was never sure what to do with that. What are your thoughts?"

"I make pastry. Vulnerability isn't really a key qualifier in my line of work. Chefs don't care about feelings." Daphne put both elbows on the table and interlaced her fingers. "But let me guess. The people who offered you this 'helpful feedback' were both men?"

Austen nodded.

"Can you imagine any man saying to another man, 'dude, you really need to show more vulnerability?' No freaking way. It's so sexist." Daphne pulled her hair back away from her face, as if to clear her thoughts. "You should have just told them you'd work on that and then crushed a beer can on your head. Men sometimes."

Chiara laughed and then asked, "What was the context?"

"I was talking to one guy back in the States about a prospective next job. It was a manager role for a big team, and he wasn't sure I was suited for it because 'I wasn't good at showing vulnerability.'" Austen chewed on her thumb nail as she tapped into the memories. "I was so annoyed. Why do I have to be able to cry on-demand to manage a team?"

"I don't think that's what he meant," Daphne chided.

"I've gotten the same feedback, and yes, it's almost always from men. But there's a fine line between vulnerability and authenticity," Chiara said, spreading butter onto a piece of baguette. "Sometimes it's more about the latter and being willing to admit when you don't have all the answers. It's easier for people to relate to someone they can appreciate as imperfect."

Austen nodded and continued. "The other was an odd, passing comment by a peer. He said my confidence was intimidating, and I'd be better liked if I showed up as more vulnerable from time to time. I don't need everyone to like me, but I don't want to scare people."

"Nonsense," Daphne exclaimed. "Look at Gordon Ramsay. No one is telling him to show vulnerability. He is a total despot in the kitchen and gets Michelin stars for it."

The discussion on vulnerability nagged at her. She had a high-powered, big job that required her to master many things and project confidence while representing François as she arranged his various speaking engagements. There was no margin for error. But the question snagged in her mind of how to find that balance between being respected and being feared.

"I don't want to be Gordon Ramsay, but do I have to show weakness for people not to feel threatened?" Austen genuinely wanted to crack this code.

Daphne leaned in. "If other people are threatened by your power, that's their problem."

Her first instinct was to agree, but then she reflected. *I terrified that guy Gildas who asked me about the guns in Texas. This isn't just a professional dilemma.*

Gazing off into the distance, Austen said, "It'd be easy to believe that and brush this whole topic off as nonsense, but if it's blocking me professionally or personally, for that matter, shouldn't I be doing something about it? I must be doing something wrong."

"The mere fact that you're taking this to heart and trying to process it shows vulnerability, as far as I'm concerned. And vulnerability isn't weakness." Chiara rested her hand on top of Austen's. "Just be you, and maybe ask for help when you need it. The second you stop trying to project perfection, you're already doing yourself a favor. I mean, no one is perfect."

"True. But I must say that you two are pretty damn close," Austen declared, squeezing Chiara's hand and smiling at Daphne. "I guess I do spend a fair amount of energy and money trying to cover up my flaws with the right clothes, or accessories, or vacations, or wine, or whatever feels like the right kind of armor. Maybe I need to drop the bullshit and just be real."

"Austen, accessories are not bullshit." Chiara clutched her vintage Chanel black leather handbag to her chest to illustrate her point. "And tomorrow, we shop."

CHAPTER EIGHT

Retail and Other Kinds of Therapy

Chiara and Austen met the next afternoon on the Avenue des Champs-Élysées. Chiara wanted to do some "competitive intelligence" shopping before they went to Isobel's gorgeous apartment on the Boulevard Saint-Germain for a dinner party. They hit the flagship Louis Vuitton store where Chiara carefully examined every detail—from the handbags to the way the salespeople interacted with customers. Austen admired her commitment to professionalism on a Saturday, but after an hour inside the store, she hit her limit and went outside to get some air.

Standing on the sidewalk on this storied Avenue, she watched the tourists buzz up and down the street. *It's sad that only tourists shop on the Champs-Élysées anymore*, she thought. The same shops could be found in every major city in the world. But Louis Vuitton and Cartier, just a block away, were two of the more French of international brands. *Cartier. Alain. That watch.*

It had been eight months since Alain took her to the Cartier on Rue du Faubourg Saint-Honoré. She still needed a new watch and hadn't seen anything she liked more than the Tank. *Accessories aren't bullshit. Chiara said it, so it must be true.*

She pictured herself old and gray, wearing the watch and telling the story to some old biddy she met on the golf course. "My first French lover took me to Cartier on our second date, and we swilled champagne while I tried it on," she would tell her old new friend. *I could get a lot of mileage out of that story over the years,* she thought.

When Chiara finally emerged from Louis Vuitton, Austen hooked her arm into her friend's and declared, "We're going to Cartier, and I'm buying the watch."

Chiara squealed in delight as they set off down the street, their heels clicking against the sidewalk.

The Cartier boutique sat in the shadow of the Arc de Triomphe, one of Austen's favorite monuments in all of Paris. It sat at the center of the Étoile, a massive roundabout with 12 exits which was absolute chaos and Parisian drivers' worst nightmare. Every time she rode around that perilous circle in a taxi, a hundred other cars and scooters whizzing by, she hardly ever noticed the pandemonium because she was always staring out the window at the Arc.

Napoléon Bonaparte commissioned the Arc de Triomphe in the early 1800s to commemorate his war victories, but Austen's favorite part was the ceiling under the arch, which was carved with 21 perfectly sculpted roses. She loved the juxtaposition of the hard-fought-and-hard-won battle themes carved on the outside for all to see and the delicate flowers carved on the underside of the arch, only visible to those who breached the inner circle. Tough on the outside. Soft on the inside. She saw something of herself in the architecture.

She thought happily about those flowers as she walked into Cartier with her fiery Italian friend and politely asked the saleswoman if she could try on the ladies' Tank. An all-black-clad saleswoman poured Cartier's house brand of champagne while they waited, and the two friends clinked glasses.

"Are you bringing Nico to Isobel's tonight?"

"Oh no, *cara*, that ended weeks ago," Chiara said very matter-of-factly.

Austen leaned in to whisper urgently, "What happened, and why didn't I know this?"

"We were out dancing salsa, and this guy Emmanuel asked if he could cut in," Chiara explained, her voice becoming animated. "The way he danced was so powerful I fell for him practically on the spot. He slipped me his number, and I broke up with Nico within the week."

"Why didn't you tell me—tell us—last night at dinner or at any point today?" Austen stammered.

"I guess it slipped my mind. But good thing you asked. How embarrassing would that've been at Isobel's tonight if someone asked me where Nico was." Chiara grimaced and took a sip of champagne. "I should probably tell her before we show up, so she's not surprised. Anyway, it was never going to last with Nico. He was way too young."

"And Emmanuel is how old?" Austen asked.

Chiara grinned. "He's so much more age appropriate. He's 33. Seven years difference is so much better than 12."

Austen was perplexed about how a breakup and meeting someone new could slip a girl's mind so easily. She silently admired her friend for being able to keep the excitement of a new relationship to herself. Austen could barely keep it to herself when she had an interesting conversation with someone online. Her romantic side got excited too soon, and she always wanted to analyze the conversation with her friends, either to get their read on the prospective new man or for advice on how—or if—to proceed. *Chiara is clearly much better at living in the moment.*

She banished the thought when her new watch showed up in the perfect square red velvet tray. She tried it on and loved it even more than she remembered.

Austen admired her new watch in the sunlight as they left the store together. "I really should tell Alain I bought it," she told Chiara.

"Definitely. He'll be thrilled that you did."

As they walked, Austen popped off a text.

> I just bought the Tank. You were right. 😊

Wonderful news. You must come by the restaurant one of these days soon and show me.

> I definitely will. Thanks again for the reco.

"Are you going to go see him?" Chiara asked.

Austen was sure she would, and soon. She couldn't imagine that his life had settled much since their split, but she was curious. She didn't like the way things ended between them. It felt unfinished, and she had just nudged the door back open.

But for the time being, she had a dinner party to get ready for and an outfit to build around her shiniest new piece of body armor, the aptly named Tank.

That night, Austen found herself the seventh wheel to six couples—Isobel and Luc, Chiara and Emmanuel, and a friend of Luc's named Sébastien, with his girlfriend Céline. Whenever Austen was the only single at a table full of couples, they all wanted to hear her dating stories, curious about what they were missing and/or seeking validation of their choice to live in coupledom.

Isobel got the storytelling ball rolling while serving the first course of smoked salmon on blinis with crème fraiche and caviar.

"Austen started a fucking hilarious blog with some of her dating stories; they're so damn awful. I wouldn't believe them if I didn't know they were true."

Céline placed her hand on top of Austen's. "You poor thing. It's awful out there. I was single for a long time before meeting Sébastien, and you know you're lucky that your couple friends still invite you to dinner parties." She looked earnestly around the table at all the other couples. "When I was single, I was never invited to nights like this because someone was always worried about me stealing their man."

Everyone's eyes grew a bit wide at her statement, but she continued talking to Austen, unaware of the stares. "Don't you just hate not having someone in your life?" There was an air of grave concern in her voice.

Austen got this question a lot and always found it annoying, especially when asked in a tone she'd come to identify as superiority disguised as sympathy.

I just met you. You don't know me, and your assumptions piss me off. She removed her hand from Céline's grasp.

"I live in the most beautiful city on Earth. I have a job that I love that pays me well, so I have financial security. I have great friends. I have family who love me. I have my health. Most people on Earth can't say two of those things, so I think I must be the luckiest girl alive."

She paused to let that sink in, taking a long sip of wine. "Would I like to have someone in my life? Of course, but I was married once to the wrong guy, which is worse than being alone. I don't want kids, so have no ticking clock. And I've got way too much to give to end up alone. I'll meet the right person one day. And until then, my life is pretty fucking great."

Chiara and Isobel raised their glasses to toast her well-rehearsed and often-used answer. Austen raised her glass in return.

Céline was momentarily speechless and looked like a deer in headlights. She eventually raised her glass to join the group and said in a patronizing tone, "Good for you for having that perspective."

She doesn't believe anything I just said, Austen thought to herself.

Every word of her reply to Céline had been true, but she admitted only to herself that she wanted that missing piece very badly—someone with whom she could share her life. When she married Brad, she'd thought she'd found her partner for life. She considered the breakup of her marriage a profound personal failure and was still surprised every day to wake up alone. But because she recognized her privilege in so many other things, she didn't allow herself to whine about not having love.

Maybe she's sharper than I thought and just saw right through me.

They were well into the main course—steak with peppercorn sauce—when Isobel's boyfriend, Luc, said, "I can't understand why you're still single. Are you maybe being too picky?"

She started to cut her steak and explained, "I want someone who challenges me intellectually and has a good sense of humor. That's it. And I'll confess I prefer someone who is neither shorter nor skinnier than me. Is that being too picky?"

Sébastien threw his hands into the air dramatically. "You're in the wrong country if you want tall. We're all descendants of Napoléon who was famously short. Deal with it."

He was at least three inches shorter than Céline.

"No offense, Sébastien." Austen put down her cutlery and raised her hands in surrender. "It's me. There's just something I love about being pressed against a tall man's chest, wrapped in his arms. It makes me feel safe and small."

Her mind darted momentarily to Matt and the fantasy she still had of falling under his protection and love. But she only disappeared for a moment.

"I think it's a pretty reasonable list," Luc offered. "I don't get it."

"And no one seems to know any good single men. Do any of you know any?" she asked.

Heads shook all around the table.

Austen continued, directing a disclaimer to Emmanuel and Sébastien. "I don't know either of you, so at the risk of further insult, I will share my theory about why there are no single men in France."

The whole table leaned in, eager to hear it.

"Relationships are trees, and in each perfect tree, there are two monkeys, all loved up in the beautiful branches, far above ground. If the male monkey gets unhappy, he will leave his tree by taking a giant swing toward another tree—toward another woman. He has a genuine fear of his feet touching the ground—otherwise known as being single."

Austen scanned the table to make sure everyone was following. *They're with me so far,* she thought, seeing smiles and nodding heads.

"However, if the female monkey feels unsatisfied, she climbs down the tree to walk around for a while to reground herself. When she eventually starts looking for her next monkey man, she is disappointed in what she finds on the ground."

"Why is she disappointed?" Isobel asked, keeping the conversation flowing.

Swallowing the last sip of the superb *Châteauneuf-du-Pape* in her glass, she continued. "Excellent question. It's because all the male monkeys on the ground are there because they got kicked out of their tree or fell and hit their head on something. The vast majority are suffering from a primate concussion which leaves them fundamentally flawed and totally undatable."

Sébastien moved to refill her glass and braved the first reply. "I think you're right. I know one single guy, and he is undatable. And if I think about it, most of my friends who've left relationships recently did go directly into a new one. And I left a relationship to be with Céline. You may have nailed it."

Austen couldn't help but notice that Céline seemed to bristle at the anecdote. Her shoulders hunched inward.

"It's true that men are not as good at being alone," Luc conceded. "You're probably on to something there. So now Iso, we just have to think about whether any of our friends are about to leave their wives or girlfriends, who might be a good match for Austen."

Isobel patted him on the arm condescendingly. "Sure, honey. Let's root for the demise of our friends' relationships so we can shuffle them around to our other single friends. That'll make for some fucking great dinner parties in the future and send absolutely no one into couples' therapy."

Everyone laughed, except for Céline, who Austen noticed was becoming increasingly agitated. She'd started to scratch furiously at a spot on the tablecloth, with her light pink fingernail.

All other eyes went to Emmanuel as the one man who hadn't weighed in. His gaze darted around the room as if he was looking for an answer. He then said, "You're right that it's easier to leave one relationship for another. Who wants to be alone? You don't, because here we are talking about this. So, I'll offer you my own theory in return, about why." He raised one eyebrow at Austen, almost daring her to object.

She liked the challenge and nodded in encouragement.

"I dated an American girl before Chiara," he began.

Chiara feigned shock, exclaiming, "I thought you'd never met another woman before me."

He kissed her forehead. "Yes dear, it's only ever been you. Just don't listen to this story." As he continued, he kept one hand on Chiara's thigh, which Austen found an adorable gesture of reassurance.

"What I observed was that for you American girls, love somehow needs to be all or nothing. It's fireworks, hearts, and flowers, or it's a no-go. For us French, there are many in-between possibilities, which can be right under different circumstances," he explained. "She told me that when you were little girls, you pulled petals off flowers, saying, 'he loves me; he loves me not.' Do you know the equivalent for French girls?"

She shook her head.

"In France it's '*Il m'aime un peu, beaucoup, passionnément, à la folie, pas du tout.*' He loves me a little, a lot, passionately, madly, not at all. It isn't black or white, you see? It's at least five shades of gray, and any of them can be good for a given moment—except perhaps the 'not at all' bit. So, four different shades, but that's twice as many as you Americans have."

"I thought there were 50 shades of gray," Luc cracked.

"I've got your 50 right here." Isobel kissed Luc square on the mouth, and he pulled her into his lap.

They're adorable, Austen thought, before turning her attention back to Emmanuel.

"Maybe you just need to adapt to the French way and open up to the possibility of something in the middle being enough," he concluded.

I'm logging that one for later. Gotta think about it. Very interesting.

Chiara broke her train of thought, taking the conversation back to fashion. "You need to start trying men on like t-shirts from Zara. It's Zara, so who cares if you only wear it once. But maybe it becomes a favorite t-shirt you wear for years. You never know until you try it on. Not everyone needs to look or feel like a Chanel suit to be worth a go. Even Kate Middleton wears Zara from time to time."

"There's the solution. Wear Zara and find my prince," Austen exclaimed, banging her flat hand onto the table. "Thank God we got that sorted. What would I do without you people?"

Everyone seemed to have enjoyed the fashion detour, save Céline, whose smile had grown increasingly pained as she drained her wine glass. As Luc brought in a decadent plate of perfectly stinky French cheeses, Céline leaned into Sébastien and whispered accusingly, "I'm just a Zara t-shirt to you, aren't I?"

The entire table was startled to full attention, but no one more so than Sébastien.

"Where on Earth did that come from, Céline?" He put both hands forward, seeking an answer, as his forehead crinkled.

Her eyes narrowed. "You left Juliette to be with me; a monkey swinging from one tree to the next, just like Austen said. But it wasn't because you loved me *passionnément* or *à la folie*." Her voice started to crack. "You wanted out of that crappy relationship, and I was a conveniently nearby tree wearing a Zara t-shirt."

"My love, I think you're mixing your analogies there. Maybe drink some water." He filled her water glass and then rolled his eyes.

Céline abruptly stood up from the table and stormed toward the front door of Isobel and Luc's apartment. Sébastien let her go, exhaling in exasperation.

He reached for the wine bottle, this time to fill his own glass, just as the door slammed.

"Sorry, guys. Céline is all drama, but usually in a good way. The mention of couples' therapy triggered her, I think. She's been trying to get me into couples therapy because she thinks I'm never going to marry her."

The whole table was speechless.

Isobel broke the awkward silence, sounding uncharacteristically remorseful. "I'm really sorry I upset her, Sébastien."

"Not your fault. Talking about therapy in France is hardly taboo. Everyone I know sees a shrink."

That much was true. It had always surprised Austen how easily French people talked about their therapists. It did seem everyone had one, except for her.

Sébastien continued. "Don't worry. She'll calm down. Or she won't. But I know you made crème brûlée for dessert, so there was no way I was chasing after her."

Isobel nodded and jumped up to prepare the dessert, and Sébastien offered to help.

He has his priorities, and Céline doesn't seem to be one of them, Austen thought. *That relationship will never work.*

With Isobel and Sébastien out of earshot and in the kitchen, Luc leaned over to Austen and asked, "So if Céline dumps him, should I give him your number?"

Chiara and Austen simultaneously barked "Luc," in staccato reprimand.

"What, too soon?" he asked, with a dry yet puzzled look.

"Too soon. Also, he's too short." Chiara looked at Austen for confirmation.

She laughed and patted Luc's shoulder. "Yes. Both of those things, but thanks and good looking out."

"Trying to be helpful, my friend. We're determined to find you a man," Luc smiled. "Right, Iso?"

Isobel and Sébastien returned to the dining room with the crème brûlée and a bottle of Dom Perignon.

She untwisted the champagne cage and said, "Absolutely. Maybe you'll meet someone at our wedding."

She lifted her left hand to reveal an insanely large diamond ring. The entire room burst into cheers, congratulating Luc and Isobel on their engagement. Austen jumped out of her chair to hug her friend.

"About damn time," Isobel whispered in her ear, returning the hug.

"We all knew you'd wear him down eventually," Austen murmured back.

"It's going to be one hell of a party," Isobel declared to the room.

CHAPTER NINE

Frenched Again

August

When she wasn't working or traveling, Austen continued to swipe left and right until she matched with Grégoire, a morning radio deejay on Radio France. Their first date started like they all did, over one glass of wine. He chose Le Fumoir, a chic yet unpretentious see-and-be-seen bar and restaurant. Austen loved to go there to "people watch," a term which curiously didn't have a proper translation in French, despite France being the birthplace of sidewalk café culture.

As they settled into their outside table with a view of the Louvre, she noticed he had one perfect brown freckle on his left eyelid that she instantly wanted to kiss. She observed as he ordered a bottle of *Côtes de Provence* and a plate of charcuterie and cheese for them to share.

He's got a perfect voice for radio, but those poor listeners sure are missing out on the view, she thought.

"So, what's it like being a radio deejay?" she asked him, sipping her rosé.

"It's fast-paced. It's fun. It forces you to be on your toes and on top of current events. It's the only thing I've ever wanted to do," he told her.

This, she thought silently to herself, with the corners of her eyes smiling upward. *And inner monologue isn't a good dating tactic. Unmute yourself.*

"It's so nice to meet someone who loves what they do. So many people are just punching a clock, it seems. I couldn't live that way."

"Agreed. Also, I love music of all kinds and discovering new artists. Do you know French music well?" he asked.

She shook her head. "Not nearly as well as I should."

"I'd love to teach you."

She was suddenly desperate to be the teacher's pet. She imagined the two of them arm-in-arm at concert venues across Paris, listening to all the best bands with backstage passes hung around their necks. As her mind swam in the imaginary music and stage lights, she recognized a familiar pattern. She did this when she met someone new—projected too far into the future, imagining what life could be like with them. She inevitably did it too soon, before she knew them, and then struggled to rationalize reality with the fantasy. She knew she shouldn't, but she couldn't help herself. Suffice it to say, her imagination was healthy.

"Tell me about what you do. It was something in communications?"

The question referred to the text exchanges before their date. *He remembered.* In her online dating exchanges, she often had the impression that many men were chatting with too many women and couldn't keep any details straight before they met in real life.

Austen made a habit of re-reading her full text exchange with any guy she'd met online before their first date, to make sure she didn't forget any important details. She was a diligent studier in school, and often felt like dating was the adult version of trying to pass a test.

"I'm a speechwriter for a tech executive who gives lots of speeches all over the world. My job is to decide which stages he stands on and then make sure the right things come out of his mouth once he's up there," she explained.

"So absolutely no pressure or stress in your life," he quipped.

He has a sense of humor. Thank God.

"You said you like your job because it forces you to be on your toes. I can relate," she said with a wink.

Did I just wink? Other than regular use of the winking emoji, I'm not a winker. Am I having a facial tick, or is this guy getting to me? Mental note: do some research later on why people wink.

"And why France?" he asked her, mercifully unaware of her increasingly weird inner monologue.

"It's a long love affair which started from a rebellious streak at age 13. I grew up in Texas, where everyone took Spanish because it was practical. I picked French to be a rebel," she explained, shrugging her shoulders.

"I like a rebel," Grégoire confessed with a smile.

"An exchange program to Lyon in high school sealed the deal. My host family—the Sharpes—were so warm and welcoming. Hélène was the daughter, and we hit it off instantly. My two weeks with them marked me in a way I can't explain. It was serendipity."

"*Sérendipité.* It's a beautiful thing." Grégoire put the stem of his wine glass between his index and middle fingers and pushed it toward the center of the table, resting his freckled hand close to hers.

She pretended not to notice his subtle movement toward her and casually continued. "I kept studying the language, so I could get better at communicating with them. And when it was time to declare a major at university, I picked French."

"Why?" Grégoire asked incredulously. "It's so impractical."

"I wanted to study something I loved and trust the universe to sort out the rest. And here I am living and working in Paris, so I guess it all worked out." She leaned back and took a sip of her rosé, letting him take her in.

"So, I have the universe and the Sharpes to thank for your presence here?"

"Indeed, you do," she confirmed. "I visited them right after I moved to Paris and told them that my life might have taken an entirely different path if they hadn't been so wonderful to 16-year-old me."

"I'm very grateful to the Sharpes of Lyon," he said, releasing his wine glass to slowly interlace his fingers in hers.

The night with Grégoire flew by without any additional involuntary winking (or voluntary winking, for that matter). He drove her home and parked in front of her apartment. The streetlights shone warm yet dim light into the car.

"It was a really nice evening, thank you," Austen said, unbuckling her seatbelt.

"The pleasure was all mine."

He unfastened his seatbelt and looked at her with hungry eyes. He paused, giving her the opportunity to exit, but she sat still, silently inviting him to make his move. He reached for her, cupping her face in his palm and they kissed softly, then passionately. She was already looking forward to their second date as the lights faded on their first.

The pleasure feels pretty darn mutual. Yum. So tempted to invite him up and never let him leave, she thought, as his fingers pushed through her hair. *Don't want to be a one-night stand. Ugh. Must disengage and send him away, or the second date may never happen.*

Her strategy worked. They met a week later at Le Perchoir du Marais, a hip rooftop bar that overlooked the Hôtel de Ville. She arrived first and sat in the fading sunshine to wait.

A few minutes later, he greeted her with a slow, sweet kiss on the lips. "I saw you sitting here from across the bar, but your head was turned, so I didn't realize it was you. I said to myself, 'Check out that bombshell of a girl.' And then you turned, and I thought, 'Wow, that's *my* bombshell.' How lucky am I?"

Her smile stretched to the far corners of her face and never left for the rest of the night.

As the sun set and Paris began to sparkle below them, they continued the dance of getting to know one another. Over their third cocktail, he told her about a guest he'd had on the radio that morning.

"This woman has lost consciousness 14 times in the Louvre simply from being overwhelmed by the beauty of the art," he recounted.

"And she keeps going back?" Austen asked. "Dangerous habit. Talk about killer beauty."

He continued with a tone of admiration. "She has a master's degree in art history from one of the best schools in the world, so she knows her stuff. Each time she enters the Louvre, she has this involuntary reaction to the art and just passes out."

Austen was skeptical and was about to tell him that this woman must be a total fraud, when she remembered her wink from their first date.

"You know, there may be something to this idea of involuntary physical reactions. I winked at you on our first date, and I don't wink. I had to look up 'why one winks' afterward, and do you know what I learned?"

"Please do tell." He put his hands on her knees and leaned in, running them up her thighs.

"Apparently, when humans are aroused, their pupils dilate, which causes more blinking, and in some cases, winking." She rested her hands on top of his and leaned in closer toward his face. "It is the physical equivalent of 'more please' as a response to whatever it is that is pleasing, to allow the eyes to take in even more of the view."

He used two fingers to slowly move a strand of her hair behind her ear, leaning in to kiss her neck in the space he'd just cleared.

"You're exquisite," he whispered. "I've been working hard all night to keep my hands off you, but I've lost the fight. Can I take you home with me?"

"Yes. More please," she whispered into his ear.

That night he became her second French lover, and by then, she had upgraded her lingerie.

They picnicked in a park on the tip of the Île de la Cité a few nights later, setting out a blanket, a bottle of Bollinger Brut Rosé, and various nibbles in the late summer sunshine.

As she opened a small dish of figs, she mentioned, "My grandparents had a fig tree in their backyard, and my grandmother always made fig preserves when I was little. I can't smell a fig without thinking of her."

He picked up her hand and kissed it. "My grandparents had a fig tree too and did the same, thousands of miles away in the South of France."

She kissed him and reveled in the discovery of common ground from their childhoods. For her, the simple suggestion of shared life experience brought comfort into a budding relationship. It held a promise of more common ground to be discovered and shared.

She'd often wondered if she'd chosen her ex-husband, Brad, because they both grew up as Army brats. They'd spent much of their respective childhoods moving from one location to the other. The transience gave Austen her resilience and independence. It also gave her a deep desire for stability—the one thing she never had in her youth. She started to believe she might find it with Grégoire.

They'd been dating for a month when Austen decided to host a dinner party—an excuse for him to meet some of her friends. He was the first to arrive. When she opened the door, he handed her a small box. In it, she discovered a fig-scented candle.

"A smell that reminds you of home, to keep in *this* home," he explained.

The thoughtfulness of it made her glow. She buried her smiling face in his neck and thanked him, as he wrapped his arms around her.

Her guests arrived and introductions were made. Daphne's husband, Jean-Marc, asked a question they hadn't anticipated. "How did you two meet?"

They hadn't discussed whether either cared about sharing the truth. For some, meeting on a dating app was still taboo, but Austen preferred the truth. It was easier to remember.

"We met on Bumble," she offered, while pouring Chiara a glass of Brouilly. Her voice was casual, but she carefully checked Grégoire's face for a reaction. *Did I just step in it?*

He cleared his throat loudly and said, "We should come up with a different version of that story soon. Maybe we can say we met at a bookstore or in the grocery aisle?"

"Everyone meets on dating apps these days. It's the way of the world," Daphne assured him.

"Did you all meet online?" Grégoire asked, looking between Daphne, Jean-Marc, Chiara and Emmanuel.

They all shook their heads.

"So not everyone."

While he laughed it off, Austen could tell he wasn't at ease. "Sorry," she mouthed to him.

He put his arm around her and kissed her temple. "We'll do better next time."

As the night went on, he relaxed as he interacted with her friends. He was making an effort to be part of her life, and things felt like they were falling beautifully into place—a new boyfriend, good friends, and a fig candle. *What more could I need?*

"You can keep him," Daphne whispered into Austen's ear as she and Jean-Marc said their goodbyes. "We approve."

She squeezed her friend and closed the door behind them, just as Grégoire took her hand and led her toward the bedroom.

He did early morning radio so was always awake and out the door hours before her. When she woke, she turned on the radio and picked up her phone to text him.

> Good morning, again. The
> bed is lonely without you.

Morning darling. Keep
listening. Don't tune out.

OK. 😊

She closed her eyes and stretched into her bed, taking in his voice through the speaker. He started to describe a new exhibit of Gustave Caillebotte's paintings. She had one of his prints, *The Floor Scrapers,* hanging in her living room, which she had studied in an art history class at Stanford. He admired it once while they were curled up on her couch.

"The exhibit opens at the Musée Marmottan this weekend in Paris," he announced. "Maybe you're a fan of Caillebotte and have one of his paintings, like *The Floor Scrapers*, hanging in your living room. If so, you're in luck, as his collected works will be on display starting this Friday and running for the next three weeks. Don't miss it."

I just got an indirect shout-out on Paris morning radio, linked to a Caillebotte painting, she thought, pulling the covers over her head. *Color me an artist's muse.*

She was smitten.

That weekend, Grégoire traveled to the South of France to see his parents, so Austen made dinner plans with Isobel. They sat on the terrace at Gigi on Avenue Montaigne, with a superb view of the Eiffel Tower.

"Show me a picture of the new man," she requested. "I'm sorry I missed the dinner party and the chance to meet him."

Austen was all smiles as she retrieved her phone to pull up Grégoire's profile picture from Bumble. In addition to the photos, the app also used geo-location to indicate how far away a person was. Her face dropped as she noted his distance: three kilometers—the distance between his apartment and hers.

"He's supposed to be in the South of France," she said, pointing to the screen.

"Maybe there's an explanation. Maybe the app is broken," Isobel offered, looking doubtful.

There isn't, and it isn't, Austen thought. "Or maybe he's just a lying piece of shit," she replied.

"That's possible too."

Austen deflated. "I think I just got 'Frenched' again."

Isobel nearly spit out her wine, trying to hold back her laughter. "Frenched? Please explain because I'm thinking so many things right now, and none involve geo-mapping."

Austen laughed. "It means 'screwed' and not in the good way. It's an expression I made up to explain things that can't be explained logically."

"OK?"

"It usually applies to ridiculous idiosyncrasies of French bureaucracy like how you have to schlep to the bank branch to sign paperwork in hard copy—in triplicate—for the most insignificant transaction, but I think I can apply it here as well."

Isobel nodded. "Yep. You may have just gotten Frenched. Sorry, friend."

Austen hated few things in life more than liars. He didn't even bother trying to explain when she called him out for it. He simply accepted that he'd been caught and walked away.

Is it inevitable that losing French lover number two sends one back into the arms of French lover number one? A week after her split with Grégoire, Austen was walking home after dinner with friends in the neighborhood of Alain's restaurant. *He's*

probably just starting to wind down his service. I think it's time to show him the watch, she thought.

"Well, look what the cat dragged in," he said with a leisurely grin, as she entered.

There were two small tables of customers left in the back of the restaurant, so it was quiet but filled with lingering smells of the night's menu. He put down the glass he was drying and came out from behind the bar, greeting her with a hug.

There's something unmistakable about a former lover's hug—something that makes their familiarity clear to anyone paying attention. It is as if their limbs recognize each other and long to stay close, even when they pull apart.

Brad pointed out this "tell" one night in San Francisco, after they ran into an ex of hers from university. After observing their brief interaction, he'd asked her if they'd dated. "You stood closer to each other than people normally would," he'd noticed. If anyone in the restaurant had been watching, they'd have witnessed the same phenomenon between Austen and Alain.

He knew why she had come without her saying it, so he reached for her wrist and pushed back her sleeve to admire the Tank.

"As I knew it would be, it's perfect for you. I'm really glad you bought it," he told her, still holding her hand as he admired the watch. "Can I get you a glass of wine?"

Just as Alain knew why Austen had come, she knew he'd offer her wine. She happily installed herself on a bar stool while he poured a glass of a *Saint-Joseph* he knew she liked. It was the first time they'd seen each other since they broke up, and the chemistry was still there. She could see the heat in his eyes as he resumed his drying, watching her wordlessly.

Once the final customers left, he joined her for a second glass of wine. It was after midnight, and they settled cozily into a round booth in the window of the dimly lit restaurant. The other server and both cooks went home for the night. They were alone, sitting only inches apart. When he spoke, she couldn't keep her eyes off his lips, remembering how they felt on her skin.

"Let me see that watch again," he said.

She extended her wrist, and he glanced at it perfunctorily before pulling her into him, kissing her fiercely. She melted into his arms, luxuriating in the familiar feeling of his hands on her body. Chemistry had never been their issue. Only the timing had been off. The subsequent nine months and litany of horrifying dates had given her a new perspective on Alain.

Maybe we could give it another go. Maybe it would be different now that he and his son are more settled into their new life.

Alain dragged her by her Cartiered wrist out of the booth and upstairs into the office, away from the windows to the street. He picked her up and put her on the desk, pulling her dress over her head and arching her backward. She inhaled deeply and relaxed back onto the desk as he cascaded kisses down the entire length of her body.

You better notice this sexy AF black and gold lace ensemble, she thought.

He read her mind. "You've turned the lingerie game around, I see." He righted himself to get a full view. "This is very hot," he said admiringly while unbuttoning his shirt. "And now it must go."

A while later, they were lying on the carpeted floor of the restaurant's back office, catching their breath. Austen felt perfectly relaxed and satisfied.

Alain propped himself on one elbow and dragged a finger down her torso toward her stomach. "Have you gained weight?"

And just like that, she was back to their first night and "bra-gate," again hearing the sound of the record needle scratching off its vinyl track, interrupting what had been until that second, a charming melody. This time she didn't freeze.

"Seriously? You're an ass," she exclaimed while getting up and shimmying back into her dress. "Thanks for the sex and the reminder that you aren't my guy. I'm leaving."

"Come on, Austen. Don't be so dramatic. It was an honest question. I'm not allowed honest questions?"

He got up and lit a cigarette by the cracked-open window.

"Not that one and not while I'm naked. I don't know what's culturally acceptable for French girls, but you never ask an American girl if she's put on weight in the two minutes after sex. So rude."

She opened the door and purposefully slammed it shut behind her.

The following morning, she woke up and rolled over to grab her phone, looking for an apology text. There wasn't one. And so, she found herself "Frenched" again.

That's what I get for looking for happiness in places I've already lost it. Never again.

CHAPTER TEN

An Australian in Paris

Two months later

Austen and Chiara had a regular Saturday ritual of shopping and champagne. When she ordered champagne after their first shopping excursion a year prior, Austen had looked at her quizzically and asked, "Are we celebrating something?"

"Yes. Waking up to live another day."

Chiara lost both her parents when she was in high school and a good friend to cancer during her university days, so she took no day for granted, a trait Austen admired. And so, with that simple declaration, "Champagne Saturdays" had been born.

On a Saturday in November after successfully attacking Le Bon Marché, the two friends collapsed into a table by the window at Sip Café Babylone, tossed their shopping bags into the corner, and ordered a bottle of Nicolas Feuillatte.

"Sam is coming to town on Thursday for work," Austen told her friend. "We spoke a few nights ago about whether he should stay with me or in a hotel."

"Stay with you? After what happened at New Year's? Was that almost a year ago already? Do you think he wants to press the issue, and by that, I mean press his body back into yours?" she said, eyes wide in feigned shock. "Why else would he propose staying at yours? If he's coming here for work, surely his company would pay for a hotel."

Austen had wondered the same when they spoke on the phone. In the end, it felt like too much pressure, so she suggested he get a hotel room. He was sweet and understanding, as always. They hadn't seen each other since the kiss, and she was nervous about the reunion.

"What else is going on? Any dates recently? Any good stories for the blog? I haven't checked it lately," Chiara admitted.

"Tomorrow I'm meeting some Australian guy named Kevin. He's my friend Charlotte's friend and coming to Paris for the first time," Austen explained. "I met Charlotte through Peter and Sam, of all ironies. Anyway, I looked at his picture online, and he seems meh, but Charlotte is a lovely human, so I agreed to show her friend around. If only he'd been hot."

"What about dates with guys who live here who might actually be available to you for real?" Chiara asked.

"I'm supposed to be looking for someone that has actual potential for something meaningful?" Austen asked sarcastically. "I think you may have found the last one." Austen felt herself dropping into a moment of self-pity. "Or something is horribly wrong with me, and I just suck at love."

"Nothing is wrong with you, and you don't suck at anything. You have standards, as well you should," Chiara offered. "It only takes one, and he could be right around the corner. You know the saying, it's always the darkest before dawn."

The next night, she met Kevin at Germain on Rue de Buci. He was a tall and strapping Aussie lad with sandy blond hair and dark brown eyes, and as he shook her hand hello, she could feel positive energy bounding out of his every pore.

Wow. Turns out my judgment on photos is totally off, which may explain why my online dating game is so terrible, she thought.

"What do you think of Paris so far?" she asked.

"Just got in an hour and a half ago," he told her. "I'm seeing you before even seeing the Eiffel Tower."

"I feel honored to be prioritized above *The Gray Lady*. She's kind of a big deal around here," Austen cracked. "What's your plan while you're in town?"

"I was in gelato school in Italy for two weeks, and now I'm doing some market research, jumping around European capitals, and playing tourist," he explained, looking at the menu. "I'm going to launch a gelato business back in Oz when I get home."

How delicious, she grinned to herself. *Both you and your entrepreneurial path.* Entrepreneurs were bold and confident, and she liked those qualities in a man.

"I don't know why I'm looking at this menu. I can't read a word of it. I put myself entirely in your hands. What should we have?"

"Anything you don't like?"

"I like whatever you like tonight," he replied.

Austen was chattier than usual with the waiter, aware that the French language sounds like sex to anyone who doesn't speak it. She could feel Kevin's eyes on her as she deftly placed their order. His energy was already rubbing off on her. Her skin tingled.

They bantered back and forth, laughing easily, over shared plates of burrata and cherry tomatoes and pork terrine, paired with a bottle of *Haut-Médoc*. The conversation was effortless. He was witty and sharp, and she felt a natural connection to him—the kind she hadn't experienced in a long time.

About an hour into their evening, her mobile phone rang, disrupting the conversation. She quickly declined the call.

"Sorry about that. My friend Daphne. I'll call her back later and turn off my ringer," Austen apologized, clicking the button.

"Tell her you're on a date," he said.

"I didn't know I was," she replied coyly, cocking her head to one side.

With a catlike grin, he shook his head and said, "I didn't know either, but you definitely are now."

So, yeah, this is going well.

"I must say, this is the best date I've been on in ages," she told him. "It makes me realize how exhausting it is to date in French."

"First of all, I'm glad to know our spontaneous date is going well." He raised a glass and toasted her. "Less importantly, but tell me anyway, why is dating the frogs so exhausting?"

"It's not them; it's me. I'm not as quick on my feet in French as I am in English," she conceded. "I get frustrated when thoughts come out too slowly. It's refreshing to be able to banter at the speed of my brain and not the speed of my language."

"You give good banter," he said approvingly.

"There's not even a word for 'banter' in French. Quick wit repartee is not a thing here. Everyone is so serious all the time," she observed.

"What's dating without banter?"

Exactly, she thought, abandoning her previous commitment to only date French men. *Kevin has just turned me into an equal opportunity dater. Game on.*

After two bottles of wine, a series of "get to know you" stories that only made her want to learn more, and not nearly enough food, Austen looked at her watch and realized it was 20 minutes until the top of the hour. Her hand shot into the air, flagging the waiter for the bill.

"Are we done?" he asked.

"Absolutely not. We're going to the Eiffel Tower," she declared, looking back at her watch. "It sparkles at the top of every hour for five minutes, and you must see it. We've got exactly 19 minutes to get there."

"I would follow you anywhere, Ms. Keller. Lead the way."

They paid the bill and ran into the street to hail a taxi. Kevin helped her into her jacket and took her hand. If it was possible to swoon in the 21st century, she did. A taxi appeared, and they hopped in, Eiffel Tower-bound, and fingers comfortably intertwined and resting on her leg. Her smile turned shy, and the energy between them turned up—buzzing in that fleeting way that only exists in the short window of time between a first touch and a first kiss. *If someone could bottle and sell this kind of energy,* she thought, *they'd be an instant billionaire.*

Arriving with seconds to spare, they walked to the Tower's base, just as the lights started their sparkly dance.

"Wow. This is the right way to see the Eiffel Tower for the first time," he declared.

Standing side by side, they tilted their heads back and he put his arm around her waist, holding her hip to his as they watched the lights twinkle against the ink-blue sky. The Tower held his attention for two minutes, after which he leaned in for an incredibly cinematic first kiss, with its lights still flickering above them. The kiss made her feel like she was sparkling just as brightly as the Eiffel Tower. Everyone and everything else fell away, and they stayed pressed into each other until long after the lights went out.

The next morning, he showered first, and when she got in her shower, she noticed that the shampoo wasn't where she always put it. Her first impulse was to be annoyed, but as she lathered up, she self-corrected.

Unclench, Austen. You like him, and who cares where he puts the shampoo. God, I've gotten comfortable being alone. Her thoughts stalled, as concern creeped in. *Have I gotten too comfortable to make room in my life for someone else?* She resolved to believe that for the right person, she would want to create space.

After work, she raced across town to meet Kevin at Little Red Door, a bar in the Marais. She had been turned on all day, thinking about his hands on her. Knowing their story was destined to be brief, she decided to follow Chiara's lead and live fully in the moment. She burst through the door and was greeted with a passionate kiss.

"Why don't you ditch the Airbnb and stay at my place? Stay as long as you'd like," she offered, as soon as her breath returned.

He took a sip of his cocktail and leaned back into his chair with a broad smile. "This is one of those moments when I really enjoy being my own boss. I'll get my stuff out of there tonight. And now that you mention it, three nights in Paris doesn't seem nearly enough."

Having bought themselves some extra time, the energy between them naturally slowed from a violent boil to a strong but steady simmer.

I'm going to relax into this and enjoy every second, she thought.

That evening, they barhopped around the Marais, telling each other every ridiculous and endearing story from their past, laughing their faces off, and falling into long, lazy, and increasingly intense kisses. They were that annoying couple that couldn't keep their hands off each other in the streets. Finally, she was feeling that "City of Love" vibe and thoroughly enjoying it.

On their third night together over glasses of *Saint-Emilion* and burgers under the orange ceiling lights of Le Select Montparnasse, the conversation turned more serious.

"You've never been married?" he asked.

"No, I was. We got divorced a little over a year ago. What about you?"

"I was. We got married and planned to have kids, or at least I thought we had," he shared. "We were married for two years, and then she told me she didn't want kids after all. So, I left her three years ago. I really want to be a dad."

Austen was rattled. The story held eerie echoes of hers with Brad, and her mind hadn't wavered on kids.

"Yikes. Very similar story with me," she admitted.

"How so?"

"We got together in our mid-twenties, and he was clear that he wanted kids one day. I assumed that I would wake up one day and want it too—everyone around me did—so we got married." She shrugged. "Every year on our anniversary, we checked in to see if either of us was ready. For years, we weren't."

"Until one day he was?" Kevin asked.

"Not exactly. I was almost 35, and I still had no desire. I felt guilty for not wanting what everyone else seemed to want, but guilt seemed like a pretty crap reason to have a kid," she mused. She took down her ponytail and let her hair fall like a shield, protecting her from the memory. "I told him I didn't want him to wait for something that maybe wasn't coming, and that was it, really. It took a little while for us to split, but if I look back, that conversation was the beginning of the end."

Kevin's face had gone dark as he listened. "You did the right thing to tell him." He paused and then shook his head and shoulders violently before continuing, "How did we get on this topic on night three? Damn. We definitely need more wine."

He flagged their waitress, bursting the bubble of seriousness. She was relieved. *How did we get there? This is temporary and should be light and fun. No more Brad stories.* They'd quickly fallen into the easy pattern of two people who had known each other for years, despite it having been only days.

Two nights later, they were lying in her bed, recovering. She was on her stomach with her face turned away from him, as he picked up a strand of her hair and twirled it around his finger. "So, what are we doing tomorrow night?" he asked.

She'd been waiting for the right moment to bring up Sam, and there it was.

"Actually, I have a friend in town tomorrow." She rolled over to face him. "We have some things to catch up on, so would you mind terribly if I ditched you, just for one night?"

"You're ditching me. I wasn't expecting that, but yes of course I can fend for myself for one night. OK if I'm here when you get home?" he asked.

"Yes, please be right here, in this bed, when I get back," she purred into his ear.

Sam almost stayed at my apartment. So glad I pushed him to the hotel. This would have been hard to explain, she thought, with her hand on Kevin's bare torso. She hated to pull herself away from him for one of their precious few nights together, but for Sam, she wanted to go. She knew the affair with Kevin was fleeting, and Sam was something more.

She also felt anxious, scared Sam would somehow be able to sense all the sex she'd been having. From the office the next day, she called Daphne for support.

"I don't know why but I'm nervous about being alone with him. I feel like the whole Kevin story will burst out of me if we're alone, and I don't want to hurt him. Please come with us to dinner and save me," she begged. "I booked your favorite—Septime."

"You're a wimp, but you had me at Septime," Daphne said. "I'll call Bertrand and tell him to add an extra spot to your reservation."

Bertrand was the chef, who Daphne knew through her professional circle. He embraced her warmly when they entered the dining room that evening, with its perfectly appointed wooden tables and steel spiral staircase winding upward in the corner. Knowing the chef and being a gorgeous blond have their perks, and so their evening passed deliciously with a few extra exquisite nibbles and a truly divine *Bas Armagnac* on the house. They devoured the food, drink, and conversation, and Austen felt no awkwardness with Sam. Daphne had provided the perfect buffer.

When the food was gone and the glasses empty, Daphne thanked Bertrand and said goodbye to Austen and Sam at the restaurant door, to make her way to the Metro.

"I booked the hotel we stayed in for New Year's in your hood. Want to share a cab back? Maybe have a nightcap at yours?" Sam asked.

Kevin's there waiting, so that's not an option, she thought nervously. *Tell him or don't tell him?* Austen hated a lie, even if only a lie of omission, so she decided to tell him the most toned-down version of the story she could muster.

"There's someone at my apartment right now waiting for me." She felt heat creeping into her ears. "He's a friend of Charlotte's, visiting from Sydney. We're 'involved.'" She used air quotes to make the point she didn't want to verbalize. "I abandoned him tonight because I really wanted to see you, but he's there now."

Sam's eyes grew wide, but he spoke quickly, diffusing the tension. "Good for you. Raincheck on that nightcap, and thanks for breaking away to see me. I'm honored and will keep you no longer."

A cab pulled up, and he opened the door, gesturing for Austen to get in.

"I'll get the next one." He kissed her on the cheek and whispered into her ear, "He's a lucky bastard. I hate him."

Austen's heart clenched, and she softly squeezed Sam's hand before climbing into the cab. She didn't want to hurt him, but he still lived on the other side of the world, and Kevin was waiting for her on the other side of town.

She returned home to find him naked on her couch, drinking Sancerre.

Good decision not bringing Sam back for a nightcap, she thought. She kicked off her boots and crossed the room, unzipping her black leather pants.

The next night, Austen brought Kevin to a party at Isobel's fabulous apartment. This soirée was a trunk show for her jewelry-designer friend Shelly, to showcase her latest Shel Couture collection as part of Paris Fashion Week.

Isobel had a habit of collecting new friends randomly in the streets, which always made her parties a delightful mix of eclectic souls. The apartment was filled with Shelly's Fashion Week acolytes, Luc's suited and booted corporate lawyer friends, and Isobel's pack of glorious strays. The room pulsed with energy, and Austen was in heaven.

Her ex-husband, Brad, had been a wild introvert, always shrinking into himself during evenings like this one, so she was quietly thrilled to see Kevin working the party—filling up her friends' champagne glasses and casually making conversation with everyone. When he fell into a deep discussion with a shoe designer, she slipped away to look at the jewelry.

Austen fell in love with one of Shel's necklaces. Its long chain was made of sparkly green Swarovski crystals, and it had a gold snake curved at the end, which hung at her pelvic bone.

"It's so sexy, but too expensive," Austen lamented to Isobel. The Cartier watch had not broken her aversion to spending big on jewelry.

"Be a model for us. Wear it tonight at the party and show it off," she suggested.

"Well, if you insist," Austen giggled, slipping it around her neck.

Isobel gestured toward Kevin. "He fits right in."

He was chatting with Daphne, Chiara and Emmanuel and looked up to find both women watching him. He raised his glass and smiled, with fire in his eyes.

Hiding her mouth behind her champagne glass, Isobel quietly said, "My God, he is looking at you like you're dessert."

"Honestly, the sex is off the charts. We've had more sex in the last six days than I thought was humanly possible," Austen whispered, shaking her head. "I finally get what people have been talking about when they rave about sex. I've never been so sleep-deprived, sore, and blissed out all at once."

"Fan-fucking-tastic. Get back over there to him," Isobel insisted, with a light nudge to Austen's back.

Kevin watched her as she sashayed across the room to re-join him, champagne glass in hand. "Nice necklace."

"Thanks. It's on loan. I'm modeling for the crowd," she laughed, displaying the gold snake in her palm.

"Best looking model in town," he said, leaning in to kiss her.

"Get a room, you two," Luc shouted from across the apartment.

At the end of the night, Austen went to say her goodbyes to Isobel and started to slip the necklace off to return it.

Isobel shook her head and pushed it back around her friend's neck. "I've been watching you two all night, and I know what you're going home to do right now. You should do it wearing this necklace—and only this," she said with naughtiness glimmering in her eyes.

Austen felt heat rising from her toes to her temples as the visual crystallized in her head. "I do like the way you think," she gushed. She pulled out her wallet and paid Shelly for the necklace, the earlier sticker shock entirely forgotten.

They arrived back at her apartment, and as soon as the door closed, he picked her up by the hips, and she wrapped her legs around his waist. They careened down the hallway, banging into walls as they hungrily made their way to her bed. Every ounce of clothing hit the ground, but the necklace stayed on, with the snake snaking down her body as he laid her down on the bed. The night was the stuff of legends.

The next morning, they emerged from the bedroom and giggled at her boot marks which had scuffed the hallway walls in multiple locations between the front door and her bed-room—evidence of their haste and desire. As they stood in the bathroom brushing their teeth in the morning light, she watched him in the mirror, shaking her head in wonder at whatever it was that was happening between them.

He caught her gaze, and with his toothbrush still in his mouth asked, "What's going on in that insane bedhead head of yours? We really did a number on your hair."

She spat and picked up a hairbrush to work out the tangles. "I didn't know it could be like this. Is it normal for you, this kind of connection?"

"Definitely not. It's you."

"But why?" she asked, genuinely looking to understand.

He moved behind her, so they were both facing the mirror, and wrapped his arms around her waist. "Just look at you. You have no idea how sexy you are, and that makes me want to both never stop fucking you and protect you at the same time."

She blushed and closed her eyes, leaning into him. Kevin desired her in a way she'd never experienced. It made her want to open her entire soul to him. She couldn't recall ever feeling so exposed and so safe at the same time. The protective shell she'd built around herself was fracturing, and even with her eyes closed, she could see the light shining through the cracks.

Even still, she knew the end was near—that he'd leave soon. She had artfully avoided the subject for days, but that night over buckwheat crepes and Norman apple cider at Crêperie Mad'eo on Rue de Cadix, she had to ask. "Where will your travels take you next, and when?"

"London. I was thinking of going the day after tomorrow," he said.

Austen's heart leaped. "Well, isn't that interesting? It just so happens I'm headed to London on Thursday with François for a speech he's giving."

"Ms. Keller, are you suggesting an international fling?"

She could hardly contain her excitement. "Why yes. Yes, I am." *Thank God, it's not over yet. I've still got him for a little while.*

"You know Charlotte is in London this weekend too," he pointed out.

Charlotte was the mutual friend who fatefully introduced them a week prior.

"Yes, she's staying with my friend Peter. God, the world is small," Austen exclaimed. "I feel a fun surprise coming on."

CHAPTER ELEVEN

An Epic International Fling

A few days later

Kevin flew to London on Monday to take care of his gelato business, and Austen took the early Eurostar on Thursday morning with François. She sat on the train and sipped coffee while he reviewed his speech, her mind already done with the workday and looking forward to dinner.

She took advantage of the silence and texted Milena, one of her best friends from university. Milena lived in San Francisco but was coincidentally in London as well for business. They discovered the overlap in their business travel agendas a month earlier and made plans to meet for dinner that night, which was Milena's last night in town.

> I'm on the train and will be
> there soon. Can't wait to see
> you.

Me too. And I'm so excited
to see Peter and meet Kevin.

It's going to be a fabulous
evening.

See you at Duke of Wellington
at 7:30!

Kevin and Austen coordinated their plans for the evening and conspired to surprise Charlotte. They were meeting in Notting Hill at seven p.m., so Austen arrived 15 minutes later and found them standing at the bar, their backs to the door. She tapped him on the shoulder, and he turned around casually.

"Hey there," he said with absolute nonchalance.

Charlotte exploded in delight and grabbed her for a hug. "Austen oh my God; I didn't know you were in town."

As Charlotte released her, Kevin picked up the relay and pulled Austen in for a kiss, which he planted directly on her mouth.

"OK, so this went well," Charlotte deadpanned, punching Kevin in the arm.

"Surprise," Austen answered, with jazz hands.

Peter arrived next, followed by Milena, and they grabbed a round table for drinks and dinner.

"You two went to uni together?" Kevin asked, gesturing between Austen and Milena.

"We did, and then we were roommates in San Francisco after school before she married Brad. I met Peter in San Francisco too, before he absconded to London," Milena explained. "How did you and Charlotte meet?"

"Through mutual friends in Sydney," Kevin said. "Boring story actually."

"Which then led to what appears to be a significantly less boring story when I introduced you to Austen," Charlotte joked.

"True. I'm very grateful for our boring story leading me to this spicy one," Kevin said, winking at Austen.

"She's a spicy one," Milena confirmed, raising a glass to her friend. "And Peter, how has ex-pat life been treating you since you abandoned us in San Francisco? Matteo and I are thinking hard about a move to Asia. Austen's given me all her ex-pat-living advice, and now I want yours."

"Best decision I ever made," Peter declared. "As you can see, everyone passes through London eventually, so I don't have to miss anyone or anything for too long. Where in Asia are you thinking?"

"Hong Kong. Matteo's company has an office there, and they've been talking about transferring him. We're on the fence but leaning in that direction," she explained.

"Do it. I'm in Sydney now, but I lived in London for a few years and the experience abroad was so enriching," Charlotte effused. "This is where I met Peter. You'll never regret living abroad. And Hong Kong is one of my favorite cities. You'll love it."

Austen wondered what was going through Kevin's mind as he listened. He'd only ever lived in Australia. *Would he ever consider moving to Europe?* She hadn't dared to ask. *He's an entrepreneur, so he could come up with a business idea for something to do here.* They'd known each other for all of a week, but she couldn't help but imagine what their European life might be.

In a perfect display of bestie-brain-meld, Milena turned to Kevin and asked, "What about you? Ever thought about leaving Australia for a stint abroad?"

Kevin replied without hesitating, "I've never thought about it before this week, but this one has me thinking all kinds of crazy thoughts." He put his hand gently around the back of Austen's neck and leaned over to kiss her temple.

Austen felt hope rise in her belly, and Milena's face lit up like a Christmas tree. *That girl should never play poker*, Austen thought, returning her friend's smile.

When Kevin excused himself for the restroom toward the end of dinner, Peter took advantage of his absence. "Austen, this is the kind of guy I've always imagined you with. He gets you, and it's wonderful to see you so happy. But what happens next?"

"No idea," she confessed. "I'm trying to live in the moment and not think about it."

Milena nodded her head aggressively. "That is one thousand percent the right call. Don't think. Just enjoy it to the max. And you know what I like best about him? He's the total opposite of Brad."

"I never met Brad," Charlotte interjected. "Did we hate him?"

"No, I liked Brad, don't get me wrong. He wasn't a bad guy," she recalled. "But there's some obvious fire with Kevin, which I don't think I ever saw between you and Brad."

Peter finished the dregs of his beer. "I didn't know Brad as well as Milena did, but I'm going to agree. I've never seen you so lit up."

She knew they were right. After so many years of neglect by Brad and the past year of dating misery, her heart and her soul finally felt awake again.

Austen met Milena for breakfast the next day before her flight. Milena wanted to hear all the juicy details of Austen's tryst, and she wanted to hear all the latest thinking on their evolving plans for Asia.

"Matteo's boss really wants him there. The deal is getting sweeter by the week, but if we go, I've got to quit my job," she explained. "I've been working for 17 years, so it's scary but also exciting to be the one that quits with nothing to fall into. I've never been unemployed."

Austen hadn't either. They both started work straight out of university at age 22 and never took breaks between jobs. But with her fortieth birthday looming next year, she'd been thinking that a break could be a good idea.

"I applied for a sabbatical from work a few months ago, and if I get it, I was thinking about spending the time traveling in Asia, so I'll come visit you," Austen promised.

"A sabbatical? How long? What made you want to do that?"

"It'd be two months. I guess I'm feeling a bit run down and overstressed since the divorce. One of my colleagues took a sabbatical recently and came back looking so refreshed. I thought it could be a good idea, so I applied on a whim," Austen shared.

"That'd be amazing. I hope you get it. We'd have such fun." Milena put both hands on the table and leaned in. "Speaking of having fun in fabulous places, I've been thinking about our fortieth birthdays next year. I want to come to France. Let's convince Liz and have a girls' trip. Maybe the Côte d'Azur in August?"

Austen squealed, "I'd absolutely love that. If Matteo and Andrew are willing to part with you both, I'd be in heaven. I'll call Liz when I get home and start the pressure campaign."

"Fab. I love planning to meet up in marvelous places all over the world. And I love being here now. I'm so glad this weekend happened, so I got to meet Kevin. Wasn't he quite the delightful surprise?" Milena asked rhetorically.

"I finally understand what it feels like when something just works," Austen declared. "And the sex is the best I've ever had."

Milena clapped her hands together, grinning ear to ear. "It's about time you got a taste of this. Nobody deserves it more." Her face then slowly faded from glee to concern. "I know I said last night to just enjoy it to the max, but can I also ask you to please be careful and protect your heart?"

"I'm afraid it may be too late for that, my friend," Austen conceded.

"Is this it? Just another two nights in London?"

"I don't know. We haven't talked about it yet. He's got an open ticket back to Australia, so I'm hoping he'll stay forever," Austen admitted with a defeated smile.

She woke up with her head on Kevin's chest on their last morning in London. He was already awake, stroking her hair.

"Good morning," she mumbled into his chest, squeezing her body tighter to his.

"I'm thinking about going to Madrid for the weekend," he casually stated.

Even though he couldn't see her smile, she knew he could feel it.

"I could come to Madrid." She kept her head down so he couldn't see in her eyes how badly she wanted to go.

He hesitated, and she held her breath.

"I'm falling for you," he whispered into her hair. "Another few days would be amazing, but to what end?"

She sat up to face him. "It's going to end no matter what, so why not have a few more days of fun in country number three?" She pushed the sheet out of the way and straddled him. "Emotionally, we were both probably screwed before we even left Paris, but we ignored it and came here. Let's go to Spain and ignore it for a few more great days. Because we can."

He flipped her onto her back and kissed his way downward.

"I guess we'll buy tickets later," she exhaled in pleasure.

She returned to Paris on Sunday night, powered through the week, and took a vacation day on Friday. She caught the last flight out to Madrid on Thursday night. When he answered her knock on the hotel room door, she found a room service dinner on the settee and the bed already turned down.

Everyone eats late in Spain, she thought, pushing him toward the bed.

The next day over tapas and a pitcher of sangria, he asked, "Do you think maybe you just didn't want kids with him, rather than not wanting them at all?"

It was a question she'd heard before. "If I was with the right person, would I feel differently? It's possible, but I can't say for sure. All I know is that I've never felt that pull—in my uterus." She was trying to get a laugh but only got a sad smile in return.

"Is it because of your job? Are you worried about missing some career opportunity if you had kids?"

"One time when I was still married, I went to refill my birth control and my gyno asked me if I didn't want kids because of the guy or because of the job. I told her it was the guy, and she handed me my prescription directly," Austen recalled, taking a bite of chorizo. "She was going to try to convince me to go for it if I'd said the job, but because I said the guy, she was happy to refill it. I always appreciated how she handled that."

"Gynecologist stories, always a fan favorite," he smirked.

"I've got a good one about a dentist too if you want," she returned playfully.

"How could I say no?"

"I have this metal bar on the inside of my bottom teeth to keep them straight, and one day it came loose on one end and was scratching up my mouth, so I made an appointment. After he fixed it, he said he needed to stick his tongue in there, just to make sure it was smooth," she recounted.

His jaw dropped. "You're making this up."

"Sadly, it's a true story," she replied, sipping sangria. "I've since changed dentists."

"Holy hell. Well, I suppose I'd better stick my tongue in there and verify his work," he said, pulling her toward him.

Once they came up for air, she returned to their more serious vibe. "Do you think you'll ever reach an age where you'll decide you're too old to have kids?"

"It's a good question. Maybe." He looked down and picked at the seat of his wicker chair.

"Maybe that'll happen right around the time I decide my love affair with Paris is ending, and I'll move to Australia, and we'll live happily ever after," she offered enthusiastically.

"It could happen," he said in return, although with significantly less conviction.

The next two days were a blur of sex, sangria, and stories. One of his on their last day in Madrid was about a short-lived idea he'd recently harbored to write an advice column for women.

"I was going to call it *The Anonymous Man*. Women could write in with their man troubles, and I was going to give them the male point of view. I think it could've been brilliant," he told her.

"What made you decide to deprive the women of the world of your wisdom?"

Scratching his head, he replied, "I got too deep into the gelato idea, so I let it go. Who knows. Maybe I'll revisit it one of these days."

"I think you should also revisit Paris," she said out of nowhere. "Like, this week. Come back with me for a few days. I'm not ready to say goodbye."

He caressed her face with one hand. "I've got to get back to London for a meeting tomorrow afternoon. I set it up when I was there last week."

She nodded quickly, trying to suppress her anxiety. "Come to Paris after London then. Daphne is hosting expat Thanksgiving next weekend. Ever been to an American Thanksgiving in Paris?"

"Can't say that I have," he replied snarkily.

"Well then you must," she stated.

"Maybe."

He'll come. This isn't how it ends.

They said goodbye at the airport in Madrid. She kissed him briefly and said, "See you when I see you," tossing a sultry smile over her shoulder and waltzing away. She was certain their reunion would be imminent.

Two days later, he texted.

I'm headed home on a bird
tonight. I'm scared that if I stay,
I will make the same mistake
that I made with my ex-wife.
I want to be a parent. We live
in different hemispheres. It
doesn't work, so I've got to go.
But I will miss us.

She stared at the text in disbelief, but also knew his decision was made.

> We'll always have Paris. And
> London. And Madrid. 😣 🖤
> Safe travels home.

As she hit send, her heart deflated to the sensation of a million tiny pin pricks.

She surprised herself by how hard she took his departure. She spent the next two weeks moping around her apartment after work in the evenings, missing him. He opened something inside her heart that had been closed for a long time— or perhaps had never been open at all. Now, that space felt hollow.

Before she met him, she would often find herself sitting across from someone on a date and asking, *Could I like him?* It hadn't occurred to her yet that this was a question she should never have to ask.

Now I know. When it clicks, it's obvious. And I don't have to look so hard.

She resigned herself to be grateful for that learning and accept that hers and Kevin's love story was over.

The acceptance was short-lived.

A few weeks later, she was restless. She missed him terribly and didn't want to let him go without a fight. So, she sent him an email.

Dear Anonymous Man,

I recently said goodbye to a guy with whom I had an epic international fling. Three countries in two weeks. Massive intellectual connection. Amazing sex. The whole package. We said goodbye without belaboring the point because we live on opposite sides of the world, and he wants kids. I'm pretty sure I don't.

With two weeks of retrospect, which I recognize isn't much, I can't stop thinking about how incredible our time together was. So, I find myself asking some tough questions.

It's almost Christmas, and I have two weeks off. The only place I want to go is to see him. He hasn't said anything about seeing each other again, and I know it's (at least in part) because of the kids thing. It seems to be a real deal breaker for him.

Also, he nearly didn't want to go to our third country in the two weeks because he said he was worried about getting attached, given our geographic challenge and mismatched reproductive inclinations. Adding a fourth country to our list would certainly make saying goodbye a lot harder. And then there's the fact that I love the city I live in and have no real desire to move. So, this doesn't work, right?

But what if it does? Truth is, we're already both emotionally involved. So, what if, after two more weeks together, I feel differently about the kids thing? I think he's the type of guy who could make a girl change her whole life plan. I mean, how often do you find this kind of connection with someone? Not often, as far as I can tell.

It's all a bit crazy, but I know for sure that I don't want the story to be over. I don't think he does either, but I understand

and respect why he's nervous. It just feels a bit foolish not to take the risk and try to figure it out.

What do you think I should do? Take the leap and ask for an invite to come visit? Or wait a few months and see if we're both still missing each other?

— Girl from the Wrong Hemisphere

His response was simple and clear.

Austen, I just can't see an us in any way. I'm sorry.

K

The end.

She was devastated and thoroughly confused. She didn't understand how he could walk away so easily from a connection that felt so strong. When they were together, she'd tricked herself into believing it was all just casual fun. It was her way of protecting her heart. But in the time since, she'd realized it had been the mythical "love at first sight," at least for her.

I know he felt it too. Maybe he's scared. Or maybe he was lying all along.

That thought chilled her. She wasn't sure which truth would be more painful. But whatever his reason, there were two certainties: her heart was broken, and she'd never felt more alone.

But even through her sadness, she knew she'd never regret the epic international fling. Kevin had, with no hyperbole, brought her back to life. For the last few years of her marriage, Brad neglected her. Kevin made her realize that those years of sleeping next to someone who wanted nothing to do with her sexually had left a deep and dark emotional mark. His desire and attention had both revealed the wound and simultaneously started to heal it.

CHAPTER TWELVE

The Bodyguard Returns

Two months later

On a cold and snowy day in January, Austen found herself in Davos, Switzerland, for the World Economic Forum, a highly prestigious annual gathering of the world's business, institutional and political elite with the goal of creating solutions for the world's biggest problems. She had to guess that the event had the highest bodyguard-per-capita ratio anywhere on Earth, so naturally, Matt was on her mind. It had been nine months since their Senegalese tarmac goodbye.

While many people believe in manifesting—to make something happen just by thinking about it—Austen wasn't a believer. And yet, when she took her coat and laptop bag off the security belt and started to walk to her first meeting, there he was, standing by the door. He was as gorgeous as ever and still pulling off a suit in a way rarely seen off an Armani runway.

They caught eyes and stared at each other for a few seconds, smiles creeping slowly across the full expanse of both of their faces.

"I can't believe it's you," he stammered.

She held up the name badge hanging around her neck, to prove her identity. "In the flesh." *Maybe manifesting is a real thing after all,* she thought. *I should try that more often.*

"What a nice surprise."

As the words left his mouth, a man's voice called his name. His eyes darted quickly between her and the voice in the crowd.

Must be whoever he's here protecting this week.

"Sorry, gotta go. I hope I'll run into you later," he said, as he strode quickly away.

Her heart pounded as she walked in the other direction toward her meeting. *What are the chances? But push him out of your mind. François is waiting. Get to work, girl.*

Later that morning, as she walked through the snow-covered streets toward her next session, he appeared, again, exiting a hotel with Bastien. She approached them and exclaimed, "Well, if it isn't a Dakar reunion here on the snowy streets of Davos."

"Can you believe it?" Bastien asked. "We just ran into each other when I was coming out of my last meeting. Small world, eh?"

"Matt and I actually ran into each other earlier today in a security line," she replied, before turning to look at Matt. "And here you are again."

Bastien's smile went sideways as he looked back and forth between Matt and Austen.

"Right. I've got to run to my next meeting," he muttered while backing away. "Great to see you again, Matt. Take care." He nodded at Austen. "See you later at the thing."

She waved her gloved hand.

"Pretty crazy to run into each other twice already today. In an event with how many people?" she asked.

"Three thousand," he stated, crossing his arms across his broad chest. "Still with the same team, I see. Big 'thing' later?"

"François is speaking on a panel on the ethics of artificial intelligence later this afternoon at the English Church," she explained.

Matt nodded knowingly. "The guy I'm here with is going to that one. I guess I'll see you there."

I wonder who "his guy" is this week. Probably someone famous. François doesn't even request a security detail here; the place is so secure.

As a preemptive apology, she explained, "I'll probably be pretty busy at that one. It's a press event, so I need to be 'on' the whole time."

"Of course. I get that. I think my next few days are going to be intense too."

Pulling up the collar of her parka against the cold, she decided to once again be bold with him. "If you find yourself with a free moment some evening, let's get a drink?"

"I'm not super optimistic about having any free time, but if I do, you'll be the first to know. I've still got your number," he told her, looking at his watch. "I've gotta move. Meeting my guy in just a few minutes."

"See you in church," she grinned.

He laughed as he walked away. "See you."

She sat down in a café to warm up and grab a quick bite before her afternoon meetings. She scrolled through her phone as she ate her pumpkin soup and found Matt's number. She couldn't help herself, so she texted him.

I have to ask. After I left
Senegal, I sent you an email
saying I was coming to
Joburg. I never heard from
you. Did you get it?

Did I not reply? I'm so sorry. I
thought I had. Yes, I got it.

No worries. But I've always
wondered about the answer
to my question. I asked if
you were (A) married, (B)
had a girlfriend, or (C) wildly
uninterested. So, which was it?

It was B.

Well, at least it wasn't C. 😊
Hope we can make that drink
happen.

I still love your fearlessness.

I will definitely try. And either
way, see you later at the panel.

The English Church sat just outside the security perimeter of
the main WEF event, so supplemental security was high. Austen
and Bastien escorted François there well in advance to get him
mic'd up and fully prepped. With ten minutes to go before the
panel's scheduled start time, the church was packed, with a line
of security guys standing against the walls. Once François was in
place on stage, she took her seat in the front and casually turned
to scan the line of dark suits. She didn't find him.

The panel discussion began, and she focused on François, taking notes on his key points in case there were any questions afterward from the press, who filled the front three pews. The discussion was lively and engaging, and as soon as it ended, a small press swarm headed to the stage for additional questions. She quickly made her way to join the boss to manage any follow-ups that might be required.

From the elevated position, she saw Matt watching her from the back of the room. He raised his hand to wave and then turned to leave. She briefly watched his broad shoulders make their way through the door and into the snowy streets, and then refocused on the press.

She didn't hear from him after the panel, and their paths never crossed the next day. That evening as she was heading to a networking cocktail event, she texted him.

> Hiya. Hope things are going well. I'm headed to the Hotel Belvedere for a drinks thing the Wall Street Journal is hosting. Any chance I'll see you there?

Afraid not. My guy has a dinner at another location tonight, and if last night is any indicator, he'll be hitting the bars after. He's here to party.

> Late night?

Painfully late.

> Not super fun for you. Sorry.

That's the gig. I'm at his
mercy.

Have fun for me tonight. I'll
ping you if I get lucky and he
turns in at a reasonable hour.

We did run into each other
twice already, so maybe luck
is on our side this week?

Maybe. Let's see.

The next day, she was walking with the team when she saw Matt for a third time. *It's a trifecta*, she thought. He was standing by a meeting room door in the conference center, most likely waiting for his client to emerge. She couldn't stop as they had a meeting to get to, but she slowed her pace to put herself one step behind François and Bastien as they passed by Matt. He saw her coming. She wiggled three fingers near her face and mouthed, "three times" as she passed.

He returned her smile and shook his head. Then, he re-opened the text volley.

I do enjoy watching you walk
away. Nice view. 😊

Must say, I'm both sorry and
not sorry about the long hours
this week.

It's a good thing we've not
ended up in the same bar

any night this week. It would
not have been good for my
career.

Or for my girlfriend.

Sitting next to Bastien during their meeting, Austen read
his texts and built up her courage to reply.

So how much do you really
like this girlfriend anyway?

Because honestly, running
into each other three times
in three days at an event this
densely packed, in a country
on another continent than
the one on which we first
met...

Don't forget our run in at
church.

See. Even God wants to see
us together.

And who am I to argue with
God?

Don't you kind of have to
wonder if it's not fate?

I have thought that. How
could I not? It is–you are–
incredibly tempting. I must
admit, you ensorcell me.

Her breath caught in her throat at the word "ensorcell." *That's not a word I hear every day. Or any day for that matter. And it sounds more like the devil's work than God's, but whatever. Great word.* She rolled it around in her head, enjoying its implications and imagining the sound of it falling off his tongue.

I guess I should be glad
this guy has me on call at
all hours. Otherwise, I'd be
tempted to break all my rules.

OK, fine, but let's make a
deal. If you ever end things
with her and find yourself
anywhere in Europe, you call
me.

Deal. 100% yes.

"Who are you texting?" Bastien whispered to her as the meeting dragged on. "Can I guess?"

Austen put her phone in her lap and tried to make her face tell a different story. "A friend back in Paris," she lied.

"I was going to guess Matt." His face was an open question, looking for an answer. "We walked by him when we were on our way in here, and I saw him lock on you. He likes you."

Austen elbowed him lightly in the ribs and shushed him. "Pay attention to the meeting and stop imagining things." She kept her face stern, but on the inside, she was beaming.

On their last night in town, Austen, Bastien and François had a working dinner at Ochsen Steakhouse to debrief on their sessions and start triaging action items.

"Thanks to you both for the good support this week." François raised his wine glass to them in appreciation. "It was an intense few days, but I'm happy with the outcomes."

"Glad we could help," Bastien said, returning his toast.

"I've got some news for you, Austen, which I think you'll like," François continued. "I approved your sabbatical request."

"Oh wow, thank you." Austen's mind flipped into overdrive. *Two months off. What a dream. Can I go now?*

"Not this year though," he interjected, reading her thoughts. "We need to plan this for some time next year, so we can get a backup plan in place for while you're out."

"Of course. Next year will be amazing. Thank you. I'm thrilled."

As their tiramisu was served, her excitement over next year's sabbatical was replaced by the thought that they were leaving Davos tomorrow. She reached for her phone and discreetly reopened the nightly texting ritual with Matt.

	Last night….
Last night.	
	How's it looking? Any chance you'll be able to break away?
It's looking grim. 😟	
	So much for our good luck.
I know. I'm really sorry.	

She returned to her chalet and went to sleep feeling frustrated and horny over Matt but ecstatic about the sabbatical. She slept fitfully.

Her eyes snapped open the next morning at the sound of her phone buzzing. She reached for it on the nightstand and saw Matt was texting.

On the plane, barely alive,
about to roll out. I think I got
maybe 90 minutes of sleep.

I don't know how this guy
does it. He's an animal.

I've spent the last four days
protecting him, and now all I
want to do is murder him for
the sleep deprivation.

And for keeping me from you.
Would that be wrong?

She laughed groggily at his morbid joke, knowing he could do it, probably without breaking a sweat.

That might limit your
professional references for
your next gig. Maybe best not
to? 😊

Hard to argue with that. 😊 In
my line of business, satisfied
clients are rarely murdered on
my watch. But damn. I really am
sorry we didn't get that drink.

Me too, Matt. More than you
know.

Another time. Another
country?

Third time will be the charm?

That's what they say. Bon
voyage home, Austen. Back
to Paris for you. I'll be thinking
of you there.

She didn't reply. It seemed like a good message to end with, at least for that day. *Frustrated goodbyes from tarmacs is apparently our thing*, she thought. *It's for the best. I like him more for not actively trying to cheat on Girlfriend Option B.*

With men and sex (or even the potential for it), she knew that where there was a will, there was always a way, even if it meant knocking at her door in the wee hours of the morning. She would have opened it, and he must have known that.

He is one of the good ones—that tragically got away. She let out a long sigh and then peeled herself out of bed to head back to Paris.

The "ones that got away" theme followed her home. When she landed and turned on her phone, she found a text from Kevin, back in Australia.

Just woke up from a
particularly naughty dream in
which you were the star.

A montage of their greatest hits flashed through her mind as she disembarked the jet at Le Bourget airport, warming her up on the cold tarmac. Kevin still affected her, even with the time and distance between them. Also, she was feeling horny from the last few days of frustratingly little satisfaction with Matt.

Kevin was already on her mind because of the sabbatical. Australia was a probable destination. *Not thinking of going there because of him,* she thought loudly. *With two whole months of play time, it's only logical to travel to faraway places and discover new things.* So, she decided to start her planning.

> Always nice to be a star.
> Hope we both got a happy
> ending.

We did.

> Wonderful.

At least a version of me is getting laid somewhere, she thought. *And what better time than just after giving him a dream-orgasm than to start talking about a visit? Here goes nothing.*

> In other news, I just got a
> sabbatical approved for next
> year, and am thinking I might
> want to visit Oz.

Next year sounds like a solid
plan.

She could hear the relief in his typing that she wasn't trying to come sooner.

> When is the best time of year
> to come?

February is your best bet. Not
too hot. Not too cold.

OK thx. Just starting to think
about plans.

Keep me posted.

You know I will.

She was already anxious about one aspect of her sabbatical—traveling alone. She had done it exactly twice in her life.

The first solo trip was before she was married. The boutique PR agency she worked for in San Francisco forced a week-long closure for cost-cutting measures, and none of her friends could escape that week. Liz encouraged her to go somewhere solo, and she settled on San Diego.

"Excellent choice. It's full of hot surfers. Go hang on the beach. Pack your Kindle and some condoms. You'll have a fabulous time," Liz declared.

In the end, she ate every meal alone and read a lot of books. In her "normal" life, Austen was outgoing—someone who easily connected with others. But as a solo traveler, she became someone else—a quiet, shy person who didn't engage. She told herself it was for safety reasons. As a woman traveling alone, she didn't want to be too friendly, lest she invite the crazies in. The result had been a relaxing but lonely week, which she didn't enjoy. She wrote off solo travel after that trip—a choice made easier by her marriage to Brad.

Her second solo travel experience came just as things with Brad were falling apart. They had planned a weekend on Île de Ré but got into a spectacular fight right before the trip. She couldn't even recall what it was about now, but she was mad enough to uninvite him. It was, unsurprisingly, another unpleasant solo travel experience, with her walking on beaches alone.

Now she was single again, and for a two-month trip, traveling solo for at least some part of it seemed inevitable. *I'm older and wiser now, so I'll do it better this time. It'll be good for the soul*, she tried to convince herself. *But I'll start planning now to recruit as many friends as possible to join me along the way.*

She decided to take Kevin's advice and start in Australia next February. She promised herself repeatedly she wasn't chasing him. She chose New Zealand, Thailand, and Cambodia to round out the trip and in early February, sent an email to all her favorite girlfriends laying out the tentative itinerary which was exactly 12 months away. "Join me for any or all parts of it," her email said. The implied part of the message was, "Please don't let me spend two months alone."

CHAPTER THIRTEEN

Loyalty

Two weeks later

Riding the bus across Paris, Austen passed the Corvisart Metro stop. Her first French crush was Maxime Corvisart, a schoolmate of Hélène's in Lyon who captured her young heart during her high school exchange. Her mind's eye flashed to his wavy blond hair, his beautiful green eyes, and the longest eyelashes she'd ever seen on a guy before or since.

All those years ago, they'd spent their hours in class passing notes and peeking at each other from behind textbooks. His English was better than her French, but she'd tried to impress him with whatever sentences she could string together. She'd eagerly accepted his offers to correct her vocabulary and syntax, even as he'd laughed at her in his charming, superior, teenage-boy way. They'd been smitten. But, he had a girlfriend.

On the last night of that formative stay in France, teen-Maxime sneakily decided to not invite his girlfriend to the farewell party. He'd wanted to spend the evening hanging out with Austen. He'd also wanted to kiss her goodbye; he'd made it clear. But his plans were foiled when another class-mate casually mentioned the soirée, and the inconvenient girl-friend showed up unannounced. Their goodbye that night was furtive, while the girlfriend was in the restroom. It held all the imaginable teenage angst, including a few tears on her part. Missed opportunities for love are devastating when you're 16. They wrote each other love letters for nearly a year after she left, full of "if onlys."

Eventually, the letters stopped, and they lost touch. That's what happened before the Internet. She'd thought of him often over the years, whenever the stereotypical French boyfriend ap-peared in a TV show or movie. She'd also heard the occasion-al story about him through Hélène, who remained her close friend. He, too, had been married and divorced, and she knew he was a lawyer living somewhere in the South of France.

Back in the present day, as she stared at his family name from the bus window, she looked him up on Facebook on a whim. She found him easily, and his photo showed he'd aged well. She sent him a friend request with a message.

Yes, this is the Austen you knew from Texas when we were both 16. Hope this message finds you well.

He replied about an hour later.

What a blast from the past. Send me your number. We must catch up.

He called that evening, and when she saw the 05 number indicating Bordeaux, her heart jumped into her throat.

"This is Austen," she answered, trying to sound chill.

"Austen Keller," he stated. "Back in my life after 23 years. I almost drove off the road when I saw your message pop up."

"I'm glad I didn't cause an accident. Geez. It's been a while." She hopped out of her chair and started to pace around her living room. "How's life treating you?"

"I can't complain. I'm a criminal defense lawyer living in Bordeaux now. I've got three great kids, one less-great ex-wife, and just bought a house down here with my girlfriend," he told her. "And you're in Paris."

"I am. I've been here a few years now. I'm sorry I didn't look you up sooner." She meant it. *Might've gotten in before the new girlfriend. Why is there always a girlfriend?*

"Better late than never. It's wild and wonderful to hear your voice. You sound exactly the same," he noticed.

"You do too. Do you ever come to Paris?"

"I'll be there next week for a legal conference. Let's make that happen. I mean it," he insisted.

"OK, you're on," she confirmed. "Really looking forward."

When the night of their reunion rolled around, she slipped into her favorite black jeans, black-and-white striped V-neck, black blazer, and ankle boots, and applied her brightest red lipstick. She called Hélène from the cab on the way. "Guess who I'm meeting for a drink in ten minutes."

"I have no idea," Hélène replied.

"Maxime."

"What? Oh my God, how did that happen?" she asked, laughing.

"I looked him up on Facebook, and we reconnected last week. He's in town for some work thing, so we made plans. It's going to be nuts," Austen enthused.

"You're such a stalker. Twenty-three years later, wow. You must call me tomorrow and tell me all about it. I'm sure he's still gorgeous," Hélène said. "Don't do anything I wouldn't do."

Austen hung up and giggled in the back of the cab. Her romantic self was hoping for fireworks—for the undeniable pull that made them both decide on the spot they wouldn't let each other slip away again. *This could be like a movie,* she dreamed. The realist in her usually did a good job keeping her romantic side in check, but this night, she was hopeless.

Austen and Maxime met at Le Fitzgerald in the seventh for a pre-dinner drink, and it took all of 30 seconds to know that the chemistry between them was alive and well.

"Look at you. Still gorgeous," he said, kissing her on both cheeks.

"You're looking quite handsome yourself," she smiled. "Is this place OK for you?"

"It's perfect. What a treat to have a local tour guide to show me hip places that aren't near the dreaded convention center. Thank you for enabling my escape tonight, my American in Paris." He pulled out a bar stool for her.

"Thank you, sir." She propped herself onto the stool and crossed her legs toward him. "I'm so glad this worked out. I travel a lot for work, so it's lucky I'm in town."

"I never travel for work, anywhere except Paris," he explained. "But right now, Paris is more than enough. I can't believe I'm seeing you—and we're adults."

"Who would've thought. Tell me everything about your life," she insisted.

Maxime's stories wound back time to when he became a lawyer, met his wife, had his kids, got divorced and moved to Bordeaux.

No mention of the new girlfriend in tonight's tale, Austen noticed.

In return, she told him about the twisting road of her life which had finally brought her back to France, including her divorce and the demands and rewards of her job as a speechwriter.

They finished their drinks and relocated to Le Petit Varenne, a nearby bistro. The wine poured in, and the conversation poured out as they sat at the tiny candlelit table. She took in every detail of his face as he talked—the fine lines that had formed around his eyes, his one crooked tooth, the way he licked his lips after each sip of wine. His body leaned in as he talked, but Austen made sure she stayed behind the invisible line that divided their table in half.

One fingertip across that line and you're a goner. Don't break into jail. He's with someone else.

As the waiter cleared their dinner plates, he leaned back into his chair and said, "You haven't changed at all, except that now you're even more intimidating."

Intimidating? Is that for real or is he trying to butter me up?

An uncertain smile crept across his face, and he slowly set his wine glass down, pondering. "It's clear you've become a very independent woman who needs nothing from anyone. That's probably hard for most men to accept. Doesn't every man want to be needed?"

She leaned in, intrigued by his question, and said, "But wouldn't you—OK maybe not you, so let's generalize— wouldn't any man rather be wanted than needed? Wouldn't you rather have an equal partner than a dependent?" She paused, watching the wheels turning in his head. It was clear he didn't have an answer yet, so she continued. "I want to share my life with someone who challenges me to be the best version of myself. Isn't that more interesting than being needed, hypothetically?"

Maxime's gaze had turned quizzical as he listened to her long-drawn-out question. "You're a rare one, Austen. To be honest, I don't know. I've never known anyone like you who seemed so utterly capable. I'm not sure what I—or rather, this generic guy we're discussing—could offer that you don't already have." He shrugged and scratched his head. "Men are supposed to be hunters and providers. It's wired into our genes. Without the certainty of that job to do, I think a lot of guys would be lost. But I like the idea of the challenge, hypothetically."

He finished that one strong.

When the bill was paid and they made their way into the street, she buried the girlfriend in the back of her mind, thinking about the kiss they never got to share as teenagers.

"One more drink somewhere, or shall we call it a night?" she asked.

"I should probably call it. Early morning tomorrow."

"Of course," she chirped, trying to keep the surprise and disappointment from her voice. "I'm so glad we got to see each other again."

He took both of her hands in his and leaned in slowly to kiss each of her cheeks. With the first kiss, their fingers weaved together, and with the second, they pulled apart slowly, like two dryer sheets sparking against the resistant pull of static cling.

"Thank you for a night that I won't soon forget," he said, as he walked away.

She walked in the other direction, simultaneously disappointed and relieved about not becoming "the other woman" on that Parisian street corner.

Once home, she fell into an uneasy sleep and woke the next morning to a series of texts.

I can't believe I left and didn't
get that extra drink with you.

I thought I should be good
and get some sleep before my
conference today, but I have
to tell you, I couldn't sleep.

I couldn't stop thinking about
you, my dear Parisienne.

I have to see you again. And
soon.

What have you done to me?

Her heart and mind raced awake as she bolted upright in bed, reading and re-reading his messages. *Is this really happening? Nope. Girlfriend. Remember the girlfriend.* She decided to proceed with utmost caution.

It was really good to see you
again, Maxime. I had such a
nice night. But it's probably for
the best we left it where we did.

Why? I have spent the last 23
years regretting not kissing
you. I made a promise to
you 23 years ago, but I
made another promise more
recently. I was really torn.

She had no recollection of his childhood promise, but she guessed it had something to do with not letting her get away if they ever met again. Part of her wanted to swoon. *Kind of romantic?* But the other part of her had to ask. *Did this just get cheesy? Where is the line between romance and cheese for a French man? Am I too cynical?*

Feeling overwhelmed, she again decided to be pragmatic.

I think the more recent
promise usually wins out. I
wasn't planning to hold you to
any 23-year-old promises.

I hate myself for letting you
walk away last night, but
something told me you were
holding back. Honestly, I can't
figure out why. What are you
scared of?

It was a legitimate question that the two warring halves of her brain debated at length before she replied.

I wanted it to happen too,
but I know myself, and I don't
share well.

You're with someone. I
don't want to be the other
woman.

I have to see you again.

Why don't you come down to
Bordeaux and stay with us for
a weekend soon? We have an
extra room.

The war in her head stilled, and the smoke cleared.

Us? You want me to come
down to visit you and your
girlfriend?

Yes, why not?

Because you and I both
just admitted that we're still
attracted to each other?

Why would you want to put
yourself in that situation,
spending a weekend all
together?

If I'm going to fall out of love
with her, I'm going to fall out
of love with her.

It could happen with you
or the girl who works in the
bakery down the street. I'm

not going to NOT buy bread
because of this risk.

Things happen, and we
must let them. I really don't
understand your hesitation.

I don't understand why you
want to tempt fate.

So, we can't be friends just
because we're attracted to
each other? Why did you
bother reconnecting with
me if you don't want to be
friends?

Austen stared at his last text. It was so typically French, like he was screaming: "What's the big deal if we slip into a torrid affair? Let it play out." But she couldn't. It was all too hasty, too cavalier.

Late that night, she met her Parisian tribe at Chez Janou in the 3rd arrondissement and recounted the story over an excellent bottle of *Bandol* and the restaurant's legendary bottomless bowl of chocolate mousse.

"If he were my partner, I'd kill him. I mean, what the actual fuck?" Isobel growled, baring her teeth.

Chiara shook her head. "I can't believe he invited you down there to spend time with the two of them. What does he think happens in that situation?"

"A threesome?" Austen guessed. "I can't even." She shoved a heaping spoonful of chocolate mousse into her mouth.

Daphne exploded with equal parts furor and flair. "He's so incredibly lame trying to have it both ways. He's like a Catholic girl who only has anal sex, so she can say she's still a virgin."

Chocolate mousse very nearly flew out of Austen's nose. After the laughter died down and everyone's breathing returned to normal, Daphne continued, "Seriously, avoid. This guy has tried to cheat on two women for you over the years. It would probably be a piece of cake for you to go down there and steal him. But then how could you ever trust him?"

Austen took a big gulp of her wine and wiped her mouth with a napkin.

"Of course, you're right. But the romantic in me wanted the dream. Twenty-three years later, they reconnected and instantly knew they were meant to be. Violins playing in the background and all that shit." She mimicked someone playing a violin, her head waving to the imaginary tune. "I wanted the fairy tale."

Daphne was resolute. "This one is no prince, my friend."

"Nope. He's an unavailable monkey man trying to swing out of his current tree into mine, probably more out of boredom than any real feelings." Austen was sure Daphne was right but had another question lingering in her mind. "What do we think, girls? Once a cheater, always a cheater?"

"Once a cheater, always a fucking cheater," Isobel declared, banging her fist on the table, and sending the wine in their glasses sloshing.

Chiara shrugged. "Unless you're *the one*. I'm not saying you're Maxime's 'one' but sometimes cheaters cheat because they find their soulmate."

"What kind of excuse is that?" Austen asked, exasperated. "Break up with the first one and then go live happily ever after with your soulmate. Why is that so hard?"

"Kids. History. Comfort. Because they think they won't get caught. There are a million reasons people cheat," Isobel offered.

Austen was a deeply loyal person—to all her friends and boyfriends. At Stanford, she had a friend named Jane whose boyfriend cheated on her. Austen's outrage burned inferno-hot on her friend's behalf. Even when Jane forgave the boyfriend for the transgression, Austen remained mad about it until, eventually, Jane asked her to call off the dogs.

"I love you for hating him and wanting to protect me from that hurt. But I've forgiven him, and I need you to too now," Jane calmly asked.

The request made Austen think hard about why she was holding on to anger when poor scorned Jane had let it go. She understood even then it was about values. Austen valued loyalty above everything else, because she'd felt the sting of disloyalty from supposed friends in her youth.

Austen started high school as one of the "cool kids," but she'd always been innocent. She inherently trusted people to be good, and in her freshman year, she trusted the wrong person once—her mom.

After a night out with friends, she told her mom that some of the kids had been drinking on the train tracks behind the movie theater—the height of teenage rebellion. Her mom relayed the story to another mom, who relayed it to her daughter, who relayed it to the whole school, resulting in Austen's absolute and final social ex-communication.

That fateful day as she entered the school's main courtyard, every kid in the place dropped into silence and stared at her, until one of them shouted "narc." Then they all turned their backs to her, never to return.

She spent the rest of her high school years as a social outcast, wondering why those she'd believed were her friends refused to acknowledge her. One mistake erased all loyalty and forced her to redefine her sense of self. She had to become a different version of the girl she thought she knew.

It wasn't until years later that she understood it to be the defining moment of her youth. It got her out of Texas, landed her at Stanford, and reset her future. It defined her values system, placing a premium on friendship, loyalty, honesty, and empathy in her relationships.

When she started dating Brad after university, he confessed that he'd never been faithful to any girlfriend before her. She told him, wholeheartedly believing it, that he simply hadn't met the right girl. She'd held a youthful certainty that people in love didn't cheat on one another—that cheating was a symptom of love lost. Time had hardened her against that naïveté, but she still desperately wanted to believe that devotion was possible.

By stereotype, French men were reputed to be disloyal. Maxime proved the stereotype true. Austen shut down their conversation, once she understood there was nothing remotely romantic in his approach. His invitation to Bordeaux was all haste and drama. They hadn't seen each other in 23 years, and after one night out, he casually suggested that they drop a proverbial firebomb into his household.

If he'd put in the effort to rebuild a friendship, gradually eased toward her, and then declared that they must be together, she probably would have fallen for it.

But not like this, she thought. *The right one will put in the time and effort to build something that will last.*

CHAPTER FOURTEEN

The Sex Friend

March

On Friday night, Austen sat alone at a high round table by the window at Chez Nous on Rue Dauphine. Isobel was late, so she was watching the door when the definition of "tall, dark, and handsome" walked into the wine bar. He cut a fine figure in a well-tailored jacket, nicely pressed shirt, and dark jeans, and she watched as he made a lap around the bar, presumably looking for whoever he was there to meet. As he completed the circle and arrived back at the door, he greeted another man who had just arrived, and they moved toward the table next to hers.

Bingo, she thought.

He looked her way as they approached, and she smiled. He returned her smile and sat down in the chair closest to hers, just as Isobel blew through the door.

"Sorry I'm late," she huffed. "I was being the perfect step-mom, watching Amélie, and Luc was late getting home."

"No worries. I was enjoying the view," Austen whispered, subtly gesturing to the table next to theirs.

"I see." Isobel winked. "What are we drinking? Where's the wine list?"

"No wine list here," Austen explained. "We just tell the server what we're in the mood for, and he makes recommendations. It's the best for discovering new wines."

Moments later, the waiter arrived at the table next to theirs and began discussing options with the two men. Austen put her finger to her ear and leaned their way, indicating to Isobel to listen in.

"I'd like a red—something on the dry side and medium-bodied," said Tall, Dark, and Handsome. "But nothing organic. Maybe just me, but I think organic wine tastes like dirt."

Perfect entry point, Austen thought as she casually pivoted her body toward him.

"Sorry for eavesdropping, but I can confirm it's not just you. Organic wine absolutely tastes like dirt."

"Thank you," he smiled.

The waiter objected. "I have an incredible natural red that tastes nothing like dirt. I'm going to have you taste it. It's just become my mission to change your minds."

"OK, let's see what you've got," Austen challenged.

The handsome stranger leaned toward her. "I guess we're in this together now. I'm Clément and this is Olivier. Would you two ladies like to join us?"

"I'm Austen, and this is Isobel," she returned.

She didn't need to ask Isobel. Friend code implicitly states that "when a handsome stranger invites you and your single girlfriend to join their table, the answer is yes." Isobel was already shifting her chair to combine their tables.

The waiter returned with a bottle of grenache. "Try this. The grapes are organically farmed." He poured a small taste into four glasses. "It's Domaine de la Damase in the Vaucluse. The guy is a fifth-generation wine maker and knows his stuff."

Clément spun the wine in his glass and tasted it. "It's a bit on the lighter side of 'medium-bodied,' but it's not awful."

"High praise," Austen cracked.

She took a sip and let the wine swirl in her mouth. Clément raised his eyebrows in anticipation of her verdict.

"Entirely drinkable," she declared. "I feel like I should make some kind of dirt joke now, but I'm drawing a blank."

"Dirty jokes so soon? We only just met. Let's have a proper drink first," Clément teased.

"Oh, he's good." Isobel raised a glass to Clément.

Witty, handsome, a wine connoisseur, and possibly a dirty mind, Austen thought. *Nice combo.*

"What do you two gentlemen do in life?" Austen was thirsty to know more.

Olivier responded. "We work in catering—private events mostly."

"Chefs?" she asked.

"Of a sort. We mostly prep and serve," Clément explained. "Having my own kitchen is the dream though. Maybe one day."

"That's wonderful. I have zero culinary ability," she confessed.

Clément leaned toward her. "I have a feeling you have other skills."

Wouldn't you like to know? she asked with her eyes.

"And you ladies? What do you do?" Olivier asked.

"You deal in food. I deal in words. I'm a speechwriter for a technology exec," Austen explained.

"I deal in apartments," Isobel said. "I'm in real estate."

"Now that the job interview portion of the evening is out of the way and it's clear none of us is hiring, we can all finally relax," Clément cracked.

"Sorry, she's American," Isobel interjected. "The Americans always go straight to the professional stuff."

Austen cringed. *Another cultural faux pas? Am I not supposed to ask what people do for a living?* She looked toward Isobel for reassurance, but Clément stepped in.

"I was joking. You can ask me anything you want. Professional or otherwise." His intonation suggested he preferred "otherwise."

Phew.

After a few bottles and several small plates of nibbles, Clément had a proposal.

"A friend of mine is playing in a jazz band tonight on the Péniche Marcounet, just on the other side of the Seine. Do you know it?"

She shook her head.

"It's a jazz bar on a barge docked on the Quai de l'Hôtel de Ville. Would you like to come? Olivier and I promised we'd make an appearance," he explained.

"You go," Isobel insisted. "I'm going to head out. Call me tomorrow." She pointed both index fingers at Clément and Olivier. "You'll take good care of her?"

"I promise. She's in safe hands," Clément assured her.

Austen hugged her friend goodbye.

She sat in the middle seat of the cab on the way to the boat. When it took the first turn, she allowed the centrifugal force to push her body into Clément's. He took her cue and propped his arm on the seat behind her, pushing his hand gently under her hair and placing it on the back of her neck.

She was certain he could feel the tiny hairs stand to attention at his touch.

They boarded and took their seats by the stage, set in the belly of the barge. He held her hand and gently tapped his thumb against hers, to the beat. Moonlight sparkled off the Seine through the porthole windows, and music reverberated off the boat's steel hull. As the band played on, his hand made its way to her thigh. The music and the movement of his fingers against her leg heightened all her senses.

The concert ended at the stroke of midnight, and they made their way out, back onto the quai.

"I'm not ready to say goodnight. Are you?" he asked into her ear.

She shook her head, and they made their excuses to Olivier before jumping into another cab. She gave the driver her address.

Kevin had technically been the first man she'd brought home on the very night they met, but he was "qualified" since he was a friend of a friend. Clément was a total stranger. *This is reckless and entirely necessary,* she thought.

They were already kissing by the time the cab crossed the Pont Marie.

He peeled off his shirt in her bedroom, revealing muscles she didn't know existed. She nearly started to drool, but luckily his mouth was on hers fast enough that it went unnoticed. He was attentive but not communicative—more tactile than verbal—and in that moment, it was enough.

She awoke the next morning to his hands once again exploring her body. They say idle hands are the devil's playthings. Clément was anything but idle, and she was in heaven. She enjoyed it so much she barely noticed just how few words passed between them—at least until he left. She made coffee and called Isobel to debrief.

"How was he? Tell me everything."

"He was divine but quiet." As a professional communicator, Austen was uncomfortable with quiet. "I honestly have no idea what this is."

"How did you leave things?" Isobel asked.

"We exchanged numbers and said we'd talk soon. He texted as soon as he was out the door, so that's good," Austen said, more to herself than to Isobel.

"You're in a relationship," Isobel declared. "One-night-stand-guy wouldn't have even asked for your number."

Austen wasn't convinced.

However, he proved otherwise. They continued to see each other over the next few weeks, almost always at his apartment, for champagne-fueled nights or weekend afternoons. They always started in the bedroom, then moved to the living room where they danced in their underwear, drank more champagne, and ate delectable little snacks that he whipped up.

At Austen's apartment, "snacks" were olives, store-bought hummus, and crackers. At Clément's, it was roasted pears and ricotta on crostini drizzled in honey, or something similarly elaborate. Once their food hunger was sated, their sexual hunger pushed them back to the bedroom. It was a consistent loop. If someone had been watching them through the loft windows, they would have believed no one in Paris was having a better time. But despite many evenings spent together and many orgasms, she still knew shockingly little about him.

One Sunday afternoon in April, Austen met Daphne for a stroll through the Tuileries, where spring flowers were just starting to bloom in the manicured gardens.

"I feel like I've been stuck in the bowels of the Ritz for weeks, up to my eyeballs in icing sugar. It's so nice to escape. How's your heart since Kevin left town?" Daphne asked.

"You *have* been stuck in the bowels of the Ritz. There's a whole new series of sexcapades happening with a new guy named Clément."

"Sexcapades?"

"Sexual escapades." Austen rubbed her palms together, smiling.

"Here I was, thinking we'd wander the Tuileries while I tried to help mend your broken heart. But no, there are sexcapades," Daphne exclaimed. "You're my hero."

"You know what they say—best way to get over someone is to get under someone else," Austen cracked. "Pining for someone on the other side of the planet was doing me no favors. And then Clément appeared. In a wine bar."

"There was wine. Thank God. No good story ever started with someone drinking water," she declared. "Do tell all."

She brought Daphne up to speed on the last few weeks of adventures with Clément, explaining how they'd met and how they'd spent their time together since.

"Champagne, spontaneity, and sex. That's exactly what I said I wanted in a relationship when things ended with Alain, but isn't it strange that we hardly ever talk about anything that matters?"

"You're not in a relationship. You've got a sex friend," Daphne told her.

"A what?" Austen had never heard that term.

"In the U.S., it's called 'friends with benefits.' Here, it's called 'sex friends,'" Daphne explained.

"Hang on a minute. Isobel told me that in France, after your first night together, you know if you're either a one-night stand or in a relationship," Austen stammered, trying to process this new information.

"Isobel forgot about the magical mystery of door number three. It's a perfectly legitimate option." Daphne paused and then raised a finger. "Just as long as neither of you want it to be something more. That's always the rub. Do you want more?"

"I don't know," Austen conceded. "I keep thinking I should, but as much as I enjoy the sex, I'm not sure I do."

"You have a stressful job and need an outlet to help you unwind," Daphne offered. "You're allowed to just enjoy the sex. A girl's gotta eat."

"Clément is a damn good cook," Austen laughed. "But it's funny that you asked about Kevin. The big difference between them is that I could talk to Kevin for hours. He lit up my brain and my body." Austen threw her head back and looked up at the sky. "I think this thing with Clément only makes sense in the bedroom."

"Intellectual connection matters," Daphne confirmed. "We're smart women. We need both."

Things between Austen and Clément continued at the same pace for another few weeks until he did something unexpected—he suggested they graduate from snacks and have a proper dinner.

Like a real date?

"I'll be at your apartment tonight at eight o'clock," he told her.

He's picking me up and taking me out. She was shocked that he wanted to break their usual habit of staying at his place. She was also sucked into nostalgia of her Southern youth when boys picked girls up in cars for dates. Hardly anyone had a car in Paris, so this almost never happened. Her heart soared higher than she cared to admit. *Maybe this could be something more.*

She grabbed her purse when the doorbell rang, ready to go. Opening the door, she found him holding a bag of groceries.

"I'm cooking for you," he announced. "We're having lasagna."

Dueling senses of disappointment and delight flooded her brain. *He said dinner. He never said we were going out*, she realized. *But it's still dinner.*

"I went to the Italian deli and even did some prep work," he said, as he removed various sacks and containers from his bag. He took her purse out of her hand and set it aside, before picking her up by the hips and placing her on the kitchen counter.

"Just sit there and look beautiful. I've got it all under control."

She watched quietly as he opened a bottle of wine, poured two glasses, fired up the oven, and slipped on the crisp white apron he pulled from his bag.

Yeah, OK. This is good. Get out of your own head and enjoy this gorgeous man cooking dinner in your kitchen.

He deftly chopped, sautéed, and stirred. She drank and observed.

This is the most action this kitchen has seen since I moved in. What would he say if he knew I can barely boil an egg?

He removed the pans from the stove and kissed her as she sat on her perch on the counter. Her legs wrapped around his waist, pulling him in. Things escalated quickly; lasagna be damned. Her shirt hit the kitchen floor, and before long, they were in her bedroom in some certain kind of ecstasy.

They laid in bed for a few minutes after, recovering their breath. Then, he extricated himself from the tangled bedding.

"Take your time getting up. I'm going to finish dinner."

Good sex. No conversation. So strange, she thought.

She meandered out of the bedroom on still unsteady legs and found his clothes strewn across the hallway, mixed up with hers. She reassembled her outfit, step by step, and then found him in the kitchen, wearing the apron and nothing else, his bare ass hanging out the back in all its toned perfection. He handed over her shirt and kissed her with his whole mouth which had, up until seconds before, been aerating wine. She hopped back onto her place on the counter with a satisfied smile, and he refreshed her wine glass with a devious licking of his lips, before returning to their meal.

He pulled the bubbling, cheesy masterpiece out of the oven and announced, "Dinner is served in 30 seconds—just as soon as I put my pants back on."

They sat at the table and dug into the delicious lasagna. Austen was still searching for common ground between them.

"What's your ideal vacation? Beach or mountains?" she asked.

His answer was immediate. "If we're camping, either is great. I love being in nature and sleeping under the stars. Put me in a tent in the forest or on a beach, and I'm happy."

Austen had never camped for a day in her life. She leaned toward five-star hotels. She wordlessly sipped her glass of *Mercurey.*

"You're probably not big on sleeping in the dirt," he correctly observed.

"And we've now come full circle on the topic of dirt. I don't like it in my wine or in my bed." She shrugged and smiled. *What are we doing together?*

The morning light brought the clarity she needed. As they laid in bed, Clément said, "We've been seeing each other for a while, and we should probably talk about what's going on between us."

She sat up and wrapped the sheet around herself as the flimsiest armor, bracing for what was coming.

"This is all I can give. Emotionally, there's nothing more here." He tapped four fingers on his chest, near his heart. "I like spending time with you and want to keep doing it, but I'm not in a place for a relationship, and I want to be honest with you about that."

"OK, thanks for telling me. I get it. It's fine," she said quickly.

"Are you sure?"

She thought about it for a beat too long, during which the atmosphere between them changed. She felt cold and wanted him gone.

"I'm sure. Of course, it's fine. But for now, I think you should go." She jumped out of bed, threw on a robe, and went to the kitchen to make coffee.

He met her there a few minutes later. "OK I'm leaving. Will you call me?" he asked, putting the ball in her court.

"Sure. I will," she replied hastily.

He looked at her skeptically, kissed her softly on the cheek, and showed himself out.

She moved to the couch, sipped her coffee, and tried to process her feelings. *"Sex friends" is fine. I know he doesn't fit in my life. But why doesn't he want me in his?*

With that last question, a lightbulb went off. It was her pride that was hurt—not her heart. That realization made the bitter pill easier to swallow.

She spent most of the next week in Lisbon for work, where she emptied her mind of all things personal. On the jet home, she thought of him again—mostly about his beautiful body. In her younger days, Austen believed that being "sex friends" was entirely untenable, as someone would inevitably get emotionally involved. But given how little they had in common, that risk seemed low.

"Sex friends" can work, if neither of us wants anything more, and neither of us do. So why not enjoy it?

And so, she resolved to joyfully enter door number three. With her girlfriends, Austen's advice was always the same: "Have fun until you're not having fun anymore."

I'm going to be 40 soon. I should prioritize fun. You only live once.

Once back in Paris, she called.

When she came through his front door, he kissed her urgently. "I'm so glad to see you. I wasn't sure I would."

She nodded, acknowledging the weirdness. "I needed a few days to reset my expectations. But they're reset. I'm good with what this is. It doesn't need to be more."

He smiled with relief in his eyes and then flung her over his shoulder and carried her to his bedroom.

Eventually, the relationship with Clément ran its course and faded to black. She wanted more—good sex, intellectual connection, and emotional availability.

Does such a man even exist or am I hunting unicorns? she wondered.

She chose to believe he did and that he wanted to find her as badly as she wanted to find him.

CHAPTER FIFTEEN

The Wedding

June

Isobel and Luc's wedding was destined to be the event of the century. The venue was the uber-glamorous Château des Joyaux in the Loire Valley; they expected 100 guests. Since Isobel was British, all the ladies would wear hats. Austen had her fascinator and couldn't wait to celebrate.

Daphne, Jean-Marc, Chiara, and Austen took the train together to Angers and rented a car to get to the chateau, where they were also sleeping. While she was thrilled to go, the timing was terrible. Work was exceptionally crazy, and she had been traveling non-stop for weeks, bouncing between countries with almost no downtime. She even had to beg out of a work trip to Munich; she wouldn't miss this celebration for the world.

Luc and Isobel arranged a dinner for their closest friends on Friday night before the wedding. Getting there on time meant catching the train at four p.m., which was turning into a challenge for Austen, as she had several urgent end-of-week deadlines. She spent the 90-minute train ride down with her nose buried in her laptop, responding to emails, and trying to clear the decks so she could spend Saturday without worrying about work.

Bastien tried to call her four times while she was in transit, but reception is never good on a fast-moving train. She returned his calls the second they rolled to a stop.

"Just arrived and just got a signal, sorry. What's up?" she asked.

"François and I just landed from Munich, and on the plane, he decided he isn't happy with the speech for next week in Delhi at the Ministry of Health. He wants one of the customer references changed. I have notes. Do you have a pen?"

She climbed out of the train and followed her friends. "I'm on the move getting out of the train station. Can you just talk me through the issue?"

"He thinks that instead of talking about the program in China that's using AI for predictive healthcare, we should talk about something local—something smaller scale that's happening in India. He doesn't think that Minister Singh is ready for something that big."

Austen let out a sigh of relief and said, "Well, he's wrong. I spoke with Singh's Deputy Minister two weeks ago, who specifically asked me to include that example in the speech because she's been studying it and has laid the groundwork to sell it to him." She switched the call to her earphones and stuffed her phone in the pocket of her linen pants as they hit the stairs leading from the train platform toward the station. "She sees it as a huge opportunity for India and wants to make a full court press. She has his ear. If François lands this case study with some color, there's a solid chance Singh will buy it.

Trust me. I've vetted the speech with his Deputy, down to the last comma."

She could hear the smile in Bastien's voice on the other end of the line. "I'll let François know. Sounds like you've got this buttoned up. Go have a great weekend, Austen."

She hung up feeling victorious and tossed her phone in her Moynat tote bag as they arrived at the rental car desk in the small station. She looked up to find all three of her friends staring at her.

"You spoke with India's Deputy Minister of Health two weeks ago? Who are you?" Daphne asked with a smile.

She looked flatly at Daphne and said, "Didn't you bake a wedding cake last weekend for the daughter of the CEO of L'Oréal—one of the biggest companies in France?" She turned to face Chiara. "And wasn't Marion Cotillard photographed last week at some movie premiere with a bag on her arm that you designed? We're all just making a living here."

Jean-Marc looked at the three women and said, "I swear, you three could take over the world if you joined forces for good. Or for evil, for that matter."

Austen let out an evil laugh. Jean-Marc shook his head and advanced to the rental counter to collect their key.

The 30-minute drive from the station led them up a tree-lined road that dead-ended at the glorious chateau, glowing in the summer sun. Austen adored an opulent wedding, and this one promised to be nothing short of spectacular. *I feel like I'm driving into a fairy tale*, she thought. *Thank God I don't have to spend my weekend rewriting the Delhi speech.*

It was the first wedding she would attend since her divorce. Austen and Brad's wedding took place at a winery in Napa. It was a beautiful affair for 75 of her and Brad's people, overlooking the vineyards. Even though the marriage failed, she remembered the day as magical, with everyone she loved in one room for the first and last time. Maybe it would happen again for her funeral, but she doubted she would enjoy that day nearly as much.

Her memories of that day were altered after Austen told her parents that she was getting divorced. Her mom had burst the bubble: "I never told you this, but at your wedding, Brad's mom said to me, 'He needs her much more than she needs him.' I couldn't believe she said it."

"Mom! Why did you tell me that?" she had demanded to know. Her eyes bulged out of her head, and she threw her hands into the air.

"What? Why are you so upset?" her mom had asked.

Austen let out a disappointed sigh. "Because you're telling me that his mom knew all along that we weren't well matched. And I didn't see it."

She had convinced herself that their marriage failed because Brad had changed. Her mom's story turned that idea on its head, and the memory was still raw.

She snapped out of her recollection as the woman at the chateau's reception desk handed her a heavy, gold-plated skeleton key. She walked up the spiraling stone staircase, appreciating every detail of its magnificence and history. She turned the key in the lock and entered her room to find beautifully vaulted stone ceilings and a canopy bed worthy of royalty. There was also a well-appointed desk and chair which she slid into to finish the business dealings of the day.

Dinner started at eight p.m. in the courtyard of the chateau. It was a perfect summer evening; the weather gods were smiling on Isobel and Luc. Austen emerged punctually from her room in her favorite little black dress and made her way to the courtyard. A loose canopy of little white lights hung over two long tables topped with candles and all-white floral arrangements, creating a magical ambiance. She scanned the space looking for her friends but didn't spot them, so she casually made her way to the bar and picked up a long-stemmed flute of champagne.

She set her glass on one of the tables to take a picture of the light canopy and the medieval courtyard walls when she heard a deep voice behind her.

"Friend of the bride or the groom?"

She turned around to find an attractive gray-haired man who was probably 15 years her senior. "Both actually. We're all friends in Paris. I'm Austen."

He leaned in for the traditional French greeting of a kiss on each cheek, overwhelming her with his cologne. "I'm Luc's uncle, Etienne—his mother's brother. I live here in Angers and own a winery nearby."

Wine is my love language, Austen thought. She instinctively checked his left hand—no wedding ring.

"I'd be happy to give you a private tour of the caves one day, with a full tasting, of course. Maybe even on Sunday after the wedding," he suggested.

Austen found the offer, his tone of voice, and his exaggerated smile equal parts charming and strange. *Clearly a confident guy, but maybe too confident?* she thought. Her guard was officially up, but she was intrigued despite herself.

"That's a very generous offer. Thank you," she replied.

Etienne adjusted the crisp pocket square in his suit jacket and asked, "How did you meet my nephew and his lovely bride?"

"Isobel and I happened to sit next to each other in a café in Paris one day and started talking," Austen explained. "I met Luc through her."

"A fated meeting in a Parisian café. It's almost romantic," he declared.

"If only we'd fallen in love," Austen cracked, before taking a sip of champagne.

"Are you a lesbian?" he asked, abruptly.

Austen choked on the question and covered her mouth with her hand, to prevent the champagne from escaping. *Wow. Just went there, didn't he?* "Uh, no. I was joking—responding to your suggestion it might have been romantic."

"Well, that's excellent news," he smirked.

Chiara appeared moments later and introduced herself to Etienne. She hooked her arm into Austen's and asked Etienne, "Would you mind terribly if I borrowed her?"

"As long as it's only temporary."

Austen waved goodbye to Etienne as her friend led her away.

"Don't you dare ditch me for that guy this weekend," Chiara exclaimed, dragging Austen toward the bar. "I don't want to be the only single person at this whole wedding, sitting alone at a table tomorrow night while everyone else is dancing."

Austen wrapped an arm around Chiara's waist. "I'm sorry you and Emmanuel broke up. Are you sad?"

"I will be impossibly sad if you ditch me."

"I'll do no such thing," Austen promised, giving her a squeeze.

The courtyard slowly filled up with guests, and everyone made their way to their seats. Austen and Chiara found

Daphne and Jean-Marc at the far end of one table, sitting with Céline and Sébastien. They'd apparently made up since the weird dinner party fight about Zara t-shirts and monkey men.

There were 40 people in the courtyard for dinner that night, and Luc and Isobel made their rounds, saying hello to all their guests and accepting all the exuberant well-wishes. Isobel looked stunning in a lace, ice-blue cocktail dress, with her blond wavy hair falling loosely around her shoulders. Luc looked equally dashing in dark slacks, a bespoke shirt in a shade of blue that perfectly complemented Isobel's dress, and a gray sport coat. They were a handsome couple, and watching them glide from guest to guest, Austen felt a pang of jealousy for their happiness, which she quickly suppressed.

When the blissful couple reached them, Luc leaned in to speak discreetly to Austen. "I hear you already met Uncle Etienne. Do what you want, but fair warning: He's a player. I love him, and he is very generous with the women in his life, but it's always women—plural. Don't you dare tell him I told you that, or he'll kill me."

"We can't have you getting killed. You're getting married tomorrow. Therefore, my lips—and probably my legs—are sealed. And thanks for the warning. You're a good man." She stood up to hug him and then turned to Isobel. "This place is kind of a dump," she cracked, exaggerating a double thumbs down.

Chiara stood and joined in on the joke. "It's wretched. I don't know how we're going to make it through the weekend."

Isobel laughed and took both of her friends' hands, looking earnest. "I'm sorry we couldn't do better for you guys. Thanks for struggling through."

"I'm over the moon for you," Austen told her.

"Thanks, friend. I wish I could sit down and hang with you guys all night, but we've got to circulate. Enjoy dinner."

When Austen sat down, Jean-Marc stared at her flatly. "Probably your legs?"

She shrugged with a coy smile, and scanned the room to find Etienne, subtly raising his glass to her from the other table.

The next day, the ceremony started at six p.m. in the expansive, manicured gardens of the chateau. Austen wore a tea-length, midnight-blue, sleeveless dress and black stilettos, which would inevitably be killing her feet by the end of the night. Her fascinator was a matching blue, completed by a small but fabulous peacock feather. She sat on the aisle next to Chiara, Daphne and Jean-Marc, tissues at the ready. Austen always cried at weddings. Etienne was just across the aisle from her, wearing a light gray suit that perfectly complemented his gray hair, with a crisp white shirt and a black tie.

Super handsome, and he knows it, Austen thought.

Isobel floated down the aisle in an ivory, floor-length, high neck, sleeveless lace concoction that deserved to be in a movie. Her hair was pinned into an elegant chignon, and she carried a bouquet of deep purple orchids. Luc wore a dark suit and a purple tie which matched the flowers. The smiles on their faces as they promised to love and honor one another were undeniably genuine.

Watching them exchange vows, Austen involuntarily returned to memories of her own wedding and marriage. She believed in the vows she made that day and that they would grow old together. She was young, of course, and life often zigs when you expect it to zag. She chose Brad thinking they would successfully navigate the zigzagging of life together because their life goals were similar.

They met with a marriage counselor once, toward the end, who asked Austen what she wanted out of life. She replied, "I want to go everywhere, see, smell and taste everything, live the biggest, loudest life I can and slide into home plate at the end exhausted and happy."

The counselor asked Brad, "How does that make you feel?"

"Like we're completely fucked."

Brad wanted a quiet life. At the end of their hour together, the counselor said, "I can't help you. My job is to help people communicate, and you're communicating very well. You just don't want the same things."

Once she let that sink in, Austen knew she had to walk away, to live the life she wanted. In her parents' generation, walking away was a harder choice. Many married couples were too comfortable, even in their discomfort, to take the leap. Austen abhorred complacency, even if the idea of rebuilding a life alone was daunting. Life was simply too short to be unhappy.

Nearly two years had passed since her divorce, and her love life since then had left a lot to be desired. Her relationships with Alain and Grégoire had lasted two months each. Her time with Kevin was even shorter. *They didn't love me. No one has fallen in love with me since Brad—and that was 12 years ago. And I'm not sure he loved me for very long.* Tears escaped as she watched Isobel and Luc seal their union with a kiss. *I don't feel unlovable. But all recent evidence is to the contrary.* She'd never felt less like a party in her life.

As they made their way up the aisle toward the party, following the newlyweds, Daphne grabbed Austen's hand, looking concerned. "Are you OK? You look like your cat just died."

"I don't have a cat," she said, forcing a smile. "I'm fine."

As they walked toward the chateau, Austen resolved to end the pity party in her head and enjoy the actual party that awaited them. She locked arms with Daphne and Chiara, and they made their way toward the waiter with a tray of glittering champagne flutes, which were calling their names.

A black-and-white checkered dance floor sat at the center of the reception, with ten round tables, opulently covered in orchids and tealights, surrounding it. Heavy crystal chandeliers marked the four corners of the space. It was the definition of elegance. Austen and the Paris contingent sat together again. The food and the wine kept coming for hours, with some guests hitting the dance floor in between courses.

After the cheese course, Austen had drunk enough wine to believe she could dance, so she pulled Chiara and Daphne onto the dance floor. They twirled around each other giggling and were having a great time when Etienne appeared, alongside a waiter holding a tray of four glasses of champagne.

"You beautiful ladies look like you need some refreshment. I took it upon myself to recruit Thibaud here to come to your aid," he said, gesturing for the women to take the offered glasses. Etienne took the fourth glass and inserted himself into their dancing circle. Jean-Marc joined them seconds later.

So protective, Austen thought. *It's very sweet.*

Etienne's dance moves didn't disappoint. He took Austen's hand, gave her a spin, and pulled her close to him. "You shouldn't be allowed to be more beautiful than the bride. It's distracting. I haven't been able to take my eyes off you all night."

"You certainly aren't shy." She smiled and spun out of his grasp.

"And she pulls away. You're difficult to read, *madame.*" His face looked smug, as if he enjoyed the challenge too much.

"What do you think about that wine tasting tomorrow? Can I tempt you?"

"I'm traveling back to Paris tomorrow with my friends," she told him.

"Bring them," he said, still brimming with confidence. "Or don't. Take a later train. I'll drive you to the station myself."

Austen saw the cake being served to their table and used it as an excuse to escape without answering. "Time for cake," she grinned, grabbing Chiara's hand and moving them away from an unsatisfied-looking Etienne.

Back at the table, Daphne asked the question in everyone's mind. "Is there something brewing between you and Luc's uncle? Are we having a wedding fling? Everyone loves a good wedding fling."

"Listen, he's tempting. I mean, he's a handsome, wealthy, older guy with a vineyard. A lot of girls would go for that in a heartbeat, but you heard what Luc said. And he's given me a weird vibe since we met," Austen explained.

"Who cares if it's just a one-night thing? I say you should enjoy it so we married folk can live vicariously," Daphne said, batting her eyelashes.

"I don't need a one-nighter, and he seems like more trouble than he's worth," Austen concluded. "If there had been no Clément, maybe, but I've exceeded my sex quota for this quarter."

Jean-Marc shook his head. "Spoken like a true businesswoman—your sex quota for the quarter. I swear."

"Also, I told her she couldn't ditch me," Chiara added.

Austen took Chiara's hand and said, "Yes, I promised not to ditch her, knowing very well that if I wanted to, she'd let me."

"I would have, and I only would have hated you a little. And just for tonight," Chiara joked, pinching her friend's cheek with her free hand.

Austen knew that if it was love she wanted, Etienne was a highly unlikely candidate. He seemed like the kind of guy who would always love himself more than anyone else he might let into his life. Seeing Sébastien and Céline across the table, she flashed back to the conversation at Isobel and Luc's apartment about the expression "*Il m'aime un peu, beaucoup, passionnément, à la folie, pas du tout[3].*"

Even being loved "un peu" would be enough for now, she thought. *But Etienne is a "pas du tout" guy. I've had enough of "pas du tout."*

Later in the evening, the entire group of friends, including Isobel and Luc, were bouncing around the dance floor to Beyoncé's "Single Ladies" when Etienne came up behind her and intrusively wrapped his arm around her waist. She once again pulled away and turned to face him.

"Etienne, thank you so much for the nice offer for the wine tasting tomorrow, but I'm afraid I can't accept," she explained. "I've got to get back to Paris."

"You're missing out," he told her flatly, confirming her suspicion that he was an egomaniac.

"It will surely be my loss," she muttered insincerely.

Jean-Marc, vigilant as ever, offered his hand and spun her back toward the group as Etienne slunk away. "Good girl," he beamed.

Austen gave him a hug in appreciation. *Daphne is lucky to have him in her court. He's one of the good ones,* she thought, as she continued to dance the night away with her friends.

---

3   He loves me a little, a lot, passionately, madly, not at all.

At the stroke of midnight, the DJ blasted Luciano Pavarotti's rendition of "'O Sole Mio" and a spectacular display of fireworks set the sky ablaze over the chateau. Daphne, Jean-Marc, Chiara, and Austen put their arms around each other, heads tilted upward, and let the light pour down on their faces.

CHAPTER SIXTEEN

Desert Heat

The last weekend in July

Isobel and Luc's wedding was the start of the summer of celebrations. Austen and many of her friends were turning 40, and people were celebrating in style. Sam was celebrating his fortieth in Palm Springs with a group of ten friends, including Austen and Peter who had decided on a whim to make the trek across the pond for the milestone.

Austen arrived just after five p.m. at the Colony Palms Hotel, jet-lagged but excited. She went to her room and jumped onto the bed. *So comfy*, she thought. *Austen, do not fall asleep.* She texted Sam.

I'm here. I'm awake (sharing to convince myself more than you.) What's the plan for tonight?

Welcome! Can't wait to hug you. Meet in the lobby at

7:15. Dinner at a Mexican
place in town. Your fave.

> Mex? God bless you. See you
> in 2 hours.

Two hours. Definitely will fall asleep if I'm not moving. Shower now then go get a coffee in the hotel bar, she thought. *Then Mexican. Mmm. I miss Mexican.*

An hour later, she sat under the fans in the hotel bar and ordered an iced coffee. She took her first sip and pulled her hair into a ponytail to help cope with the heat.

"Please tell me you're not drinking coffee. The Austen I know is a wine drinker."

The voice was right behind her. She turned to find Logan, a banker friend of Sam's from San Francisco who she met a few times before moving to Paris. He was originally from the South like her, so she found him to be familiar—even though she ran screaming from Texas as soon as she got her high school diploma. There was something about him that felt like home. It was a feeling she rarely—if ever—had with French men.

"Logan, hi. Good to see you. Sit." She patted the seat next to her. "Yes, coffee. I know, but jetlag is tacky. I need caffeine."

He ordered a whiskey on the rocks and settled in. "How long have you been in Paris now?"

"Almost four years. Time flies. How are you? How's San Fran? Seeing anyone?"

"You sound like my mother," he cracked. "Life is good. Work is busy, and I'm always seeing someone but rarely seriously. No one is meeting Mom any time soon."

She turned up the Southern accent she spent years working to neutralize. "Those Southern mothers—livin' for the weddin' and then those grandkids. I'm not sure mine will ever forgive me for not having any."

"Nice drawl. It's true what they say: you can take the girl out of Texas, but you can't take the Texas out of the girl. Anyway, if we had kids, we wouldn't be here doing this for the weekend," he observed, raising his glass.

They toasted, while she declared, "Hear, hear. Sorry not sorry, Mom."

"Sam told me you've got your own fortieth bonanza next week in the South of France. Do you ever work?"

"I work my ass off, thank you very much. But I live in France where we believe in a little thing called vacation time. I get eight weeks every year, and I take my vacation just as seriously as I take my work," she grinned.

Austen loved and admired many things about France, but her favorite was that the French knew how to draw clean lines between work and play. Her American friends were glued to their phones 24/7; she'd operated the same way when she worked Stateside. In France, no one expected it, so she gratefully dropped the habit and embraced the joie de vivre.

"I'll have what he's having," a man said to the barman as he pulled up next to Logan. The two men shook hands.

"Do you know Austen?" Logan asked the new arrival. He leaned back in his chair and pointed to her.

"We haven't had the pleasure. I'm Parker." He extended his hand which she shook.

Vive le handshake, she thought. *So much less invasive than the kissy French way.*

As she released his hand, she saw Peter and Sam heading straight for them, alongside Sara and Gillian, two of Sam's friends from the Bay Area who she knew well. She stood to hug them all.

"Thank God. Paris has arrived to raise the culture quotient in the group," Sam declared, returning Austen's hug.

Peter threw his hands into the air in an exaggerated shrug. "What about me? I'm European. I'm cultured too, damn it."

"You're from Idaho," Logan blasted back.

"I da ho? No, you da ho," Sam laughed, pointing at Peter.

Peter rolled his eyes. "Hilarious. Never heard that one before."

"It's so shocking to find you three in the bar," Sam quipped. "It's time for dinner. Drink up, pay up, and let's roll."

Austen sat between Gillian and Logan in the tall orange booth at Tac/Quila; Sam was across the table from her, between Peter and Chris. Tacos, tamales, guacamole, enchiladas, and quesadillas kept coming from the kitchen, and margaritas flowed from the bar. Austen was in Mexican food heaven.

In between bites of his taco, Logan asked, "How many beaux do you have in Paris? They must be chasing you through the streets with their baguettes and berets and B.O."

"Nice stereotypes, Logan," she laughed. "I wish I had something juicy to share with you, but honestly, so far, French men have left a lot to be desired. And B.O. isn't the problem."

He refilled her margarita and asked, "What is the problem?"

"I wish I knew. There's a definite cultural mismatch because I'm American."

Logan leaned back into his chair and looked at her closely. "That's strange because you seem very European to me."

"How so?"

"For starters, you're wearing a black bra under a white shirt. American girls don't do that." He pointed toward her chest.

She looked down and frowned. *He's right. I never would've worn this when I lived here. France is rubbing off on me.*

Logan held his hands up in surrender. "Don't get me wrong. I'm digging it, and I'm sure every guy in this place is as well."

Parker was sitting across the table next to Chris, and he'd been listening. "I'm with Logan. Dig it," he said while staring at her boobs.

Austen shot Parker a look. *Nice to meet you too, slightly too pervy guy.*

She looked at Sam who was smiling playfully at her. He'd heard the whole exchange. He held her gaze for a few seconds, said nothing, and then turned to listen to Chris extol the virtues of Mezcal to Sara.

"So, what's the deal with you two?" Logan asked quietly, gesturing toward Sam. "He talks about you all the time, and you flew here from the other side of the world for his birthday."

"We're very close. Have been for years," she replied cagily. "Peter crossed the ocean too, I'd point out."

"But how close are you?" Logan pried. "Like, how often are you in touch when you're in Paris, and does it ever turn into sexting?"

She punched him in the arm. "If it did, I wouldn't tell you, but no. He's just a good friend. We talk on the phone every two or three weeks."

Did Logan buy that? Do I even buy that?

"That's more than I talk to my parents," Logan admitted.

"Well, then, you're a truly terrible son," Austen joked.

She looked toward Sam to make sure he didn't hear the exchange. She was relieved to find his head turned away, talking to Chris.

As tres leches cake and churro ice cream sandwiches hit the table, Sam stood up and clinked his glass with a knife to get everyone's attention.

"I'd like to make a toast to all of you fine people who have flown here to celebrate with me, with blatant disregard for the health of your livers."

Everyone raised a glass and pounded a fist on the table in response.

He continued, "I'll give a special shout-out to Peter and Austen, who both crossed the pond and the country for this event. I really appreciate all of you being here and am looking forward to a great weekend."

Glasses clinked up and down the table. When Sam's glass reached Austen's, he winked at her with a smile that made her heart rise into her throat.

Her hand covered her neck, almost reflexively, as if to protect it. She couldn't help but watch him out of the corner of her eye as he continued to make the rounds of the table, toasting his friends, and enjoying the celebration.

The margarita-jetlag combo was brutal, so Austen was the first to get up from the table. "Sorry guys. I'm crashing early tonight but promise to do better tomorrow."

"I thought you said jetlag was tacky," Logan shouted.

She tossed some cash on the table and threw her crossbody bag over her head. "It is, and I did. I'm horrified with myself. But I've got to call it. Goodnight."

"Rest up. You've got a full day of this tomorrow." Sam's smile held equal parts mischief and sympathy.

Peter added money to the pile Austen had started. "I'm out too. European solidarity."

"You da ho," Sam bellowed at Peter.

Austen laughed and blew kisses to the group before gratefully taking Peter's arm to make their way back to the hotel. As soon as her head hit the pillow, she was dead to the world.

She woke early the next morning, made coffee in her room, and played back the memories of the previous evening. She felt fortunate to be there, as part of Sam's inner circle, and her heart was full—oddly full. She also felt uneasy but couldn't put her finger on why.

Maybe it's jetlag. Or the tequila. I should stick to wine.

There were no clouds in the powder-blue sky; dry heat permeated everything. Austen and Peter were already lounging by the pool under a green-and-white striped umbrella when the rest of the group began to reassemble around 11 a.m.

"Late night?" she asked, as Sara, Gillian and Chris approached.

"Very late. We need a recovery day and some serious hair of the dog. I will not be leaving this pool today," Chris declared.

Gillian's skin looked green. "I feel like death. Whose idea was tequila?"

Sara flopped down on the lounger next to Austen. "We're not 22 anymore. We're 40. Ugh."

Austen sat up and stretched her arms into the sky. "When I was leaving for university, my dad imparted these words of wisdom: You can't be drunk and hung over at the same time, so you might as well keep drinking."

"Smart man, your dad." Chris's shoulders slumped as he plodded toward the bar.

Sam emerged 20 minutes later, with two waiters each carrying a magnum of rosé in an ice bucket. They set the bottles on tables under two adjacent pool tents, complete with couches and chairs covered in a green palm tree motif.

"The tents are ours for the day and the rosé is going to keep coming. Both are there to save us from the heat," Sam announced as he put ice in a glass.

He spent the day in "entertaining mode," floating around his group of friends in high spirits. The final guests—Heather and Bill, two of Sam's friends whom Austen had never met—arrived around lunch time. The group plunged alternatively between the pool, smoked chicken sandwiches, french fries, and the bottomless California rosé.

After lunch, Sam was sitting under the tent in his swim trunks, talking with Chris, Heather, and Bill, when Austen came in for a refill. He poured her wine and then pulled her onto his lap in the armchair, resting a hand on her back.

"Hello, birthday boy," she purred. "Are you having a good day?"

"It doesn't suck." He leaned in, to whisper in her ear. "I think Parker has a thing for you. He's been watching you all day."

She pulled back to look him in the eyes. "You're watching Parker watch me?" *I kinda love that.*

"He's not subtle." Sam broke her stare and reached for his glass. "Anyway, how's Paris? How's your Australian?"

Kevin. "In Australia and not mine. He's been gone eight months. It was just a couple weeks of fun. What about you? Been dating?"

"Dating? What's that?" he asked sarcastically.

Austen felt flooded with relief. *Obviously, he's not dating anyone. She'd be sitting on his lap right now instead of me.*

She forced herself to respond lightly. "You sound French. Did you know there's no word for 'dating' in the French language?"

"How do relationships start then?" he asked.

"I wish I knew," she sang, leaning the side of her head into his.

He kissed her cheek. "They're all idiots for not snapping you up, as far as I'm concerned."

It was 90 degrees in the shade that day, but she hadn't noticed the heat until that moment.

"I'm going to jump in the pool," she announced, unsticking herself from him.

She tossed her cover-up on a lounger and glided into the water, floating in front of Sara, Logan and Peter who were on the steps of the pool, half-submerged. She looked like she was listening to their conversation, but she was lost in her own thoughts. Her sense of unease was building.

Being with him is uncomfortable comfort, she thought. *Such an odd feeling.*

She had felt this before with Sam, after the New Year's Eve kiss, but the discord of her feelings was coming on stronger than usual.

She drifted to the edge of the pool and hung on to the side, perching her chin on crossed arms while her legs floated behind her. Sam, Heather, and Chris were still sitting in the pool tent. She couldn't hear their conversation but was soaked in the sounds of their laughter.

Heather noticed her and came to sit on the pool's edge, putting her feet in. "I've heard so much about you from Sam over the years. It's great to finally meet you."

"That's so nice," Austen replied. *Awkward. I've never heard of you.* "His birthday is a fantastic reason to get the whole gang together."

Heather leaned back on her hands. "You two have serious chemistry. I couldn't help but notice when you were sitting on his lap."

"We're just close friends," Austen casually replied.

Heather cocked her head skeptically and took a sip of rosé. "Hate to break it to you, but that's not friendship—whatever is going on there. I think you two are just a matter of time."

Austen smiled awkwardly and let go of the pool wall, letting herself sink to the bottom. Water filled her ears, and in the silence, she was alone with her thoughts.

Is she jealous? More importantly, is she right? Does it matter when I'm still in Paris?

When her air depleted and she surfaced, Sara and Gillian were gathering their things from the lounge chairs.

"We're going to nap before dinner. Day-drinking must be managed," Gillian announced. "We need to power back up."

"I'm coming with you," Austen shouted, making her way up the pool stairs, and quickly drying off.

"Seven forty-five in the lobby," Sam announced. "Taxis will be waiting."

The three women waved their acknowledgment and retreated to their rooms.

After her nap and shower, Austen arrived in the lobby feeling fresh and relaxed in a red corset top and black crepe pants with high slits up both legs. Her hair was piled on top of her head, and she wore oversized gold hoop earrings. Half of the group was already down, including Sam.

"Don't you all clean up nice?" Austen observed. *Especially you, Sam.*

He stood up to hug her and took a deep inhale against her neck.

"You smell good," he whispered.

Her skin caught fire.

The courtyard at Tropicale was a lush garden of green plants interspersed with tables draped in white tablecloths and surrounded by high pink walls. It was packed with other diners, and even before they sat down, the atmosphere was festive. It was a perfect spot for a birthday party. Austen sat between Sam and Peter, with Gillian, Chris, and Logan directly across from them. Once drinks were ordered, Peter needed advice from the group.

"I met a girl in London—Bridget—and we've been out a few times, but I can't tell if she likes me," he lamented. "She takes a day and a half to respond to a text. Is that normal?"

"Maybe she hates texting," Gillian offered. "Have you tried calling her?"

Peter's brow furrowed. "Like, on the phone? Does anyone do that anymore?"

"No, they don't. But why not?" Austen demanded to know. "It's a lost art, and I think Gillian is onto something. You should call her, Peter."

Logan's face lit up. "Speaking on the phone is now considered art? I've always felt like I had an artist's soul. I just never knew my medium, until now. Thank you, ladies. I feel artistically validated."

Austen showed her palm to Logan—the stop sign. "Texting is the communications equivalent of making art using those thick pencils for toddlers. Speaking on the phone, you graduate to crayons. You've got a way to go before you're Picasso, buddy."

"I've seen toddlers that can draw just as well as Picasso. That guy never did put a nose in the right spot on someone's face," Logan retorted.

Peter raised his voice to bring the group's attention back to him. "Would you believe that Bridget is an artist? We met at a gallery opening. She paints."

Sam nearly spat out his margarita. "I'll be damned. You've been to an art gallery? Maybe you do have some culture after all."

"You've got to show her what she's missing, man. Take a picture with Austen and all the other beautiful ladies here tonight and send it to her to make her jealous," Chris suggested.

Gillian stared flatly at Chris. "That is terrible advice."

"The worst," Austen concurred.

Sam could only agree. "Peter, seriously, look around the table at who you're asking for dating advice. When was the last time you knew any of us to be in a good relationship?"

Everyone scanned the table—a group of perpetual bachelors and bachelorettes—and burst into hysterics. Clearly no one in the group had any of the answers.

The evening flew by in a sea of coconut shrimp, chicken satay, tempura green beans, baby back ribs, cocktails, and wine. Austen stuck to the wine—and to Sam. It was easy to get away with—he was the birthday boy so deserved to be the center of everyone's attention. When the massive chocolate cake topped with vanilla buttercream and sparklers arrived, no one sang louder than Austen.

When the sparks died out, Gillian cut the cake. She was passing plates down the table when Peter stood up to make a toast.

"I want to thank Sam for getting us all together, to ring in your new decade. I'm a few years older and wiser than you, so I can tell you it's all downhill from here. You're already looking decrepit. Happy birthday, buddy."

Austen stood up next, shaking her head and giving Peter an exaggerated frown. "Thank you, Peter, for that sentimental toast."

She looked around the table at everyone's smiling faces, and then raised her glass to Sam. "The friends you keep reflect the person you are, so it's only fitting that you find yourself surrounded by such a smart, accomplished, warm and totally attractive group. I think I can speak for everyone and say we're honored to be here. There's nowhere I'd rather be. To Sam."

"To Sam," everyone cheered, glasses raised in the hot desert air.

Sam rose and wrapped his arms around her waist, holding her tightly. She threw hers around his neck, careful not to spill her wine.

"I adore you," she whispered into his ear.

He again kissed her cheek. "Back atcha, baby."

Logan smiled at her with a raised eyebrow when she sat down. She quickly looked away, flagging a waitress for more drinks.

The group returned to the hotel late, but Austen wasn't tired. She had her eyes on the back of Sam's head as he meandered through the lobby with the group. *Turn around and slow down. Let everyone else disappear so we can be alone.* Her heart leaped as he turned, as if he'd heard her.

"Goodnight, friends, and thank you for a wonderful evening," he shouted, hands in the air. He turned on his heels again and disappeared down the hallway.

Austen deflated. She said goodnight to everyone and ambled to her room. Phone in hand, she climbed into bed and typed and deleted the same message four times: "I don't want this weekend to end."

What am I doing? I'm leaving tomorrow morning. Don't start something you can't finish.

She tossed her phone on the nightstand and closed her eyes.

The next morning, she was checking out at the front desk when Sam appeared. "How was your stay, madam?" he asked, imitating the staff.

"Too short," she said, giving him a quick hug.

"I'm so glad you came, but I know the South of France awaits. Tell the girls hi for me."

"I will. You've set a high bar for the fortieth celebrations. We shall endeavor to maintain or exceed your standards." She tilted her head forward in a mini bow.

"Ten days on the Côte d'Azur with Milena and Liz? I think you'll exceed. I miss you already. Hope to see you again soon."

He gave her a fleeting peck on the lips, followed by a long hug which pressed her full body into his.

Austen walked away trembling, knowing already that "soon" wasn't going to be soon enough. Her head spun as the cab pulled away from the hotel.

She had been in the air for an hour when she pulled out her laptop and started writing him an email. She still hadn't finished it when she landed in Nice 15 hours later. After multiple drafts and a few fitful hours of sleep, the one thing she knew for certain was that she was in love with him and had been for a long time.

I was just never ready. But I am now, and I have to figure out how to tell him. Thank God Liz and Milena are here. They'll know what to do.

CHAPTER SEVENTEEN

The Big 4-0

The next day

Austen jumped in a cab at the Nice Côte d'Azur airport and gave the driver the address of the small villa they had rented on Castle Hill, overlooking the Old Town. Liz and Milena were already there waiting for her. They'd all studied in France at different stages of their university years, so it held a special spot in their hearts, and she was bubbling over with excitement, anticipating their destined-to-be-boisterous reunion.

It's been too long since we've all been together, she thought.

Austen's taxi parked inside the stunning arched entryway to the villa. As the driver opened the trunk to retrieve her bags, the front door burst open.

"You're here," Milena squealed, arms outstretched. She was wearing a wide-brimmed sun hat, a long white cotton dress and platform espadrilles.

Liz was right behind her, barefoot and wearing a blue sundress and a matching blue and red print silk scarf tied around her head to tame her wild chestnut hair. She had an open bottle of champagne in her hand. "And we're fucking 40."

Austen flew toward them, returning their squeals, and they fell into a tight group hug. Once their voices returned to a regular decibel, Austen paid the driver and Milena wheeled her bag inside.

Liz was already pouring champagne into glasses when Austen got to the kitchen. "At least we're all equally jet-lagged. No French home court advantage for you."

"Here's to having no idea what day or time it is," Milena cheered.

Twenty-four hours later, after a good night's sleep, they were eating seafood at La Terrasse, overlooking the teal-blue Mediterranean, when Austen could no longer hold it in.

"I'm in love with Sam," she blurted out, bursting into tears.

Saying it out loud released all the anxiety that comes with the combination of uncertainty and love. She looked through her tears at their smiling faces and saw that neither of them was surprised.

Liz leaned back hard into her chair. "Well, it's about damn time you admitted it to yourself. It's been screamingly obvious to the rest of us for years."

Milena nodded in agreement. "Duh."

Austen pushed all ten fingers into her hair. "I don't know how to tell him. I started writing him an email on the plane, and it all came gushing out in a jumbled mess. I'm freaking."

"He's going to freak when he gets it—in the best way." Milena wrapped her arm around her friend. "That man has loved you since the day you met, and you two are going to live happily ever after."

"Where is the wedding going to be? Oh, this calls for champagne." Liz flagged the waitress.

Austen buried her face in her hands, her mind racing. She'd introduced Sam to Milena and Liz shortly after they'd started working together and become friendly. They'd spent time together frequently during her San Francisco years. Her friends' reaction validated her beliefs.

They're not just telling me what I want to hear. They've seen it. We're going to live happily ever after.

She was doing that thing again—projecting forward in her mind to her perfect, future life. That life would be back in California since Sam didn't speak French. Once more, she was ready to choose love and walk away from Paris.

"He's the one. And I think it is finally the right time."

The next few days along the Côte d'Azur were sun-soaked and champagne-filled. They spent their days talking and laughing about the ups and downs of life and how on Earth it was possible that they were all 40. They gambled in Monaco, swam in the infinity pool by the sea at the Hôtel du Cap-Eden-Roc in Antibes, walked the Croisette in Cannes, and had cocktails on the beach in Saint-Jean-Cap-Ferrat. They ate more fresh seafood and giggled more than any three women should be allowed, and each day was better than the last.

Austen remembered when her parents turned 40. They celebrated with black balloons and "over the hill" signs, as if life was beginning to end. But not for these ladies. They were on a five-star trip with the best of friends, looking and feeling fabulous.

One afternoon, in the shade of a blue-and-white striped beach umbrella on the rocky beach in Cannes, Austen broached a topic Milena had artfully avoided for days.

"How is ex-pat life in Hong Kong? Are you and Matteo adjusting?"

Milena dropped her head. "I'm 40, have no friends, no job, and no clue what I'm doing. I know you've been through this so please tell me—when does it get easier?"

"It takes a year to figure out which way is up in ex-pat life. You've only been there a few months. It does get easier though." Austen gave Milena a reassuring pat on the knee. "I remember when I went to the grocery store for the first time in Paris. I was exhausted and wanted to make pasta with parmesan. I wandered the massive French cheese aisle for nearly an hour looking for the green can."

"The Kraft can of parmesan. It's green." Milena nodded.

"Exactly. It's the brand I'd bought my whole life, and I couldn't find it. Kraft doesn't sell parmesan in France. I had to read every cheese packet in the whole damn aisle to find some, and it felt like such a struggle," Austen recalled.

Milena gave a sad laugh and shook her head knowingly.

Despite her oversized Gucci sunglasses, Austen could tell she was on the verge of tears. She squeezed her hand tightly, hoping to reassure her.

"Eventually, you'll make friends, learn what the parmesan packet looks like, find new favorite shopping neighborhoods, and discover all the best spots for dim sum. You'll get there, I promise."

"I know, but why is it so lonely and hard?"

Austen propped herself up on one elbow and thought about Milena's question until she was sure of her answer.

"The last time you started over with a truly clean slate was at Stanford when we were 18. We were all clueless, friendless, and grasping for a lifeline. When everyone is in the same boat, it's easier to adjust."

Liz rolled over on her sun lounger. "I'm so glad I found you two at freshman orientation. How lucky were we to meet right at the beginning?"

"So lucky," Austen confirmed. "Then we graduated and moved to the city together. We had a basic network in place, so that change was evolutionary. Now, you've quit your very big job and taken a revolutionary step with no safety net, except Matteo. Revolution is a big deal."

Milena sighed deeply. "And I feel like such a fraud as a Chinese American in Hong Kong. People speak to me in Cantonese, and when I ask them to speak English, I get the nastiest, most disapproving looks. I feel like I'm back on the playground at school with mean kids calling me a Twinkie."

Liz cocked her head to one side. "A Twinkie? What does that mean?"

"Yellow on the outside and white on the inside," Milena explained. "People look at me and expect me to speak the language, but because he's not Asian, Matteo gets a pass. If he manages to eke out "thank you" in Cantonese, they ooh and aah over him like he solved world hunger. It's really triggering."

Austen tried to put herself in Milena's shoes but found it hard to imagine. Racial discrimination wasn't something she'd experienced. Her white privilege was showing.

"I don't know what that's like; it has to be tough. But if anyone can handle it, it's you. I'm so proud that you and Matteo took the leap and went. You're going to be settled before you know it, and now you have this amazing opportunity to explore your roots," Austen said.

"I'll be fine, but I'm so happy to have a break from it all and be here with people who love me no matter what color I am, inside or out," Milena breathed.

"We love you to the moon and back. And Twinkies are magical," Liz exclaimed. "Anyone gives you shit, you tell them I am a doctor, and I said so."

They left the beach and drove back toward the villa, stopping for pizza and wine on the way. They decided they needed at least one night in, to enjoy the sunset from their ocean-view terrace.

As they munched on pizza and the sun started to dip below the horizon, Liz let out a dramatic sigh.

"Who was the bitch that said we were supposed to want it all? I swear there are days where I want none of it. I want to be able to sit on the couch in my pajamas all day for one Saturday—just one—and have no one need anything from me."

Milena looked alarmed. "What's happening? Where did this come from?"

Liz jumped out of her chair and started to pace. "I'm a doctor, a mom, a wife, a daughter, a sister, and a friend. Most days, I love wearing all those hats, but lately, it feels like a lot. When people ask me how I'm doing, I say 'I'm just ducky.'"

"Ducky?" Austen and Milena asked in unison.

Her arms started to move in slow, horizontal waves. "On the surface, I'm gliding across looking all smooth, but underneath, I'm paddling like hell."

"That's a good one. I'm going to get you a small army of yellow rubber duckies for Christmas," Austen cackled.

Liz collapsed back into her chair. "Oh God, don't make me think about Christmas—with all the presents and lights and caroling and baking and Jesus. The pressure."

"Did you mean Jesus, the birthday boy, or are you cursing?" Milena asked, with a laugh.

Liz let out a scream. "Both. Jesus. Why are we talking about Christmas?"

Austen tried and failed to suppress her giggles. "Duck army. Sorry. No more Christmas. Seriously, what's going on with you?"

Liz took a slow, deep breath. "This week with you two is the most relaxed I've been in years."

"You don't seem that relaxed." Austen scrunched up her nose and cocked her head. The gesture turned her statement into a question.

Liz guzzled rosé. "I love my family and my kids in all their insane, glorious splendor. I love my job, working with these elite athletes. I'm so lucky Andrew is willing and able to be a stay-at-home dad." Her voice trailed off.

"But it's a lot of pressure on you," Milena guessed.

"Yes. Sometimes I think it'd be easier if I could love it all a little bit less," Liz confessed. "I wouldn't trade any of it for the world, but damn I really needed this trip."

Austen rubbed Liz's back in a circular motion. "All that pressure is one of many reasons I never had kids. Also, I like sleeping in, my perky boobs, and not sharing my ice cream."

Milena threw her a "you're not helping" stare.

"I hate you," Liz replied, smiling. "Seriously, how the hell are we 40 years old? Weren't we young and carefree at university, like, 15 minutes ago? Adulting sucks. I constantly feel guilty for not being able to give everyone 100 percent of my energy. Is that terrible to admit?"

"Absolutely not," Milena insisted. "Everyone needs and deserves a break."

Austen spread her arms wide toward the horizon and the speck of sun that was rapidly descending into the sea. "Look where we are. Does adulting suck, really? We have the privilege to take time for ourselves, which makes us better at being all the things we need to be. No one can do it all, all the time. So, we do this. We're mere mortals, despite what we may want others to believe."

They were all quiet, reflecting for a few moments, until Milena broke the silence.

"I read a quote recently from this writer in Uruguay, Eduardo Galeano. He said, 'We are all mortal until the first kiss and the second glass of wine.' Isn't it perfect?"

"Is he single?" Austen asked. "He sounds like my dream guy."

Milena laughed. "I think he's in his seventies."

"I thought Sam was your dream guy," Liz interjected, killing the laughter. "When are you sending the email?"

Austen stood up and pulled the bottle of *Minuty* out of the ice bucket on the table.

"I'm not ready yet. Still thinking. Constantly. For now, I will follow Eduardo's and Milena's lead and have a second glass of wine in the noble quest for immortality."

She took a dramatic bow.

CHAPTER EIGHTEEN

The Love Bomb

On their next to last night in Cannes, Liz and Milena were getting ready for dinner in their rooms, and Austen was in hers, putting the finishing touches on the email to Sam. There was so much she wanted to say, but she knew she couldn't overwhelm him so had to pick her words carefully.

She shut her computer to think and laid in bed, eyes closed. The fantasy of their future life together played like a movie rolling fast-forward across the insides of her eyelids. Theirs was the house all their friends wanted to come to for barbecues and birthdays. It was always full of laughter and had a big yard on the water somewhere. They cheered each other's victories at work and held each other close during disappointments. Each maintained their independence, but they prioritized time together too. They had fantastic sex, then snuggled in bed and read each other interesting passages from books or magazines, discussing the more thought-provoking bits. She could read his thoughts and anticipate his needs in a way that no one had before, and he loved her for it. They took regular trips to Europe to visit her Paris friends and discover beautiful corners of Italy, which they both loved. Their families met and adored spending time together. It wasn't always easy, but they both put in the work because they knew their match was as good as it could ever get.

It was a gorgeous fantasy, but she held it for herself, at least for now. To him, she wrote a simple love letter.

Subject: So there's this

This shouldn't be an email, but it's a lot, so I thought you might want some time to process.

I'm in love with you, and I think (God, I hope, otherwise, this is super embarrassing) you feel the same way. I finally admitted it to myself when I left Palm Springs.

The truth is my heart has been yours since that New Year's kiss almost two years ago, but our timing was all wrong. My head only just caught up to my heart. Sorry for being so slow.

I love Paris, and being there has made me happy, but a lot has changed in the last two years, and now, I just want to be with you.

I know this is messy and inconvenient but love often is. It will take some time and serious air miles to figure this out, but I am willing to move back to California to make it work.

There's so much more I want to say, but I'll stop here for now. The rest is probably better discussed live.

I'm back in Paris late my time on Saturday. Let's talk then?

For now, breathe. And I'll try to do the same.

A

She emerged from her room to find Milena and Liz in the kitchen, their backs to her, opening an umpteenth bottle of *Minuty*. "I sent it."

They both spun around quickly to face her.

"Holy shit," Liz exclaimed, inhaling dramatically, and jumping up and down.

Milena, always the calm force, simply smiled. "How do you feel?"

"My stomach is in knots." Austen dropped into a crouch, hugging her knees.

Milena stepped toward her and pulled her up, squeezing her arms. "It's early in California. He's probably just waking up. He loves you, and you'll hear from him soon."

They each tossed back a glass of wine and meandered down the hill into the steamy streets of Nice's Old Town, on their way to a foodie restaurant called L'Alchimie. Austen was buzzing like a bumble bee on amphetamines, her mind in overdrive.

Alchemy—the attempt to turn something basic into gold. How appropriate for tonight. Sam and I are going to turn this thing into shimmering gold.

She felt elated and hopeful, despite the knots in her stomach. She was sure sending the email was the right thing to do, and her phone ringer was on full volume, anticipating his call.

By the time the molten chocolate cake with crème anglaise was served, her nerves were starting to fray. *It's been hours. Why haven't I heard from him?* Her friends' frown lines showed they were equally concerned, but no one dared to voice it. Surely there was an explanation for his hours of silence. They returned to the villa, still waiting.

"Try to get some sleep. You'll hear from him by morning," Milena assured her.

Austen tossed and turned all night. It was six a.m. in Nice—nine p.m. in California—when she heard her phone beep with an incoming email. It had been 12 hours since she sent hers. When she saw his name on the screen, everything in her body seized. She sat bolt upright in bed and started reading.

Subject: Re: So there's this

Good morning, your time. I'm still breathing, so the shock of your email didn't kill me, which is a good start. But yeah, I'm shocked. I don't process this kind of thing quickly so I'm sorry for what will inevitably be a far from perfect reply. Here goes.

First, this is incredibly courageous. That's not surprising because you're you, but I wanted to give you credit.

Second, I do adore you, a lot.

Third, you're right that timing has been a challenge for us. Maybe we're destined to be star-crossed in this way. I just started a new job and am nervous about overcommitting myself—trying to be great at that and be a worthy partner to you, with a nine-hour time difference. I fear we'd be setting ourselves up to fail.

After New Year's in Paris, you were fiercely protective of your need to create a life for yourself there, which I understood. Now I might be in that same boat.

I'm not saying never. If we do this, I want the timing to be right. You're too important to me to mess this up. Let's talk when you get back to Paris. And please refer back to the paragraph starting "second."

In the meantime, go and enjoy your last day with the girls. You deserve it.

S

She read it five times and grew more nauseous with each pass. She felt like she was sinking through the floor. *"Not saying never." Does that mean he does love me? No, he said he adores me. Twice. That's not the same.* On top of the early feelings of heartbreak and embarrassment, fear started to creep in that she had killed their friendship.

She stumbled out of her room and made coffee, sitting alone in the early morning silence of the villa. Liz emerged from her room two hours later and found Austen staring at the wall.

"I'm getting Milena. Hold on." Liz flew to her room.

Austen heard Liz's wake up call.

"Get up. Something bad happened with Sam. I can tell from her face."

She heard mumbling and the rustling of bed sheets before they emerged from Milena's room, sleep in their eyes.

"Tell us," Milena said.

She read Sam's response, and looked into their faces, silently begging for comfort.

Tell me I'm wrong. Tell me it's not as bad as it seems.

Liz spoke first. "He's in shock. Absolute medical possibility. It wasn't a great reply, but you did drop a bomb on him."

"You'll talk when you get home. He'll have had some time to process. It's going to be OK." Milena tried to sound reassuring.

Austen's fingers were interlaced, her elbows on the island countertop and her hands covering her mouth. She wanted to cry but desperately clung to the hope her friends had tried to offer. After a few moments of awkward silence, she jumped up.

"It's our last day together, and no man is going to ruin it. Let's get to the beach."

She pushed Sam to the back of her mind, despite the ache in her heart. *Do not spoil the last day of the trip for the girls.*

They spent their final day together wandering Nice, soaking up the sunshine and the memories of the previous ten days, before traveling back to Paris together. Charles de Gaulle airport was the scene for their teary goodbyes before Milena flew east and Liz flew west. Austen hugged Milena tightly.

"You're going to be in love with Hong Kong before you know it. I have faith in you and Matteo. You'll find your place there."

Milena wiped a tear out of her eye. Austen wasn't sure who she was crying for.

"I will, and I'll tell you all about it in Cambodia in March. Keep me posted on Sam."

Austen turned to Liz. "You are Superwoman, and you've got the best support in the world with Andrew. There's nothing you two can't handle. I've never known a couple who was better matched. I envy your love."

Liz squeezed her tightly. "I want to be you when I grow up. Thank you for this trip. I'll never forget it. And what's meant to be will be with Sam."

They finished where they started—in a group hug—until all the air had been squeezed from their lungs. Austen boarded her flight to Paris in a puddle of tears, shed for already missing them and for her fears of what would come next with Sam.

She decided to leave the ball in his court and waited for him to reach out. He called four days later—voice only, no video. *That's a bad sign,* she thought before picking up, already feeling fragile and vulnerable. Anticipation of their impending conversation had been haunting her sleep.

"Hi, sweets," he said. "How's re-entry been, and how was the trip?"

She forced a smile into her voice as she perched precariously on her couch. "It was epic. I couldn't have asked for anything better."

Silence followed, punctuated by static on the phone line. She held her breath.

"OK, I've been processing," he finally said. "And you really did surprise me."

Austen exhaled while her hands clenched into fists, her fingernails digging half-moons into her palms. "I know. I'm sorry for the love bomb via email. Can I ask—what was your initial reaction when you read it?"

"Surprised and flattered. Who wouldn't be flattered getting a letter like that from you?"

She waited, hoping for something else, but was met with more awkward silence.

"But?" she prompted.

"Listen, of course, there's always been something between us. I think I'd just convinced myself it would never happen since you live on the other side of the world. Would you really want to move back?" He voiced the question cautiously.

"I would for you."

"It's a lot of pressure, Austen. You love Paris, and I'd never forgive myself if you gave it up for me, and things didn't work out. You know I don't have a great track record with relationships."

He's not wrong. I've never known him to have a girlfriend.

"I know, but this thing between us has been there for a long time. It feels worth the risk to me. Life is short, you know?"

"My new job has me working brutal hours," he told her. "Like I said in my email, I worry that I will disappoint you. But if anyone was going to be worth this kind of effort, it would be you. You've got my head spinning."

She felt hope rising in her chest. *I'm worth it. We're worth it. Take the leap.*

"Mine is spinning too, Sam. Fast."

"Let's try to slow down the spinning before we both throw up."

Sam was always the jokester who got everyone laughing. She was usually the first to giggle, but today, the tension was too high. She noticed she was holding her breath again.

He continued, "If we start this and it goes how I think it would, that's it for me. You're it. But I could start ring shopping for you tomorrow, and it would still take you a year to get back here."

The words "you're it" and "ring shopping" shot her hopes even higher into the stratosphere. *He does love me. I knew it. I'm not a total fool.*

"I just don't want to fuck it up by starting at the wrong time, so let's take it slow."

Her rising hopes suddenly fled her body like a balloon releasing its helium. *Take it slow? He could start ring shopping tomorrow, but he wants to take it slow? What is that?* Her mind raced. *OK Austen, get practical.*

"I'm not sure what that means. What happens next?" she asked.

He sighed. "I don't know. This is uncharted territory. Can we just keep talking and see how we feel?"

Despite her uncertainties, she saw no other choice than to agree, so he quickly ended their call and promised they'd talk soon. When she sent the email, she'd imagined him reading it, jumping on the next plane to Paris, showing up at her door, and carrying her to the bedroom where they would've stayed naked for days. It had been quite a vivid—and perhaps crazy—fantasy. She never imagined he'd say, "Let's take it slow." Slow was rational, and in her mind, love sent people running headlong toward all nature of crazy.

She didn't hear a peep from him for the next five days. Every morning, she reached for her phone hoping to find a message, only to sink back into her pillows feeling slightly more defeated than the day before. *This is not how two people starting a relationship act. Maybe he just needs some time to get his head around all this.* It took every ounce of her willpower to not text him every day.

On Friday night, after a few glasses of wine with Isobel, her self-control ran out.

Hello you. How's everything
going at the new gig? Buried?

Three dots appeared on her screen as he typed his reply.
Her heart rose into her throat.

Hey baby. It's going well.
Hours aren't too crazy this
week.

*"Baby" feels positive, but he's been calling me that for years.
And if work hasn't been busy, why has he been radio silent? This
feels bad. Just try to be cool.*

Good then. Glad you're
finding your rhythm.

How are you? It's late there, no?

It's midnight. Just got home
from dinner with a friend. I
will admit to having had a few
glasses of wine. 😊

I would be disappointed if you
hadn't. Good girl.

I aim to please.

I'm actually just about to head
out to play golf with Logan.
Catch you later?

That was all she was going to get tonight—not even the
slightest reference to the monster "will we or won't we" question that occupied every corner of her mind. It was the kind of

WILL THERE BE WINE?

chat they would've had on any other Saturday for the past few years. Except, before, Sam would have responded to a comment like "I do aim to please" with some mild sexual innuendo. Tonight, he ignored it. Austen felt like she'd been punched in the gut. She could feel him retreating.

> Sure. Have fun. Hi to L for
> me.

She promised herself she wouldn't be the one to reach out next. Seven agonizing days later, Sam finally texted her again.

Hey doll. How's your week
been?

> It's been OK. I've been
> missing you.

What's on tap for the
weekend?

If the conversation had been live, Austen might've convinced herself that he didn't hear her say she missed him, but with it staring back at her in unavoidable black text—four of seven words she'd typed—it was clear he'd chosen to ignore it. Tears welled up in her eyes. If she could've jumped through the phone, she'd have screamed, "Did I drop acid and hallucinate a conversation two weeks ago about us slowly starting a relationship? Because you're acting like that never happened." *That probably wouldn't go over well.* So instead, she typed.

> Shopping & champagne
> tomorrow with Chiara. Dinner

with Daphne & Jean-Marc,
and a museum on Sunday
with Isobel. Should be good.
How about you?

Sounds very French. I'm
doing the San Francisco guy
equivalent — golf and beers
with the boys tomorrow. Enjoy
yours, and we'll talk sometime
soon.

Call me Sunday?

Sure. I'll call you when I wake
up?

Yep, sounds good. Talk then.

She re-read their exchange and then scrolled back through their texts from the pre-love-bomb era. The tone was very different. They'd always been flirty, fun, light and easy. Now, everything felt stilted and wrong.

When Austen met up with Daphne and Jean-Marc for dinner at Restaurant Coco at the base of the Opéra Garnier, she was a wreck. It was the first time she'd seen them since she got back from the Côte d'Azur, so she filled them in on the whole chaotic story.

"Wow, Austen, you just threw your heart out there, didn't you?" Daphne asked, with what seemed like equal parts pity and admiration in her voice. "You've got balls, girl."

Jean-Marc's eyes bugged out of his head. "You American girls, you're not scared of anything. But you're scary. I'm trying to imagine what I'd feel in his place, and I truly can't. It's a lot to throw at a guy."

"I was sure he felt the same way. In Palm Springs, we were attached at the hip, like always. You guys saw us at that New Year's. He makes me feel like I'm the only person in the room when we're together. Could I have gotten it this wrong?"

Daphne grabbed Austen's trembling hand.

"You told me he's never been in a relationship as long as you've known him. There's probably a reason for that."

A tear rolled down her cheek. "I thought it was because he was waiting for me. He said 'ring shopping.'"

"Oh, honey. I so wish that was it, but everyone knows actions speak louder than words. He's showing you how he feels. Now, you need to believe him."

Austen dropped her face into her palms until she felt Daphne gently pushing a glass of wine into her forearm. She looked up and gratefully accepted it, drinking half the glass in one gulp. Jean-Marc smiled sympathetically and refilled it.

"We're supposed to talk on the phone tomorrow. I want to ask what the hell he's thinking, but I know I shouldn't press."

Jean-Marc jumped in. "I only met him once, but from a guy's perspective, one thing to consider is that he might be slowly backing away, trying not to damage the friendship. He keeps up the casual banter forever and hopes you'll eventually get the hint?"

How did I become the girl he needs to slowly back away from?

All the lights in the restaurant seemed to dim. Austen felt like she was sinking again and grabbed the edge of the table to steady herself as Jean-Marc continued.

"You'll probably have to be the one to bring it up but go easy on him. Try not to back him into a corner. If you do, based on how he's acting so far, I can almost guarantee he'll bolt."

The pity in Daphne's eyes made Austen want to burst into tears.

This isn't going to end well.

In anticipation of their Sunday call, Austen sat at her kitchen table with a steaming mug of mint tea which she thought might calm her nerves. She ran her fingers back and forth across the table's wood grain, eyes glazed, as she replayed every conversation they'd ever had in her head, cataloging all the reasons she'd believed the feelings were mutual. When he finally called, she filled her lungs with all the air she could capture and dove straight into the abyss.

"Sam, our conversations over the past two weeks have been so awkward. We've spent the last two years flirting non-stop, but ever since I sent that email, you've become an exceptionally polite stranger. I think that you changed your mind about wanting to start something—however slowly—and haven't figured out how to tell me. If I'm right, just say it."

He exhaled and didn't say anything for a few seconds.

That's a long pause, she thought as her heart started beating faster.

"I was so shocked and flattered by your email, but the more I thought about it, the more I realized that I never really felt that way about you."

Her head felt like the inside of a pinball machine, his words hurdling violently in every direction, crashing into her skull. She was speechless.

"I'm sorry," he added softly.

"Fine, ok, thanks for letting me know. I've got to go."

"Austen—"

She hung up before he could hear her sobs. As she gasped for breath through her tears, she thought she might never recover.

After four days of crying, she decided to call Peter. She felt blindsided and needed his take on the situation. The three of them had been close for years, and he knew Sam better than anyone. She called him on a Thursday night, playing back the key details while fighting back the seemingly endless flood of tears.

"Wow. I don't even know what to say, sweetie. I always knew there was something special between you, but I never thought it was that. I just don't see you two together. I've always seen you with someone like Kevin. But I'm so sorry you're hurting this much. What are you doing this weekend?"

"Crying on my couch," she sniffed.

"No, you're not. I'm buying you a Eurostar ticket right now, and you're coming here. Let me take care of you for the weekend."

She couldn't refuse.

They spent the weekend wandering the streets of London, playing back all the events that had led her there. Over beers at Peter's local pub, he asked, "Are you sure you're in love with him? Maybe you're just bored or lonely?"

It was a fair question. She'd mistaken boredom and friendship for love before. Most people make that mistake at least once. The distinction between them was crystal clear in her mind.

"This is love—the kind that consumes."

"You'd miss Paris too much," he said.

Austen had always said that if she ever left Paris, it would be for a big job or a big love. While she treasured the life she had built there, her Army brat upbringing had taught her that she could thrive anywhere. Twice now, she'd asked someone to love her, willing to uproot her life and leave Paris to be with them, and both Kevin and now Sam had brutally turned her down. She couldn't believe it had happened again.

Paris was holding on to her, but she couldn't fathom why.

CHAPTER NINETEEN

Gravity

December

On a frigid Wednesday night, Austen was in the Metro on her way home when she noticed an Emirates Airlines advertisement for travel to the Seychelles, a perfect mid-winter getaway. She and Brad had often talked about going but never did.

She took a photo of the ad and opened an email to him, attaching it. She typed, "Have you been yet? It still looks like heaven. Hope you're well." She stared at the email on her phone, her finger hovering over the send button, and then deleted it.

The next morning, as she stood in front of the bathroom mirror brushing her teeth, it occurred to her: *That was the beach ball.*

Just over two years earlier, Brad had asked her for the extra money and that angry beach ball had exploded into the proverbial sky. She'd been furious, but Liz had promised her that one day, when she was least expecting it, the beach ball would fall down in front of her, and she would realize she wasn't angry anymore. "Because gravity," Liz had said. It had finally landed on that cold Metro platform.

The next weekend, Austen sat on Chiara's couch under a wool blanket and told her about Liz's theory and the email not sent.

"It was a relief to know that anger was finally gone, but I didn't want to reopen the door with him, so I didn't send it," she explained.

"That's a big deal and an important step in putting that whole relationship behind you," Chiara agreed.

Austen leaned onto the back of the couch and stared at the ceiling, tears welling up in her eyes. "At least there's one thing I've put behind me."

Since things had imploded with Sam, she'd struggled to mend the pieces of her broken heart, mourning both the lost opportunity for love and the lost friendship. "Champagne Saturdays" had been replaced far too often with "Kleenex Saturdays," with Austen disappearing into the cushions of her friend's couch under a pile of tissues.

Chiara patted her leg sympathetically through the thick blanket. "Anything new on the Sam front?"

Shifting her position on the couch, she looked earnestly at Chiara. "I don't understand why I'm still so upset. The relationship never even started. Why can't I get a grip?"

"*Mia cara*, I think it comes down to expectations. They're always high at the start of relationships—people hoping for the fairy tale. Over time, if they start to disappoint each other, expectations are gradually lowered until they break up." Chiara raised one hand high in the air and brought it down gradually as she spoke. "By the end, they don't have far to fall."

"Gravity again." Austen reached for a Kleenex and wiped her nose.

"Yes, but that slow descent can be useful. With Sam, your expectations were sky high, and his response knocked you off a very high ledge. It's not the kind of fall you just pop up and walk away from. You need time to lay there and heal, and that's OK. You will get up again. I promise."

That's it. I got my ass kicked by gravity and am now a pile of shattered bones lying on the ground, with my guts oozing out. It's not a good look.

Austen knew better than to try to fight gravity. Emotionally, she had stayed on the ground for months, waiting for her heart to heal and analyzing what had happened. She trudged through work, trying her best to put on a happy and professional face. Faking it took a lot of energy; she felt like a zombie at the end of every day.

Any spare ounce of energy went toward her sabbatical planning, which was rapidly approaching. Australia would be her first stop in February. As she looked at the hotel and sightseeing options there, her mind naturally went toward Kevin. As she thought about him on one side of the world and Sam on the other, she recognized a pattern.

I've fallen for two men who live as far away from Paris as possible. Am I unwittingly sabotaging myself by choosing the geographically inconvenient? Do I not want love? I swear I do. I always have.

Austen flashed back to a conversation she'd had at university with Milena, after they'd both read an inevitably academic article in *Cosmopolitan Magazine*. The article stated that most women would fall in love three times in their life. Neither of them had been in love yet, so they daydreamed about who their three loves might be and when and where they'd meet. Milena had a youthful certainty that at least one of hers would be a ski instructor, another an investment banker, and the third would be unexpected. She hit the first two targets like a champ in her twenties and married the mystery guy—the supply chain sustainability expert whose career had taken them to Hong Kong.

Austen had been less sure of her three, but her naive, 20-something romantic heart had been sure she'd find all three when the time was right. Brad had been her first love. When they married, her over-achiever persona was thrilled to have nailed it on the first try. Except she didn't. Since then, she'd fallen in unrequited love with Kevin and Sam.

Remembering the rule of three, she panicked.

Does it count if they didn't love me back? Did I blow my last two chances?

A few nights later, she met Isobel, Daphne, and Chiara for dinner at Monsieur Bleu at the Palais de Tokyo, questions still burning in her mind. The Eiffel Tower glowed warmly in the night sky through the restaurant's frosty windows.

"How many chances do you think we each get at love?" she asked her friends, after the waitress had poured their Pomerol.

"A million," Chiara answered confidently.

Austen pouted. "I'm serious."

"You're asking the wrong question," Daphne said. "There's no answer to that one. What you really want to know is if you'll fall in love again, and of course, you will."

"OK, different question—do you believe in soulmates? Is there one person for everyone?" Austen asked.

Isobel raised a finger, drawing all eyes to her. "No way. The concept of soulmates is based in reincarnation—that couples find their way back together in the next life, but the math doesn't work out on one-for-one soulmates."

The women stared at Isobel, listening intently, and trying to determine where math and soulmates would come together in her story.

"Think about it. There are way more people in the world today than thousands of years ago. If every newborn gets occupied by an old soul, the souls would've had to split into many pieces over the decades to accommodate all the new humans," Isobel explained.

A light went on in Austen's brain. "So, your original soulmate's soul is now split into God-knows-how-many different people, and you could be happy with any of them."

Isobel raised her glass. "Exactly."

"Ooh I like that idea," Chiara grinned. "Broken souls are floating around the universe, searching for someone who is broken in the same places as them."

The idea gave Austen a sense of peace. *Maybe souls have their own kind of gravity, pulling toward each other through space and time.*

"Since we're going all metaphysical tonight, let me ask a question," Daphne interjected. "How do we feel about fate?"

"As in a predestined path?" Austen asked.

Daphne pushed her wine glass away. "I shouldn't be drinking. Jean-Marc and I have been trying to get pregnant for two years now. We tried IVF a few months ago, but no joy. He said that maybe we're not *fated* to be parents, and I've been bummed out ever since."

"Fate's got nothing on science." Isobel reached across the table and squeezed Daphne's hand. "Try IVF again. The marvels of modern medicine can bend the universe to your will; I'm sure of it."

Austen had always been a fatalist. For every apartment, job, or guy she'd thought she wanted and didn't get, there had always been a better one just around the corner. Fate had steered her life well, so she rarely bothered contemplating the road not taken. She believed whole-heartedly in "what's meant to be will be." In the aftermath of Sam, she'd been reminding herself of this belief often.

"I see this vivid future life, watching my little one push those wooden sailboats around the fountains in Luxembourg Gardens," Daphne said wistfully. "I want it so bad I can taste it."

Isobel nodded. "Luc and I take Amélie to do that. It's as Parisian as it gets in parenting."

The haunted film of her imagined life with Sam started to replay in Austen's mind as Daphne spoke about her Parisian parenting dream. And then, something caught in her mind like a hangnail snagging on linen trousers. It was the house she'd imagined living in with Sam—on the water, with the big yard and the barbecue. The image was the polar opposite of her life in Paris, where she would undoubtedly always live in an apartment and never own a grill.

Daphne's fantasy life is 100 percent Parisian. Why isn't mine? Do I still belong here, or is my subconscious telling me it's time for a change, even if it's not with Sam? But if I left Paris, I'd sure miss these girls.

Austen refocused on her friends. She reached over and slid Daphne's wine glass toward herself. "If you want to be a mom, I am going to help you in any way I can, starting with drinking this wine for you."

The women laughed, and Daphne leaned over to hug her. "You're a good friend. Thank you."

Austen returned to Texas for Christmas where she spent a quiet holiday with family. On the plane ride back to Paris, heading into a new year, she finally felt ready to put Sam behind her. She had one month left before her sabbatical, and she needed to snap back into the zone at work, to tie up any loose ends before she disappeared for two months. Heartbreak has a way of dulling all the senses, and she was sure her work had suffered.

She headed into the office on Monday morning wearing the black suit that made her feel most powerful, along with her gravity-defying ultramarine stilettos. She'd paid extra attention to her hair and makeup that morning and breezed into the office with her head held high and her shoulders back, determined to regain control.

"You must've had a good holiday." Bastien leaned back in his chair and looked Austen up and down. "You finally look like you again, thank God. Who was that girl sitting in your seat for the past few months with a ponytail and the dead eyes?"

"I was having a bit of a personal crisis, but it's over. I'm back, and you and François will get 100 percent of my energy and attention between now and the sabbatical," she committed.

"Good. I was worried about you. You seemed to have the weight of the world on your shoulders. Anyway, it's nice to have you back—and not a moment too soon." Bastien handed her a thick stack of folders. "We just booked trips to Dublin, Chicago, and Shanghai, all before you go. There are speeches. Many speeches. Details are in those."

She took a deep breath and dove in, clearing the emotional cobwebs from her mind.

New year, new me, she decided.

CHAPTER TWENTY

Tranquility and Tarot Cards

January 31

Isobel sat on Austen's bed, drinking Chablis as she packed; the long-awaited sabbatical started the next day. Austen was nervous about spending the first five weeks alone in Australia and New Zealand, but also incredibly excited. And she was already looking forward to meeting up with friends in Thailand and Cambodia for the final three weeks in March.

"Are you seeing Kevin in Sydney?" Isobel asked.

"Yes. I'm staying with our mutual friend Charlotte when I get in, and she told him I was coming. He sent me a text last week saying he wanted to see me. I honestly wasn't going to reach out, but then he did," Austen explained.

"Well, that's some weird self-restraint. Why the fuck wouldn't you have reached out? And now that you're seeing him anyway, are you packing the snake necklace?"

Austen hucked a rolled-up pair of socks at her and laughed. "No, I'm not. You're so bad and yet oh so good. I hope Luc knows how lucky he is to have you."

"Oh, he does. Don't you worry, my friend," Isobel said with a wicked smile.

"Kevin's been radio silent for the last couple of months, so I think he's seeing someone. I'm trying not to have expectations," Austen admitted. "This trip is about me, not about men. He walked away, and I'm not going there to chase him. I wouldn't mind some closure, though, to understand what really happened. I'm convinced I still don't have the full story."

"No expectations is good. Closure is good; I hope you get it. But no matter what happens with Kevin, remember what you just said. This trip is about you. And I can't wait to see you in five weeks in Thailand."

On her first day in Sydney, Austen and Charlotte strolled along the coastline catching up on each other's lives, including a thorough debrief on what had happened with Kevin. Charlotte had arranged drinks and dinner for the three of them the next night.

"Do you know if he's seeing anyone?" Austen asked.

"I'm not sure, but if he is, I feel sorry for that poor girl now that you're in town. I remember what you two were like in London. That kind of chemistry doesn't just disappear."

Austen wondered. *Is chemistry a constant, or can it be changed by time and distance? I guess I'll find out soon enough.*

Charlotte hooked her arm into Austen's. "I plan on being fashionably late to drinks tomorrow. I am going to give you two a little time alone before I crash that reunion."

The next day, she was a bundle of nerves as she walked onto the rooftop at The Glenmore, wearing a white cotton summer dress that showed off her legs. She ordered a glass of the local Shiraz and tried her best to relax, taking in the view of the Opera House and the harbor. Kevin arrived a few minutes later. She watched him smile and look down at his feet as he walked toward her. The smile was genuine, but so was the avoidance of eye contact. When he reached her, they hugged, and she took in his familiar smell.

He's still sexy as hell.

Austen took her seat, angling her body toward him. She could immediately see that Kevin was on edge. His eyes darted around the bar, looking for a waiter. While they waited for his beer to arrive, the small talk was cursory and tense—nothing like the easy flow they'd had in Europe.

He's seeing someone. He won't even look at me, Austen thought.

It took five minutes for him to confirm her suspicion.

"I've been seeing this girl, Jenna. She's got a couple of kids, so I'm getting a taste of that dad thing I was craving." He traced the top of his pint glass with his finger.

Austen leaned toward him across the small table, suddenly curious. "*Was* craving? As in, now that you have it, you're not sure you want it?"

"You always did jump right to the heart of the matter," he said, shaking his head and looking deep into his beer. "Jenna is great, but they're not my kids. I want my own, and she doesn't want any more. We'll see. It's only been a few months."

Austen uncrossed and recrossed her legs and moved them to the other side of the table, out of his view. The idea of Jenna and her brood was now firmly seated at their table for three, and it felt crowded.

Why did he bother reaching out? We didn't have to do this.

Charlotte finally arrived and kicked the phantom girlfriend out of the third chair, breaking the tension. When her gin and tonic arrived, she started to reminisce.

"That was a fun night we had in London with Peter and your friend Milena. How are they doing?"

"They're well. Peter's happy and seeing a new girl, Bridget, and Milena and her husband Matteo moved to Hong Kong nine months ago. She and I spent ten days on the Côte d'Azur in August with another friend from college celebrating our fortieth birthdays. It was fab," Austen shared.

As Charlotte recounted her own fortieth birthday celebrations in Bali, Austen watched Kevin over the rim of her wine glass, taking a slow sip. He caught her staring hungrily at him. A slow, sexy smile spread across his face and crept all the way into his eyes, confirming that the spark between them hadn't faded.

But as soon as he finished his beer, Kevin stood up abruptly. "I've got to go. You ladies enjoy dinner. Great to see you, Austen." He hastily kissed them both on their cheeks and raced out.

"What the heck was that?" Charlotte asked.

Austen tossed back the rest of her wine. "No clue. But his loss. I'm starving. Let's go eat."

She decided to push Kevin (and Jenna) from her mind, at least for tonight.

The restaurant Charlotte had reserved smelled divine but looked oddly precarious. The interior was held up on all sides by scaffolding. They were going through a major renovation but carrying on amid the chaos.

Charlotte sat down and took in the scene around them. "Well, if this isn't the perfect metaphor for how one must live life."

"How do you mean?"

"The staff's doing their thing, despite the place being a construction zone. I guess that's life, right? Just get on with it, even when your guts are exposed."

Austen nodded. "You're so right. I'll take reality every day and twice on Sunday, over some fake facade hiding whatever's crumbling inside. I'd rather know what I'm dealing with, flaws and all."

"Cheers to that," Charlotte said, raising a glass. "Speaking of flaws, how did it feel, seeing Kevin again? Are you disappointed that he didn't stay for dinner?"

"I don't know," Austen admitted. "You were right about the chemistry—it didn't disappear. But he chose someone else. At least that's closure."

"So, you're over him?" Charlotte asked. "I must say, it surprised me how hard you fell. He's a fun guy but a bit directionless for you, I think."

"Interesting assessment," Austen noted. "In those few weeks that I knew him, I suppose I interpreted it as 'limitless.' He had a million ideas of where he might go, and all that energy felt exciting—like he could do anything."

"I think he's got a severe case of attention deficit disorder and will likely drift for the rest of his life. I think you dodged a bullet."

"Maybe so. But guess what. He's not the only one you know who's broken my heart lately," Austen confessed.

"What? Who?"

"Sam," Austen said flatly. "And that one was way worse."

"San Francisco Sam? What happened?"

Austen played back the whole story, and Charlotte's jaw dropped a centimeter more with each detail.

"Wow. I can't believe he let you slip through his fingers. I remember the night we all met for the first time at Peter's in London. It must've been right before your divorce. I could've sworn he had a thing for you."

"I thought so too, but sadly, no," Austen lamented. "I have this theory about emotional baggage that people bring into relationships. I used to think there were three kinds—carry-on, which is divorced, no kids; checked baggage which is kids; and odd-sized other window baggage, which is lunatic exes who make your lives hell."

"I've dated all of those guys," Charlotte laughed.

"But I think there's a fourth kind: invisible baggage. That's the kind carried by men over 40 who have never been married, like Sam and Kevin. It's the thing that's kept them from settling down their whole life, but it's nothing you can spot on sight."

"I think you're onto something there," Charlotte said, smiling.

She climbed into bed that night exhausted, tipsy, and thinking about Kevin. But she didn't allow herself to text him. But his text was waiting for her the next morning.

It was really good to see you last night.

> Lovely to see you too, albeit briefly. What was so important that you had to run off and miss dinner with us? Meeting your parole officer?

You know those parole meetings. Can't miss them.

She stared at the message, perplexed, and decided to wait for him to make the next move. Four days passed, and he never did. *I said I wanted closure. Looks like I got it. He's not the one.* It was officially time to focus on herself. She left Sydney without saying goodbye.

Byron Bay was her next stop—a hippy beach town one of her Australian colleagues said was not to be missed. Walking on the beach, she saw a sign advertising a tarot card reading. She'd never had one but had always been curious.

What the hell. Why not?

She sat down for the reading at a wooden table in a surprisingly sparse room, and the woman explained that tarot cards worked best if she asked a question for them "to answer."

"OK. Will I live in Paris forever?"

The reader spread the tarot cards on the table and examined them carefully. "One hundred percent, yes."

"One hundred percent? Well, that's definitive."

Austen hadn't expected certainty.

"It's right here, plain as day," replied the fortune teller. "What else would you like to know?"

Austen felt it very cliché to be a 40-year-old woman asking a fortune teller about her love life, but she figured she was there, so might as well go all in.

"What does the year ahead hold for me romantically, according to the cards?"

The woman turned out a new set of cards and reviewed them carefully, frowning. "Not much is going to happen for you on that front this year."

Again, the reply was unsettlingly definitive, but Austen wasn't surprised, given her unfortunate track record. The reading suddenly felt more credible.

At least this lady isn't blowing sunshine up my ass, telling me what I want to hear.

"But a bit further down the road, there will be a third. I'm seeing something to do with the number three."

"A third what?" Austen asked.

"I'm not sure," the woman replied unhelpfully. "In numerology, the number three represents social interaction, optimism, and tolerance. I can't say what it may indicate about your love life, but I definitely see a three."

I definitely see a three? For fuck's sake.

Safe to say, the reading didn't do much to curb Austen's skepticism about the mystical world or the wisdom of numerology. But later that night, as she laid in bed listening to waves crash into the beach, she thought back over the woman's words, and her mind caught on "three." She again flashed back to her *Cosmopolitan Magazine*-inspired conversation with Milena.

Three loves. Brad. Kevin. Sam. Fortune teller lady said there was a three in the future, so maybe there is hope for me yet.

Everyone always says hope isn't a strategy, but they also say you can't strategize love. So there in that hippy hotel room bed, she chose to hold on to hope.

After Byron Bay, Austen headed north toward the Great Barrier Reef. She and Brad had been scuba certified before their honeymoon to Belize. The last time they dove together was in Hawaii, six months before they moved to Paris. Austen had hyperventilated at 60 feet, due to a series of unfortunate events, none of which could have been predicted. She managed through it as per her training—no harm done—but she hadn't been back under water since. The incident had shaken her, and she'd been waiting nearly five years for "perfect conditions" to get back into it.

She routed herself to the Great Barrier Reef, determined to get back on the (sea)horse, conquer her fears and stop waiting for perfection to resume an activity she'd once loved. She was anxious when she got on the boat that day and signed up for a "skills refresh" with a group of beginner divers. For the first 15 minutes of the dive, she stayed close to the instructor and breathed heavily into her regulator, readjusting to the equipment and water pressure. But it didn't take long for her to get comfortable and start freely exploring the depths.

Surrounded by truly exquisite and totally silent nature, she was alone with her thoughts. It created a violent contrast to her life in Paris, where she was constantly surrounded by people, concrete, emails, deadlines, swirling cigarette smoke, and the chaos of Parisian ambulance sirens, car horns, and ringing phones. There under the sea, she could hear herself think for the first time in ages.

When she climbed back into the boat and took off her heavy oxygen tank, she felt unburdened in ways she couldn't yet explain.

Austen spent the next two and a half weeks exploring vast expanses of untouched nature in New Zealand. She visited vineyards on Waiheke Island across the bay from Auckland, paraglided off a mountaintop in Queenstown, and tramped around Mount Cook. "Tramping" was the Kiwi word for hiking. It didn't mean "slutty walking," as she had initially guessed.

Being alone in nature gave her the opportunity to reflect on her life and relationships. One afternoon at Lake Wanaka, she sat on the rocks looking at the lake's main attraction—a willow tree whose roots are submerged in the water. Her gaze wandered from that extraordinary tree to a small patch of dandelions—a common weed—growing between the rocks.

She recalled a conversation she'd once had with Liz about adaptability and resilience.

"There are two kinds of people in this world: orchids and weeds," she had explained. "Orchids need very particular circumstances and care to thrive. They're finicky and delicate and ephemeral. Then, there are weeds. Those things can grow and thrive anywhere, no matter the conditions. You, my friend, are a weed."

Austen had nodded, instantly understanding.

"You are wired to choose happiness, and you will thrive no matter where you find yourself. That's a gift that will serve you well in life," Liz had told her.

Brad was an orchid. His inability to thrive in Paris or in their marriage had frustrated her to no end. In those quiet weeks of reflection, Austen finally understood that during their Paris years, she had been waiting for him to see *what she saw* in the place. He never would have or even could have seen things her way. They were fundamentally different people who needed different circumstances to thrive.

Austen was sure her ideal partner would also be a weed and was quietened by the knowledge that there were millions of varieties of weeds in the world. She simply had to find that one weed with the qualities that best complemented her own, so they could thrive side by side. Her fingertips danced across the tops of the dandelions on that rocky lakefront, and as she watched the winged seedlings float off in the breeze to find a new spot to thrive, she resolved to embrace her inner weed.

The five weeks of solo travel flew by faster than Austen had expected. Every day she had been journaling—documenting her activities and thoughts. Several of her early entries reflected days where she did nothing but read a book. On those days, she had systematically struggled with guilt, feeling she should've been doing something productive. But as the weeks passed, she had relaxed into the quiet days. It was as if her brain had downshifted into lower gears—gears she barely remembered she had. Austen's life motto had been "work hard, play harder" for as long as she could remember. "Slow" wasn't usually her style.

As she packed her bags to move onward to Thailand and her friends, she contemplated the contrasts in life—between living fast and living slow, but also between quiet versus loud love.

Her mother was an extrovert like her, and she had always loved Austen loudly. She couldn't resist telling every person she met that her daughter lived and worked in Paris as a successful corporate speechwriter. She would tell the checkout girl at the grocery store if she could find a way to work it into their brief conversation. She was incredibly proud and told Austen every time she had the chance.

Austen's father, on the other hand, loved her quietly. He was an introvert who rarely said much. As a child, she felt loved through his actions, but she craved hearing the words.

She had a distinct memory of the first time she told her dad she loved him. She was 12 years old. Her parents had put her to bed, but she'd lain awake for 20 minutes listening through the wall to the TV show that he was watching, working up her nerve.

When she finally came out of her room and peeked her head around the corner to say those three little words, he reacted simply. "I love you too, sweetheart. Now go back to bed."

At age 40, she questioned why her 12-year-old heart had needed to hear it so badly that night. Perhaps being loved loudly felt safer, less difficult to doubt.

Brad had loved her quietly too. She fell asleep that night wondering. *What would it be like to be loved loudly by a partner?*

CHAPTER TWENTY-ONE

Togetherness

The next day, she arrived in Thailand to meet Isobel and Daphne, who had flown in from Paris for ten days. They checked into their hotel in Phuket and immediately headed to Café Del Mar, to get their toes in the sand and Mai Tais in hand.

"You survived your five weeks solo. How was it?" Daphne asked. "Any problems? Were you lonely, or was it all as fabulous as it looked on Instagram?"

"No problems. Everything went according to plan. Honestly, it was incredible. Paragliding in Queenstown and diving the Great Barrier Reef were the major highlights."

"You didn't get eaten by a great white shark. Well done you," Isobel exclaimed.

"And to my great surprise, I enjoyed the alone time. I read books and wrote in a journal—pen on paper. I can't write as fast as I type, so that daily ritual made my brain slow down. I didn't know how badly I needed that."

Isobel grabbed Austen's arm. "Did you see Kevin?"

Austen nodded. "I saw him once. For one drink. He's seeing some girl named Jenna, playing dad to her kids. And you know what? I hardly thought about him after I left Sydney."

"You got the closure you wanted," Isobel noted.

She nodded. "It seems I did."

"How do you feel after five weeks out of the office?" Daphne asked.

"This is the longest break I've taken in 18 years of working, and I've disconnected 100 percent," Austen said. "At the beginning of week six, I've gotta say, I feel pretty freaking Zen."

Daphne raised her Mai Tai. "You look amazing—tan and relaxed. I'm thrilled for you that it's been such a great experience. And you've still got three weeks to go."

Austen toasted with her friends. "And work carries on without me. I've gotten a friendly text or two from Bastien, assuring me the business is alive and well. I'm not thinking about them at all."

"This is one of many things I love about my job," Daphne said. "When I'm out of the office—the kitchen in my case—I'm out. There's no remote work in baking. No temptation to check some email or whatever you office workers do."

"Your temptations come in other forms," Isobel cracked. "I'd want to eat everything I baked if I had your job. But I'll admit it now—I'll inevitably check email while we're here. I have such a hard time disconnecting."

"Early in my career, Brad and I were supposed to be taking off for a long weekend, and some work shit hit the fan. I felt I had to be there to save the day, and he looked at me and said, 'Austen, stop being such a martyr. If you got hit by a bus tomorrow, that company would continue to function, without missing a beat.'"

Daphne frowned. "Well, that was rude."

"I had the same reaction initially but then realized he was 100 percent right. It was probably the best thing he ever gave me—the understanding that it's OK to disconnect from time to time and let someone else deal with things. No one is irreplaceable," she concluded.

"Cheers to that and to the glories of vacation time," Isobel shouted.

Austen dramatically set down her glass. "Enough about me. What's been going on with you two? How are things back in Paris?"

Isobel slathered sunscreen on her face and arms. "Amélie spent all last week with us on her school holidays. We went to the Maldives because it was on the way here, so I left Luc there with her yesterday and flew here to meet you two beauties."

"A week in the Maldives followed by ten days in Thailand? You poor thing. Life is hard," Austen laughed.

"Look who's talking, girl who's traveling for two months straight to nothing but exotic climes," Daphne exclaimed.

Austen smiled and shrugged. "Sorry not sorry."

"Yes but, the Maldives is supposed to be romantic. Having her with us killed that vibe, but it was still beautiful. Is it horrible to admit that I'm glad we don't have her full time?" Isobel folded her hands in prayer and raised her eyes to the sky. "God protect that girl's mother, so she's always around."

"Have you and Luc talked about having one or two or seven of your own?" Daphne asked.

"Seven. Good God, you shut your mouth. One, yes, we have, and I'm sure we will eventually. But I'm not ready to be done jetting off on girls' trips," Isobel explained. "Anyway, we haven't even been married for a year, and I'm only 36. I've got time, right?"

"Of course, you do," Daphne reassured her. "However, this may be my last girls' trip for a while." A broad smile spread across her face.

"Oh my God, you're pregnant," Austen shouted. "And you're here."

Daphne nodded, and they hugged and clinked their cocktails, realizing only then that Daphne's was a mocktail.

"I wouldn't have missed it. I'm 13 weeks and due in September. My doctor gave me the all clear," Daphne said, grinning ear to ear. "It happened maybe a week after that night I was whining about it at Monsieur Bleu."

Daphne's news made Austen equal parts thrilled and glum. This happened every time a close friend shared their pregnancy news. She was delighted because they were, and she wanted her friends to get all their hearts' desires. But every new baby meant the loss—at least for a few years—of another carefree, kid-free pal with whom she could travel and day-drink.

But we're all here now, and we're going to make the most of it.

They spent their days in Phuket between the beach, sea kayaking through hidden lagoons, scuba diving and Singhas for Austen and Isobel and snorkeling and mocktails for Daphne. They had Thai massages nearly every day and ate an excessive amount of shrimp pad thai and green papaya salad.

Austen was genuinely thrilled to be with her friends but couldn't help but notice that they moved at the frenetic Paris speed she'd left behind. One morning after breakfast, Isobel and Daphne decided to hike up to the Big Buddha.

"You two go," Austen told them. "I'm going to sit at the pool and read."

Daphne's brow furrowed. "Are you feeling OK?"

Austen reassured them. "Perfect. Just want a down day after yesterday's kayaking adventure. But you two go. Enjoy."

Six weeks ago, she would've felt compelled to join them, to maximize every minute of every day. But now, she felt perfectly content to lie low. Zen suited her.

After five days on Phuket, the three friends moved to their next destination, the island of Koh Tao. The last flight out of Phuket got them to their hotel after dark. When the bellman showed them to their suite, the black sky was filled with a million stars and a nearly full moon reflecting off the ocean in a sparkly path toward the horizon.

In the morning, they awoke to find themselves directly on the beach, in front of the most turquoise waters they'd ever seen.

Austen had chosen Koh Tao for several reasons, one of which was the diving. On their second morning there, they arrived at the boat dock and were greeted by two tanned and painfully attractive dive masters who were at least ten years their junior.

The taller of the two spoke first. "Hello ladies. I'm Axel, and this is Ethan. Welcome aboard."

Ethan extended his hand and helped them climb into the boat. The women exchanged silent but knowing smiles.

They're both easy on the eyes. It's a good day to dive.

As the boat sped toward the reef, Ethan gave the briefing on the boat's safety and other features.

"There's a toilet under the deck. Please put nothing in it except for your business and the associated paperwork," he cracked.

"We've got a funny guy," Isobel smiled.

"Is that a New Zealand accent I hear?" Austen asked.

Ethan nodded. "Kiwi born and raised."

"I just spent a few weeks there. Beautiful country."

Daphne leaned toward Axel, shouting slightly against the wind. "Where are you from?"

"Denmark. Copenhagen. Been out here now for three years doing this," Axel explained, gesturing toward the sea. "Can't beat it. Where are you ladies from?"

"Paris," Isobel answered. "Daphne and I abandoned our husbands to join Austen here on her two-month epic travel adventure across Asia Pacific."

I love that girl. She casually drops "our husbands" into the conversation to take herself and Daphne out of the equation.

Axel turned his full attention toward Austen. "Making your way across the Pacific to dive all the best spots?"

"Not exactly. We dove in Phuket last week, and I dove in Australia last month, but Koh Tao is the last dive spot on the trip."

"We'll do our best to make it memorable then," Axel smiled.

Daphne snorkeled on the surface, due to the bun in the oven, as Austen and Isobel dropped in, following the group. As soon as they were underwater, they knew they were in for something special. They swam through massive, swirling tornadoes of multi-colored fish—more than either of them had ever seen in their scuba diving lives. They exchanged looks of pure delight through their masks.

During their third and final dive of the day, Axel abruptly turned toward the group and banged a metal tool on his tank to get their attention. He pointed to something in the distance ahead of them. They swam toward him, eager to see whatever had him so excited, and as Austen approached, she saw something *massive* swimming toward them.

There's an underwater sign language divers use to communicate, and when she got to him, he made the sign for whale shark—both hands' index fingers and thumbs creating the W shape against his forehead. Austen excitedly repeated the sign for Isobel who had just swum up beside them.

A whale shark is the Holy Grail of dive sightings, and she had never seen one. Her heart leaped into her throat as she watched the magnificent beast slowly swim toward them. Whale sharks are the size of a three-story building laid on its side, and when something that massive swims directly over one's head, it's a true marvel.

Austen splayed out on her back, suspended in the water, and opened her whole soul to the experience. Her heartbeat throbbed in her ears and bubbles poured out of her regulator as she watched the creature lazily passing above. Once it did, she righted herself, looking for Isobel. They swam to one another and had an awkward underwater dance party, effusing the joy of the moment.

Axel swam by and briefly joined in, moving his arms in an underwater hula dance. When he looked her way, Austen let her eyes go cartoon-sized, to silently communicate her excitement and wonder.

She came out of the water elated, hitting the surface with Axel as Isobel ascended slowly beneath them. They met at the stairs on the back of the boat and dropped their regulators.

"Not bad, eh?" Axel kindly took hold of her fins as she took them off.

"Absolutely stunning. I've never seen one before." Austen reached for the boat's ladder and climbed up, beaming. "It was the most amazing thing I've ever seen. I'm over the moon."

He climbed up the stairs behind her and helped her out of her BCD, putting her oxygen tank and his own into the rack.

Austen helped Isobel out of her gear and turned to find Axel, wetsuit unzipped to his waist, his tan and toned torso exposed.

"I'm delighted we could deliver for you, especially in March. We usually don't see whale sharks until April or May. You got lucky."

Axel was visibly pleased with himself and the local fauna, as he reached down off the back of the boat to pull in the ladder.

Isobel and Austen rejoined Daphne and told her about their whale shark sighting.

Daphne spoke to her stomach. "Listen up, baby. You're not even here yet and already making me miss things. What the heck?"

"He or she will be worth it," Austen assured her.

Isobel nodded. "Whale sharks are totally overrated anyway. Just kidding. No, they're not. Sorry, Daph."

Daphne rubbed her stomach and smiled. "You got a whale shark. I get a baby. I'm cool with that deal."

"You know what I love most about diving?" Austen asked the group, ready to answer her own question. "We have no business being down there or seeing any of that. We're only able to do it because of technology. So, every experience, like that freaking whale shark, is such a privilege. I'll never forget today. Thank you," she said to both Axel and Ethan.

"The pleasure is all ours," Ethan said, with a genuine smile. "And you're right. Every day is a privilege—to be lived to the fullest."

Axel sat down next to Austen. "On that note, what are you three up to tonight? We were thinking about hitting Maya. There's meant to be a great DJ spinning. Want to join?"

Austen looked toward Daphne and Isobel and saw agreement in both their faces, so plans were made to meet up later that evening.

The women arrived at the beach club just as the sun was setting, wearing their beach party best. They found Axel and Ethan at the bar, having also cleaned up nicely. Drinks were ordered, and the music bounced its way down the beach as the group of five found a table.

After a few drinks, they made their way to the dance floor, and Austen's energy rose with the beat. When the guys went to the bar for another round, Isobel grabbed Daphne and Austen's hands and said, "I love right now."

"I love right now too," Austen screamed into the sky as the dance floor throbbed around them. "I'm so glad you two are here."

"A couple of beautiful men in the mix also doesn't hurt," Isobel continued. "Which one is your pick?"

"Why do I have to pick just one?" Austen asked with a sarcastic grin.

Daphne danced in circles around them both. "You said you haven't gotten any action on this trip, so I say go for it. I predict you can have your choice, based on how they're both acting. I'm married and knocked up, so let me live vicariously through you," Daphne insisted.

"I'm not going to ditch you two to get laid. You flew halfway around the world to spend time with me," Austen said. "That would be so lame."

"I don't care. If you want to, you should. We have a three-bedroom suite. We'll sleep with earplugs," Isobel offered as she and Daphne giggled conspiratorially.

The idea blossomed in her mind as she watched them, standing at the bar.

I suppose I could have one sabbatical fling. Axel is bolder and the obvious choice, but Ethan has something quietly attractive about him too. Dilemmas, dilemmas. Must pay more attention to their dance moves to inform my selection.

The guys returned to the dance floor with the drinks, and Daphne decided to take a break, returning to sit at the bar with her mocktail. Ethan danced with Isobel, and Axel stayed close to Austen. He took her hand and spun her around, pulling her into his chest with one hand as his other arm wrapped around her waist. Leaning into him, she noticed he smelled like all the best parts of saltwater, sweat and sex.

After a few minutes, Ethan grabbed Austen's hand off Axel's shoulder and executed some kind of spin-swap, switching their partners. She found her arms around his neck without understanding how they got there, but she didn't mind. Axel seemed to have not missed a beat and was dancing with Isobel inches away.

"Looks like you two have done that before," she said to Ethan with a suspicious smile. "Quite the team."

"You have no idea," he whispered sultrily into her ear.

Austen's skin started to tingle. They danced on for another minute, his hands on her hips, until she felt Isobel tap her on the back.

"Daphne just flagged me down. I think she's pregnant-tired and wants to go."

"OK, then we should head out," Austen said to no one specifically.

"You stay if you want," Isobel offered. "I can get her home, and I'm sure one of these nice gentlemen can make sure you're OK?"

"We certainly can," Axel promised. "We'll take excellent care of her. Don't worry about a thing."

"Are you sure?" Austen asked Isobel while looking toward Daphne at the bar.

She nodded and waved a "you stay here" hand gesture.

Isobel leaned in for a hug. "Have fun. Keep your phone on. Be safe. Use a condom." She pranced away, throwing Austen a wink over her shoulder.

"And then there were three," Axel said.

"So it seems."

She was full of energy and having a ball dancing and laughing with the two easy-going, attractive, and attentive men. She danced until she couldn't dance anymore, at which point she made a dramatic gesture grabbing onto both of their shoulders in a fake collapse.

Axel took her cue. "Want to walk down to the beach to cool off?"

"Great idea," she breathed.

As they made their way toward the ocean, Ethan peeled off to make a final run to the bar for beers. She and Axel made their way to the beach and kicked off their shoes. As their feet hit the cool sand, he took her hand. She let her fingers lace into his.

"Will Ethan be mad at you?" she asked, motioning toward their joined hands. "I've spent the whole evening wondering which one of you was going to make a move."

"Well, he'll surely try to make the next one." Axel gave her a cautious smile. "And that's OK with me if it's OK with you."

"Oh yeah? You're willing to surrender if I were to choose him? Just like that? Easy come easy go?" Austen asked, faking offense.

"I never said surrender—more like share. You can have us both if you want—together or separately."

Austen's eyes popped out. "Wow. Umm. Do you two do that a lot—share conquests?"

She didn't even try to hide her shock.

"Sometimes we do. How do you feel about that?" He dropped her hand and moved his onto the back of her neck as they continued to walk.

Austen was so taken aback that she wasn't sure how to answer. In her moment of stunned silence, Axel pulled her toward him and kissed her.

Holy shit. But he smells so good.

She wrapped her arms around him and kissed him back, her mind spinning on what he'd proposed and increasingly conscious of the muscles rippling down his back. After a minute, she stepped away.

"Have you two discussed this—about me specifically, tonight?"

"We have. He's hanging back to give me some time to feel things out with you," he confessed. "We decided you were down for something with at least one of us and gave it a 40 percent chance you might be open for more of an adventure."

"Forty percent chance of a threesome?" she blurted out, her blood pressure rising. "What are the indicators there? I mean, academically speaking, what put me at 40 percent?"

Axel laughed, picked up her hand, and kept walking. "You're a total flirt, so that got you 15 percent. When we saw how you moved on the dance floor, your percentage went up to 30," he explained.

I wasn't the only one imagining how the vertical dance moves translated to horizontal, she thought, quietly laughing at herself.

"OK interesting. What gave me the next ten points?"

"You stayed when your friends left, and you've been paying equal attention to us both. Your flirting game is strong," he said with an admirative tone.

"Who me?" She leaned toward him to dramatically bat her eyelashes.

His attention turned her on. She reveled in it, while silently questioning whether she was as adventurous as they thought.

"Yes you. But I thought I might have a slight advantage after our whale shark sighting together, so I drew the lucky straw to make the first offer."

They continued to walk in silence.

"We're nice guys, I promise. We'd be very gentle, unless of course, you didn't want us to be. Either way, you'd be fully in charge. No pressure to do anything you didn't want to do. Have you had a threesome before?"

"Never," she quickly confirmed. "This is the first time one's been on offer."

He took both her hands in his and spread their arms wide. "You'd never seen a whale shark before today either. Maybe today is just one of those days that's made for epic new experiences."

Austen threw her head back, searching the sky. Axel softly pulled her in and kissed lazily down her neck. As he did, she saw Ethan out of the corner of her eye, casually strolling toward them, beers in hand. She tensed, and Axel looked up without releasing her. To the left, he saw Ethan coming.

"Or he will disappear if you want him to, and it can just be you and me. Your call," Axel said quietly.

Still unsure what she would do, Austen freed herself from his grasp.

"How's it going?" Ethan asked them both, handing over the cold beers. He sat down on the sand. "Shall we sit?"

Axel followed his lead, leaving enough space in the middle for her to sit between them. She remained standing, trying to get a better read on them.

"Austen wanted to know how she got to 40 percent likely," Axel grinned. "Very intellectual, this one."

"It's an inexact science," Ethan acknowledged. "Are there any other questions we can answer for you?"

Austen pursed her lips and started to slowly pace back and forth on the beach in front of them. She was working up the courage to ask what she really wanted to know.

"Yes. This is obviously not your first rodeo. So, when you're doing whatever it is that you do, are you both on the girl, or are you guys hooking up too? Sorry if that's awkward. Just trying to understand the dynamic here."

Ethan leaned back on his hands. "It's up to you, really. We're down for any version of this. Whatever gets you excited. You'd be in charge."

"Axel mentioned that. It's nice you two are so in sync on your messaging strategy," Austen said, her professional verbiage leaking into this decidedly unprofessional situation. "Another question if I may. What is the minimum 'percent likely' you assess someone to be before deciding to extend this kind of offer?"

"Forty," they both said in unison.

"Got it. So, I'm as unlikely a candidate as you'd ever propose this situation to," she said, moving her index finger to point between the three of them.

She continued to pace slowly back and forth, alternating her gaze between them and the ocean, her mind in overdrive.

"I'm going to take a quick swim." Axel stood up, squeezed her shoulder, and planted a slow kiss on her neck. He whipped off his shirt and casually strode toward the ocean under a starry sky, leaving her alone with Ethan.

"So, this is how it works? Time alone with each of you? Now I know what you meant when you said I had no idea what a good team you two are."

Austen was flustered and increasingly aroused. Her curiosity was getting the better of her, pushing her forward.

"How many times have you two run this game? No, scratch that. I don't want to know."

Ethan silently motioned for her to sit with him in the sand, which she did, her feet tired from dancing. He scooted close to her until their shoulders touched but kept his gaze on the ocean.

"You know what? I think you're more like 45 percent likely, now that I look around," he said.

"And why's that exactly?"

He pointed up to the sky. "Full moon. Everyone is hornier on a full moon. It's a well-known fact."

She laughed and tilted her head back to look up at the giant moon in the sky. As she did, he traced one finger from her chin down her neck and in between her breasts before pulling her gently toward him and kissing her. Before she knew it, their bodies were pressed against one another, lying in the sand. As they kissed and his hands explored her body, she began to ease into the idea of having four hands on her at once. She was buzzing.

"Son of a bitch," Axel yelled from the water, bursting the bubble.

They both sat bolt upright and looked toward him in the dark.

"Fuck. I just got nailed in the face by a giant motherfucking jellyfish," Axel said as he made his way up the beach toward them, dripping wet. His pace was frenzied; he was clearly in pain. As he approached, they could see the welt forming by the light of the full moon.

"I'm not pissing on your face," Ethan said, trying to hold back his laughter.

"No, you're not. Goddamn it. I need to go deal with this. You two stay." He grimaced and looked at Austen sadly. "I can't believe *this* is going to be the reason I don't get more of you."

He shook his head and walked away.

Austen was speechless and horrified. The spell was broken.

"Shouldn't you go help him?"

Ethan turned toward her and tucked a strand of hair behind her ear. "Nah, he'll be fine. I'd be happy to take you home though."

"I think I should call it a night. You should go make sure he's OK."

Ethan sighed heavily. "Damn. You sure? Things were getting pretty good there before jelly face ruined it."

She stifled a laugh. "I've always been a big believer in signs, and if a jellyfish sting to the face isn't a sign that things should stop, I'm not sure what is. But thanks for a truly memorable evening."

She gave him a quick goodbye kiss, grabbed her shoes, and ran up the beach toward the lights of the street to make her way back to the hotel.

The next morning over coffee and a plate of tropical fruit, she recounted the story to Isobel and Daphne, who couldn't believe the offer and laughed hysterically at its conclusion.

"If that jellyfish hadn't made its mark—literally—across that poor bastard's beautiful face, would you have gone through with it?" Isobel asked.

Austen took a slow sip of her coffee, considering. "I guess we'll never know. There was only ever one of them with me at a given time, so I didn't have to decide. But it's going to be one hell of a memory. Let's go make some more today, shall we?"

The three friends clinked their coffee mugs.

Their final days in Koh Tao passed quickly. They chose not to dive again. Instead, they went paddleboarding and took a Thai cooking class. They lapped up the sunshine and the time together in paradise before parting ways at the airport—Isobel and Daphne back to Paris, and Austen onto Cambodia to meet Milena and Liz for the final ten days of her sabbatical.

CHAPTER TWENTY-TWO

Gratitude

Austen arrived first in Siem Reap. Milena and Liz were still a few hours out, so she had time to settle in quietly before their arrival. She wandered around the tranquil resort grounds soaking in the quiet after ten brilliant but loud days with Daphne and Isobel. She walked through a lotus garden and came across a large stone Buddha. In its left hand was a message, written on a piece of paper:

"Live with no excuses. Travel with no regrets."

She sat on a bench for some time, facing the statue and contemplating the message. *I think I'm doing a pretty good job living up to your counsel, mister Buddha.*

As she reflected, a woman from the hotel staff approached. "Hello madam. I hope you are enjoying the gardens. Do you know the meaning of this particular Buddha statue?"

Austen shook her head. "I don't, but I'd like to."

"This is a Teaching Buddha. It represents wisdom, understanding, and fulfilling destiny. Maybe you have traveled here to Cambodia to seek these?"

"I hope so. Can you tell me about the scroll in the Buddha's hand? I love the message."

"Buddha speaks to our guests through these messages. There's a new one every day, so you should come back to visit him. You never know what wisdom he may impart. I wish you a wonderful stay at our hotel."

The woman folded her hands into a prayer position and bowed her head.

Austen thanked her and turned back to contemplate the Buddha's two-part message. Regret was an emotion she rarely, if ever, felt. It was her fatalistic side—the belief that what was meant to be would be. She saw no room for regret there. It felt like a waste of time.

However, the first part of the message was something she'd not yet mastered. Austen still made excuses regularly—for herself and for the people around her. As a professional communicator, she could find a way to justify almost anything. It was a skill that didn't always serve her well, especially when she wanted to avoid certain truths.

"Living with no excuses" seems like a perfect goal, coming out of this trip. I can take that to heart, she thought.

She wandered out of the lotus garden and into the hotel lobby just as Milena walked in, suitcase in tow. Seven months had passed since the fortieth birthday celebrations in the South of France, so Milena and Matteo were now nearly a year into their Hong Kong adventure.

Once they'd put Milena's bags in the room and she'd freshened up, the two friends made their way to the hotel bar to wait for Liz's arrival. Fans circulated humid air through the high archways, and each table was topped with a lotus flower floating in a crystal vase.

Austen approached the bartender and said with a smile, "Hello. I miss wine. What red do you suggest?"

"We've got a lovely Australian Pinot Noir from the Yarra Valley," he said. "I've got a bottle that's slightly chilled, since it's so warm today."

"Sounds perfect. We'll take two glasses." She turned to Milena. "How's Hong Kong treating you? Feeling more settled?"

"Yes. I feel like I've finally figured out who I'm supposed to be. I can't explain it, but life makes sense to me now in a way that it never did before."

Austen saw a serenity in Milena's face that hadn't been there in the South of France. Emotionally, they'd both come a long way since that trip.

"Matteo is killing it at work. I'm making friends. I have a few leads on potentially amazing jobs, so I'm confident my career will get sorted soon. It's all coming together, and honestly, I don't think I've ever felt happier."

"It's ex-pat living," Austen exclaimed. "When you're surrounded by nothing familiar, you have to learn to rely on your instincts. And when those prove correct, your confidence goes up and you just become more sure of your place in the world."

"That's exactly it," Milena agreed. "I'm figuring it out."

Austen smiled warmly at her friend. "My heart is so happy for you, seeing you blossom like this. And it's only just begun."

"I remember when you came back to Stanford Toulouse. You seemed so confident, so poised, so European," Milena recalled. "I was jealous that you were that comfortable in your skin when I felt so awkward, but now I get it. Ex-pat life changes you."

"Welcome to the club, lady. It's the place to be—fabulous ex-pat women living their best lives. And jetting off to Cambodia because they can, when their friends are just a few countries away." Austen laughed and hugged her friend. "I'm so proud of you for making it over the hump toward feeling settled there."

Milena grabbed Austen's hands and squeezed. "You've been such a help as I've fumbled through this. People who haven't lived abroad don't get it, but you do. I've never felt closer to you than I have since I moved there. You've been a lifeline, and I'm so grateful."

"I've always considered you one of my best friends, but I have to agree. I've never felt closer to you either," Austen acknowledged.

"Cheers to us and to Cambodia. This is going to be epic."

As they clinked glasses, a voice behind them asked, "Where's mine?"

They turned to find Liz, wearing enormous Prada sunglasses and a sleeveless floral romper, one hand perched on her roller bag. Austen and Milena jumped up to hug her.

"We're all here now, so let's go to the pool. It's hotter than Hades," Austen said.

"Bikinis, Christ. It's only March so my summer body couldn't make the trip. But my winter body is here, and she likes wine," Liz cracked.

The last leg of the sabbatical had officially begun.

The Angkor Temples were the centerpiece of their planning. They hired a guide to show them around, and they toured each temple with an overwhelming sense of awe at their history, architecture, and longevity. Each temple was more impressive than the last. They watched the sunrise over Angkor

Wat—the most famous of them all—but it was the Bayon Temple of Angkor Thom that impressed them the most.

They wandered around its 54 towers which were carved with 200-plus smiling faces, believed by some to be King Jayavarman VII, the man who commissioned it in the late 12th century. It was a stunning work of art, even if requesting 200-plus carved likenesses of one's face seemed like an over-stretch by current standards for ego.

"Can you imagine, Austen, if you went on a date and ended up back at his place, and he had 20 giant statues of his face scattered around his apartment?" Liz joked.

Austen looked up at one of the many carvings and laughed. "I think that might be a minor red flag. But I'm guessing King Jayavarman didn't have trouble getting women. The ladies of the late 12th century probably didn't have the same concerns over the male ego."

"What *do* we think Cambodian ladies of the late 12th century were concerned about?" Milena asked.

Liz trailed her fingers along the ancient stone walls. "Finding and keeping a husband, making and raising babies, trying to find Zen—probably not all that much has changed since. Except now, they have to do it while holding down a full-time job."

"Speaking of jobs, dare I ask?" Milena looked at Austen. "Are you ready to go back to work, or will you be opening a beach bar in Thailand soon?"

Austen waited for a trio of orange-clad monks to pass and then replied. "I'm not really a 'beach bar in Thailand' kind of girl, but I have been thinking about what makes me happy. And you know what I've decided?"

"Tell us," Liz insisted.

"I love my life and my job. While this trip has been full-on amazing, I'll be ready to go home after these days with you two. The time away has just validated that my life is pretty damn good."

Milena put her hands on her hips in Superwoman pose. "That's an incredible outcome. I think there are not that many people who'd reach the same conclusion if they allowed themselves to deeply ponder that question."

Austen looked at her friends and did a slow 360-degree turn, taking in the majesty of the temple. "I don't know what I've done to deserve this life, but I'm just so grateful."

The three friends stood motionless for a moment, taking in the sentiment.

Liz broke the silence. "You work your ass off. You're a good human. You deserve all of it and more."

Austen shook her head. "A lot of good humans work their asses off and don't have a fraction of what I have. A lot is dumb luck, for being born when and where I was. I'm reminded of that whenever I travel, especially in less developed countries."

"No doubt we're extremely lucky," Milena agreed. "But not everyone who is lucky is grateful, and you are."

"The benefits of being a fatalist. I look back now with 20/20 hindsight on things that once really disappointed me, and I know that everything happens the way it's supposed to," Austen said.

"Such as?" Liz asked.

"I never would've moved to California—where I met you two—if my mom hadn't thrown me under the social school bus in high school. Or if Sam or Kevin had said yes, I'd be back in California or in Australia now, probably in a relationship that was falling apart and hating myself for leaving Paris."

Milena inhaled deeply. "God, you're right. And if you'd not taken the job in Paris, we wouldn't be here right now."

"Here is pretty great, eh? It's all butterfly effect, so I'm going to be grateful and trust the universe," Austen declared.

"I think you're right. You're exactly where you are supposed to be, which is here in temple heaven with us," Liz said, raising her arms to the sky.

"Before Paris, I remember thinking that if I died, I'd regret never having lived there. But with that box checked, I can't think of anything I'd regret *not* doing if I died tomorrow. Except maybe visiting the Taj Mahal."

"Why the Taj Mahal?" Milena asked.

"My wanderlusty, romantic side. It's a monument to love. The Shah built a freaking palace to show how much he loved his wife. How dreamy is that?" Austen asked.

Liz rolled her eyes. "You're hopeless."

"Totally hopeless. And yet, still full of hope. Ain't love grand?"

Austen twirled in a circle and leaped through the intricately carved South Gate of Angkor Thom, topped by four faces of King Jayavarman, one looking in each direction, surveying the landscape. They emerged onto a bridge with carved figures lining both sides.

"The mean looking ones on the right side are the Asuras— the demons," their guide explained. "And the more serene looking ones on the left are the Devas—the gods."

Milena surveyed the bridge. "A long line of gods and demons. Reminds me of your love life, Austen. Are you going to get back on the dating apps when you get home?"

"Nice segue. Geez. But yes, I will. The quest for love must go on."

On the morning of their last day, Austen woke up early and wandered back into the hotel's lotus garden to see the final message from the Buddha. It read:

"Travel makes one modest. You see what a tiny place you occupy in the world."

She let her mind wander back over her favorite memories from her two months on the road, replaying them vividly. The Sydney Harbor Bridge. The tarot card reading. Conquering her fear of diving. Paragliding. Tramping. The willow tree at Lake Wanaka. Daphne's baby news. Isobel's dancing. Axel and Ethan. The temples. Liz and Milena.

Each thought pushed a new wave of calm over her soul and filled her heart. She remembered the Buddha's message from the first day and offered a small bow to the statue, committing to occupy her tiny place in the world with deep gratitude and with no excuses.

Paris was awaiting her return.

CHAPTER TWENTY-THREE

Emotional Affairs

For her first few weeks back in Paris, Austen was stunned by how quickly life swirled around her. Walking down the street, she felt like she was moving in slow motion while everything around her raced by at double or triple speed. Plus, everyone seemed really angry. All the scowling faces reminded her of a t-shirt she saw once that said *"J ♥ rien. Je suis Parisien.*[4]*"* At the time, she'd thought it was funny, but now she found it sad. It wasn't how she ever wanted to live.

Work was unrelenting. The hours were long, and she resumed traveling with François and Bastien whenever duty called. But despite the grumpy Parisians, she always felt relieved to return home. She still believed Paris to be the most beautiful city on Earth, and she couldn't help but get sucked into its throbbing energy. No one moved to Paris to live a slow life; that much was certain.

One day in late April, Austen jumped into a Parisian taxi to get to an important lunch meeting. She was wearing a navy-blue, short-sleeved dress with the black slingback stilettos

---

4   I love nothing. I am Parisian.

that usually filled her with confidence, but today she was feeling twitchy and under-prepared for the meeting. Sitting in the back of the cab, she fidgeted and ran through the objectives and desired outcomes in her mind, until the taxi driver interrupted her thoughts.

"On your way to meet a lover?" he asked.

"I'm sorry?"

"Going to meet a lover? You seem nervous."

Wow I did hear him right, and he thinks that's a perfectly acceptable question to ask. Seriously?

"Umm, no. I'm going to a meeting for work," she stammered.

"Too bad," he replied.

In French, there's an expression *"le cinq-à-sept*[5]*"* which is used to refer to a lover. Five to seven p.m. are the hours when people are often between work and family obligations. "Is she your five to seven?" one might ask.

Austen grew up as a good Southern Baptist, where getting involved with married folks was a no-go. Do not covet thy neighbor's wife, et cetera. The French relationship with monogamy, however, was tenuous at best. She often wondered if she was the only woman in Paris who *had not* had an affair with a married man.

A few nights later, she got an unexpected text from Louis—a friend of a friend she'd met at a party years earlier.

Welcome home! I was
following your pictures on
Instagram from your trip. It
looked incredible, and I'd love
to hear all about it.

---

5   The five-to-seven.

How about a drink some night
this week? It'd be good to
catch up.

He was married, of course, and gorgeous. His wife must have traveled a lot for work because she was never around, and he never spoke about her. He and Austen had friends in common so saw each other socially from time to time, but they'd never spent any time one-on-one.

Their relationship had always floated on a light undercurrent of flirtation, which Austen had never actively encouraged but had also never particularly discouraged. She'd told herself it was just the French way, so she had consciously chosen not to think about it. Married men were off limits. And yet, here he was, asking her out.

The truth was, she liked him. In addition to his striking good looks, she'd always found him kind, interesting, and very smart. He knew how to tell a great story but also how to listen, which was a rare quality she admired in people who did it well. He'd lived in the UK for a few years and in Singapore for six months—both for work—so he had an interesting international profile that somehow matched hers.

She remembered her theory. *They're all monkeys. Maybe he's about to swing out of his tree? Probably not. Don't overthink. It's just a drink.*

That'd be great. Name the
time and place.

Despite herself, she was excited to find out what it was like to have his full attention for an evening. He set their meeting for two nights later at Jaja, a restaurant near his apartment in a quiet, quaint street in the Marais.

He wouldn't pick a place so close to home if he was trying to have an affair, she rationalized. *But he's French so who knows. Maybe all affairs are hidden in plain sight?*

He was already seated when she arrived. They greeted each other with kisses on both cheeks, and she sat down, feeling flushed. A bottle of Côtes du Rhône was opened on the wooden table.

"I remembered you drink red," he said, pouring her a glass. She nodded and smiled. "Good memory."

"Tell me everything about the sabbatical. I almost unfollowed you on Instagram at least twice a week, I was so jealous."

She shared all the highlights, and he listened intently, breaking eye contact only to refill her wine glass whenever it ran low. When she finished her stories, she asked him about his work, which he skimmed over quickly.

"Work is boring. My life is boring. Tell me more about you. Meet any handsome strangers on your sabbatical?"

"Sadly, no." *No way I am bringing up Axel and Ethan. That'd be a bit much.*

"That's disappointing. What about now? Are you seeing anyone?" he asked.

She shook her head and strapped on an imaginary helmet. *Here we go. Officially headed into dangerous waters and kinda looking forward to the ride.*

"I don't understand how you're perpetually single. What's your type?"

You.

"I'll be shallow and admit—part of the problem is that French men are all so short and skinny, present company excluded. I can't date someone shorter and skinnier than me. I have a firm rule: if I can't fit into their pants, they can't get into mine."

"Good rule." His eyes lit up and he nodded, feigning seriousness, and urging her to continue.

"I think French men see me as too American, too direct. But when I'm back in the States, I feel foreign. Maybe I've become someone who doesn't belong anywhere. Not sure France is my best bet for love, though. It's rough out there."

Louis's reply was quick, and it came in the form of a belted-out song. "*We are young. Heartache to heartache, we stand. No promises. No demands. Love is a battlefield.*"

Every head in the restaurant turned toward Louis as he sang. People didn't often burst into song in Parisian restaurants. She exploded into one of her big American laughs.

"Who doesn't love Pat Benatar?" he asked.

He leaned back into his seat, smiling, as her laughter died down. They held silent eye contact just long enough for it to be strange; her pulse started to race. The waitress broke the spell by setting down their appetizers, but a charge was still hanging in the air around them.

Another couple arrived and were seated at the table next to theirs, along with their dog—a small collie. The dog immediately leaned toward Austen and Louis for a sniff, and they both reached under the table to pet him. His hand quickly found hers through fingerfuls of dog hair. She could tell it was deliberate on his part; he kept his eyes on her as he simultaneously caressed the dog and her hand. She didn't pull away. She wanted to see where it led.

That night, it led to nothing. But if it had been a date, it would have been the best one she'd been on in ages. Interesting conversation, easy laughter, obvious chemistry, but he was married. She wasn't ready to cross that line, but her inner cheerleader jumped with excitement when he insisted that they get together again soon. He proposed a date on the calendar in two weeks.

His wife's next business trip?

They saw each other every few weeks for the next three months, always going out for dinner and drinks and discussing all the subjects on which relationships are built—childhood memories, relationships with their parents, their ambitions, their frustrations, and more. Each was a fantastic non-date date. The wife was always in the back of her mind, so she never invited him to her place and continued her online dating. Her stories from those dates were always the first thing Louis wanted to hear. And whether the date had gone well or horribly awry, he always said the same thing: "You deserve so much better."

She wondered. *Does he mean him?*

In between their meetings—or let's just call them dates—they texted constantly but always in the daytime and only during the week. He became a constant in her days. Every text put a smile on her face, but she knew not to text at night or on the weekend when he was presumably with his wife. She stuck by that unspoken rule, all the while wondering why she was even playing the game.

She had countless girlfriends who had gotten involved with married men in allegedly unhappy marriages. They all promised they'd leave their wives soon. It had worked out for one girl she knew. One. For the rest, she'd seen a trail of broken hearts when the guy inevitably decided he couldn't leave the wife and/or their kids.

At least Louis didn't have kids. And he was oh-so-charming. And persistent. And he sent her greetings like "hello love," which made her heart go pitter-patter.

On their fifth non-date, they sat on high stools at the dark wooden bar of Rosebud on the Rue Delambre, sipping champagne. He took her hand and turned her wrist toward him to admire her watch—the Cartier. She told him the story of how she'd gotten it, playing up some of the sexier details of the exchanges with Alain to try and get a rise out of him. She could see it working. He adjusted his sitting position multiple times throughout the story, leaning closer to her each time.

When her story was finished, he said, "I got my wedding ring at Cartier."

She held out her hand to take his. "Let's see it."

He held the back of his left hand up toward her. She froze. There was no ring on his finger.

"Did something happen? Did you two split up?" She felt something like hope rising in her chest.

"No. I just forgot to put it on tonight," he replied casually.

The cool tone of his voice and the pinched look on his face—*was it guilt?*—didn't match. His face said he'd taken it off because he was meeting her and wanted to forget he was married, at least for the night.

OK I'm going in. It's time to find out what's going on with us.

"You never talk about your wife," she said pointedly.

He crossed his arms over his chest. "I know. It intrigues you. That's why you keep coming back."

Austen was annoyed. "Is that really all you're going to say on this subject?"

"Tonight, yes. I'm sure you have your theories, and they're probably not entirely wrong. But I don't want to do this tonight. I'll tell you next time, OK?"

She simply nodded, feeling disappointed.

The next day Austen called Daphne for a debrief, playing back every word—spoken and unspoken—between her and Louis the previous night. Daphne had seen it all, both in Austen's life and in her own ups and downs with men before Jean-Marc, so Austen valued her perspective.

She concluded her play-by-play by saying, "It feels like this is a relationship. But I can't make a move on him. He's married."

Daphne sighed into the phone. "You're having an emotional affair with the guy. You've been dating him for months, without the physical thing. We're just not sure if he is also dating you."

"You think I'm imagining this whole thing?"

"I don't know," Daphne said. "You should have made a move on him months ago. Then at least you'd know. Emotional affairs are much riskier than sex for heartache. You don't actually think he's going to leave his wife, do you?"

Austen shook her head. "No. Almost certainly not. And I've never slept with a married man, on principle. I like the moral high ground of never having gone there, but what if he's worth the risk?"

"If he calls you tomorrow and wants to come over to your place, would you let him?"

"Almost definitely," Austen confessed. "Maybe it makes me weak, but I love that he pursues me. It feels good to be wanted."

"I hate to break it to you, but that moral high ground you think you're standing so firmly on is a slippery slope that you're about one boob touch away from sliding down," Daphne cracked.

Austen let out a sad laugh. "You're probably not wrong."

"Also, you say that you love that he's pursuing you, but it sounds to me like he's just encouraging you to pursue him. Maybe so he can feel like he's less to blame for what's happening between you two."

Daphne's comments burned a hole in her brain. *But what is happening between us? If only I knew.*

"He said next time we'd talk about the wife, so we'll see," Austen said.

She saw him again two weeks later for dinner at Les Fous de l'Île on the Île Saint-Louis. She noticed as soon as they sat down that his wedding ring was back on, as if it'd never left his finger. He was his usual charming self, asking about her *other* dates, talking about work, French politics, and music.

"Who do you think is the best songwriter of all time?" he asked.

"Taylor Swift, hands down," she declared.

"What? Wrong answer. It's Bob Dylan," Louis insisted.

Austen shook her head. "No one writes about love and heartbreak like Taylor. You'll never convince me otherwise."

"Love and heartbreak." He went silent and moved his leg, so it was touching hers under the table. "What am I going to do with you?"

"Isn't that the million-euro question?"

She interlaced her fingers and covered her mouth with her hands, holding in any further words. A staring contest began. She held her breath, waiting for him to finally tell her what was going on with his wife, and therefore with them.

The waiter ended the stare-down by bringing their desserts. She moved her leg away from his, feeling guilty and terribly turned on.

Louis dug into his brownie. His next words were, "Bob Dylan has written some of the absolute best…"

She didn't hear whatever he said next. All she knew was that it wasn't what she'd been waiting for. Her eyes wandered around the restaurant, which was decorated with a consistent chicken motif.

Chickens—how fitting.

They exited the restaurant and stood in the street, facing one another wordlessly. He leaned in and gave her slower-than-necessary kisses on each cheek while his hand leisurely caressed the length of her arm, finishing with a small squeeze of her hand.

"Thank you for another delicious evening. See you next time?" he asked.

She nodded and he turned away, walking toward the Pont Marie. She stood in the street, watching him leave. Her bones felt heavy, but she leaned forward on the tips of her toes. She'd been waiting two weeks—no, for months—to finally have *the* important conversation. It felt pivotal to turning this "relationship" on or off, and the need to know became urgent.

"Louis," she called after him.

He turned, and she walked with purpose, closing the distance between them, and kissing him squarely on the mouth. He responded immediately, holding on to her like his life depended on their kiss. But after about ten seconds, he pulled back with a small groan in his throat that was full of both desire and disdain.

With one hand still tangled in her hair, he said, "This is going to end badly."

Austen heard his words but saw something different in his eyes, so she decided to play it cool to give him time to think.

She put her hands up in surrender and took a step back, freeing herself from his grasp.

"OK then. It's done. That's fine. I'm sorry," she said, not meaning it at all.

He stared at her, frozen. She could see the wheels in his head turning and the desire bubbling up from his insides. She said nothing, held his gaze and waited. It took another ten seconds before he pulled her back toward him and kissed her slowly and passionately.

They kissed in the street for what seemed like forever. Austen's instincts were battling each other in her brain while they kissed.

Take him home and turn this kiss horizontal. No, Austen, don't. He said, "This is going to end badly." Believe him.

When they finally came up for air, she searched his face for a clue as to what came next. Finding none, she asked, "So now what?" There was more longing in her voice than she'd intended.

He released her and put his hands on the top of his head, looking at the sky. "I need to go home. She's there. And I need some time to think, which I can't do while looking at you and knowing what a good kisser you are. I think I'm fucked."

He reached for her, and they kissed again deeply.

"I'll call you," he promised, before turning on his heels and disappearing into the night.

Five days passed and she didn't hear a single word from Louis—not even a text. She was slowly going insane, so insisted on meeting up with a now seven-months-pregnant Daphne to try and make sense of it all. Daphne was working, so she snuck Austen into the kitchen at the Ritz and sat her on a crate of oats next to her station, as she deftly cored cherries for a clafouti.

"Well, I could say I told you so, but I'm not going to say I told you so," Daphne smiled.

"You just said it. Twice," Austen pointed out, frowning. "Why don't you take that cherry corer thingy and dig my heart out?"

"OK, drama queen. Listen, I told you emotional affairs are a killer. Case in point, you kissed once, and now you're all over the map. I'm sorry he's gone radio silent, but who knows what's going on in his head. It could be anything," Daphne offered, while chucking cherry pits into the trash. "You were bold and made a move, so one way or another, you'll have an answer soon."

Austen buried her face in her hands. "I wasn't bold. I was an idiot. I can't imagine why he would've invested all this time with me if there wasn't something there."

Daphne looked at her sympathetically. "You aren't an idiot. But because I love you and want you to be prepared for any outcome, let me say this. Married people get bored in their relationships all the time, even if they're still in love."

She paused as another chef went by her station. She gestured toward him as he passed. "That guy, for example, is a huge flirt, but he's madly in love with his wife."

"This doesn't help me at all," Austen moaned.

"Married people get curious about whether they've 'still got it.' You may be answering that question for him. All relationships serve some kind of purpose; whether it's friendship, sexual validation, love or just distraction, it could be anything. What purpose is he serving for you?"

"He's great. And I'm lonely," Austen admitted, in a moment of extreme candor.

Daphne put down the cherries, washed her hands, and grabbed Austen by the shoulders. "Don't you realize that you're in better company alone than being with someone who only gives you a fraction of themselves? You're better than this. And after months of what he *clearly knows* has been something, he's ghosting you. He's not *that* great."

As Daphne returned to the clafouti, Austen contemplated the question of purpose, and her mind took an unexpected detour toward Kevin. Despite his actions, she'd been convinced that he felt the same thing she did when they were in Europe. After he left, he continued to reach out to her regularly, and she interpreted each of those hellos as "I'm missing you and us." But then, he barely gave her the time of day when she was in Sydney.

A realization hit her hard.

All those texts over all those months were probably just him and his ego needing a dopamine hit, wanting to know that someone somewhere wanted him. That was the purpose I served for him, and man, did I do it well. I was a fool.

Her mind then traveled to Cambodia and the Teaching Buddha, whose message about living life without excuses she'd seemingly forgotten. She realized she'd been making excuses for both Louis and Kevin—for their selfish handling of her heart. A text, an email, another maddeningly beautiful non-date date—all niceties that ultimately meant nothing. Each one she'd lapped up because she was lonely or bored or both. And in her mind, some attention had been better than none.

But now, as she looked at it all through the lens of excuses, she could make no more for Kevin or Louis or, more importantly, for herself. She wanted to scream. The thing with Louis had gone on for months, and the moment she pressed the issue, he bolted. There was no acceptable excuse for five days of radio silence. It was harsh—not how people who cared for each other handled things. She decided right then and there that she was done with Louis.

Austen let out a sigh of relief. "Daphne, you're so right. Damn it. I'm done accepting scraps. I deserve someone who will, without hesitation or caveat, choose me."

Daphne nodded. "Yes. Good of you to remember that."

Austen left Daphne at the Ritz, feeling clear-headed but angry. She flopped into an Uber to head home.

"So, Austen. You're American?" the driver asked, watching her in his rearview mirror.

"Yes," she confirmed. No French women were named Austen.

"French husband?"

"No husband," she replied curtly. She wasn't in the mood to talk.

"Boyfriend?"

"No." *Leave me alone.*

"Why?" he asked.

She shook her head and sighed deeply. "Just haven't found him yet."

The driver adjusted the rearview mirror to look her in the eye. "No, madam, he hasn't found *you*. He's looking for you, I promise."

It was the perfect response.

The right guy is looking for me. No more excuses for anything less.

She closed her eyes and let that resolution sink deep into her bones. By the time she arrived home, she was resolute—she would no longer accept this kind of bullshit in her life. She felt the bad habit fall off her like a second skin. It felt raw, but there was strength in it too.

Louis sent a text four days later, after nine days of cold silence.

Can I see you?

No apology. No context. No shame. Austen didn't respond, and he let her go without a fight, just as she knew he would.

CHAPTER TWENTY-FOUR

The Internet, Round Three

Something in Austen had known not to wait for Louis. She'd continued her Internet dating even while she was "dating" him, and the best thing she could say about it was that it made good fodder for her blog.

"Isn't Paris supposed to be the most romantic place on Earth?" Liz asked one day while they were catching up via FaceTime.

"Whoever created that marketing campaign for Paris deserves two things. First, an award for creating a universally believed image out of a truly stunning set of lies. But second, some serious jail time for the transgression," Austen exclaimed.

She knew no one who had ever been picked up in a charming French café while drinking a coffee or a glass of wine and then fallen madly in love. It happened in nearly every movie set in Paris, but never in real life.

Austen's friend Julia had been on dating apps for years and treated it like a second job and a source of entertainment. One of her strategies was to always have an "unexpected" question on hand, to make the online conversation less mundane.

Austen liked the idea and had adopted "What was your last Google search?" as hers. She liked it as a question because even if his last search had been for porn, he could choose anything as a reply, to at least *seem* interesting.

It also worked well to filter out the duds. When she asked the question to one particularly hunky fireman, he replied that he didn't understand why she was asking.

"Just a conversation starter," she answered, trying to explain without sounding patronizing.

He replied, "I don't know why that's relevant."

She sighed and unmatched him. He made her think of one of her favorite cartoon characters—Happy Bunny, a deeply sarcastic and slightly mean rabbit. Her favorite quote of his was "Let's not bore each other. You start." The fireman had flamed out.

She reentered the wretched online dating scene with the intention to be nothing but herself, deciding that if a guy wasn't interested in who she really was (70-plus countries traveled and all), she was wasting her time.

Isobel had told her once, "If someone thinks you're 'too much,' they're simply not enough. You do you."

Austen had very wise friends. And so she went, once more into the breach.

Marc, or was it, Julien? May 20

Bonjour, dear readers! Sorry, I've been away for a while, but I've been AWAY. I had the glorious opportunity to take a sabbatical from work, so I spent a few months traveling in Asia. Therefore, the blog had to take a sabbatical too. Did you think maybe I'd met someone wonderful and fallen in love? Oh, if only your beautifully optimistic hearts had been right. But no. I'm back in Paris and back on the dating scene, so here we go again.

Marc had just moved to town from Martinique. I've found that new arrivals tend to be a bit softer and kinder in how they play the dating game. Paris hardens people. He even made a classy and interesting choice on where we'd meet—La Coupole—a Parisian art deco institution since 1927, where I'd never been.

One of the first things Marc told me was that he was using the apps to build his Paris network. He was looking for friends just as much as a potential girlfriend. By the time the first glass of wine had been poured, I'd decided he wasn't a match for me. I wasn't attracted to him—at all. It happens. But I decided to stay open to the possibility of friendship. He seemed like a nice enough guy.

He was very curious about my experience as an online dater. Generally, when a guy asks me about my experience on the apps, I'm not impressed. Why ask me about my dates with other guys when *we're* on a date? But since I already wasn't interested in dating him, I decided it would be a unique opportunity to learn about the male perspective of this weird online dating dance.

He told me he'd met several women with fake profiles that bore no resemblance to reality. They turned up looking nothing like their pictures. They lied about their jobs or their age. One asked him if she could borrow some money while on their date. Another provided a specific list of gifts she wanted to receive, should they begin dating. The crazy list went on. Clearly, this online dating bonanza isn't easy on either side!

He told me that I was the most "normal" person he'd met so far, who looked and acted the same both online and in reality. Yay me? And then he said, "By the way, I should probably tell you now that my name isn't Marc. It's Julien."

I burst out laughing and said incredulously, "Really? Right now, in the middle of a conversation about the preponderance of fake profiles and crazy people doing crazy things, you're going to change your name? You do see the irony here, right?"

He attempted to defend the name change, claiming in a very circuitous way that Marc was a logical nickname (for Julien?) while also expressing concerns about his online privacy.

None of it made the slightest bit of sense, and it was more than my beleaguered online dating soul could take. Marc/Julien was done. The search continues for someone who can keep it real.

#parisdatingdisasters

Xavier, the Sexist   June 7

Occasionally, dear readers, I doubt myself. Is my list of rules too long? Am I missing out on good guys that maybe just don't look good on paper? I was in this frame of mind when I matched with Xavier. In the bare minimum of exchanges, I discovered we were neighbors, so when he very quickly asked me out, I decided to throw caution to the wind and meet him the next day for a drink.

Normally, I would've done more of a pre-qualification, but for whatever reason, the date was on. All I knew was that he lived nearby and bore a striking resemblance to Ryan Gosling, which I had made a mental note of even before he casually pointed it out.

We agreed to meet at the Parc Georges Brassens, just a few minutes from where I live. Two hours before the date, he texted me.

So how does it feel to have a
date with the best-looking guy
in Paris's 15th arrondissement?

I rolled my eyes so hard I almost pulled my eye muscles and seriously contemplated canceling but chose to reply, working against my better instincts.

Modest, I see!

He claimed it was a joke, but by that point, I was officially not feeling great about the prospects of the afternoon. I arrived at the entrance to the park and, seeing no sign of him, sat down on a bench to wait. Immediately my phone rang.

"I see you. I'm by the fountain. Come on in," he said.

I got up feeling slightly awkward, knowing he was watching me walk toward him, well before I was able to spot him. We'd agreed to meet outside the park gates, presumably to head to one of the two cafés just opposite, but clearly, he had other ideas.

We said our hellos, sat down on the bench, and started the small talk. He said he'd brought a blanket if we wanted to sit on the grass and talk, or we could go to a café as we'd discussed. I was wearing a short dress, so I pointed out that sitting on the ground maybe wasn't ideal.

"Don't worry. I won't look," he replied.

So, the grass it was! Awesome.

The small talk shifted to work, and he told me about how he'd just been let go from his job. He was pretty incredulous about it, saying that the boss had it out for him and spending a lot of energy explaining the office politics between this guy and that girl and the other one, none of whom I knew, obviously. He was clearly not happy with the situation, so I tried to turn the conversation around by asking him what he loved to do and, therefore, what he thought he might do next.

"I'll stay doing what I'm doing now, of course. But there are just not that many jobs out there where you make 100,000 euros a year," he replied.

French discussions of money have always fascinated me. Some claim that the subject is totally taboo—that no one talks about how much money they make. But Xavier wasn't the first man to tell me his salary very early in a potential relationship. It was weird.

But the conversation continued, and about an hour into the date and pretty much out of nowhere, he said, "I find you very agreeable. I think we should see each other again. Do you agree?"

I hesitated for a bit too long, and he looked genuinely perplexed by my reluctance. Furrowed brow and everything. I decided to proceed with caution as my Spidey senses had started to tingle.

"I'm not sure yet," I replied, honestly.

"Why?" he demanded to know.

They say feedback is a gift, so I decided to just shoot straight.

"Well, Xavier, I mentioned that sitting on the grass wasn't ideal for me since I'm wearing this dress, and yet here we are. I've mentioned twice that I recently went on a great vacation, and you didn't even ask me where I went. And you've spent most of the past hour talking about yourself, so I think that maybe you're just a little too focused on you."

"That's just not right," he returned snippily. "We've only been talking for an hour, and of course, I was going to ask about you eventually. You can't decide that I'm not for you after only an hour."

I decided not to tell him it usually took 15 minutes or less for me to know if there was going to be a second date. But he spent the *next* 15 minutes explaining that we were both attractive, smart, and interesting, so clearly, we were a great match.

I played nice and eventually made my excuses to go, saying I had plans to meet a friend. He asked me again as I said goodbye if we were going out again. I smiled, said we'd text, and walked away. And then the text storm started.

I said I'd like to see you again,
with pleasure. So, the ball is
in your court.

I admit I don't understand
your hesitation but will respect
it, of course, if you don't want
to see me.

But at least my point of view
is clear.

I didn't respond straight away because (a) I wasn't interested but also (b) I was indeed in transit to meet my friend. And then, 30 minutes later, a second ping:

I'm waiting for an answer. It's
not normal to hesitate when
a date was that good on so
many key criteria.

It's a yes or a no. Don't
overcomplicate things.

> Listen, Xavier, it's a no. You're a
> nice guy but not a match for me.
> Sorry. Wishing you lots of luck
> personally and professionally.

And then the texts just started flying in, one after another:

Can you tell me why?

I'm bilingual, good job, good-
looking Parisian guy.

So, where is the problem?

It's frankly humiliating for me.

Who do you think you are?

I'm not enough for you?

Incredible. I've never
experienced anything like this.

No wonder you're alone. You
must have a crazy collection
of sex toys!

Incredible

Too bad I was only interested
in your big boobs anyway.

Bye

But I want a valid reason. I
can't believe you walked away
from me like that.

No one does that to me.

> The "bye" followed by the "but I want a valid reason" was truly
> where he hit his low point, and he'd already set the bar quite
> low. And it wasn't over.

I'm waiting for a reason. Or
several. Go ahead.

I'm waiting. I hate cowards.

So?

What is your problem?

Is it that I make more money
than you?

> After that last message, I blocked him. And not because he *didn't* have a good job or make more money than me. But really, in the history of time, has *any* woman *ever* had a problem with a guy making more money than her? It was all just so ridiculous.

> I briefly considered sending him a reply saying, "Oh honey, you don't make more money than me." Or perhaps less snarkily, "Remember an hour ago when you said you'd respect my choice if I didn't want to see you again? Is this what you think respect looks like?"

> But the poor thing was clearly a fragile narcissist with anger management issues—and my neighbor—so I decided the better choice was to take the high road and put a giant roadblock up behind myself so he couldn't pass. Now, I just have to pray to the gods of the 15th arrondissement that we never cross paths in the streets close to home.

#parisdatingdisasters

Guillaume of the Gym Shorts   June 21

Guillaume suggested we meet at the Metro stop. *Oh God, not again*, I thought to myself. I almost canceled, but once more, I failed to trust The Rules. **Spoiler alert** It was a mistake. Clearly, I am an overly hopeful idiot. In an admittedly weak attempt at my own defense, it was a beautiful summer night, and he'd picked the Odéon Metro, which is surrounded by a lot of good places—some of my favorites, in fact.

We'd been chatting online a decent amount. He worked in commercial real estate and seemed to have a decent head on his shoulders, and not an unattractive one at that. He was also allegedly in his early 40s, but when he showed up, I was sure he couldn't be a day over 27. Normally when people lie about their age online, it's in the other direction, wanting to be younger, right? This one was breaking that rule too, but more than the shocking lack of facial hair, I was dumbstruck by his outfit.

He was wearing what French men wear to the gym—a short sleeve white polo shirt, khaki shorts, and white tennis shoes. I must've given him a full up-and-down stare of disbelief because he quickly and happily announced he'd just left the gym.

Thanks for the effort, I thought to myself, cringing. For the record, I was properly dressed for a date. I was wearing perfectly hip-hugging dark denim jeans, a sleek white top that showed just a hint of cleavage, a black blazer, and high-heeled boots. Expectations were clearly misaligned.

After the pleasantries of nice to meet you, etc., I asked if he had any idea of where he'd like to go. He looked at me, raised two fingers into a V shape, and pointed them to my eyes. "Right there," he said with a smarmy smile.

I almost barfed on his white tennis shoes before replying, "Well, there's not a lot to do there, so what's plan B?"

He was another one from whom I should have immediately turned on my heeled boots and walked away, but my upbringing wouldn't let me. Damn Southern manners. Note to self: you really must get rid of those; they're not serving you well.

We wandered around (as—surprise—he had no plan) and settled on a relatively charmless sidewalk café where we ordered two glasses of Beaujolais. Over wine and small talk, he eventually asked if I wanted to see a magic trick. My immediate thought was to look around for Ashton Kutcher, wondering if I was being punk'd or on some other form of Candid Camera. But sadly, no. Guillaume just didn't get it.

He pulled a deck of cards, a pen, and a piece of paper out of the pocket of his gym shorts (what?) and asked me to write down a number on the paper, fold it up and put it under my glass. I did as instructed, and he proceeded to do something with cards that eventually matched my number. I wish I could retell the story better, but honestly, I'm not sure what the hell he did. The whole thing was weird.

Our one-hour date was exactly 59 minutes too long. No more exceptions to rule #11 will ever be made. I know I said that once before, but this time I really mean it.

#parisdatingdisasters

Parker, the Long-Distance Loser   July 19

I travel around Europe a lot for work, and with French men continuing to disappoint, I started to consider trying to date men in neighboring countries. Dutch men are really tall, which I love. There's a (more or less) common mother tongue with the Brits. And Brussels was a quick train ride away. I'm in all three countries fairly regularly, so the logistics seemed manageable. I started to experiment, swiping left and right while on the road. I had a few matches, but work trips are always jam-packed with meetings and dinners that don't leave a lot of time for spontaneous dating.

Just when I was about to give up on the idea of long-distance love, I got a ping from Parker, a guy I'd met a year earlier in Palm Springs at a friend's birthday weekend. I was totally crushing on someone else at the time, so I'd barely clocked Parker, but it turns out he had definitely clocked me.

After that weekend in the desert, Parker sent me a Facebook friend request. He had sent me the odd Facebook message from time to time. I could tell he was interested, but he wasn't pushing it and he was in Boston. Our conversations had all been fairly benign. However, this time, I was feeling open to faraway possibilities.

Maybe he's the hidden gem that's been lurking right under my nose for a year, I told myself optimistically. Silly me.

After some small talk back and forth, he asked me if I was seeing anyone. When I said no, he said, "Well, this may be strange, but I've been wanting to ask you out for a year. Would you consider a trip to Boston?"

I was flattered but found the idea of taking a transatlantic flight for a date a bit desperate. I started to hedge, so he came in with the hard sell.

He typed, "You wore a lacy black bra under a white shirt the night we met. I remember it like it was yesterday. I asked Logan about you that night because I thought you were beautiful, funny, and interesting. I remember catching your eye for a few seconds across the room after dinner that night. You smiled at me, and my heart skipped a beat. But then you left with some other guy from the group. I've thought about it a million times and regretted not coming after you."

It takes a lot to render me speechless, but that did it.

"How about a video chat/date to start?" he proposed.

I was stunned that someone I'd met once a year earlier had been working up the nerve to ask me out ever since, so, despite the ocean between us, I agreed. We set it for a few days later on a Sunday, when the six-hour time difference would matter less.

Sunday rolled around, and I got ready for my video date as if it were a real one. I put on a shirt with a pretty neckline, carefully did my makeup, and even painted my fingernails. With all conventional methods of meeting people failing me, I was ready to give this a go.

And then he stood me up.

I sent him a text ten minutes after our appointed time, trying to strike a light note.

> Stuck in traffic on your way to meet me? 😊

Thirty minutes later, when he still hadn't replied, I wrote again.

> I guess I got stood up? Hope you're OK.

I went to sleep that night feeling disappointed and confused, but assuming there must be an explanation. After all, he'd been waiting a year for his shot with me. I woke up the next morning to a text.

Hi Austen. I'm so sorry. It's been a really hard weekend. A good friend of mine got into a bad car accident. I need a few days to regroup. I won't ever do that again. Can't wait to talk.

Forgive me?

Of course I did and felt a bit relieved. If ever there was a legit excuse for standing someone up, that was it. And so, we rescheduled for the coming weekend.

How about 4 p.m. my time on Saturday or any time on Sunday?

4 p.m. for you is 10 p.m. for me, so I'll probably be out on Saturday, and even if I'm not, it's a bit late to start a date, so let's do Sunday, your morning.

Why don't you just ping me whenever you're up on Sunday morning, and we can be spontaneous?

Perfect. I'll call you then.

The next Sunday rolled around, and I again went through the routine of "date prep" and was all dressed up with no-where to go, from his 9 a.m., which was 3 p.m. my time. I kept the phone nearby and waited. And waited. Seven hours later, when it hit 10 p.m. my time, there may have been actual steam coming out of my ears. I was furious, having now been stood up twice.

I think this is something guys don't understand about dating. When a girl gets ready for a date, she typically puts in some serious prep—hair, makeup, clothes, nails. I'll admit I didn't bother shaving my legs for the video date, but other than that, I'd gone through the whole process twice, to be left sitting alone on my couch. Have I mentioned how much I hate wasted time? I'm a busy girl with a busy calendar, and when I carve out time for someone, I expect them to show up. And not be wearing gym shorts. Is this too much to ask? No, my friends. It is not.

He did eventually call, 40 minutes later. When I saw his name light up my phone, I angrily hit decline. He sent a follow-up text.

I just tried you on FaceTime. It said the call was declined. It might be a bit late for you. Headed out now but will try you again tomorrow. Sweet dreams!

I responded immediately.

When you proposed 4 p.m. on Saturday, I told you 10 p.m. my time was probably too late to start. So you called me at 10:40 p.m. today? After standing me up last Sunday and agreeing we'd speak today in your morning?

It's 4:40 in the afternoon in
Boston.

Not cool. Really, don't bother
calling tomorrow.

His reply annoyed me even more.

I guess I lost track of time.
And my stand-up was a
pretty unique situation, in my
opinion. But, I'll leave you be.

Not even a hint of an apology or a mea culpa or anything resem-
bling an explanation for why the whole concept of "his morning"
was too much to handle. A guy who claimed to have been pining over me for a year effectively stood me up *twice*. For a
video date. Nothing about this makes any sense to me or to
any of my friends to whom I have retold this tale. The mys-
teries of the male species—French, American, pretty much
all of them—keep piling up, with no answers to be found, no
matter how hard or where I look. I'm starting to think I should
just stop looking.

#parisVIDEOdatingdisasters

Emile, the Over-Sharer   August 5

And yet, I keep looking because I really do want to find love. I own it. And so, the search swipes on.

Things with Emile were going relatively well. He was in his late 40s and a musician, a profession for which I have a lifelong weakness. We'd even made it to a *third* drink at the Terrass" Bar in Montmartre. The majority of my dates are "one drink and done," so I was feeling good. The conversation was easy and interesting, although I was still on the fence about whether I was attracted to him. But I'd pushed that to the side, enjoying his sense of humor and storytelling. I believe attraction can build over time as you get to know someone.

While on the topic of past relationships, I casually mentioned that I had been married once and asked if he had. He hadn't. With two and a half glasses of wine flowing through my veins, I decided to dig a bit deeper and asked how long his longest relationship had been. Nine months, he said. He readily acknowledged that wasn't long, so I felt like I had an opening to ask one more question. "So why do you think that is—that you've never had a long relationship?"

"Well, I was the product of my mother's one-night stand, so as a result, she basically never loved me, and that has damaged all my relationships with women and probably always will," he stated, all in one breath.

I instantly regretted the question. I *had* asked, and gosh, if that wasn't an honest answer, but the alarm bells were going off in my head. I looked over my shoulder at the door and briefly considered running, but then I felt really sorry for the guy. His mother never loved him? It's utterly tragic, of course, but really, who is that honest about their damage on a first date?

"Do you want to see a picture of her?" he asked.

The look on his face made me feel like he was reverting back to his traumatic childhood right before my eyes.

"Of your mother?" I asked, not quite believing where this was headed.

And sure enough, he pulled out his phone and showed me not one but eight pictures of his mother. I give the guy all the credit in the world for his self-awareness of the root cause of all his relationship issues, but wow, this was some serious mama drama! It was like he ripped the invisibility cloak from Harry Potter off his invisible baggage a bit too soon, exposing himself to a mere Muggle who knew no magic. I want to be a believer in magic, but with this one, I just couldn't. It was too much.

#parisdatingdisasters

Emile had Austen's head spinning for some time after the date, as she homed in on one true difference between herself and the majority of French men she was meeting. It was a fundamental difference in world view. Hers was one of inherent optimism and belief that good things were always ahead. Emile, and many French people, seemed to live under a dark cloud of inherent pessimism.

Where is the light, Frenchies?

A few days later, she sat in Café Bonaparte reading an interview in a newspaper with French author Sylvain Tesson. He coined the phrase "France is a paradise inhabited by people who believe they're in hell." It struck her like a cultural lightning bolt of truth.

In the interview, Tesson explained that he'd come to this conclusion after extensive travels abroad. He now understood how good life is in France—universal healthcare, excellent public education, heavily subsidized childcare, remarkable unemployment benefits, not to mention all the incredible food, wine, and culture. Despite it all, he noticed that the French too often exhibit an inherent displeasure with their lives.

The cultural gap between Austen and France felt like it was growing wider. Was she doomed for being an optimist? She'd been playing the Parisian dating game for three years now, and she was losing. *I hate losing.* The last "relationship" she'd had was two years ago with Grégoire, the radio guy. Thinking back, she realized she hadn't had a second date since him. The thought was almost enough to knock the optimism right out of her head.

CHAPTER TWENTY-FIVE

Office Romance

Late September

Chiara and Austen sat by the window at La Boissonnerie after stopping by the hospital to meet Daphne and Jean-Marc's adorable baby girl, who they'd named Sylvie. The two women were deep into conversation and deep into the bottle when they heard a tap at the window from outside. They looked up startled, ready to be outraged by this strange break in French decorum, when she saw Bastien smiling at her, clearly drunk. She waved him and his friend inside.

The guys slurred their bonjours and clumsily pulled over two chairs. She'd never seen Bastien drunk or even unshaven. He was always so buttoned-up in the office, but today, she was seeing a different side of the man. Austen couldn't decide if he seemed happy or sad. Mostly he just seemed drunk.

Once they were seated, Bastien tried for some semblance of sobriety, rather formally introducing his friend to Austen. "Thomas, please allow me to introduce Austen Keller of the Texas Kellers."

A flicker of recognition flashed on Thomas's face as Austen leaned in for the traditional French hello of kisses on both cheeks.

"So, this is Austen." He nodded with a jagged smile to himself and then turned to Bastien. "Yeah, I get it now."

Bastien kicked his friend under the table and shot daggers at him with his eyes. He wasn't sober enough to be subtle.

Austen suddenly felt very awkward, but her good friend stepped in.

"I'm Chiara. Lovely to meet you both. We're drinking a gorgeous Pinot Noir from Burgundy. Shall we get two more glasses?"

"Yes, let's. We're celebrating," Bastien announced as he tousled his hair violently.

Austen flagged the waiter. "Great, what's the occasion?"

"My bitch of a soon-to-be-ex-wife is banging some other guy and leaving me. We're drinking to their future happiness." His voice dripped with sarcasm and hurt.

"Oh God, Bastien. I'm so sorry." Austen's eyes went wide, and her hand reflexively covered her mouth. "I don't know what else to say."

She knew nothing about Bastien's wife or their marriage, so she was at a loss. Chiara was equally stunned into silence. Thomas wasn't helping. He simply stared at the exposed beams in the ceiling.

Bastien's eyes seemed to go in and out of focus while she searched his face. His mouth opened as if to say something, then snapped closed as he looked between her and Thomas.

Just as the waitress set down the two extra glasses, Bastien grabbed his friend's arm and stood, dragging him out of his chair. "We've gotta go. Sorry."

Thomas shrugged at Austen and Chiara over his shoulder, and the two men disappeared into the Parisian evening.

"Poor guy. But quite good-looking. And seemingly single now," Chiara said with a smirk.

"You think he's cute?" Austen asked. The pity she felt for him was quickly replaced by curiosity. "I've never thought about him that way."

"Maybe you should start. His friend had clearly heard your name before. Maybe he's got a crush," she theorized.

On Monday, back in the office, Bastien stopped by her desk mid-morning, leaning in for what she knew would be a quiet apology.

"I'm so sorry about that scene on Saturday. I'm embarrassed."

Austen waved her hand dismissively. "Don't be. Already forgotten. It was nothing."

He nodded with a tense smile and quickly walked away.

For the next few weeks, she had the impression he was avoiding her. She figured his pride was suffering, so she gave him a wide berth; however, she often found herself watching him when he moved around the office. She wondered how he was coping with his heartbreak.

Chiara's comments had led her to notice things about him she'd never seen before, like how there was a bit of red in the stubble on his chin at the end of a day, and how his hands seemed rougher than the hands of someone who worked at a computer for a living. She'd started to wonder what he did with those hands when he was outside of the office.

Maybe he has an ancient French country house where he spends his weekends refurbishing things and working in the garden. I miss having a garden. That could be nice.

She was doing it again—fanning the flames of her imagination. Her inner storyteller had crafted many magical tales over the years about her future happiness with one guy or another. The stories she'd imagined with Sam and with Kevin were worthy of Scheherazade, without the happy ending.

Reflecting on this bad and overly romantic habit, she told herself to stop thinking about Bastien that way. *Office drama is the last thing I need. And he's been nothing but professional, albeit slightly on edge, since "the incident."*

She'd seen him snap unnecessarily at a few underlings in recent weeks, probably taking out his personal frustrations on the poor young things that got in his way. He always caught himself after and apologized, but she could tell he was tense. Remembering her own state of mind after her heartbreaks, she empathized.

Six weeks later, François pulled Austen and Bastien into a meeting to brief them on an upcoming event.

"I've agreed to host a full-day event at the Louvre in January, focused on European sustainability efforts. It's going to be attended by a lot of high-level people from business and government, as well as some royalty and celebrities. I want a full day of meetings booked." François looked pointedly at Bastien. "You can skip the celebrities for the meetings."

He nodded. "Understood."

"I'm going to have to open various sessions throughout the day, meaning quite a few speeches and a lot of protocol around the government dignitaries. And that evening, there'll be a black-tie gala, honoring a set of these people for their contributions to the cause. I'm hosting that one too," he explained.

"Sounds exciting. When can we dig in?" Austen asked.

"I'll send you an email with the contact details for the organizers. I need you both all over this ASAP. There's a lot of potentially very valuable connections to be made there for our business," François said.

Austen left the meeting smiling at Bastien like a goofball and buzzing with energy. *It's not every day one gets to be at the Louvre in formal wear,* she thought.

"This is going to be amazing and way better than Davos for the famous people factor. I wonder if Leo will be there," she enthused.

He rolled his eyes. "You're such an American. It's going to be a lot of late nights, you know."

"I know, but we'll smash it and have fun along the way," she assured him.

Things between her and Bastien remained entirely professional over the next intense weeks of prep. But as Christmas approached, she felt like something had shifted in their relationship.

Maybe we're becoming friends?

They were working together better than ever, sharing their wins and their challenges as the event took shape. His small displays of impatience had started to wane, but late at night when they were both still in the office grinding through work, he occasionally seemed a bit tortured. It made her want to comfort him.

They worked all through the Christmas break, and before they knew it, the big event was only two weeks away. They'd been asked to attend a smaller-scale and significantly less formal event at the Louvre, to help them get the lay of the land. It was a dry run of sorts.

They spent the afternoon moving around the facilities with the event staff, watching how foot traffic flowed between the event spaces, noting transit times between venues, and walking all the public and staff passageways to determine the best routes for getting François from one meeting to the next. The logistics needed to be flawless, as his schedule was tightly packed. They spoke with the tech crew, and tested lighting and acoustics in the bigger rooms that weren't in use for that day's event.

They'd walked the length of the event space about 25 times that afternoon when the evening event set-up started, and a waiter passed by with a tray of champagne flutes.

"I'm just going to grab two of those," Bastien casually yet confidently said to the waiter. Glasses in hand, he turned to Austen. "Let's grab our coats, take these, and duck into that side garden we passed earlier for some fresh air."

Austen was dead on her feet, so she welcomed the suggestion, and the two headed off down the long, carpeted corridor. As he opened the door, the winter air hit her face, sending a charge of energy back into her tired body.

He sat on a stone bench and motioned for her to join him. "You've been incredible on literally everything that's been required to get this event together."

Tucking her scarf into the collar of her coat, she looked up at the blue-gray winter sky. "I appreciate that, especially from you. It's been fantastic working with you on this thing. I've learned a ton, and we're ready. It's going to be epic. So yeah, we should probably start a mutual appreciation society."

She turned toward him, smiling with the satisfied confidence and the nervous energy she always felt before a big event. He looked back in a way that destabilized her. His eyes were soft, and his lips parted. It was a look of barely masked, unmistakable desire. She looked away, suddenly feeling tension hanging in the air. He stayed quiet.

Where did that look come from? Is it what I think it is?

Curiously and cautiously, she allowed herself to look back toward him.

"To be honest, I've been a close observer of your work— no, of *you*—for a very long time. I remember the day you breezed into our hallway to join the team. You were all light and energy, and I felt somewhat blinded. And not entirely in a good way," he admitted.

She could feel him building toward something, and her insides were in tumult, unsure of what was coming.

"I'm Parisian. We don't do light and energy. We do conflicted and broody," he quipped.

She laughed to try and break the tension, but also because what he said was true, even more so since his split from his ex. There was something hard about him, which she found herself wanting to soften. Humor was her tool of choice.

"The grand irony of the City of Light is that you don't 'do light.' No wonder I always feel like I'm flying blind."

His brow crinkled. "I hate that you feel that way about Paris, but I guess I get it. You're an anomaly, but one I've always been drawn to. When I was allegedly happily married, it was easy to brush it off as cultural curiosity about the oddly sunny American in our hallways."

Austen wasn't sure she was ready to go wherever he was leading her, so she turned the conversation back toward him.

"I'm really sorry about what happened with your ex-wife."

He stood up and started to pace around the small garden. "Soon-to-be-ex-wife. Technically we're still married, but anyway, I'm not sorry. It was a blessing in disguise. We didn't want the same things."

She nodded. "I get that. Same thing happened with my ex-husband."

"I remember when you got divorced. One day I noticed you weren't wearing a ring anymore, but I never dared to ask what happened. How'd you figure it out—that you didn't want the same things?"

"One session of marriage counseling," she replied. "The counselor asked what I wanted out of life, and I said I wanted to try, taste, see, smell, and enjoy absolutely everything life had to offer and slide into home plate at the end utterly spent and blissfully happy."

A smile crept across Bastien's face. "There's all that blinding light again."

He's got a pretty sexy smile. Oh man.

Austen pretended to ignore his comment and continued. "The counselor asked him how that made him feel, and he said, 'Like we're completely fucked.'"

"Ouch. Are you sure he wasn't French? He sounds French." Bastien offered her a pained look while he tried to suppress a laugh.

"Nope, definitely American. He wasn't a bad guy. He just wasn't *my* guy," she said.

He returned to the bench and sat down beside her, taking a deep breath. "Do you think maybe *I* could be your guy?"

Chiara was right. Woah.

Looking at her openly, he confessed, "Over these past few weeks, as we've spent all this time together and gotten to know each other better, my interest in you has only grown."

She was stunned, speechless and frozen by his boldness and the winter air. Her teeth started to chatter. *I did not see this one coming.*

"Sorry, you're freezing. Let's go inside."

He opened the door back into the museum and let her go in first. The wheels in her head spun at the speed of a Le Mans racecar. She hadn't yet found her words.

Closing the door behind them, he said, "I get that we work together, and that can be complicated, but watching you float through these hallowed halls today, I decided I had to take the leap. So, here I go. Can I take you to dinner some night soon, with entirely unprofessional intentions? Say yes."

He landed his request with such confidence. She found it irresistible.

"OK, yes. But—"

He jumped on top of the word. "No buts. Let me just hang onto the yes. We'll take it slow."

She couldn't stop her mouth from opening and putting another "OK but—" into the air between them. He quickly reached out and lightly pressed her lips closed between his freezing thumb and forefinger, smiling.

She wanted to set some ground rules—to try to control the direction or the speed of whatever was coming—but he clearly wasn't going to let her. Her thoughts were zigzagging through her head, but with her lips held lightly closed and an intriguingly playful look in Bastien's light brown eyes, she decided to put them away for now.

She nodded, so he let go of her lips which quickly curled into a smile.

"So that's settled then. Excellent. I think it's time we get out of here. It's been a long day." He gestured toward the exit, and they set off walking silently, side by side.

When they reached the taxi queue, he opened the car door for her and then leaned in to give her the traditional goodbye kisses on each cheek, which they'd never done at work. The custom was social, not professional. He then picked up her hand and kissed it lightly. "I'll look at my calendar and text you a date or two for our dinner?"

"Sounds good. Have a good evening," she said, climbing into the cab.

As the car pulled out, she turned to watch him walk away, with a decided spring in his step. She abruptly faced forward and felt every muscle in her body tense. *What just happened?* She was suddenly a bundle of nerves and wasn't sure if they were the good or the bad kind.

He's smart, confident, tall, and cultured. On paper, he's perfect—other than the small technicality of him still being married. That'll be sorted soon enough. And that we work together. Is that why I'm hesitating or is it something else?

It was time to bring in the big guns for counsel.

Two nights later, she met Chiara and Isobel for dinner at Freddy's, their favorite haunt for small plates and amazing wine on Rue de Seine. They sat at "their" table—the round wooden one in the far back corner where they always felt at home. Austen recounted her conversation with Bastien from earlier in the week, as well as her apprehensions.

Isobel was first to state one potentially obvious issue. "You've been single for a long time. Do you think maybe you're just nervous that you've finally met someone *right* for you, and what that might mean for your sense of independence and control? I think you might just be nervous about letting someone else in."

She'd considered that fear—not just with Bastien but with others who had come before him. She'd grown exceptionally used to her own company and having her own space. Kevin moving the shampoo in her bathroom had freaked her out.

Chiara supported Isobel's theory and pushed Austen to let this one play out. "What have you got to lose? He's very good-looking, smart, and not intimidated by you. All good things."

"I think the thing that I like the most about him in this particular moment is that he's choosing me. In the relationship game, I feel like I'm back in middle school, being picked last or never for kickball on the playground." Austen reflected quietly while sipping her wine. She could feel them waiting for her to finish her thought. "Here's someone finally choosing me, but I can't decide if I'm just grateful to be chosen, or if I'm excited about playing the game."

Chiara was quick to jump in. "You're always telling me to have fun until I'm not having fun anymore. Follow your own advice. Go play the game. It's a date, not a marriage proposal."

"Fishing off the office pier is risky," Austen said.

"Yes, OK but remember, the game here in France is simple," Isobel reminded her. "Maybe you'll be a couple after the first date, but you can end it as quickly as it begins if you want to. It doesn't have to be dramatic. Be smart but roll with it."

And so, she decided to roll.

Bastien proposed that they wait until after the big event for their date, knowing they'd both be working long hours until then.

Practical, she told herself, *and it gives me a bit more time to think.*

As the days ticked by, he got even bolder, sending flirty texts from down the hall or even from across the conference room table during meetings. They were sweet and felt like courtship—not like the aggressive attempts to lead into sexting that had become all too commonplace in her online dating interactions. He texted things like:

You should wear that color
of blue more often. It really
brings out your eyes.

For all the time I've spent
observing you, how have I
never noticed the freckles on
your neck?

Can you please repeat here
via text whatever you just said
in this meeting that everyone
seemed so excited about? I
was very carefully watching
your lips move but somehow
didn't hear a word you said.

With each exchange, her heart opened a bit more to whatever was happening between them.

We've been working together for three years. How am I only seeing his charms now?

After her divorce, Austen had subscribed to the theory that if a relationship didn't start in an explosion of fireworks, there was a very small chance that the passion would continue to burn for the long term. She and Brad had started off as friends, after all, and the flames went out of that relationship very quickly.

But there are exceptions to every rule, so let's give this one a chance.

CHAPTER TWENTY-SIX

A Night at the Louvre

January

The big day finally arrived, and everything was running smoothly. Austen and Bastien worked side by side to help François be the perfect emcee, and he was infinitely pleased with the business opportunities being surfaced. He'd been generous with his praise of their two-person power team throughout the day. They were at the top of their professional game, and the heady combination of business success and underlying sexual tension was intoxicating. They still hadn't even kissed.

She was highly caffeinated and moving fast when she returned to her apartment in the early evening to get ready for the gala. Several last minute, high-profile RSVPs had come in, which meant adjustments needed to be made to the evening's speeches, to account for all the protocol.

She stood in front of her antique dresser, her iPhone on speaker, dictating changes to the speeches to a junior staffer while applying her eyeshadow into a flawless smoky eye. With the help of Chiara's shopping genius, she'd found the perfect long black dress that hugged her curves in all the right places, providing the ideal balance between bombshell and businesswoman. She was determined to be both tonight.

When the final changes had been made, she rushed back to the Louvre, with François's speech for the gala on a USB stick stored safely in her favorite Valentino clutch. It was a moonless night, and the air was cold when the cab dropped her off. The glass pyramid entrance to the museum was lit from the inside, golden light pouring out onto the centuries-old facade of the building. *The staggering beauty of this place will never get old,* she thought. Racing toward the entrance, she couldn't have wiped the smile from her face if she'd tried.

With adrenaline and anticipation racing through her veins, both for the final event and for Bastien's reaction to the dress, she breezed through the doors and threw her all-access pass around her neck. She headed straight backstage, first to the tech stand to load the speech notes into the teleprompter, and then to the green room to make sure François was ready. They went over the final changes; she straightened his bow tie and wished him luck. In that moment, she was the bombshell businesswoman of her own dreams.

She walked into the ballroom, which was elaborately covered in gilt accents from floor to ceiling. Full of perfectly lit people in formal wear, it was even more impressive than when she'd seen it at the dry run. Bastien had saved her a seat in the front row. As she made her way down the aisle, she felt like all eyes were on her. She slid into her seat next to him just as the lights began to dim and watched as he scanned her from head to toe.

He's gawking. This dress was worth every euro, she thought, smiling.

"You look perfect," he whispered, lightly kissing her cheek.

She reached down and squeezed his hand gently, letting it rest there for a few seconds longer than would've been professional. "Looking quite sharp yourself," she smiled.

François delivered his speech flawlessly, and the night's awards celebration and entertainment—a mesmerizing opera singer performing selections from *Carmen*—took her breath away. Throughout the event, she could feel Bastien watching her out of the corner of his eye. She was enjoying his attention and increasingly conscious of how close his hand was to her thigh. The venue and the way their story was slowly unfolding felt utterly enchanted.

François closed the event by thanking everyone for attending and inviting them to the champagne reception under the pyramid. As the house lights came up, she threw Bastien her most flirtatious smile and quickly darted to the stage door to manage any follow-up that François might need. She made a few notes on his asks, all of which could wait for the next day, and left him rubbing elbows with someone from Sweden's royal family.

With her professional duties complete, she worked her way back through the crowd to find Bastien in the reception. She spotted him across the room, talking to a broad-shouldered man in an impeccably fitting tux whose back was to her. The stranger's profile gave her an eerie sense of familiarity as she approached.

Bastien saw her coming, and he gave her an almost defeated-looking smile, which she didn't understand. When the other man turned slightly, she noticed a clear, curly cord stretching from his ear into his jacket. Then, it hit her like a bolt of lightning.

It's Matt.

Her breath caught in her throat as he turned and their eyes locked.

"And there she is. Again," he said with a smile, extending his hand for the most professional of handshakes.

Austen couldn't believe it was him. For the third time.

"Well, I'll be damned," tumbled out of her mouth as they stared at each other, hands clutched and softly shaking, sending an electric current straight up her arm.

Bastien cleared his throat, startling Austen into dropping the handshake and momentarily placing a hand on his shoulder. She removed it quickly, feeling awkward.

"So nice to see you. What are you doing here?" Austen asked Matt.

"Just took a new gig working for one of tonight's award winners. Permanently, as a matter of fact," he explained. "He's based in Paris, so I moved here two weeks ago."

Holy bombshell news. Matt lives in Paris. And good God, the man can wear a tux.

Bastien spoke first. "We should grab a beer some time. Let me give you my number."

"Very kind of you, man. Thanks. We should do that," he said, pulling his phone out of his pocket.

As Bastien typed his number into the phone, Matt turned to Austen, looking at her with hooded eyes.

"I still have your number."

An invisible filament of electricity shot between them. She was certain the entire room felt it, especially Bastien.

I just don't feel this same spark with Bastien, as much as I might want to.

The realization screamed at her like a banshee inside her head. Staring at both men standing directly in front of her, the contrast was stark and unavoidable.

Matt took his phone back and said, "It was great to run into you both, but I've got to get back to work. Hopefully, we can catch up another time soon now that I'm local. Have a great night." He smiled at them both and disappeared into the crowd.

"Matt again. What are the chances?" Bastien asked rhetorically.

He looked nervous. She could see him searching her face for a reaction. After all, he'd been there in Dakar and in Davos and had noticed a vibe between her and Matt on both occasions. He'd come right out and asked her about it on the plane as they left Dakar and again in Davos while she was texting Matt from one of their meetings. The look on his face said that he remembered those interactions almost as well as she did.

"Infinitesimally small," she replied, still stunned.

"Let's get you some champagne," Bastien suggested. "I think we both deserve some, given tonight's excitement."

She nodded and they made their way to the bar, where they ran into François. She was relieved by the professional intrusion, as it took Bastien's focus off her. And since she'd already done her debrief with François at the stage door, she stood back and let the two men talk. Sipping her champagne, she scanned the room and spotted Matt standing about 20 feet away. He was scanning the room as well, presumably for whatever it was he looked for when on security detail.

Or is he looking for me?

Bastien and François finished their debrief quickly.

"Thanks again for all the great support today. You both were indispensable," François said graciously. "I'm going to sneak out of here and get some sleep. See you both in the office tomorrow. Enjoy the party."

Bastien put his hand on Austen's back and guided her toward the center of the room, where they could have the best view of the pyramid.

"Congratulations on a very impressive and well-executed day of events," he said, raising his glass to her.

"And to you," she said, clinking her glass with his.

As she took another sip, exhaustion washed over her. The music from a string quartet echoed throughout the room, and the melody lulled her. The cumulative impact of two months of hard work finally hit, with a vengeance. She leaned against the spiral staircase that climbed toward the pyramid's apex.

"You look tired," Bastien observed. "Do you want to go?"

"Gosh, it just hit me like a ton of bricks. I think all my adrenaline just ran out," she admitted.

He took her hand in his—a first—and they headed toward the exit.

We're holding hands. François is gone, so I don't need to worry about him seeing this. That'd be awkward. But Matt's here somewhere. Holy shit. Matt.

As fate would have it, they were walking right toward him, hand-in-hand, and he saw them coming.

Austen tried to pull her hand away, but Bastien possessively held it tighter. As they passed by him, Bastien acknowledged Matt with a nod. "See you soon."

Matt locked eyes with her as they passed, and she involuntarily turned her head to maintain their stare over her shoulder, even as Bastien swept her away. She was certain that her look conveyed equal parts defiance, shame, and lust.

They arrived in the same taxi queue that they'd stood in just two weeks before, on the day this part of their story had begun. He ran his fingers through his hair before taking both of her hands in his.

"Let me say again how beautiful you looked tonight, Austen. You were the belle of the ball, hands down. And an exceptionally talented speechwriter, I must add."

"Thank you, Bastien."

She was freezing, exhausted and her feet ached from the heels. Her mind raced over Matt and the dilemma his appearance tonight had created. Up until about 45 minutes earlier, she'd been optimistic about where things were heading with Bastien. But now, as he held both of her cold hands in his, all she could very eloquently think in her mind was: *Fuck.*

What am I doing? Matt could be in Paris with Girlfriend Option B. She could be his wife by now. Crap, why didn't I check for a ring? Can I really let a chance encounter with Matt—but oh my God, it was a third chance—throw off what could be the start of something good with Bastien?

She saw the wheels turning in his head, just as surely as he saw them turning in hers. Her mind flashed back to the moment with Alain on Pont Neuf, right before their first kiss. He'd asked if he could kiss her, and she'd wished he'd dared to do it without asking. The memory then jumped to her first kiss with Kevin, who hadn't hesitated under the sparkling lights of the Eiffel Tower.

Neither relationship worked, but doesn't fortune favor the bold? Wait! Fortune.

Her roving stream of consciousness took her back to the tarot card reader in Byron Bay who'd predicted a "third something" in her love life.

I just ran into Matt for the third time. In a third country. Could this be it?

Bastien touched her face with one hand and pulled her closer to him with the other, snapping her back into the present. Their eyes met, and he leaned toward her, albeit with hesitation.

He wants to kiss me, but he's not sure, and neither am I.

She moved her face away from his hand and went in for a hug—a very American move. He'd hesitated too long, and her mind was too distracted; the moment wasn't right. A cab pulled up, and she quickly said goodnight and jumped in, thankful for the escape.

When she got home, she peeled herself out of her gown and stood in her bathroom in her underwear, staring at her reflection in the mirror, her hands resting on the sink. She reminded herself of the important lesson she'd learned from Kevin: When it's there, you don't have to ask. There's no reason to hesitate.

But we both did.

Her thoughts shifted back to Matt, lighting every cell in her body on fire in a blinding flash. She washed her face and rubbed her eyes repeatedly, trying to make sense of it. Nothing could have prepared her for such an unexpected finale to that night at the Louvre. She dried her face with a towel, stumbled into her room and collapsed onto the bed, emotionally and physically spent.

CHAPTER TWENTY-SEVEN

Chemistry

The next morning, she woke up early and stretched out diagonally across the bed, a luxury she'd come to appreciate while sleeping alone. She eventually rolled toward the window, and her face touched the cold side of the pillow. The chill brought back the memory of Bastien's cold hand on her face, and how she'd pulled away—because of Matt. She replayed the evening in her mind as she watched dust float through the air in the few beams of sunlight flooding through the cracks in the carelessly closed curtains.

Her date with Bastien was planned for the next day—drinks first and then dinner at Soho House in South Pigalle, or SoPi, as the cool kids called it.

I should keep it. But when Matt shook my hand, I swear I felt sparks fly. Did he feel it too? And more importantly, where is Girlfriend Option B? She must still be in the picture. He's been here two weeks and hasn't reached out.

At that instant, her phone buzzed on the nightstand. She sat up in bed and looked at the screen. Seeing Matt's name, her heart started to pound.

Good morning. Just wanted
to say how nice it was to see
you last night.

I spent two months preparing
for that event. I looked at a lot
of possibilities for how it could
play out. Running into you
was not on my list.

But it was a pleasant surprise.

We do seem to have an odd
dance going with fate, don't we?

So it seems. I still can't quite
believe it was you. And that
you live here now.

It's been hectic getting
settled, but I did think about
calling you. We had a deal.

OK here we go. Deep breaths. Play it cool, Austen.

Did we? What deal was that,
exactly?

That if I was ever single and in
Europe, you'd get a call.

He remembered. Is this "the" call? Gotta ask.

Well technically, a text isn't a
call, so I'm not sure what I'm
supposed to think just now.

She stared at her phone, waiting for the three little dancing dots indicating he was writing back, but then it rang. She answered immediately.

"And then he called," she said, making sure he could hear her smile.

His sexy baritone voice came through the speaker. "I'm hoping the call will solve the mystery for you."

She screamed silently into the air over her bed. *He's single. And here. Mind. Blown.*

"So, last night wasn't a dream. I woke up unsure," she said.

Matt cleared his throat. "I have a confession to make. I knew you were going to be there last night."

Austen threw off the covers and headed to the kitchen to make coffee. *I need to be awake to process this.*

"How did you know that?"

"I got the registered attendee list about a month ago, as part of my advance work. Your name was on it, so I went into the event looking for you," he confessed. "I saw you breeze into the room and take your seat up front, right before it started."

She heard a smile in his voice, which immediately made hers grow wider.

"Now I know why I felt like I was being watched," she said, turning up the flirtation in her voice.

"You looked beautiful. I can guarantee I wasn't the only one watching you."

A frenetic energy was building in Austen's body as she listened to his voice. She switched off the coffee machine. It wasn't necessary. Every cell in her body was wide awake.

"So, you knew a month ago that we'd be running into each other *and* remembered our little deal, but still didn't want to give me a heads up?"

He took a deep breath in and out. "It's been two years since Davos, so I wasn't sure what was going on in your life. I didn't want to presume. And then I saw you with Bastien."

He saw us holding hands.

She sat down carefully on her couch. "I know what you saw, but we're not exactly together."

"Not exactly?"

"Things have been heading in that direction. We're meant to have our first official date tomorrow," she explained. "The hand hold you saw was a first, and I'm quite sure it was a territorial move which he made specifically because you were there."

"Bastien's a good guy. I'm happy for you," he said, sounding anything but.

"Are you?"

Matt laughed and then hesitated. "Do you want me to be?"

His question made her skin burn. A combination of desire, guilt and hope raged inside her, stunning her speechless.

He charged forward into the gap created by her silence. "I'm going to let you off the hook on that one and ask another question. Can I take you to dinner tonight?"

"Tonight?" she stammered.

"I'm not usually keen on playing dirty, but I see a very small window here, and I'm going to take it if you let me. I'm kicking myself for not calling you at *any* point in the last month. It was stupid."

"Yes," she said.

He laughed. "Yes, it was stupid? Or yes, to dinner?"

"Yes to both."

"Good. There's a place near Invalides I've been wanting to try. I'll text you the address. How's 8:30?" he asked, the confidence in his voice growing.

Can he hear my heart pounding through the phone line?
"Eight thirty is perfect. See you tonight."

She hung up and ran back into her bedroom, taking a flying leap onto the bed. She screamed into her pillows and kicked her feet in excitement.

Once her pulse returned to a normal pace, she flung open her closet and pulled out her favorite dark green dress. It showed just the right amount of cleavage and perfectly complemented her green eyes and red hair. She hung it on the door, and flopped back onto the bed, her mind racing. She rolled herself into the covers like a cocoon, grinning ear to ear.

Shit. Bastien. Can't deal. Gonna work from home today, she decided.

The workday passed in a flash, and before she knew it, she was walking into Matt's chosen restaurant—L'Ami Jean, a gastropub on the Rue Malar. She spotted him immediately as she walked in. He was a large presence in a small room, and he stood as soon as he saw her. He was wearing a beautifully cut suit without a tie, and his smile made her weak in the knees.

When she reached him, he took one of her hands and gently pulled her toward him as he kissed her on both cheeks in *not quite* the typical French style. Air kisses were the standard, but his lips landed lightly on both her cheeks, and she felt her blood rush to meet them. He pulled her chair out and sat opposite her, leaning back to take her in.

With perfect nonchalance, he said, "So we're finally getting that drink. It only took two years."

"Three, if you count from Dakar." She felt like her face might explode, she was smiling so hard. "But who's counting? Better late than never."

"Quite right," he replied. "Something tells me it's going to have been worth the wait."

Austen and Matt stared at each other silently. *Good God, he's beautiful. I can't believe he's here.*

"How did you end up living in Paris?" she asked, resting her chin on her hand.

"I'd been doing contract work for this guy in Joburg for years, and he got a job here and asked me to come with him and his family, mostly because I speak French. I was ready for a change, so it was a good deal." He paused before adding, "And you were here."

She shook her head. "Me being here did not factor into your decision."

"No, I didn't move to the Northern Hemisphere to chase you," he said. "But you *were* my first thought when he told me Paris was the destination."

"I better have been," she cracked.

They exchanged another silent, smiling stare while Austen worked up her courage to ask her most burning question.

"Can I ask what happened to Girlfriend Option B?"

The waitress arrived to take their order, just as the question left her mouth. Austen waited impatiently for her to leave so she could hear his answer. He had implied he was single in their phone conversation that morning, but he hadn't said it officially, and she was dying for confirmation.

As soon as the waitress walked away, he said, "Her name is Eve. We broke up about a year ago. Life just took us in different directions. She's still in South Africa, and we're still friends."

"Friends is good," she smiled. *Phew.*

"I'm not going to ask you about Bastien."

"There's no need."

She held his gaze silently for long enough to ensure he knew she meant it. The arrival and pouring of their Pouilly-Fumé ended the silence.

"It's wild being back in Paris," Matt said, after taking a sip of the wine. "My grandparents—my mom's parents—lived here so I came every three or four years as a kid, but it's been an age."

"Your mom grew up here?" Austen asked.

"She did but she moved to South Africa in her twenties. My grandpa was South African, but Grandma was French, and Mom went to medical school down there," he explained. "That's where she met my dad."

He's got a strong, working mother. Excellent. Not intimidated by powerful women.

Austen looked toward the ceiling, searching for a memory. "Didn't you tell us in Dakar that you grew up in French Polynesia?"

"Good recall," he smiled. "Yes, Dad's Tahitian. They met in Jozi but then moved to Papeete after they got married. I grew up an island kid, but then moved to South Africa for university."

"It's all very exotic relative to my life. Born in the States. Now live here. The end. I feel very plain in comparison," she laughed.

He stared at her intently. "You couldn't be plain if you tried."

Austen lowered her eyes, smiling. The electric shock she'd felt when they shook hands at the Louvre was back but had turned into a slow and steady current, which flowed across their small table and kept her tethered to him for the rest of the evening.

After swallowing his last bite of roasted partridge, he told her, "I talked to my parents earlier today, and I told them about you."

Austen was taken aback. "Really? What did you tell them?"

Matt used a small piece of bread to sop up the last of the sauce from his plate. He popped it in his mouth and chewed, as if to buy time before he answered her.

"That I was finally having dinner tonight with the most fearless woman I've ever met." He paused again and smiled at her quizzically. "It's strange. I'm not usually one to go loud about something like this, especially to my parents, but for whatever reason I couldn't keep it quiet. What do you think that's all about?"

Austen picked up her napkin to wipe her mouth, examining his face as she did. She knew it wasn't love (at least not yet) but his story made her think of her mom, who loved so loudly, utterly unable to keep her love quietly inside. It was how Austen wanted to love and be loved—in the biggest possible way. *Maybe Matt is someone who loves loudly,* she hoped.

"In a military context, isn't the expression 'to go loud' something to do with starting to shoot?" she asked. He nodded and continued to look at her with the most curious of expressions. "My dad is ex-Army. One of his favorite expressions to use, when anything is taking too long to get moving, is 'Let's stop the saluting and start the shooting.' Maybe your need to 'go loud' with your parents was just the last three years of anticipation finally getting the better of you?" she postured.

"I think you might just get me," he grinned.

When the wine was drained and the bill paid, they made their way out onto the sidewalk. It had started to rain lightly, so he opened her umbrella over them both. He tucked his free hand into his pocket, and she held the strap of her cross-body bag in both of her hands, like a shield over her heart. Their bodies were only inches apart, but they didn't yet dare to touch.

He looked into her eyes and asked calmly, "So what now, madam? Would you like to call it a night, or can I tempt you back to my place for a nightcap?"

She released one of her hands from her purse strap and placed it lightly on his chest as she rose onto her tiptoes and kissed him. She could wait no longer. He returned her kiss eagerly, pulling her tightly into his body with one arm while keeping the umbrella aloft with the other. The rain, the traffic, and Paris itself faded to black, and at that moment, they were alone in the world. And the world wanted for nothing.

When they pulled apart and refocused their eyes on each other, their smiles said everything. It was utter perfection. Matt nodded his head slowly, staring at her.

"What?" she asked, smiling with her entire face.

"So worth the wait," he said, leaning in to kiss her again quickly before turning his attention to the street to flag a taxi.

She was in violent agreement.

A taxi stopped, and he opened her door, put her in the cab, and walked around to get in on the other side. He gave the driver his address and claimed her hand as his, lacing their fingers together. Without words, he checked her face to make sure that the decision to go to his place was mutual. She squeezed his hand and turned her bedroom eyes up to full tilt to assure him it was. As they rode through the darkened Paris streets, the butterflies in her stomach felt like they were flying through a tornado. She was suddenly a tightly wound bundle of the best kind of nerves.

By the time they arrived, the rain had stopped. His apartment was in the 17th arrondissement in a turn-of-the-century building that had a magnificently ornate door. He held it open for her, revealing a cobblestoned inner courtyard full of plants and flowers. These hidden courtyards existed in many buildings in Paris, but not hers. Any time she caught a glimpse of one, if someone had left a door casually ajar, she felt compelled to stop and peek in. She imagined them to be a magical haven for the residents of these buildings, providing a transitional space between the tranquility of their homes and the chaos of Paris's streets.

As they passed through Matt's courtyard, she felt a total sense of calm washing over her. The tornado of butterflies in her stomach fell into a much more serene flight path, even as her body temperature rose. In some way, she felt she'd been on her way to exactly this place for years, and she couldn't recall anything ever feeling so right.

"Can I take your coat?" he asked, as they entered his apartment.

It was sparsely decorated but still elegant—modern furniture set in classic Haussmanian architecture. Boxes were stacked against the far wall by an empty built-in bookcase, and out the window, she could see the illuminated top of Sacré-Coeur basilica peeking through the neighboring buildings.

She turned her back to him and untied the coat belt. As he peeled it back from her shoulders, she shifted her hair to one side, exposing her neck and the zipper to the back of her dress.

"You can take the dress too," she said, keeping her back turned.

Her coat landed in a soft thud on a nearby chair and she felt his fingertips and lips gently caress the tops of her shoulders before he slowly lowered the zipper. She kicked off her heels and stepped out of the dress as it hit the floor at her feet, turning to face him.

Taking a half step back, he let his eyes travel the length of her body while he removed his suit jacket, tossing it on top of her discarded coat.

"I've fantasized about this moment more times than I'll admit, but my imagination paled in comparison to the reality," he said admiringly.

He then quickly closed the distance between them and picked her up by the hips. In a flash, her legs were wrapped around his waist and her back pressed against the wall as they began to devour one another.

An alarm went off after shockingly few moments of sleep. She rolled onto her side to face Matt, who she found smiling sleepily, eyes half opened.

"Good morning, lovely," he said.

Austen reached for him and buried her face in his neck, kissing him from his ear to his collar bone. He pulled her on top of him, and the next thirty minutes instantly disappeared. She wanted to never leave his bed, but duty called.

Hopping into a cab outside his apartment, Austen felt like she was floating on air. But when she pulled her phone out of her purse and looked at it for the first time since dinner, her spirits crashed rapidly to the ground. Bastien had texted at some point in the evening, to confirm their date for tonight.

I have to cancel. What am I going to tell him?

He'd done nothing wrong, but the night with Matt and the cumulative lessons she'd learned over the years about chemistry, attraction, timing, and fate had brought extreme clarity. *He's just not the one.*

It was nearing lunchtime when he approached her desk in the open space. "You're alive. I was worried since you never replied to my text last night." His fingers combed through his hair, as they always did when his nerves were playing up.

"Sorry to worry you, Bastien. I was out with Matt," she said in a quiet apology. *Brutal honesty is going to be the strategy, it seems.*

"Oh. I see." His shoulders slumped and his eyes cast downward. Then, his head snapped back up, and she saw anger in his narrowed eyes.

She got up from her desk and steered him by the elbow into a small conference room, seeking privacy.

Bastien started to pace as she closed the door behind them.

"So that's it? It's over before it even starts? Perfect. I'm beginning to understand why you've been single for so freaking long. This could have been good—you and me," he said, gesturing between them.

She wasn't sure if it was his heart or his ego talking. Either way, she'd hurt him, which she'd never wanted to do. But his jab at her singledom reminded her that there was something hard in his personality. She'd seen hints of it but pushed them aside— it's easy to ignore the things one doesn't want to see. Now, it was inescapable. And since their professional relationship had to continue, she knew she had to let him down carefully.

"Bastien, I'm so sorry. Matt showing up really threw me for a loop. There's something there that's bigger than me; I couldn't ignore it. I don't know what else to say."

He raised both hands, palms to the ceiling, and an increasingly pained look on his face. "I'm in love with you."

Woah. No one has said that to me since Brad. And I feel nothing, she realized, her face blank.

He continued to pace. "I hate myself for it, but it's true. This could have been great, and you're tossing it away? I can't believe it."

"Does it matter that I really *wanted* to love you?" she asked, leaning against a wall, her hands folded behind her back. "You're a great guy, and I know you're going to make someone else very happy one day."

He didn't respond. He just stared at her, almost in a challenge.

Austen smiled apologetically and then slowly walked out of the conference room, knowing there was nothing left to say.

He said he loves me. God. Unrequited love is awful.

Bastien had said exactly what she'd wanted to hear from Sam and from Kevin. She suddenly understood how they must have felt, knowing they couldn't return her love. She *had wanted* things to work with Bastien, but they simply didn't.

Once back at her desk, her mind returned to Matt's bed, retracing the memories of his hands tracing her body. They'd barely slept. They couldn't stop touching each other, talking, and then doing it all again until the wee hours. She'd been held rapt all night, physically and intellectually. Her mind and her body were in full throttle, and she'd never felt more alive. And this time, she had no doubt that he felt it too. It was chemical—whatever existed between them. She could see it so clearly in the memory of his face in the early morning light.

The City of Love and the City of Light. She finally understood how Paris could be both things. Chemistry created the light that could lead to love. It was an illuminated path she'd not understood or even seen until that morning, but now it was clear as day, in her mind's eye.

She reached for her phone and texted Matt.

Did you ever study chemistry?

Does bomb training in the military count?

Yikes. Violence. You're scary.

Don't be scared. I was trained in precision bomb making — the kind that explode in a very controlled way to achieve a targeted objective, like opening an important door. It's an art.

I didn't know you were an artist. You're full of surprises.

Why are we talking about bombs? Or chemistry? Or was it art? I'm lost.

I was just thinking about ours. Chemistry. It was pretty good last night.

It was downright explosive. (See what I did there? 😊)

But then again, it always was.

True story and an excellent continuation of the analogy. This is fun. You're delicious.

Speaking of delicious. When do I get to taste you again?

How about tonight?

I thought you had plans tonight?

It's crazy, but a bomb went off and just plain destroyed those plans.

I've never been so happy to hear about an explosion. Assuming you're fine from its aftermath? No damage done?

I'm great. And I think no permanent damage was done. Anyway, nothing that can't be fixed with some time.

Glad to hear it. I like Bastien. I felt a bit bad for stepping in between you. But the feeling didn't last cause, well, I like you a lot more than I like him.

I think he'll probably renege his invitation to help me get settled and grab a beer.

I'll help you get settled. I can drink beer.

I'm so looking forward to tonight. But first, I really need a nap. I don't think I've ever felt this tired and this awake at the same time.

Me either. Nap first, then
late dinner at mine, around 9
p.m.?

Deal. Text me your address.

Later that night, as she awaited his arrival, she was more nervous than she could ever recall being for a date, but his kiss hello instantly put her at ease.

"How was your day, dear?" he asked with a grin.

Austen led him into the kitchen and started to open a bottle of champagne. "It started exceptionally well. Some stuff happened in the middle. And I feel like it's going to end on a high note. And you?"

He took the offered champagne flute and clinked it with hers. "Much of the same."

"Remember in Dakar when I sent you that text about being back in my room? I shaved my legs before sending that," she admitted with a grin as they moved toward her couch. "It was an invitation. You knew that, right?"

She was holding on to the elevator story, unsure if she should bring it up or wait for him to confess.

"I knew," he replied, with a smile reaching all the way to his ears. "But even if I hadn't been with Eve, that little dalliance could've gotten me fired. No shagging the clients—house rules."

"Stupid house. But that did cross my mind. Also, for the record, I don't usually offer one-nighters to men I've just met. But you were irresistible." She sat up straight and did her best to look innocent. "Also, Georges had threatened to go after you himself if I didn't."

His laughter pierced the air and the light around them in a way that made everything look and feel warmer. But then his playful face turned serious, and she held her breath in anticipation of the confession she hoped was coming next.

"I came very close to knocking on your door that night," he confessed.

Austen exhaled and smiled knowingly.

Curiously surveying her face, he continued. "I came down to your floor while you were texting me. I wanted you too. But I got two steps out of the elevator and then turned back around and left," he said, almost blushing.

"I know. I was watching you through the peephole," she admitted. "I heard the elevator ding through the wall and jumped to the door but didn't dare open it. I just watched you, willing you to take those few more steps."

His jaw dropped open. "You were watching me? God, that's embarrassing. I was really frozen there for a minute or two, absolutely torn." He paused, lost in the memory.

She watched his smile fade and set down her glass, wondering where his head had gone.

"I'm glad it didn't happen like that," he said quietly. "If it had, I don't think we'd be here right now. And I have to tell you, I'm really happy to be here."

"I am too," she said in her exhale, her heart beating out her chest. "Timing is everything, isn't it?"

"And location. Paris for the win."

"Don't forget chemistry." She mimicked a small explosion with her hands and whispered, "Boom."

He laced his fingers into hers, which were still splayed out in explosion form, pulling her toward him to kiss her hard on the lips. He stopped briefly, holding her gaze without letting go of her hands, and then went back in for a second kiss, which was soft but deeper.

When they stopped, he asked, "Do you know the expression '*jamais deux sans trois*?'"

She nodded. Its literal translation was "never two without three," but its English equivalent was "everything happens in threes."

In Paris, she had survived two failed forays into that crazy thing called love, both with men who lived elsewhere. And there was Matt, in Paris by way of Dakar and Davos, who fate had now brought to her for a third time.

As he leaned in for a third kiss, she whispered into his lips, "Third time's a charm."

THE END

Acknowledgments

For being the original three readers of my brutally rough first draft and encouraging me to continue, I'm deeply grateful to Heather Knox, Tom Pilla and Katrine Prien.

For taking what I vomited out onto the page and teaching me how to turn it into a novel, I'm forever indebted to my brilliant editors, Rozi Doci and Holly Ingraham.

For my cover design and interior typesetting, I want to thank Danna Mathias Steele, a wonderful collaborator.

For the proficient proofreading, I send my thanks to Manda Waller.

For being my expert wine advisor, I want to thank Erica Guries.

For the culture context consultation, I'm grateful to Nicole Mott.

For being my investigative team in the U.S., I appreciate Elise Enriquez and Nichole Peterson.

To all my friends and family who supported me and patiently listened while I jabbered on incessantly about the long and winding road to publication, thank you so much.

And last but not least, to every guy who goes on a date with me at any point in the future, thanks for having the courage to do so, knowing you risk ending up in a sequel. Kidding. Maybe.

About the Author

Whitney Cubbison is a dual American and French citizen living in Paris since 2009. She grew up in Texas and California and graduated from UCLA with a degree in French. She started her career in Communications working for high-tech PR agencies in San Francisco and eventually joined Microsoft where she worked for sixteen years, thirteen of which from the Paris office. During that time, she held various international roles that encompassed public relations, employee communications, executive speechwriting, and social media.

She left Microsoft in July 2022 to focus on completing her first novel, *Will There Be Wine?* The story, while fiction, is deeply inspired by Whitney's own experiences as an ex-pat divorcée living in Paris and trying to navigate the cultural minefield of dating in a foreign country.

When she's not writing, Whitney can be found sitting in Parisian cafés and restaurants with her friends, drinking wine.

For more, including links to all Whitney's social media sites, please visit Austen's blog – www.DatingDisasters.Paris. For anyone who is a fan of visual storytelling, don't miss Whitney's Instagram @whitneycubbisonwrites where she shares her own photos and anecdotes from many of the places Austen and her friends visit in *Will There Be Wine?*

Printed in Great Britain
by Amazon

17303616R00221